JAMES CHRISTIAN

AUDREY'S BONDS

WORKBOOK PRESS LLC
187 E Warm Springs Rd,
Suite B285, Las Vegas, NV 89119, USA

Website: https://workbookpress.com/
Hotline: 1-888-818-4856
Email: admin@workbookpress.com

Ordering Information:
Quantity sales. Special discounts are available on quantity purchases by corporations, associations, and others.
For details, contact the publisher at the address above.

ISBN-13:   978-1-955459-18-1 (Paperback Version)
                978-1-952754-44-9 (Digital Version)

REV. DATE: 28/07/2020

San Antonio: August, 1985

Shirtless and barefoot, wearing only faded Levis, Jack McCall leaned on the stone balustrade at the far edge of the pool patio. The Levis hung on his hips, his normally lean frame now shading toward gaunt. His dark brown hair, still thick but shot through with fresh strands of gray, had grown over his ears and twisted and waved in unlikely places. Since that morning last month when the Federal Deposit Insurance Corporation had shown up on the doorstep of First Mission National and told him they were closing him down, he hadn't wanted to face anybody, not even his barber.

He turned back toward the rambling house tucked in among the live oaks. Too extravagant for a man alone, but he'd felt full of himself, wanting to prove something, that he wasn't a loser. And then he turned out to be one.

Squinting, he saw that the morning sun had sprinkled the ruffled surface of the pool with diamonds of hard light. In the shadows of his mind he saw the swaying, half-naked ghosts of pool parties past dancing in the light of the tiki torches, eyes flashing, slick silky skin glistening. The laughter came to him then, tinkling like ice cubes in a tall glass. He had to smile. It had been a helluva run.

He made his way around the pool to the shade where a pitcher of chilled Bull Shots sat sweating on one of the patio tables. He poured from it into a crystal tumbler, took a sip and pulled back a wrought iron chair with a screech that set his teeth on edge. He swept the fallen crepe myrtle blooms from the seat, sat down and put the frosty glass against his forehead, content to be lulled by the gentle breeze rustling the leaves of the live oaks.

His reverie didn't last. The rolling slap-slap of footsteps in cowboy boots forced him to swivel slowly in the chair. There was Sam Tate, ambling along the stone walk that ran beside the house. Tall and lanky, Sam scarcely fit the lawyerly image. His boots were polished but well-worn and in a Resistol hat, pressed Levis, a blue blazer hooked on one finger and slung over a starched Lucchese shirt, he would have fit comfortably into the crowd at a high-stakes cattle auction.

"Coffee's in the kitchen, Sam. Bull Shots are out here."

"Had my coffee, Mack, and it's too early for a Bull Shot," Sam replied, taking the last few steps up to the patio and pulling out a wrought iron chair. It scraped across the limestone and McCall winced. "You just get out of bed?" Tate asked.

"Little while ago."

"I called to let you know I was coming. No answer."

"I was out here. Probably wouldn't have answered it anyway."

Sam took off his Resistol and wiped the inside band with a handkerchief. The hat left a red mark on his forehead and crimped a halo in his sandy hair. He saw in a glance what a mess Mack was. Three days of stubble on a face that was always clean-shaven, dark brown hair a tangle, the intelligent brown eyes bloodshot and puffy, looking like two pee-holes in the snow. Mack's nose, straight as a razor, was the only feature that stood indestructible, the stubborn bowsprit of the face of a man who'd lost a battle but was still fighting a war.

Sam had something to do with losing the battle. He'd pitched the bank to Mack as an investment opportunity and the numbers looked as good as Sam said they were. It was bad luck that Charlie Monroe died early. Charlie had been the bank's CEO for 20 years and was good at it, just tired of the hassle. With Mack to advise on the investment side of the portfolio and Charlie to run the loan portfolio, First Mission would have done alright. But with Mack running it all like a bull with a wild hair up its ass, it only took a couple of years for Mack and a downturn in the Texas economy to wreck it.

McCall watched Sam quietly, waiting, the only sound the rustle of the live oak leaves and the water lapping against the tile of the pool. At last, he asked, "So what do they say now? Am I going to get any of my money back?"

Sam turned to McCall and met his eyes. He shook his head slowly. "Not a nickel, podnah. They don't think there are enough good assets in First Mission to cover their cost of taking you over. No other way to say it. The people in the saddle up there think we've got too many banks, especially little ones. They're going to cull out the weak ones and let the New York boys strip the deposits and the good assets and turn the bricks and mortar into hamburger joints. No point fighting for First Mission National, Mack. This time next year, it'll be a Burger King."

"So that's it," McCall said. "Shovel full of dirt on the coffin lid."

Sam nodded and looked away. They fell silent then, staring across the pool into a bright blue Texas sky dappled with cotton-ball clouds up from the Gulf of Mexico, each remembering the times they'd spent together before Sam married Bitsy, partying around this very pool, hunting turkey and white tail deer on the ranches out around Paint Rock and Ballinger, talking business over *carne guisada* at Pico de Gallo or cold beer and barbecue at

Rudy's.

McCall tried to wrench his thoughts forward, to Virginia, to picking up what pieces were left and starting over again. But something in Sam's silence, in his reluctance to make eye contact, wouldn't let him go.

"Is there something more?"

Sam rested his elbows on the table, folded his hands in front of him and leaned forward. "They think you're an eighteen-carat gunslinger so they're not going to let you back into banking again for a long time."

"Who cares? I should never have been in banking in the first place," Mack said, immediately regretting it when his words struck Sam like the sharp point of a spear.

"Sorry, Sam. Not your fault. It was mine. I'm the one who forgot that your first loss is your best loss. I should have cut and run as soon as old what's-his-name kicked the bucket. It's obvious I don't know how to run a bank."

Tate took a deep breath, pulled out the spear and set it aside. "Well, I'm the one who got you down here. Neither one of us expected Charlie Monroe to have a coronary at the ripe old age of forty-five. I will say that I didn't expect you to try to make that little bank into a rocket to the moon. Never mind that, though. There's enough blame to go around and stirring it up'll just make it stink. We need to be looking ahead. I didn't suppose you'd care about the black list," Sam said.

"I expected it. I know it's happened to a lot of other guys. A damn good thing they can't stop me from consulting."

"Unfortunately, the black list's not the end of it."

McCall raised his eyebrows, looked into Sam's pale blue eyes and waited.

Sam leaned forward, unfolded his hands and spread them on the table top, palms down, fingers spread, bracing himself. "The FDIC wants restitution." McCall cocked his head, his eyes narrowing. "Restitution?" "The bank failed on your watch. They won't be able to sell the bad assets or the franchise for enough to cover their losses, so they're going to be out some cash. They want you to lighten the load. And if you get feisty about it, they'll make your life a living hell for the next few years. They'll write up criminal charges against you and refer the case to the US Attorney. The charges won't stick. They know that. But your legal bills will put you in hock for the rest of your natural-born life. Agree to the restitution and let me try to work out a deal you can live with."

"They can't do that," McCall said, getting out of his chair, a vein in his temple beginning to throb. "I paid the insurance premiums and I didn't do anything illegal. Sure the bank went down on my watch, but I'm losing everything. They're not paying me one red cent for my bank. I signed off on some loans that went sour in a lousy economy. So did every other banker in this state. Half of Texas is overbuilt and under water. *That's* not my fault. And there sure as hell isn't anything criminal about me or First Mission."

Sam stared at him calmly, waiting for the storm to subside. "They're not fussing about the loans on all the drilling rigs or the Mexican condos or even that damned vineyard out in West Texas. They understand the market down here. They don't understand about the exotic game ranch, though. So they think that, taken as a whole, your lending policy was 'imprudent.' It won't be any consolation, but they're putting the bite on your directors, too. "

"This is wrong, Sam," McCall growled. "They're not going to find my fingerprints on anything illegal and I never heard about anybody going to jail for guessing wrong on oil prices or the value of the fucking Mexican peso. Look, Sam, I'm out over a million bucks here and a fair chunk of it wasn't even mine," he shouted and smashed his fist on the table. The pitcher of Bull Shot bounced and an empty glass toppled over and spun around on its side. Tate flinched at the sudden outburst, but the storm blew over quickly and except for the overturned glass and a splatter of bouillon and vodka, it might never have happened.

When McCall continued, there was a cold, steely edge to his voice. "Maybe they can force me to pay something, but if you're going to represent me in this, you're going to have to convince those guys they can't get blood out of a turnip. Hang around. I've got a real estate agent and an auctioneer coming this morning." He looked at his watch and went on. "They ought to be here in about ten minutes. They're going to do an estimate for me. Maybe that'll give you some ammunition. Sam, I *really* don't want to give the Feds anything."

"I hear you. Tell me something, though, just so I'm playing with a full deck. You don't have anything stashed away in a hidey-hole somewhere that I don't know about? Like Switzerland? Or the Caymans? I'll need to make full disclosure of your assets, Mack. I won't have a shred of credibility with the FDIC if they find out you're holding back-and they *will* look."

McCall held Tate's eyes, his mouth a grim line, pausing only for a heartbeat, deciding whether or not to tell him about his stake in Banco Dorado. That was his safe harbor if everything--really everything--went to shit city. "I don't have anything stashed in Switzerland, Sam. Wish I did." The Banco Dorado shares were in Javier's name and the bank was in Panamá, not Switzerland, so maybe it wasn't an out-and-out lie.

Tate noticed McCall's momentary hesitation and knew he wasn't getting the whole, honest-to-God truth. "People lie to their lawyers all the time,

Mack. And don't get your back up," he added, raising a hand, palm outward in McCall's direction. "I'm not saying you're lying to me. Or that you would. I'm just telling you that if you have got something stashed somewhere, be real careful how you spend it."

"Why would I lie to you, Sam?"

"I don't know. I've just got a powerful feeling you're not in a law-abiding mood right now."

McCall looked away before he spoke. "The law ought to protect you, Sam. If it doesn't, it's hard to respect it. If I had a million dollars, I'd dare them to take me to court. I'd fight them to the last nickel and we'd win. You know damned well we would."

"If you had a million dollars, your bank wouldn't be broke," Sam muttered, deadpan.

****

McCall had put on a shirt in deference to the real estate lady, but he was still barefoot, standing on the grass to avoid the sizzling pavement of the driveway. One hand rested on the door of Sam's suburban.

"When are you off?" Sam asked.

"The auction's day after tomorrow. Right after that, I guess. No point in hanging around. No telling when the house'll sell. Fred's got the mortgage, so maybe he won't foreclose me."

"You going to stay with your grandfather?" Sam asked.

"No. The farm's three hours from DC. Besides, I don't feel much like facing my grandfather right now. I just pissed away a pretty big chunk of his life savings. The lease is up on my condo in Alexandria next month and I've given the renters notice that I'm not renewing it. I've got a job in Jordan for three weeks and I'm stopping in London to see Audrey for a few days on the way back. The timing will just about fit."

"You're gonna have to see your grandfather eventually. Maybe this would be a good time. Visit your roots. Might do you some good."

"Roots," McCall replied vaguely. "I don't know. Do you think there's anything in that Prodigal Son business? My grandfather's a forgiving sort, but I have a lot of hard-assed ancestors."

"Your ancestors don't have much to say about it anymore, Mack. Your roots are there whether they like it or not. At least part of you belongs there. Which reminds me. Tomorrow, you belong at my house. Bitsy wants you for dinner. Six-thirty." Sam dropped the suburban into gear and tossed Mack a two-fingered salute. "Don't be late. She hates it when you're late."

10

McCall watched the suburban glide down the driveway and turn onto the street. As he walked back toward the house, he saw a bank of dark clouds building off to the west. They'd be ugly thunderheads by afternoon.

The Shenandoah Valley

The leading edge of the storm caught up with him and the butterscotch Mercedes Benz 450SL just east of Houston. He drove through torrential rain all the way across Louisiana and stopped for the night, exhausted, in Slidell. The rain stopped and the next morning he drove in bright sunshine through the tunnel of Alabama piney woods, then ran the Great Smokies trail across Tennessee to the Virginia Blue Ridge. Now he was home, or almost home, a few miles off I-81 in the Shenandoah Valley of his birth and his youth.

McCall put two wheels off the narrow road, ran his window down and cut the engine. It ticked spastically as it cooled, joining the chirping of the insects toiling in the weeds beside the road. Sultry air, scented with hay, wafted in through the window and warmed his face. From the top of the rise, he could see the house of his boyhood through the haze and heat shimmers. The little flock of sheep his grandfather kept were grazing up the slope where the house sat and the leaves of the apple trees rustled in the vagrant breezes. The corn looked a little crispy from the long hot days of the Virginia summer. He supposed Malcolm Birney still leased the farmland, but there was no sign of him or his boy today.

He rolled his shoulders to loosen the knots that had come up from the long drive. He could see part of the gravel lane that led up to the house from the road and a soft sadness fell over him, a remembrance of the yellow school bus pulling away, heading on down the road to drop off Cat Mercer, his first-ever girlfriend. Up at the house, the door opened and his mother stepped onto the porch to watch him come up the drive. There were chores to do as soon as he changed out of his school clothes, but there was always something waiting for him in the kitchen before he went out to find his grandfather--a cake warm from the oven, an apple with a slice of cheese, a glass of milk thick with butter fat. They always seemed to be waiting on him, as if the rhythm of the farm turned as much on the school bus schedule as on the seasons. For his mother and his grandparents, the farm was the center of their universe, but not his. Some primeval force had always pulled at him, drawing him beyond the horizon toward a wider world. The few times his enthusiasm had overflowed and he'd talked to his mother about life beyond the Valley, the sadness in her eyes denied her indulgent smile.

Whatever his life was back then wasn't anymore. His mother and grandmother were both dead and Pa was eighty-something. He wondered if the old man were lonesome up here by himself. But where else would he go? He'd been born on this farm and spent his whole life here except for two years in the Army during World War I. This was his world. It was only right that he die here.

McCall thought of how the lives of the Coopers and the women they'd brought home to this farm had been. In the Cooper scheme of things, he should be here, working this farm, not Malcolm Birney. But it hadn't worked that way. He knew he'd let the family down, ignored his birthright--was that what it was called? Now he'd lost his grandfather's life savings.

If he drove up there now, he'd see it in the old man's eyes--the disappointment, the unasked questions, particularly 'when are you coming home, son?' Worse than facing that guilt, he was towing a trash bag full of failure.

He shook his head and twisted the key in the ignition. The Benz came to life, McCall dropped the gear lever into drive and eased back onto the road. He was too raw, too cut up, to meet Pa's eyes today. He'd call when he got into Washington, just to let him know he was back. Homecoming and repentance would have to wait.

September, New York City

Robert Ryder stared out of one of the fortress-like windows on the 105th floor of the World Trade Center. His view took in the haze-shrouded Hudson River as it meandered toward Staten Island and a rendezvous with the East River. The sight didn't fascinate him. He hated this office. The sub-lease would expire in four more months and he would move Ryder and Company much, much closer to the ground, somewhere on Broad Street. He had an agent looking for space now.

The firm and the office had come to him when his father died. Rob Ryder didn't reject fine things, but in his mind, his father's pretensions were an expensive vanity. He only had one client that mattered, one Rob intended to keep, but he had no intention of running the firm as his father had. He had a different client base in mind and a fancy office wouldn't impress them. On the contrary.

Behind him, the door opened and Chanille d'Orsay, his executive assistant and liaison with the covert community, slipped into the room. Not a woman anyone would easily forget. Tall and willowy, with finely sculpted features, Ryder had always wondered how she'd managed to get into the CIA or what she'd done once she was there. There couldn't have been many places outside Langley itself where she would have been useful. For him, though, her contacts in the Agency were valuable. As they were now. She was carrying a leather portfolio containing her regular report on banks recently acquired by the FDIC. How the CIA tapped into the FDIC's Resolution Trust Corporation was not his concern. That they could and that Chanille could access that information quickly was all he cared about.

"Well?" he asked, turning away from the window. "Anything interesting?"

She shrugged, tucking a strand of her honey blond hair behind an ear. "Several of the latest crop have participated in Latin American consortia. Mostly mid-size. They'll be more trouble than they'd be worth, I imagine. One small bank in Texas that would probably come cheap. A lot of international transactions, but not really Latin America."

Ryder sighed and crossed the plush carpet to his father's massive, polished desk upon which not a single piece of paper rested. "Let's have a look then."

He opened the portfolio and scanned the first extract from the RTC's computer output. Each entry displayed location, number of branches, performing assets and non-performing assets, broken down by type and marked to market, estimated value of loan and credit card servicing, correspondent balances with other banks, both foreign and domestic, valuation of fixed assets, retail deposit liabilities, brokered deposits and other short-term debt exposure, a clutch of miscellaneous data, including the size of the hole the failed bank had made in the FDIC's reserves. Add up the value of the performing assets, investments, fixed assets and correspondent balances and you could get a crude estimate of the value of the bank, hence what the FDIC might expect to get from the sale of the bank. In deciding how much to offer, prospective buyers would also be looking at the intangibles, such as how well the branch network fit with their own and whether the acquisition would serve their strategic market objectives. Was there any "synergy" in the deal?

Ryder was looking for two things, one quite tangible, the other sufficiently intangible that it wouldn't attract much, if any, competition from other buyers.

First of all, he was looking for a bank he could buy for a song and that ruled out most mid-size and larger banks with branch networks and full-service operations. That was the tangible element. The intangible aspect Ryder was interested in was a bank with international connections, particularly in shady banking havens like the Bahamas, the Caymans, Panamá and little out-of-the way places like Liechtenstein and the Isle of Man. It was an unlikely combination, he knew--a small bank with a lot of international action raised a red flag for money laundering--drug money and Mafia profits--and tax evasion, as well as flight capital.

The one bank in the batch Chanille had brought to him today was a little outfit in San Antonio, Texas, called First Mission National. No branch network, a small retail deposit base, a loan portfolio that was largely trash, which the FDIC would have to swallow. The bank had decent investments-- mostly bonds and government-backed participation certificates in mortgage pools--and, what interested Ryder, frequent international transactions evidenced by the correspondent balances in a dozen offshore banks.

Looking down the list of foreign correspondents, though, he didn't find what he expected or hoped for. The foreign banks were all in Africa and India. He looked up at Chanille.

"What the hell is this stuff?" he asked, jabbing a forefinger into the listing of foreign correspondents.

"I asked about that," she said. "If you look at the non-performing assets, you'll see a relatively large loan to an exotic game ranch. I never heard of them before, but apparently there are a lot in Texas. There's no season on exotics, so they can be hunted any time of the year. These game ranchers buy African and Indian animals, turn them loose behind tall fences and charge a big fee to hunters who are looking for a trophy. In the old days, they went to Africa to hunt big game. Now they just go to Texas."

"So it was legit?"

"I guess so," Chanille replied. "But with the recession, the fat cats don't come down so much and this game ranch First Mission lent to couldn't make the payments. The bank--I should say the FDIC--now owns a bunch of wild animals with big horns and 1,000 acres of West Texas scrub. They might be happy to have you take that off their hands, but the only market is other game ranchers and I imagine they're all in the same leaky boat."

Ryder shook his head. "What's this Mexican thing?" he asked, pointing to another line item.

"Mortgage loans to Mexicans who were buying resort property on South Padre Island. The loans were dollar-denominated, but when the Peso collapsed, the exchange rate killed the deal. The Mexicans couldn't pay in dollars, so the bank wound up with a bunch of condos on the beach."

"This guy really got hit by a shit storm, didn't he?" Ryder said.

"Pretty much. He had big ideas for such a little bank, though."

Ryder stared across the room, thinking. "Are you sure this is all there is to it? A guy like this . . . he doesn't seem like he belongs in banking."

"Want me to dig deeper?" Chanille asked.

"No, but it's curious. He doesn't seem like he did a lot about expanding the bank's footings in the U.S. Not that that would have saved him."

"He did invest in a winery in West Texas."

Ryder laughed. "A winery in West Texas? Let's see what else you've got."

"Possible acquisitions in the Caymans and Panamá. The detail isn't as good as we've got on US banks, but you wouldn't have all the regulation. You could do almost anything."

"Yeah, but transfers between US accounts and foreign banks leave a paper trail. Advantages and disadvantages either way."

"Not so much with Panamá. Their currency is the US dollar, remember."

London: September

September can be cold and damp in England, but that day the sky was a special pale blue and the air was soft and fresh through the lingering dusk. Beyond the terrace of Chilton Hall stretched one of those immaculate lawns that's been rolled for three hundred years and nourished by Britain's bountiful rain. Audrey had put half a dozen tables on the terrace, spaced for privacy, but she and McCall had it to themselves. Whatever the weather, the local hounds who made the Four Horsemen profitable preferred to drink inside, shoulder to shoulder. The sharp, sweet aroma of hops and pipe tobacco and the babble of convivial conversation drifted out through the French doors that joined the pub to the terrace.

Audrey was in her late sixties, but her silver hair was the main marker of her age. Her figure was full, the kind favored by Renaissance painters, and her bright blue eyes sparkled with spirit and mischief.

McCall turned from his fond appreciation of her and cast his eyes upward. "The sky was like this when the RAF was fighting the Battle of Britain," he said. "At least that's the way it looks in film footage I've seen. Men dying in a sky too beautiful to belong to a war."

"You lost your father in the war, didn't you?" Audrey asked in her distinctive, rich falsetto, knowing the answer.

"Uh huh. Normandy Invasion. He was a fighter pilot, but I always imagined that the day he died was gray and rainy, lots of smoke and death everywhere. Not a day like today at all."

"And you flew in Vietnam. What was that like?"

"Not like here. Except that a lot of people died. In Vietnam, people were just as dead, but why we were there wasn't clear at all_not from ground level or twenty thousand feet."

A wayward breeze swirled around the terrace, ruffling a few strands of Audrey's hair. She patted them back into place. "So unnecessary it all seems," she said. "Of course, I wasn't here to see any of it. Harold and I talked about coming home when the second war began--to stand by our England in her hour of need--but they pressed Harold into service in the British embassy in Lima and our better sense told us to accept. We were winning when Harold died, but Chilty was only five and England was no place to bring a child--there were terrible shortages and the Germans were sending those awful rockets at us."

"Why come back now?" McCall asked. "After all those years in Perú, it must have seemed more like home than England."

"Not really," she said, smiling and staring at the far horizon for a few moments before she turned back to McCall. "Like the birds, we know where we were hatched and we always try to return there. Besides, dear boy, Perú isn't what it once was. The political climate has become so much worse."

"Really?"

"Oh, yes," she said, a frown clouding her face. "Hideous things are going on between the Army and the *Sendero Luminoso*. Mostly in the mountains and the rural villages. But it's a spreading cancer that'll reach Lima soon enough." She paused. "I'm afraid it will be like Chile and Argentina--or El Salvador. Death squads and *desaparecidos*. Screams in the night. I didn't want to be there to hear it or see it." She caught her breath and exhaled slowly. "The news people here--or there, for that matter--don't report half of it. To know what's happening, you have to listen to the whispers of people who are afraid to speak out loud."

She reached across the table and patted his hand, a forced smile brightening her face. "But let's not talk about that. There are more pleasant things and better reasons to be in England again. Being home lets me see Chilty almost every week, not just on his annual pilgrimages for my birthday. And here you are. And back in Washington, which is only a few hours away."

McCall laughed. "Well, I'm sure Chilty's happy about having you here. So am I for that matter. And England seems to agree with you," he lied. She was more pale than he had ever seen her but it was no more than a passing concern that he attributed to the British climate. "Do you have a painting in the attic that's doing the aging for you?"

"Thank you, dear boy. It's charming of you to say so. I wish I could say the same of you." Audrey leaned toward him. "How are you? Truly."

McCall sighed, twisted his glass on the table top, his eyes downcast. "I'm angry. And sad. And discouraged. Nothing seems to be working out. I've lost almost everything and the damned government is trying to take what little is left." He sighed again but looked up and met Audrey's eyes. "Starting over is hard. I don't know that buying the bank was a mistake, but trying to run it myself sure as hell was."

"Is there anyone in your life these days?"

McCall turned his head to one side, his eyes twinkling in the dusk. "As far as the ladies are concerned, my dear, the ones who come for dinner and don't stay past breakfast are the only ones I'm interested in."

"I've never thought roguery suited you," she scolded. "I'd like to think there's a chance you'll find a soul mate one day. I'd like to be around to see that." She patted his hand again and added knowingly, her blue eyes fixed him, earnest and appealing.

"You can't live your life alone, Mack." "You have. For a long time, at least. Why is it alright for you and not for me? I didn't hide from the ladies in Texas. I met a lot of pretty ones, even two or three whose company I sincerely enjoyed . . . but no one I felt like sharing my life with."

"Well, I don't know what to suggest," she said, falling back in her chair, an edge of frustration in her voice. "I slept better when you were a banker. Now I lie awake nights thinking about hijacked airliners and terrorist bombs and kidnappings and your contracting some hideous disease that no one has ever heard of, much less can cure. I deplore your being perpetually and deliberately in harm's way."

"I'd never have met you if I hadn't been," he said, grinning.

"It's hardly gracious of you to remind me," she pouted, but a moment later, her high-pitched laughter tinkled across the terrace and drifted into the gathering dusk.

Audrey lit a candle at the table and McGinnis, the florid Irish barkeep with a whale's belly and a limp that was a legacy of SAS service in Aden, brought them another round of drinks. They refreshed their memories of Perú until it was time to go in for dinner.

"We have country paté this evening, Mack. Do you favor it as much as you once did?" Audrey asked.

"Indeed I do. No need to serve me anything else. But before we go in, there's something I want you to have," he said, taking an envelope from his coat pocket and handing it to her. "This is part payment on what I owe you. I guessed right on some high-yield bonds the other day. Quick in and out, tidy profit."

"*Owe me?*" Audrey asked, the candlelight flickering about her surprised face. "What on earth for?"

"For believing in me. I let you down and that's bad enough. I don't want it to cost you money as well."

"Oh, you mean my shares in the bank?"

He nodded.

She opened the envelope and took out the check. When she looked across the table, her eyes were brimming with tears. "I ca tn't take this, Mack. And I won't," she told him, holding a corner of the check to the candle's flame. "But you are so wonderful to have offered. I'll never forget that." It was his last time with her.

October, Washington

Leaving the shelter of the parking garage and heading up 15th Street, McCall popped open the black umbrella and scrunched his shoulders against a heavy drizzle falling from somber afternoon skies. The rain spoke more to the gray days of winter than to the cool and colorful days of autumn. The rain notwithstanding, for some reason McCall always looked forward to this time of year. Not today, though.

Today, meeting Chilty, he'd be reminded all over again that Audrey was gone. It wasn't that he'd forgotten her in the weeks since he stood beside her grave in the old stone church yard at Clovelly in the West Country. The sun had sparkled on the waters of Bideford Bay and he was happy she'd had fair weather. This gloomy day in Washington, a long way from Bideford Bay, it was raining and it was harder to remember the good things.

McCall furled the umbrella beneath the canopy of the venerable Madison Hotel and shook the rain from it before plunging through the revolving door, past the reception desk and straight into the Montpelier Room bar across from the elevators. It was early and the room was almost deserted. He saw Chilty right away, sitting at a table by the window watching the rain, his tall, angular frame bent into the overstuffed upholstery of the chair. Ross Chilton Chesley seemed to unfold rather than rise as McCall approached.

"Hello, Mack," he said, one long arm reaching out to shake McCall's hand.

"Hello, Chilty. Thanks for bringing your crummy weather with you. When'd you get in?"

"An hour ago. I haven't been to the Embassy yet. I had the driver pass by here first."

"The black Jaguar?" McCall asked.

Chilty raised his eyebrows and shrugged. "Are we so conspicuous? Not exactly what we pride ourselves on, you know."

"Dip plates? Some little British flag tag on the bumper? Parked in a 'no parking' zone? You think because the car's black, nobody's going to notice?" McCall shook his head and chuckled. "What you Brits call understatement is just your way of showing off. What brings you to the center of the universe?"

"Most Secret messages from the Iron Mistress to Her Britannic Majesty's ambassador. We could have brought him home, but you Yanks keep him in such a constant bother, he preferred to remain on station. It was my turn to come over. I really can't spare the time, but here I am."

"Shouldn't we have a drink then?"

"Suppose they have a decent whiskey?" Chilty asked, squinting to try to see the labels on the bottles behind the bar.

"The Madison? Not to worry." McCall turned around to catch the waiter's attention and held up two fingers. "Cardhu. Doubles. Water back. No ice."

Chilty cleared his throat and waited until the waiter was out of earshot. "Mack, I'd have wanted to see you in any event, but there's another reason for my calling you. We didn't know about the estate when we were together at Clovelly and it's not all surveyed yet, but I know you've had a run of bad luck and I wanted to tell you personally that Mum left a sum for you. Her solicitors are Llewelyn, Fisher and Cox. As I said, the inventory isn't done, but when it's complete they'll send a chap from their Washington branch to see you. Meantime, there's this." Chilty took an envelope from his inside coat pocket and passed it across the round, marble-topped table. McCall recognized Audrey's ivory stationery and her neat, spidery script. They inspired warm memories and he felt a stab of pain knowing he wouldn't see her again on this earth.

"Sorry I couldn't have given it to you before. It was tucked away at Chilton Hall and we only found it a few days ago. I'm glad I could bring it personally."

The waiter brought their drinks and disappeared. McCall held the envelope in one hand and took the heavy glass tumbler in the other. Still looking at the envelope, he said, "Here's to you, old girl. I miss you more than I can say."

McCall raised his glass and fixed his eyes on Chilty. "To Audrey."

"To you, Mum," Chilty replied and sipped his Scotch.

McCall held the envelope in the upturned palm of his hand as if it contained her ashes. Finally, Chilty asked, "Are you going to read it?"

"Yeah," he replied, sighing. The flap was sealed only at the tip but he opened it carefully, reverently, smiling at the neat slanting lines and swirls, a small echo of her life.

My dear Mack,   *September 16, 1985*

> *If you're reading this, you know that I've passed on to a more peaceful place. You've been as close to me as a son and I pray I'll be able to watch over you from some Elysian cloud that will follow*

you wherever you go. Since my guarantee of that blissful state may not be assured, I've set something aside that may clear a few of the stones from your path. Please be gracious and don't protest. Your wizardry allowed me to make a great deal of money these past twelve years and you've never let me reward you properly.

There are no strings attached, silken or otherwise, but perhaps you'll use it in some way for the beginning of the end of your vagabondage. I would so like to believe that one day you'll have a family and a normal life.

I hope you and Chilty will remain friends. You may need each other in the days to come—two lambs astray in the world without a proper shepherd—and if I can't be there, I'll rest easier knowing you're looking out for one another.

As for you, my boy, I'm so glad you were in my life.

Goodbye, dear Mack,
Audrey

McCall refolded the single sheet of heavy stationery and put it back in the envelope. He sat there feeling numb and sad, fighting the tears, glad that Chilty was across the table from him, glad it was still early and the bar was quiet.

"She wrote this right after I was there," McCall said, his voice unsteady.

"She did a lot of tidying up of her affairs about then. Wills and such. I didn't think much of it at the time. She seemed as hale and hearty as ever. Aneurysms don't telegraph their punches, so she must have had a premonition. She left a letter for me, too," Chilty added, smiling sheepishly. "Rather concerned about my marital state and such. I should have done something about it long ago, I suppose. No grandchildren for her to bounce on her knee. She would have liked that."

"I'm surprised about the money."

"You shouldn't be," Chilty said, bringing the tumbler to his mouth and taking a sip. "She told me how much she valued your advice. I should thank you, too. Although I'd have appreciated it more if you'd talked her out of buying that dreary old inn."

McCall smiled, choked back the emotion and forced himself to focus on less troubling issues. "I wouldn't worry about that. The land it's sitting on is worth more than she paid for the whole place. Why don't you just let old McGinnis run the pub and hire a manager for the inn? As I understood it from Audrey, the pub makes enough by itself to keep the operation in the black and you'll have something to fall back on when the Conservatives get thrown out of office."

"Sorry, old boy. I don't fancy myself an innkeeper, even of the absentee sort. And I'm not worried about Labour taking over just yet."

McCall finished his drink. "What about dinner? I could offer you a few well-chosen insights on the Reagan Administration's policy toward small banks."

"Sorry, Mack. Dinner with the ambassador. Since I went on the PM's staff, I scarcely have a life of my own. As for your Mr. Reagan, Mrs. Thatcher is quite fond of him." Chilty finished his drink and dried his lips with a thumb and forefinger. "Between me and thee, though, there are times she thinks his obsession with Reds under the bed is a bit over the top. This business in Central America, the Contras and the Sandinistas. Do your people really think Nicaragua is going to invade Texas?"

"First off, they're not my people. Second, they can have Texas with my blessing. But forgive me if I've misunderstood. Don't you come from the country that just went to war over some rock pile in the South Atlantic?"

"Touché. However, we won our little Falklands war. And you don't seem to be doing all that well with the Sandinistas."

"I hate to say it, but we did have Grenada."

Chilty laughed softly. "So you did. But didn't you take more casualties from friendly fire than the Grenadians?"

"A pox on both our houses then," McCall replied. "Look, I'll be passing through London the end of next week. Any chance we can get together? I'm doing a seminar in Vienna on bank management in a global economy. Imagine that. Like having a safe cracker lecture on security."

"Set a thief to catch a thief, they say," Chilty laughed. "Perhaps you have a new career ahead of you. As to getting together, my little group's going all out on something that popped up during the PM's visit to Moscow back in March. Chernenko's funeral. Remember? My lady and this Gorbachev chap get on famously and he has some interesting ideas. We're following up on one of them. Sorry I can't say more about it, but call me by all means. We'll have a meal or a midnight whiskey at least."

****

Two days after McCall saw Chilty at the Madison, Anton Becker of the Washington branch of the London law firm of Llewelyn, Fisher and Cox called to inform him of Audrey's bequest. McCall was escorted into a modest-sized corner office where he found Becker at a round oak table that served as his desk. Floor-to-ceiling bookshelves covered three walls. The fourth wall was glass--a large window, filled by a view of the offices of the Washington Post across the street.

Becker was a balding man in his mid-forties, well barbered, plump and pink-cheeked. A fresh aroma of after-shave wafted in the air around him. He rose to shake hands with McCall.

"Mr. McCall. Nice to meet you."

"My pleasure."

"Please. Have a seat," Becker said, indicating a modernistic chair at the round table. "Would you like some coffee?"

"No, thanks. I'm fine."

Becker opened the single folder his secretary had laid on the table and scanned the top document. "Ah, yes," he said, looking up to meet McCall's eyes. "Mrs. Chesley's bequest to you amounts to just over $51,000—all in cash and short-term US Treasury bills. The Treasury bills mature in a week--$20,000 there. How would you like us to make disposition?"

"Actually, I want to defer taking receipt of the funds."

Becker looked up, surprised. "Oh? For how long?"

"I don't know. Maybe several months. Can you put the cash in an escrow account in Panamá? In a bank I designate?"

"Panamá?"

McCall nodded.

"I suppose we could work that out," Becker said slowly. "I hope you don't mind my asking why you don't want to take receipt."

McCall met Becker's eyes and leaned forward. "I was the principal shareholder and CEO of a small bank in Texas that failed. Now the deposit insurance agency--the FDIC--wants the last drop of blood from my financial veins. They call it restitution. I call it extortion. Anyway, I don't want them to know I'm getting a transfusion. There's no judgment against me from a court proceeding and they don't contend that we did anything illegal. I think they're getting close to settling with me, but if they find out I've inherited more than a buck and a quarter, they might want to reopen negotiations. I'd rather that didn't happen."

"I understand," Becker said, offering McCall a sly smile and nodding sympathetically. "Our firm hasn't been involved with the FDIC, but I do read the newspapers and I live in Washington. I know what's going on. I'm surprised you aren't represented by counsel in this."

"Oh, I'm represented. Sam Tate's my lawyer in Texas and a close friend. He's negotiating with the FDIC for me. But Sam's a highly principled fellow and if he doesn't know about the money, he won't have to lie about it or be tempted to put any of it on the table. Sounds like I don't trust him, but that's not it."

"I see. Is there a particular bank you'd like us to use?"

"Banco Dorado. Talk to Javier Banderas and tell him it's for me."

****

McCall had his head under the shower, letting a torrent of cold water hammer him awake, when the phone rang. The first ring was no more than an interruption of the rhythm of the steady beat of the shower, just enough to focus his attention for a moment. Poking his head out of the shower, he heard the second ring clearly.

"Shit," he grumbled, shutting down the shower and grabbing a towel. It was only nine o'clock. Dripping through the hall into the bedroom, he picked up on the fifth ring.

"*Hola, Mack. Aquí Javier. Como estás?*"

"Hey, Javier. I'm wet, that's how I am. You got me out of the shower."

"*Hijo*, it's nine o'clock."

"Yeah, well," McCall said. "Did you get something for me?"

"I did. Overnight. It was on my desk this morning. Can you talk about it?"

"Not on the phone," McCall said.

Banderas didn't reply immediately. Then he said, "I have a meeting in New York next Monday. I could stop in Washington on the way back. Tuesday night?"

"That'd be great. Give me a call when you have a flight number and I'll pick you up."

Panamá City, Panamá

Javier Banderas put down the phone, turned in his large leather chair and stared out the picture window behind him. Over the tops of the palm trees, fronds bending languidly to the Pacific breeze, he could see the two long lines of ships standing out in the Bahia de Panamá, one waiting to enter the Canal, the other leaving, fanning out to destinations in North America, South America and points all over Asia. Even through the Venetian blinds, the bright blue of the tropical sky hurt his eyes and he squinted until they adjusted. Day or night, the scene was nearly always the same, except when the rains came and obliterated everything in an opaque, gray deluge.

It would be a week before he'd have an answer to the mystery of why McCall had chosen to hide money behind the screen of a law firm's escrow account. Panamá's bank secrecy laws were every bit as tight as Switzerland's; Mack could have put the money in his own name behind his own number and it would have been completely safe from prying eyes. He didn't need a law firm's escrow. Besides that, it was small change as secret accounts went. But whatever Mack's reasons, Javier would honor them. There were two people in the world who were important to Javier and Mack was one of them.

Mack had propped him up through college, been a true friend to a naïve, bewildered peasant from Panamá with a fragile command of English and a plodding way with his studies. And it was Mack who, six years ago, had entered into a silent partnership with Javier to buy the block of shares in Banco Dorado that made him a member of the board and all but guaranteed his future. The shares were in bearer form and only a single sheet of paper with a single typed paragraph, signed by Javier and notarized, attested to Mack's half ownership_just in case Javier were run over by a bus or done in by a jealous husband.

There were compelling reasons for doing it this way. For Javier to be a member of the board, he needed the appearance of owning the shares himself. But the arrangement also shielded McCall from the prying eyes of the Internal Revenue Service. Short of subjecting Javier to Chinese water torture, Mack's interest in Banco Dorado was untraceable. Hiding behind a law firm's escrow in a numbered account was the same thing--a double firewall. Javier just didn't know why Mack thought it was necessary.

Javier had always wondered why anyone would bother to look. Banco Dorado was a small fish in an ever-widening sea of heavy-weight international banks. It was not even among the first tier of local Panamanian banks.

It must have something to do with the failure of Mack's bank in the financial firestorm scorching the States. The thought of it gnawed at his stomach because Panamá hadn't escaped the sparks from that inferno--not just from the north, but from the south as well. The financial crises spreading over Latin America were hammering Panamá's financial sector, too.

Banco Dorado was already struggling with a growing number of non-performing loans. The bank wouldn't show a profit in the current year and Javier knew it could get much worse before it got better. If there were a storm,

Banco Dorado was no more seaworthy than a skiff at sea, particularly since Don Francisco Benedetti, the bank's hereditary chairman and major stockholder, refused to take on clients who gravitated to Panamá to launder drug money or fund the burgeoning traffic in arms to feed the war in Central America. Banco Dorado had grown out of a financiera in Colón a hundred years ago and while it had all the authorities and powers of the international banks, it remained close to its roots, providing banking services for small businesses and consumer loans for the Panamanian middle class. Banco Dorado wasn't entirely insular. It had a book of numbered accounts, held primarily by wealthy South Americans avoiding currency controls at home and shielding capital accumulated by generations of their families from the ravages of home-grown inflation. Javier saw nothing immoral, much less illegal, in what they were doing. Moreover, most of them were clients of long-standing and deserved every consideration the bank could give them.

Javier checked his watch. He was due downstairs to meet Don Francisco in five minutes. They often lunched together at the Club Union, but today they were going out to the Guest House, an acquisition of the bank in a foreclosure from a flamboyant German entrepreneur several years ago. Don Francisco used the Guest House as his personal getaway and made it available to visiting dignitaries and as a favor to influential friends and politicians. Doña Isabela had long suspected that Don Francisco used the Guest House as a place of assignation with his mistresses, but these days, it was home to their daughter, Carlotta, recently graduated from university in Switzerland.

That they were going to the Guest House for lunch meant there was a special occasion to celebrate or a matter of grave importance to discuss.

****

Vittorio, the Guest House major domo, drove the black Lincoln Town Car through iron gates controlled by an electronic signal and up a palm-lined drive to a low-lying house surrounded by tropical plants. A profusion of red ginger, purple bougainvillea and white plumeria set off glossy banana palms, veined elephant-ear caladiums and the delicate fans of leafy ferns.

Vittorio stopped in front of the entrance and allowed his passengers to alight. Javier followed Don Francisco along a flower-lined path to a long verandah spanning the front of the house. They passed through massive hand-carved double doors into a tiled foyer perched like a balcony before a two-story wall of glass. Beyond lay the deep blue of the Pacific Ocean. Below, a tropical garden swept away from the house and its open terrace. A stone patio and a free-formed pool fed by a small waterfall lay like jewels in the palm of the garden.

At the foot of the stairs on the polished, tropical hardwood floor, a young woman wearing a long white cotton dress looked up at them. Don Francisco held her eyes as he and Javier descended the long staircase from the foyer. As they neared the main floor, her smile widened and she glided toward them in easy, athletic strides. She held out her arms to Don Francisco.

"Papá," she said, embracing him. "How wonderful."

Don Francisco bent down to take the girl into his arms, his heavy features and great mane of white hair a striking contrast to her delicately-shaped face and the cascade of dark, glossy hair. Her large, brown eyes closed as she embraced him, but when Don Francisco released her, Javier found them focused directly on him--almond-shaped, shaded by heavy lashes.

"Javier, do you remember my daughter, Carlotta?" Don Francisco asked, showing the first sign of animation in their drive from the bank.

For a moment, Javier was speechless. "This is Carlotta? When I saw her last, she was in a school uniform, with knee socks and braided hair."

Carlotta laughed, and raised her eyebrows as if to say 'but no longer.'

Javier bowed and murmured, *"Encantado, señorita."*

Carlotta held out her hand to Javier, her amused smile lighting the room.

"Javier and I will be taking lunch, my dear," Don Francisco told her. "Please join us. We have business to discuss."

"Of course, Papá."

"Come along then," Benedetti said to Javier, putting an arm around his shoulders and leading him into the spacious living room. "Let me make you a drink. What would you like?"

"Cinzano and soda?"

"Excellent choice," Benedetti said, slipping behind the bar and bringing out a bottle of red Cinzano. "Carlotta?"

"Just a little Evian, Papá."

Don Francisco uncapped the bottle, poured the water into a tall glass and gave it to her. Then he filled two more tall glasses with crushed ice, poured them half full of Cinzano, topped them off with soda and added a wedge of lime. He kept one and handed the other to Javier.

"*Salud*," Don Francisco said, raising his glass.

"*Salud*," Javier replied, watching Don Francisco closely. The old man was in an unusually somber mood and Javier sensed that the occasion of their lunching at the Guest House wasn't a happy one.

"Ah," the old man said after taking a long swallow. "That's better. Now, both of you, come and sit down. I have troubling news."

Don Francisco settled in a high-backed, ornately carved straight chair at one end of the long cocktail table and faced the windows, gathering his thoughts before he began. Javier and Carlotta took their seats tentatively and watched the old man.

He took a deep breath and turned to them. "Rodrigo Morales came to see me this morning."

Javier braced himself, wary of what was coming next. Colonel Rodrigo Morales was the second largest shareholder in Banco Dorado and the patriarch of a venerable land-holding family that traced its bloodlines back to the sixteenth century, when Pablo Morales made his way to the New World as an ordinary seaman on a Spanish merchant ship. The original Morales was a bandy-legged peasant from Andalucía with the cunning of a cougar and the tenacity of a wild dog. He jumped ship in Portobelo and made his way across the Isthmus to the fledgling *entrepôt* of Panamá City. Morales prospered by bringing produce from the countryside to provision Pizarro's Peruvian treasure ships making harbor in the Bahia de Panamá. In time, he brought a bride from Spain and sired the beginning of a quiet dynasty that eventually controlled several large plantations as well as a thriving import-export business.

When Don Francisco wanted to bring the headquarters of Banco Dorado from Colón to Panamá City, Oscar Morales, Rodrigo's father, had been a logical man to turn to for the additional capital and for more than thirty years, the partnership had done well enough. Rodrigo, the oldest son, had been a disappointment to the family because he had chosen the *Guardia Nacional* as his career instead of the family business. When Oscar died, the family's interests had fallen into the hands of Rodrigo and Rodrigo's only son, Carmelo. The combination of a disinterested and untrained Rodrigo and an irresponsible Carmelo had been a disaster and a family fortune that had been four hundred years in the making was crumbling.

Panamá City is a small town to the natives and Javier, like any good banker, had followed carefully the whispers of Carmelo's disastrous investment decisions. He had a good idea why Colonel Morales had called on Don Francisco and held his breath waiting for his suspicions to be confirmed.

"Bank of America is calling in Morales' loans. He wants us to extend a line of credit to cover them." Don Francisco stared at Javier, tacitly asking the question of his Chief Operating Officer.

"How much?" Javier asked.

"Two million."

Javier's eyes widened. He'd thought perhaps half a million, but two million was out of the question.

"That's forty percent of our capital. We couldn't possibly do it. Even if it were a good loan--which we know very well that it isn't or B of A wouldn't be calling their loans. We've never made that kind of a loan to one of our directors--at least not since I've been with the bank."

"He's offering his stock as collateral," Don Francisco said.

Javier shrugged. "It hardly matters. His stock isn't worth two million and we'd have to look through the fiction of the loan to a forfeiture of the collateral. Given our earnings projections, his stock is worth less than a million and a half. At book value, only a million and a quarter. The bank is in no position to buy back his stock for a million, much less two, and that's what this would amount to."

Don Francisco hooded his eyes with heavy lids and looked down at his hands, nodding slowly. "Yes," he said. "I know." He looked up slowly and fixed his dark eyes on Javier. "He didn't come on his knees."

"What do you mean?" Javier asked, now sitting on the edge of his chair, back straight and rigid.

"He claims to have a firm offer of two million dollars for his stock from another party. He came today simply to give us the 'courtesy' of a first refusal."

"Who is the other party?"

"A *gringo* investment banker named Robert Ryder. Morales brought along the annual report. Ryder's company manages funds, but the report says almost nothing about their clients. I assume they are mainly South Americans or he would not be interested in our bank."

"So Morales would sell his twenty-five percent share of the bank to Ryder if we can't buy him out?"

Don Francisco nodded, his eyes sad and weary. "And I think Morales hopes to start a bidding war between us and the gringo. If we agreed to two million, the gringo would offer two and a quarter. If Morales weren't so stupid, he would know we couldn't afford to bid. Of course, he seldom comes to board meetings, so perhaps he is only ignorant."

"Twenty-five percent isn't control."

"Why would he offer a premium for Morales' stock if he did not want control?" Don Francisco asked. "We must assume he is not stupid even if he is a *gringo*."

"But if he isn't stupid, why would he want our little bank?"

Don Francisco raised his brushy eyebrows and put a forefinger alongside his nose. "There are many ways a bank can be useful."

Javier nodded. "Laundering money, letters of credit for illegal enterprises. I know. It can be a long list. But you have thirty-five percent and I have ten. And we hold the proxies for the other thirty percent. We would still outvote him. He would need to buy at least another twenty-six percent of the outstanding shares to take control. Do you think that would be easy? We have the only records of the shareholders. The Comision Nacional de Valores doesn't begin to have a complete registration. Our shares are almost all in bearer form anyway. Without our records, they have no way to identify the other shareholders."

"True enough," Don Francisco said. "But you forget that Rodrigo Morales has been on our board for many years. As a director, he has access to the names on the proxies. We have to assume he knows who they are."

Javier sighed and slumped in his chair. He knew who they were, too. Grandsons and granddaughters and nieces of the early investors in Banco Dorado who had received their shares as inheritances and owed no loyalty to Banco Dorado beyond the quarterly dividend. Most would have sold their shares long ago, but without a stock market in Panamá, trades were essentially private placements negotiated by the handful of stock brokers that operated in the city. There was no viable market for the shares of Banco Dorado--until now.

Carlotta had watched the exchange between her father and Javier quietly, her dark brown eyes flicking alertly from one to the other as they spoke.

"What are you saying, Papá?" she asked, speaking for the first time, her voice suddenly brittle.

"We must decide whether we can fight to save the bank or if the better decision would be to sell our own shares and begin again." Don Francisco sighed and added, "Or in my case, to sit in the sun and do nothing."

Carlotta bolted out of her chair and bent forward, facing her father, her cheeks flushed beneath the golden tan of her skin. "How can you say that? How can you think it? The bank has been in our family for a hundred years. We call it Banco Dorado, but everyone knows it's Banco Benedetti.

And you promised it to me. Why have I been away all these years in Switzerland, studying finance? Not to be a clerk in some gringo bank and be bossed around by *gringo* puppies from Harvard and Yale, thinking they can pat my behind whenever they want. We have to fight! This bank is ours!"

"Carlotta," Don Francisco said, spreading his hands out, pleading. "We are only a little bank. And there would be no need for you to be a clerk in anyone's bank. With Javier to manage the portfolio, we could all live comfortably."

"No!" Carlotta screamed, stamping her foot, her hands balled into small fists. "Why do you think they want our bank? To wash narcodollars for the Columbian Mafia and smuggle rifles into El Salvador and Guatemala. An ugly stain on the honor of our family! I will not agree to sell the bank."

Carlotta turned away from them, walked to one of the massive windows and took a belligerent stance, her arms crossed beneath her breasts.

Don Francisco stared at her for several minutes before turning back to Javier. "Can you think of any way to fight them?"

"Not really." Javier thought about Mack. Once upon a time, Mack might have been able to help, but not now. He had troubles of his own. "If we could find a white knight we could trust to bid against Ryder for Morales' shares . . . "

Don Francisco twisted his glass on the table, stirring the condensation. "Yes, a white knight from a fairy tale. Not for our little bank, I'm afraid."

"I'll be in New York next week. I can ask."

"Yes, by all means, ask," Don Francisco said, but there was no hope in his voice.

****

Lunch could have been held in a mausoleum. Vittorio served *corvina* dressed with a tangy lemon sauce that under normal circumstances would have delighted their palettes and, washed down with a chilled Pouilly Fuissé, would have filled the room with warm conversation and laughter. But Vittorio's meal scarcely penetrated the gloom around the long, polished dining table and they scarcely spoke. They ate only half the *corvina*, pushed the bulbs of buttered broccoli around on the plate and ate the *flan* out of courtesy to Vittorio. As soon as they were finished, Don Francisco excused himself to have a siesta.

"If you need to return to the bank, Javier, Vittorio will take you," Don Francisco said. A siesta, yes, but he wouldn't sleep. He'd hang up his coat, loosen his tie, take off his shoes and lie on the bed cover in the half light, watching the ceiling fan turn slowly, regretting his mistakes, feeling his life slipping away. This afternoon, he would torment himself with regret that he should have built a stronger capital base, that his employees' salaries were the highest in the city, that he'd made loans that owed more to his sympathy for the plight of the borrower than to that borrower's ability to repay. Wasn't his generosity misplaced if it meant the collapse of the bank?

As Don Francisco trudged up the stairs to the master suite, Carlotta took Javier's arm. "Please stay," she said. "I'd like to talk to you."

Javier didn't want to stay, but it would have been rude to refuse, so he let her lead him out to the terrace overlooking the garden and down to the patio by the pool.

Strong-willed women made Javier uncomfortable and he had few illusions about what Carlotta was doing. He wasn't surprised when she sat down by the waterfall on a ledge of stone jutting out over the pool and hiked up her long skirt, revealing half her thighs as she dabbled her bare feet in the water. Soft and girlish now, teasing him with the seductive movements of her legs in the water. He hardened his mind to her. Fighting for the bank or selling out would turn on issues far more important than a girl's ill-founded confidence that she could run a bank, even a small one, just because she had been to school in Switzerland and knew how to flutter her eyelashes.

First and foremost, he had himself to think of. He had worked hard to reach his position in the bank. There was sweat and sacrifice on every share of stock he owned. There was Don Francisco, just past seventy and showing less and less interest in the affairs of the bank. And Mack. What would Mack want to do? Mack might jump at the chance to sell given his financial calamity in Texas. He would have to put the choice to him in Washington next week and Mack's decision, not Carlotta's pretty face, would be a crucial factor. If Mack wanted to sell, Javier would be honor-bound to release his shares. Mack's five percent, added to Morales' twenty-five, would give Ryder thirty percent against Javier's and Don Francisco's forty. The other twenty percent would fall to Ryder like ripe fruit once the word got out. Whatever Carlotta wanted or thought she was entitled to was inconsequential.

They both looked up when they heard Vittorio coming slowly down the steps to the patio. He was bearing a tray with a pitcher of blood-red, chilled sangría with bits of fruit floating in it.

"Thank you, Vittorio," she said, rising effortlessly from beside the pool and taking the tray from him. Javier started to get up but Carlotta said, "Stay there. I'll serve you." She poured from the pitcher into two tall, frosted glasses and crossed to where Javier was sitting.

"*Salud*," she said and took a sip, watching Javier over the rim of her glass.

Javier kept his silence, waiting for her opening gambit.

"Papá seems more tired than usual, don't you think?"

Javier shrugged. "Perhaps Papá is ready to retire," she said.

"Perhaps he does not have the will or the strength to fight for the bank."

She waited for Javier to agree or disagree, but he said nothing. "If Papá retired, the bank would fall to you and me. Naturally, I would defer to your greater experience in running the bank." So that was the bait, he thought. Might as well throw some cold water on that. "Assuming Ryder and whoever he's representing aren't able to pick up the twenty-six percent they need for control."

Carlotta placed a warm hand on his forearm. "I'm sure a way can be found to stop them," she said. "But we must fight," she added, her fingers gripping his arm tighter. "You're willing to fight, aren't you?"

"We aren't ready to make a decision one way or another, Señorita Carlotta. We have to look at all the options and there are others to consider."

"Who else?" she shot back. "Papá is the majority shareholder."

"The minority shareholders, obviously. I know many of them. I need to talk to them, see whether they would stand with us. If not . . . well, the battle is lost before it begins."

Carlotta frowned and paced the flagstone patio. Finally, she said, "Go and think, then. I will think, too."

With relief, Javier rose, leaving his sangría untouched on the glass-topped table. "*Pues, entonces, Señorita. Gracias por su hospitalidad. Hasta la proxima.*"

Washington National Airport

McCall leaned against the massive window at the gate and watched the TWA flight from New York come in. It had been almost two years since he'd seen Javier, though they talked on the phone from time to time. Picking out the dots of window lights as the plane settled onto the runway, he wondered how careful he should be about meeting with Javier. He didn't think the FDIC was watching him, but he didn't want them to find out about his Panamá connection. It would raise questions he didn't want to have to answer.

He moved back into the concourse when the aircraft docked and watched the mouth of the jet bridge. The deplaning passengers were mostly businessmen, hanging bags thrown over one shoulder, briefcases an extension of their arms, another hard-fought battle in New York under their belts. Javier looked the freshest of the lot, his dark, wiry hair a disorderly bush atop his head. A mustache to match failed to hide the crooked-tooth smile when he saw McCall.

"*Hola*, Mack. *¿Como te va?*" Javier said, taking McCall's outstretched hand with his free one and turning it into a one-armed *abrazo*.

"I've been better," McCall told him with a grin. "It's good to see you. I take it you got a deposit on my behalf?"

"It's in a London law firm's escrow," Javier whispered. "What's the story?"

McCall filled him in as they joined the river of passengers flowing toward baggage claim and the exits. "The FDIC is squeezing me for restitution and they'll base what they'll settle for on what I've got left. As far as they know, that's the vested share of my retirement plan, my condo in Alexandria--which is now my homestead and therefore untouchable--and a few thousand bucks from selling the stuff from my house in Texas. They don't know about my piece of Banco Dorado, of course. But since then, a friend of mine died and left me some money. That's what I sent to Banco Dorado. It's not much, but I don't want the FDIC to find out about it before they sign off on the settlement. That's why I had the lawyers set up an escrow account with you. I haven't taken receipt of the money, so I think I could argue that it isn't mine yet. It's devious, but I don't feel obliged to play straight with the Feds when they're screwing me."

Javier nodded. "The money would have been safe behind a numbered account, but I understand that you want to be able to say it's not your money yet. I can still give you an overdraft if you need to draw it down."

"Thanks, Javier. I appreciate it. How's Banco Dorado doing?"

"There's a problem. We need to talk."

****

Chez Andrée was the closest quiet place McCall could think of. Set in a once exclusive Alexandria neighborhood, it offered excellent French cuisine and a wine list to match. Best of all, on a Monday night, the crowd would be light and they'd have enough privacy to talk business in confidence.

McCall hadn't been in Chez Andrée in more than five years and he was pleased that nothing had changed except the hostess who greeted them in the small alcove inside the front door. It used to be André's wife, Marie, a bosomy, middle-aged delight of a woman. Tonight it was an attractive, dark-haired twenty-something with a belly as flat as wallboard and big eyes under lush eyebrows.

"How's Marie?" McCall asked.

The dark eyes widened and the smile twinkled with sudden warmth. Her voice was a symphony of French accent. Just off the last flight from Paris. "Madame Marie is away this evening. I'm sure she will be sorry to have missed you, Monsieur . . ."

"McCall," he replied. "Tell her I'm back in town and I'll see her again soon. Do you have something in the corner where we can talk?"

"*Mai ouí*. It is very quiet tonight, Monsieur McCall. Please follow me."

Hips swaying evocatively, she took them to a corner table with a starched white tablecloth set with silver that glowed softly in the dim lighting. When they were seated, she gave them each a leather bound menu and took their drink order.

Javier waited until she returned with Martinis in outsized glasses, took one approving sip and then began explaining the dilemma Morales had posed to Banco Dorado. "So what do you want to do?" Javier asked when he'd finished.

McCall frowned and took a large swallow of his Martini. "I can't cash out now. The FDIC would eat me alive if they caught me with a couple hundred thousand undeclared dollars. And it would hang Sam out to dry. I told him I didn't have anything stashed outside the country. Can you put it off for a few months, until I get this thing with the FDIC settled?"

Javier shook his head. "I don't think so. As I told you, B of A is calling Morales' loans. And Morales is only pretending to ask us for a loan. He wants to sell his shares and he wants the highest bidder."

"This guy who's frothing at the mouth to buy Morales's shares--what do you know about him?"

"Almost nothing. He's a New York investment banker. Robert Ryder. Ever hear of him?"

McCall shook his head.

"The company manages funds, we suppose for South American clients, but Ryder's annual report only talks about how much money they have under management, not about the clients. Naturally." "You don't know then whether Ryder is tendering on his own account or for someone else." "Yes. That's true. We can only assume that he's not making an investment with appreciation in mind. He--or whoever he represents--wants control. Why else would he offer Morales a premium for his shares?" "And he wants Banco Dorado because . . . ?" Javier shrugged. "Banco Dorado may be small but it's a full-fledged member of the Panamanian banking system, the most secretive in the world and one of the least regulated. If you want to write letters of credit for agricultural equipment and ship AK-47s, there is very little to stop you. Panamá is close enough to Colombia and Mexico to play a role in the drug traffic. Take your pick or do both. Ryder doesn't want Banco Dorado as a straight investment." They looked at each other for a long moment before Javier spoke again. "You don't want to be part of that, do you?" "Are you kidding? Of course not," McCall said. "But how do we buy out Morales? If the bank can't do it on its own account, what about a local white knight? Even then, Ryder might raise his bid. If whatever he's got in mind is lucrative enough, a couple more million wouldn't faze him." "We were hoping you might know someone you could persuade to come in with us. Maybe some Texas oil man?" McCall grunted and shook his head slowly. "Forget Texas oil men for awhile. And where banking is concerned, Wall Street is full of bottom feeders right now. The FDIC has too many bargains on offer. I tried like hell to interest the people I knew best to recapitalize First Mission and I didn't get any takers. Granted that a bank in Texas these days and a bank in Panamá are different animals, I don't think I have a lot of credibility with the venture capital people up here. Still, I can make some calls tomorrow. See what they say."

Javier smiled his crooked-tooth smile. "I brought the latest numbers with me. Not a proposal, but you could talk from it."

McCall nodded. "Can you stay through tomorrow, in case somebody wants to meet with a principal?"

"I have a flight at six in the evening, but I could change it. Do you really think it might be possible?"

"No," McCall said, shaking his head. "I don't. All I can do is give them a chance to turn us down."

Javier's hopeful smile faded and he nodded soberly. "I understand. What about a Plan B?"

"Issue subordinated debt and buy the bastard out," McCall said. "Place it privately with some of your South American oligarchs. If they don't want your stock, maybe they'd take your debt."

"I thought of that, but the debt would still have to be serviced. Our earnings aren't strong enough now, not without getting into shady business. Don Francisco doesn't want to go that way. Neither do I."

McCall nodded and asked, "How soon do you have to make a decision?"

"Morales has given us thirty days, but if he thinks we aren't going to bid, he could sell at any time. I don't trust him."

"We don't know nearly enough, compadre. We need to find out who Ryder is and who might be behind a takeover bid if he's only acting as an agent."

"How can we do that?"

"Sam Tate, my lawyer down in Texas, used to be one of Lyndon Johnson's fair-haired boys. He knows everybody up here worth knowing. I'll see if he'll tap some of his sources," McCall said, picking up the menu. "Now let's eat. The food is very good here."

McCall had a momentary pang of concern over what he could afford, but decided this was no time to change his lifestyle because of a little thing like a shortage of funds. Might as well spend it as take a chance on letting the FDIC get their grubby paws on it. He suggested the coquille St. Jacque, ordered a bottle of Meursault from Les Charmes and changed the subject. There had to be better things to talk about than his and Javier's financial crises. But even while they talked about Panamanian politics and old friends, McCall's thoughts kept straying back to the problem. There were places he could hide the money he'd get from the sale of his stock in Banco Dorado. What worried him most was whether the transaction could be hidden. The stock was in bearer form, but a bank changing hands in Panamá . . . that might make enough ripples to stir up the Feds' interest. And they didn't know what price Ryder might be willing to pay for his and Javier's shares. If he got Morales' twenty-five percent and then went after the minority shareholders, he might try to squeeze them. Once Ryder got, say, forty percent of the stock, he might just name the price he'd offer Javier and Mack and tell them to take it or leave it. They could get royally screwed.

****

McCall put down the phone and looked into Javier's anxious eyes. "That's four, 'mano. And three others who wouldn't take my call. I'm fresh out of venture capitalists. There might still be somebody who'd be interested in a piece of a little bank in Panamá, but you'll have a better shot at finding them down there than up here."

Javier nodded sadly. "I wonder if Morales has already talked with our other shareholders. We could try to buy up some of the small holdings, make it more difficult for them when and if they go after control."

"How much cash have you got?"

"I could free a hundred, maybe two hundred thousand. At current book value, that's no more than five percent of our outstanding shares."

McCall shook his head. "That won't help much. And if Morales has already talked to them, you can bet they're not going to sell cheap."

They ate bologna sandwiches and drank beer for lunch. Then Mack called Sam Tate. They chatted for a minute or two about the progress of negotiations with the FDIC, then McCall said, "Sam, I need a favor. Actually, it's a favor for a friend. Some New York outfit is trying to put a friend's bank in play down in Panamá and he's seeing nothing but smoke as far as who this guy is or who he represents. We think it's a dirty deal, that he wants the bank for money laundering or financing the arms trade. Do you think you could make some calls? . . . Ryder. Robert Ryder. The outfit's Ryder and Company. Wall Street . . . We need it like yesterday, Sam. . . . Yeah, there's a deadline. . . . Next few days. I'm off to Vienna end of the week. . . . About ten days. . . . Thanks, Sam. I really appreciate it."

McCall hung up the phone and looked at Javier. "That's my best shot. Sam will get back to me as soon as he can. Before I leave if possible."

In late afternoon, McCall drove Javier over to National Airport to catch his Miami flight, parked and walked him to the gate.

"Let's leave it at this," he told Javier. "You keep thinking about how to find another buyer down there. We'll hang whatever Sam comes up with on the decision tree when he gets back to me. We may not have a choice here. We may have to sell. Scares the hell out of me that the FDIC might find out about my share, but between the two of us, we ought to be able to find someplace to hide it. Worse comes to worst, I'll take the money and run. Don Francisco can retire and you and I'll start another bank somewhere. The Caymans, Bahamas, somewhere like that. Don't worry, compañero, we're going to be OK."

Javier nodded and gave McCall an abrazo. "Could you meet me in Miami later this week if I come up with something?"

"Yeah, but after that you'll have to call me in Vienna. I'm staying at the Palais Schwarzenburg. I don't think the FDIC is tapping my phone in Austria, but you never know, so be careful what you say if you call me."

"I have to talk to Don Francisco. It's his bank. And it's not just up to us. There's also Carlotta. She wants to fight them."

"That's what you said. But you and I are the swing votes."

Washington

"There's good news and bad news about that favor you asked me," Sam Tate told McCall.

"What's the good news?"

"The guy is known to my source. The bad news is that my source won't talk about him over the phone or in writing. It's face to face or not at all."

"Can you do it?"

"I've got a lot of stuff going on here, Mack. How bad do you need this? I mean, really."

"My friend's on a thirty-day clock. Less than that now. And he doesn't know who he's dealing with. How'd you like to negotiate under those conditions?"

At the other end of the line, McCall heard Tate sigh. "OK. I'll do some work on your FDIC deal while I'm up there and it'll all go on your bill. Who knows, you might be able to pay me someday."

"You're a prince," McCall said. "When can you be here? I'm leaving on Thursday."

"I assume you'll be flying out of Dulles?"

"Right. I've got an eight o'clock. At night."

"Suppose you come early and I meet you there around five? The main terminal. Outside security."

****

Fall was reaching its most spectacular in Washington as Sam leaned back in the taxi and watched the Potomac go by. Golds and browns and reds were sprinkled through the trees along the Mt. Vernon Parkway and the air was brisk and clean. He'd taken the early flight out of San Antonio, changed planes in Dallas, and reached the nation's capital in time for lunch. With luck, he could get what Mack wanted, pass it on and settle into one of the big seats in the first class cabin of the six o'clock flight out of Dulles.

Sam hadn't seen Paul Clemens in years. They'd been young members of the White House staff in the late 1960s, Paul staffing Lyndon Johnson's National Security Council while Sam was earning his spurs in the White

House counsel's office. After Johnson rode off into the sunset, Paul drifted over to the CIA and Sam went back to Texas to hang out his shingle. Sam consciously used his Johnson administration connections to build a practice in Johnson's home state and stayed plugged in to Washington_once a contact, always a contact in Sam Tate's book. Whatever the problem, Sam Tate made sure he knew who to call and that included people like Paul Clemens.

Paul had risen quietly and slowly in the CIA's directorate of intelligence, the arm of the agency that analyzes information from all sources and is the keeper of the agency's voluminous files. If someone wanted a bank in Panamá, it was likely that Clemens knew pretty much everything about that person, including why he wanted the bank, or if he didn't, he knew who did and was probably on a first-name basis with him or her.

The taxi crossed the Potomac at the Memorial Bridge, threaded its way through the West End to Massachusetts Avenue and eased into the circular drive in front of the Cosmos Club, where Sam had been a member since his White House days. Henry, the six-foot-four doorman, swung wide the heavy glass door and admitted Sam into a spacious foyer flanked by veined marble columns with Ionic capitals. Outsized oriental rugs covered the marble floor and to the right, the curving foot of the grand staircase spilled its red carpet into the foyer. Leather lounge chairs and a polished library table with the day's major newspapers neatly arrayed defined an area around the fireplace where guests were obliged to wait for their hosts. Paul Clemens, distinguished by a well-barbered shock of silver-gray hair, lowered the copy of the Financial Times he'd been reading, caught Sam's eye and gave him a broad smile.

Sam covered the distance between them in three long strides, stretching out his hand, grinning.

"Paul," he said. "It's great to see you again."

"You, too," Clemens replied.

They chatted amiably as they ascended the broad staircase to the dark paneled second floor hall that contained the portraits of the distinguished members of the Club and gave access to the bar, upstairs dining room and lounge. Sam led the way into the bar and asked for a table in the corner by the windows.

They went directly to the menu while their server brought the Club's famous popovers. Paul asked for the lamb chops and an iced tea. Sam scrawled it on the order slip, adding a ham sandwich on rye and a bottle of Warsteiner for himself. He pushed the slip to one side of the table for the server to collect and leaned forward.

"I'm glad you could make this on such short notice. I hope I'm not putting you on the spot."

Clemens shook his head, smiling. "I need to get out once in awhile."

They chatted about careers and family. Paul had never met Bitsy, so Sam showed off her picture and brought him up to date. Paul's two sons were in college, one at Brown, the other at Williams. They exhausted the small talk quickly and Paul brought up the subject of Ryder.

"Some ground rules, Sam. First of all, this meeting never happened," he said, waited stone-faced for the cliché to register, then grinned. The grin dissolved and Paul added, "I don't want to mention names, so you'll have to make inferences. OK?"

Sam nodded.

"He used to be one of ours. Understand what I mean? We parted company on unpleasant terms but we keep tabs on our exes. After he left, he went in with his father. Most of the firm's business then, as now, is in Latin America. On the surface, they just manage funds, but they walk on the shady side of the street when it comes to the way the funds they manage are generated."

The server came with their lunch orders and Paul's story was momentarily interrupted.

When the server left, Sam asked, "So how's it work?" Using his knife like a scalpel, Clemens carved away a morsel of lamb from one of his chops, inspected it and brought it into his mouth. He chewed appreciatively for a few moments, then continued. "Suppose a country borrows a hundred million with a sovereign guarantee and they pay discount points up front from the proceeds of the loan. Suppose the loan carries ten points plus origination fees. Are you following this?"

Sam nodded. "So far."

"OK. When the loan closes, the borrowing country gets ninety million and owes a hundred million--plus interest, probably London Interbank Rate plus three or four, not counting the ten discount points. The loan's due in two or three years. What happens to the ten million? Well, the bank consortium gets five million—which is probably a legitimate risk premium--and they're happy. They know the loan originator--the middleman--is spreading the other five million around to the generals, but they don't care as long as they have the sovereign guarantee. Two years later, when the loan comes due, they roll it over and do the deal all over again. You can see how the minister of finance or the president or the head of the central bank could accumulate a lot of money in just a few years. You've got a pretty good nut by the time the next coup d'etat comes around and you get thrown out of office. And of course, you want to keep your stash offshore in hard currency investments."

Sam took a bite of his sandwich, crunched some potato chips and took a swallow of beer. "I get it," he said. "And you're grateful to the guy who put the deal together for you."

"Yeah," Clemens said. "And so far, no harm, no foul as far as we're concerned. But suppose one of these countries gets in over its head and--God forbid--defaults on their loans? To American banks. And those banks come screaming to Uncle Sam to do something about it. There's a chance something like that is about to happen right now—in Perú. In which case, there'd be people in our government who'd want to know how a certain country got so far in debt and why the banks weren't paying attention and if there was anybody here who had a part in it and so on. You know how these investigations go."

"How would an offshore bank figure into this? Why do you think our boy would want one?" Sam asked.

"Well, Panamá is one of two foreign countries where US dollars are the circulating medium of exchange, which simplifies a lot of things, and the country in question has an interesting set of banking laws to boot. Are you familiar with them?"

"In a general way. Switzerland South, right?"

"Close enough. But the truth is, for a straight funds management operation here in the States, you wouldn't need that. So your question set me to thinking about it. There's a lot going on in that area and they may be branching out. A bank of a certain sort could be very useful if business of a certain sort became attractive to your boy's clients. Can you use your imagination here?"

"Maybe," Sam said, knitting his brows and trying to follow Clemens' opaque scenario.

Clemens held Sam's eyes for a long time, debating with himself about the next step. At last, he decided to go ahead. "There may be another party involved here. A very powerful party, trying to run under the radar, and needing some extracurricular banking services. Are you still following me?"

Sam shook his head. "Not now. You've lost me. Are you saying there's an organization--not just a group of individuals--our boy might be representing?"

"Let me just say that he's acting on behalf of, or at the direction of, certain parties who have connections with people whose power is truly awesome. Does that narrow the field?"

Sam thought he understood. "That scares the hell out of me."

"And well it should. I won't say any more about it, but I need you to keep me informed about how this deal goes down. That's the *quid pro quo*."

"I understand," Sam said. "The thing is, though, I'm not a party to any of this. I really did mean that I'm doing this as a favor for a friend. And as far as I know, he's not a party to the deal either. It's a friend of his whose bank is in the crosshairs. So it's hard to promise a lot. I'll do what I can."

"Who's your friend?"

"A client. So I'd rather not say who it is," Sam said, grinning.

"What's the name of the bank that's being targeted?" "I don't know. But I think I can get that for you without running afoul of the Ethics Committee of the Bar Association."

Clemens nodded. "Fair's fair. But I am serious about the information. Don't just blow it off if it doesn't come easy. OK?"

Clemens gray eyes were hard for a long moment and Sam had a feeling that Mack had drawn him into something larger and more sinister than the acquisition of a little Panamanian bank by a Wall Street gunslinger.

"As I said, I'll do my best. I'm sure you went out on a limb with this for me. I won't forget."

Clemens' expression softened. "I know."

****

Late afternoon sunlight filtered through the vaulted glass windows of Dulles International as McCall paced back and forth in front of the security stations. He'd checked his bag at the curb and had only his briefcase and London Fog raincoat to bother with. The London Fog was practically the uniform of short, tall, young and old men filtering through the terminal on their way to distant points of the globe and the nation. Once, McCall remembered wistfully, Dulles had handled only international flights and the pace of passage through the dramatic terminal to the specially-designed transporters that swept passengers in comfort from the main terminal to their aircraft was leisurely. Now, to take pressure off National, long-haul domestic flights had been added to the Dulles schedule, vastly increasing the volume of traffic and requiring the construction of a mid-field terminal that, compared to the main terminal, looked like combat boots on a super model. The distinctive transporters were still in use, but they served only to move passengers from the elegant main terminal to the congestion of the concourses of the mid-field terminal.

Sam came from the ticket counters and McCall saw him as soon as he turned into the departure area. He was half a head taller than the crowd and his rolling gait was distinctive, even without the boots.

"Let's go down to the windows," he said and McCall followed him. The end of the terminal was practically deserted and they stood looking out on the roof of a lower building and the tarmac beyond.

"I've got something for you," Sam said. "But first tell me the name of the bank that's involved."

"Banco Dorado. It's a small, plain vanilla bank. Some international business, but mostly local clients. Been around for a hundred years. Definitely not a high flyer."

"So I guess a bandido could hide behind its good reputation for awhile."

"Is Ryder a *bandido*?"

"Not in the sense of 'your money or your life,' but he's a mercenary without morality." Sam went on to describe the skimming operation that channeled money from short-term foreign loans to the pockets of members of ruling military juntas in Latin America. "He manages the ill-gotten gains for these guys. My source thinks they might be getting set to branch out from stodgy old stocks and bonds. A bank like your friend's could be useful."

"Branch out into what?"

"My source wouldn't get into the specifics, but it seems to me that it might be drug money or guns or both of them together. You know there's a guerilla war going on in Central America."

"Vaguely. I've had other things on my mind."

"There's a hint also that he might be involved at some official US level. Your boy is ex-CIA, so he has the training and probably the contacts to be part of some end-run the Reagan administration might be making with the Contras. You're not personally involved in this, are you?"

McCall shook his head, lying to Sam again. "Just doing a favor for an old friend. They're trying to decide whether to sell or fight, not that they have a lot to fight with if Ryder and his friends are determined to take them over. I can't help but feel like a kindred spirit. Somebody wants your bank, so they just take it. You don't have a lot to say about it. Hell's bells, they're even trying to make me pay them for the favor. By the way, how're things going with my case?"

"I spent a couple of hours this afternoon with some of the birds working your case. They're looking at your big fat salary now, wondering how you spent it all."

"Damn it, Sam, that's none of their business. My board approved it and I paid the taxes."

"Don't get your knickers in a twist," Sam said. "I told you they'd look for money you might have stashed offshore. This is one of the ways they do it. They may have some questions to ask before long. If we have reasonable answers, they'll probably let it go."

McCall shook his head. "Is it too late to migrate to Canada?"

The loudspeakers announced Sam's flight and he held out his hand. "That's me, compadre. You'll be back when?"

"About ten days. I'm at the Palais Schwarzenburg if you need me. Thanks for the poop on this guy Ryder."

"I want to be kept in the picture on this bank deal, Mack. It's the price I had to pay for the information."

"Sure, Sam. I'll do what I can."

McCall watched him turn away, pass through the security check and stroll on to the transporters. As soon as Sam was gone, McCall went to the phone booths.

He found Javier in his apartment and passed on what he'd learned about Ryder from Sam.

"I don't know what it means, 'mano," he said. "But I think we have to assume this guy is working with at least one other group, most likely his clients. He might be doing part of the deal on his own, but I'd be surprised if his pockets were deep enough to buy control. He'd need over four million if we use his offer to Morales as the benchmark. He might not even have the two million. Can you find out who he's representing down there, where he might get the money to buy the bank?"

"I'll try, Mack. Where are you now?"

"At the airport. You know where to get me if you need to."

London: October 1985

Early Friday morning, sleep still fogging his brain from flying against the clock, McCall made his way to the taxi line and stowed his bags beside the driver. He fell into the commodious back seat of the boxy, black English cab and stretched his legs. Fifty dollars later, the doorman saw to his luggage at the London Inter-Continental and McCall phoned Chilty from his room.

"Did you just arrive?" Chilty asked.

"A couple of hours ago. I'm at the Inter-Con. What's your schedule look like?"

"Rotten. I'd rather we had time for a long lunch. Perhaps on your return. Nonetheless, I need to see you. I've a favor to ask. Could you come to Victoria Tower Gardens at half twelve?"

"Twelve-thirty? Sure. That's the park on the river by Parliament, isn't it? Opposite end from Big Ben?"

"Just so," Chilty said. "I'm meeting with one of the MPs this morning and I can catch you there before dashing back to Number Ten."

****

McCall crossed the softly-lit lobby, all polished dark wood and rich upholstery, passed through the revolving door and emerged from the porte-cochere into the clear, soft blue light of English autumn. The leaves had turned golden green and his stroll through St. James Park was balm for the tattered edges of his spirit.

Chilty had arrived first, his long frame unmistakable beside the low wall above the Thames. He had a funnel of newspaper in each hand which McCall recognized as wrapping for London's infamous fish and chips. Chilty gestured with his head to a bench when he saw McCall.

"Thanks for coming, Mack. Sorry I can't feast you at the club, but I'm awash in urgent memoranda from the PM herself. I only have a few minutes." Chilty wolfed a piece of fish and offered one to McCall.

"That's OK," McCall said, casting a suspicious eye on the spreading patches of grease leaking through the newspaper wrapping. "I'm not hungry. What's the favor?"

"Right. Well, you see, along with the other assets—Chilton Hall, you know, and the investment portfolio--Mum also passed on an awkward problem. Of course, it wouldn't be awkward if it weren't for the timing,"

Chilty said, agitated and visibly upset. "It's this project I'm working on. I mustn't have the conflict of interest."

"What are you talking about, Chilty?"

"The bonds. The Russian bonds. She's given me the bloody Russian bonds!"

"*What* bloody Russian bonds?"

"Grandfather's bonds. Didn't she tell you? You don't actually know?"

"Not about any Russian bonds. I put her into Treasuries and Ginnie Maes and technology stocks. Not Russian bonds."

Chilty sighed and sank back against the bench. "Oh, bloody hell," he muttered, took another bite of fish and gathered his thoughts before going on. "These bonds were issued before the Revolution. Before World War One even. My grandfather bought a packet of them but when the Bolsheviks overthrew the Tsar, the Bolshis repudiated the debt. Grandfather had other investments, of course, and the family did well enough during the twenties, when Mum was growing up. But the family fortune crashed when the Great Depression struck. The bonds were sort of a last hope that the Soviets would settle their old claims and the family would be able to go on. After all, you Yanks settled the cross claims with the Soviets in 1933. When we Brits didn't work it out with the Sovs then, my grandfather threw in the towel and shot himself. Surely, Mum told you this," Chilty said, turning to McCall and making it a question.

McCall shook his head.

"Well, in any event, he left my grandmother and Mum with a big house and no way to keep it or support themselves."

Chilty gave up on the fish and chips and dumped both packets in a rubbish bin. Wiping his hands on a handkerchief, he continued. "Mum was sixteen or seventeen when Grandfather killed himself. That was '34 or '35. Mum was packed off to Perú to marry Dad and through the years there was always some hope of a settlement. But there was nothing--until now. That's the project I'm working on--an agreement to settle the claims at long last. I'm drafting the protocols and the agreements that will structure the process. If it came out that I owned any of the bonds, I'd have to withdraw. And if I withdrew, no telling what part of Ten Downing's catacombs I'd be shunted off to. I might never see daylight again."

"Sell them to a stranger."

Chilty gave a half nod. "Of course that's one way. Mum's solicitors-- Llewelyn and his chaps--say I can divest or establish a blind trust. I told them I wanted to talk with you before I made the decision. If we formed a trust, I'd want you to be the trustee. And if I divest, I want you to have the bonds. I can't throw them to the wind. I'd want someone who cared about her to have them. They were special to her. They were her dowry."

"And that's why she kept them?"

Chilty nodded. "She was actually rather attached to them, which now that I think of it, is a bit peculiar. The bonds were all but worthless. Grandmother giving them to her as a dowry must have seemed cruel at the time. Not to mention being sent halfway 'round the world to marry a man she'd never laid eyes on." Chilty paused and looked out across the Thames. "Funny, I never thought much about that until lately. Growing up, I only knew that she hadn't known Dad before they married. She never talked about how she felt about that. Wish I'd thought to ask her," he muttered, almost to himself. He turned to McCall. "Did she ever talk to you about Dad?"

McCall shook his head slowly. "I never knew your father. He was 'way before my time."

Chilty was silent for a long moment, then straightened his back and consciously squared his stooping shoulders. "Well, the business at hand. The bonds are actually quite handsome. You could frame them, Mack. Put them on display."

McCall stood up and walked to the wall overlooking the Thames. The passage of a tug towing a string of barges up Lambeth Reach set off a long ripple in the murky, gray-green water slapping against the embankment. He thought for a few moments and turned back to Chilty.

"What're these things worth if there's a settlement?"

"There's no way to say. More than they're worth now, of course."

"Which is zero, right?"

"Actually, not," Chilty said, rising and joining McCall beside the low wall. "The bonds are still quoted on the London exchange. There have always been people who believed there'd be a settlement. In Paris, too. And of course, that's what I'm working on. I'm not involved in the valuation. Still, if I were an interested party, I might be able to influence the agreement to my personal benefit. That would, of course, be inappropriate."

"Yeah, right," McCall snorted. "No public servant has ever done that before."

"Mack," Chilty said, pleading. "I want to stand for the House of Commons in the next election. A scandal, even a cloud drifting through the morning of my reputation, might finish me before I'd begun. I mustn't become a scoundrel before I'm elected!"

McCall laughed and leaned against the wall, bracing himself with both hands. He looked at Chilty sideways. "Well, I guess I understand. Russian bonds. It'll make a good story."

"No, no," Chilty said. "You mustn't speak about this. At least you mustn't explain the circumstances. The settlement's not been announced and until it is, what I'm telling you comes under the Official Secrets Act. Obviously, I shouldn't be discussing this with you at all."

"Be that as it may, how much are we talking about here?"

"I don't really know. When I saw Russian bonds on the asset inventory I told Llewelyn to stop everything. I think Mum told me long ago that the bonds were originally worth about ten thousand pounds, though they were gold issues. It must have seemed rather a lot in 1910 or so, whenever Grandfather bought them."

"So suppose they settled for fifty pence to the pound," McCall said. "That'd make your bonds worth five thousand pounds. Office holders have had a can tied to their tails for less, but it's not exactly a fortune. I still think the best thing to do is divest to a stranger and be done with it. If you divest to me, it'll really look crooked if anyone puts us together."

"That's not a problem, actually," Chilty said, smiling brightly. "The only claims that will be honored will be those of British and British Commonwealth holders. And regardless of the long friendship between our two countries, old boy, Americans no longer qualify in either category. Your choice, not ours, remember. That's what makes your taking the bonds such a wizard solution. If you can't participate in the settlement, it's every bit as good as--maybe better than--divesting to a stranger because you can't possibly benefit."

"Well, I'd better pay you something for them so you can prove you divested and didn't just park them with me."

"Then write me a cheque for ten dollars. I can't ask you to keep them forever, but I know that whatever you do with them, you'll remember Mum. You'll do that, won't you?"

"Goes without saying," McCall said, drawing a check book from the inside pocket of his coat. He balanced it on his knee, scrawled out a check and handed it to Chilty.

"Thanks, Mack," Chilty said, relief and gratitude mixed on his face. "I'll have Llewelyn tidy up the legalities and send the bonds on to you in Washington."

****

In Vienna, McCall lectured on the globalizing financial system, chatted and smiled his way through the champagne receptions and cold buffets and returned to his room conference-weary and eager to fall asleep. Only twice did he relent and allow a young German from the seminar to come back with him. She was stylish, good-looking in a modern European way, dark hair cut short, heavy brows and brown eyes, slender but with flesh where it ought to be--and a creative and uninhibited lover. It was tempting to make her a run-of-the-conference event, but then she disappeared and he didn't see her again until the night before the closing session. He was having a drink in the bar and suddenly she was there beside him, pressing the length of her body, from shoulder to calf, against his. Her name was Renata Schneider. She studied in Munich, but claimed Garmisch as home. Wherever she was from, it must have been somewhere near Heaven. They made love until the first gray light of dawn filtered through the windows. Then she disappeared again.

With visions of Renata spiraling through his head, he forgot about Audrey's Russian bonds until the last session when he opened the floor to questions. A tall woman in a print dress and a gray cardigan stood up at the back of the room and in a strong Slavic accent asked, "Please explain how is global financial system if Soviet Union and People's Republic of China are outside. Without Soviet Union and People's Republic, I do not think is global market." With that, she smoothed the back of her dress and sat down.

"That's a good point," McCall said, his bleary mind racing to find a path to a cogent response. "At present, it isn't global in the fullest sense. Clearly, the economies of the Soviet Union and the People's Republic of China would benefit if they had greater access to world capital markets," he said, pausing as a plausible answer her question struck him. "There is, however, more of a global market than your comment suggests. I think you all have heard about Eurodollars. But do you know how they originated? No? Well, in 1949, when Mao Tse Dung overthrew the nationalists, the new Chinese Communist government was afraid the US would freeze Chinese dollar assets held in the United States. It turned out that the Soviet Union owned a bank in Paris, which made it beyond the reach of any American asset freeze. The Soviet Union was happy to take the Chinese deposits and keep them denominated in dollars. That was the important thing. That the funds remained denominated in dollars so that China could trade in the global market. And what do you suppose those funds came to be called?"

McCall waited, looking around the room and the attentive faces, before he answered. "Eurodollars. They called them Eurodollars because the bank was located in Europe, but the deposits were still in dollars. It's also interesting that they didn't leave these funds in the vaults. They lent them out as dollar credits and the result was the Eurodollar market-- borrowing and lending dollars without going through the foreign exchange markets. Two Communist countries, each committed to centrally planned economies, dedicated enemies of capitalism, were responsible for one of the truly important financial innovations of this century."

The woman in the print dress stood up again. "Is interesting what you say, but excuse me, these Eurodollars do not make dams or oil wells, do they? If the money is not for such things, they cannot make development, is that not so?" Again, she smoothed the back of her dress and sat down.

"Well, you know that both the Soviets and the Chinese allocate capital differently than it's done in the rest of the world. The Chinese will have an opportunity to move in the direction of market allocation in a few years when it takes over Hong Kong from the British. The Soviet Union isn't there yet. To borrow for truly long-term productive purposes outside their system, the Soviet government will have to come to the capital markets of Europe, the United States or Japan."

As the words spilled out of his mouth, the tumblers fell into place and he understood why the Soviets were eager to settle their claims with Britain. Gorbachev's *glasnost* and *perestroika* initiatives had a financial dimension. The Soviet Union couldn't enter world financial markets and gain access to long-term capital unless it refurbished its creditworthiness by settling its old debts. What Chilty was working on was a step in that direction.

The woman in the print dress asked no further questions, though he'd scarcely answered her. There were others, from Third World countries, who were interested in his thoughts about the prospects for restructuring the Third World debt burden spawned by OPEC's oil price increases. He sprinkled his answers with anecdotes from his experience and smiled his way through the closing session of the conference. Renata was forgotten as his mind exploded with thoughts of how he might capitalize on the British-Soviet settlement.

Chilty said the Russian bonds were denominated in gold. He didn't know what gold was worth in 1910, but today it was more than $300 an ounce, roughly ten times the old $35 an ounce that prevailed from the 1930's to 1972, when the dollar was floated. Ten was one hell of a multiplier and if the bonds paid in gold, they could be worth more--much more--than their face value. What if £10,000 worth of old bonds turned out to be worth £100,000? He couldn't guess how they might handle the exchange rate differences between the issue date and the present and there was that business about settling only with British holders. He thought he knew a way around that. He'd talk to Audrey's Washington lawyer, Anton Becker, when he got back.

In a best case scenario, he was still a long way from the war chest he and Javier needed to fight the takeover of Banco Dorado, but it was something. Something. He wasn't quite sure what yet, but something.

He'd taken the bonds to get Chilty out of a conflict of interest, but suddenly, he was eager to know the story and by the time he settled into his seat on the Pan Am flight to New York, he was infused with a sense of urgency. There was a chance of a two-week assignment in Egypt at the end of the month and a long line of possibles after that.

He needed some help.

Washington

His first call was to Anton Becker. "You're going to be getting a package for me pretty soon," McCall told him. "Some old Russian bonds."

"I have it already."

"Good. Next subject. What do you know about offshore investment companies?"

"It's not my specialty, but we have some clients with interests in the Bahamas and I've represented them there on occasion. What is it you need to know?"

"Would a Bahamian corporation be considered British Commonwealth for legal purposes?"

"Absolutely," Becker replied and waited for McCall to go on.

"Bahamas. That's perfect. How expensive is it to set up a company and keep it running for awhile?"

"Minimal. About three thousand for the incorporation and five hundred a year for the board of directors and the annual filings."

"Could I operate here in the States in that company's name?" "From anywhere in the world. People do it all the time." "OK. Then I want one," McCall said. "How long will it take?"

"Practically on demand. I can do it on the phone through a law firm we're affiliated with down there, have the papers sent FedEx. You sign them and we send them back. That's about all there is to it. Would you like me to handle it for you?"

"It sounds like you've got the right connections, so, yes."

"I'll need some particulars, like what you want to call the company and how you're going to capitalize it."

"It ought to be English-sounding. What about the Wellington Corporation?"

"Probably taken. Duke of Wellington, beef Wellington, Wellington boots. Maybe if you put something else with it," Becker suggested.

McCall thought about naming it for the town in the Shenandoah Valley where he grew up—Mt. Jackson—but Jackson sounded too American. Then he thought of Winchester, a town up the road where one of his Cooper ancestors had been killed in a Civil War battle.

"What do you think of Wellington, Winchester?" he asked Becker.

"It has a ring to it. We could try it. And the capitalization?"

"How about using those Russian bonds? I think they have a face value of around ten thousand pounds."

"Why not?" Becker said. "This isn't just a dummy company, is it? You're actually going to do some business with it?"

"I hope so, but I've got some research to do first." Becker nodded. "You'll want a banking relationship down there. Bahamas International Trust Company—BITCO--is a favorite. It's owned by Barclays' Bank, completely reputable, with a global reach."

"Great," McCall said. "Who would I talk to?"

"Philip Gerard is the managing director. I can set that up for you. Anything else?"

"Not at the moment," he said. "Go ahead and put it in place."

****

His next call was to the Economics Department at Georgetown University. "Kevin? It's Mack."

"Hey, stranger. We haven't seen you lately. Are you in town for awhile?"

"Not long. I just got back from Vienna and I've got a thing coming up in Egypt. Dirty job but somebody's got to do it."

"Yeah, right," Fitzgerald scoffed. "Well, let us give you dinner before you get away to the pyramids. Not a sit-down. Just cocktails and buffet on Friday. Some interesting people coming. A few from State. Some from the Hill. What do you say?"

"What time?"

"Come early. Six-thirty. You can make the Martinis and we can have a chat before the horde arrives."

"OK, but right now I need a favor. I'm looking for a research assistant to do some work on the last Russian Tsar, Nicholas II. Financial stuff. Scut work, no heavy lifting. I could do it myself, but I have to travel to pay the bills and the timing may be important. I need somebody I can trust to keep cranking when I'm out of the country. Any of your students fit that description?"

"I take it you want a grad student."

"Afraid so. An undergrad might be bright and full of spirit, but I need somebody I can leave on their own."

"Sure. Trouble is, everybody worth having already has a fellowship or an assistantship for this year. It is October, you know. There's one interesting case, though."

"Tell me about it."

"A girl. Woman really. Masters' degree candidate and a late registrant in the School of Foreign Service. Dynamite academic record from William and Mary, but she's been out and about doing different things. I gather she's just back from the famine in Ethiopia. She was actually out there feeding starving people, if you can believe that."

"Spunky."

"Spunky? Yes, I suppose so. Anyway, I have no idea whether she's qualified for your project, but William and Mary has a decent Econ department and she aced everything there a few years ago. I think the profs were a little in awe of her. When her record hit my desk, I called Murray Sanders. He had nothing but praise. She's obviously bright enough."

"How can I get in touch with her?"

"She's in my two o'clock today. Let me talk to her after class. If she's interested, I'll have her call you."

"If I'm not here, the answering machine will pick up."

"OK. Don't forget Friday. Six-thirty."

"You got it. It'll be good to see you. Oh, what's this gal's name?"

"Campbell. Paralee Campbell."

****

McCall answered the phone after the first ring. A clear contralto voice spoke to him. "Dr. McCall? This is Paralee Campbell. Dr. Fitzgerald told me you were looking for a research assistant."

"Right. Thanks for calling. I need some help on Russian finance leading up to World War I. In particular, the Tsar's foreign bond issuance. I don't know how big a job it is, but it might go a couple of months. Are you interested?"

"You bet. I'm without funding this year, so I could use the job."

"Well, I'm doing this out of my own pocket, but if it looks like we can work together, I'll match what you'd get from Georgetown. I know that's not much, but . . . "

"No, that's OK. When's a good time to get together?" she asked, her voice bright and alive.

"Right away, if possible. I live in Alexandria. Duke Street. Condo Canyon. Do you know the area?"

"Yes. But I don't have a car. I bike to school. Could you meet somewhere in Georgetown?"

"Nathan's at four-thirty? It's three-twenty now. Does that give you enough time?"

"I could do that," she said. "How will I know you?"

"I'm six foot, about one-eighty. No glasses. No beard. No mustache." He stopped and laughed. "Sounds like twenty-five other guys, doesn't it? Look, I'll wear a baseball cap with 'Alpha Tango Flying Service' on it."

"I'm wearing jeans and a blue turtleneck. My hair's blonde and cut short. Blue eyes. Five foot seven. My mother thinks I'm undernourished, but I prefer to be thought of as svelte," she added, laughing.

****

Through the panes of Nathan's windows, he watched her chain the bicycle to a street sign and tried to guess her age. She wasn't all bones, but she was very trim. A souvenir of short rations in Ethiopia? Her belly was flat and tight jeans advertised the lean of her buns and legs. The blue turtleneck she wore seemed a size too large and, tucked into her jeans, it bloused beneath her breasts. She had on well-worn hiking boots--the kind you see in the Alps, with heavy socks showing over the tops. Something--he wasn't sure what--gave her the air of a mature woman in spite of her pixie appearance.

He liked her hair. It was tousled by the wind and sun-bleached highlights spilled over honey-colored amber. Wind-burned skin more rosy than tan was stretched taut over the delicately shaped bones of her face.

She walked through the door with sure strides and stood inside the entrance, scanning the few patrons at the long, old-fashioned mahogany bar.

McCall took off his baseball cap and held it up in her direction, pointing to the lettering that said 'Alpha Tango Flying Service'. For good measure, he waved it at her.

She smiled and came toward him.

McCall had a practiced and appreciative eye for women and this one had a fresh aura that pushed aside the stale smell of the bar and opened its windows to a fresh breeze. On top of that, her eyes were absolutely striking. They weren't just dark blue. They were the luminescent color of Thai topaz when the light's just right on the stone.

"Dr. McCall?" she asked, holding out her hand. "I'm Paralee Campbell."

"Most people call me 'Mack'," he said, taking her hand and finding it cool and firm. "What'll you have to drink?"

"Ummm," she said, looking over the bottles behind the bar. "Just a beer, I guess. Corona, with a lime."

McCall waved the bartender down to them and ordered for her. She stood beside him against the bar.

"Kevin Fitzgerald is an old friend of mine," McCall began. "He said you had a great record at William and Mary and that you were someone I could count on to work independently."

She shrugged. "I'd like to think I'm a responsible person, but Dr. Fitzgerald doesn't know me very well. Maybe you'd have to take that on faith."

McCall smiled to reassure her. "I didn't mean that the way it sounded. Sorry. What I was trying to say was that you wouldn't have a lot of supervision and I wondered how you'd feel about that."

"You haven't told me much about the project yet. Just that it had something to do with Russian bonds and the last tsar. I think I could handle that." McCall rested his elbows on the bar and said, "The thing is that I came into some of these old bonds recently. Sort of an inheritance. They're in default because the Soviets repudiated the debt when they took over. The bonds are still trading on the European exchanges. Huge discount, of course, but there are people who think there might be a settlement some day and I'm trying to figure out whether they're ever going to be worth more than what they are now. "

"Wow," she said. "I did a history minor at William and Mary a long time ago, but I never had a term project like that."

"Still interested?"

"Absolutely," she said.

"OK. Kevin told me the standard rate for a half-time research assistant was seven thousand for the academic year, which is about eight hundred a month. Would a thousand be about right, allowing for the chance the job won't run more than a month?"

She smiled and put out her hand. "Best offer I've had today," she said. "What do you want me to do first?"

"Suppose we see if we can get a table on the other side in the restaurant and discuss it during dinner? The food used to be pretty good here and if you'll forgive my saying so, you look like you could use a meal."

It was early for dinner. The room was almost empty and McCall asked for a booth toward the back where they wouldn't be disturbed. He suggested veal piccata and picked a French Chardonnay to wash it down.

"Kevin said you'd been out in Ethiopia," McCall said, fascinated by her blue eyes. "I'd like to hear a little about that."

"Fitzgerald told you I was in Ethiopia?" She smiled crookedly, then looked down self-consciously at the table cloth. After a moment, she raised her head and looked into his eyes, deciding if she should go on. "Well, it's true. I tagged along with an MSF team_you know, Doctors Without Borders."

"Doctors Without Borders?"

"*Médecins Sans Frontières*--that's what MSF stands for. A group of French doctors started it. We'll have something like it in the States some day. They go wherever they're needed in the world. Politics aren't an issue. People are. And they don't charge."

"Not like any doctors I know," he said. "So what'd you do for them?"

"At first, I was just a gopher at one of the feeding stations, but after awhile, I learned enough to help out with things."

"I've seen the news footage. What's it like on the ground?" McCall asked.

She looked away for a moment, staring at the passersby beyond the windows, collecting her thoughts.

"Have you ever been to Ethiopia?"

He shook his head. "No. Lots of other places, but not Ethiopia."

"I was in Tigray Province at six thousand feet, so it wasn't terribly hot, but it was bone dry," she began. "Dust everywhere, fine as powder—in your eyes, in your mouth, everywhere. Flies all over. The stench was very bad. We were always short supplies of everything—food, medicine, clean water. Sometimes the Army let the relief trucks through and sometimes they didn't. They'd steal our supplies and . . . I don't know . . . sell them on the black market or keep them for themselves, I guess. If it wasn't the Army, it was the rebels. These were their people dying and they just took advantage of the help that was coming from abroad to keep the war going. That part made you furious, but mostly it was just bone-breaking work. You could only sleep when you were exhausted. You felt like you had no right_people were dying all around you." She swallowed hard, tucking her chin into her chest and looking down at the table. In a moment, she looked up at McCall with an expression that bespoke a remembered anguish.

"A lot of them were too near death to eat. Their bodies wouldn't take the nourishment. Their whole system just shut down." She paused, shook her head slightly as if to cast off the demons, and went on. "Sometimes, of course, if you kept trying, you'd get one of the 'goners' to take food and you'd see the spark of life come back. That was thrilling, but in the end you realized that all you'd done was to give them another day or another month. You hadn't really changed anything."

McCall listened and waited for her to go on. When she didn't, he said, "I've been in squatter settlements that were pretty foul and I've stepped over people sleeping in the street because they didn't have any place to go, but I've never seen people starving to death. It's not one of my ambitions, either."

"You try to look past their physical appearance, but it's hard. Their eyes--I can't explain it--they weren't exactly accusing, but asking a question. 'Why do you get to live and I don't?' You can't answer a question like that, particularly when it comes from a child. Sometimes it's all you can do to keep from running down the road screaming, just to get away as fast as you can," she said. "But you know you'd never make it that way. If the guerrillas or the Army picked you up, it wouldn't be pleasant, and even if you got away and all the way back home, you'd still have yourself to deal with--you know, bugging out. I wouldn't want to live with that. So once you're in it, you've got to stay to see it through. As much as you can stand. If you last six months, they take it out of your hands and make you leave."

"And you stayed six months."

"Uh huh," she said.

McCall thought his question about Ethiopia had been simple enough and he hadn't expected so frank or emotionally revealing an answer from her. In some other time or place, maybe. But not here or now. It made him see her differently. Self-confident. More than a pretty woman. He tried to imagine her in the dusty highlands of Ethiopia surrounded by starving people and failed. He could only come up with stills from an old movie--Ingrid Bergman in The Good Earth. Not a fit at all. "Kevin said you were in the School of Foreign Service," McCall said, suddenly aware he'd let the conversation die. "You don't think diplomacy keeps people from starving, do you?" "I'm not that naïve," she said, looking directly at him with a crooked smile. "But be fair. Better diplomacy might have helped, might have opened the door for people with solutions, might have scared up a few more foreign aid dollars. I don't have the answers, but I'm glad I went. There's hardly anything I look at the same way now--not a flower, not a homeless person, not a slice of bread or a glass of water. So what's 'Alpha Tango Flying Service'?" she asked, changing the direction of the conversation abruptly.

"Just some nice people down in San Antonio."

"Are you a flier?"

"I used to fly a little," he said and skirted the subject by asking her another question. "When were you graduated from William and Mary?"

She turned her eyes to the ceiling for a moment, thinking. "Spring of '76. Magna cum laude. Phi Beta Kappa. Economics."

"I'm impressed. You graduated covered with glory and . . . then what?"

"Got married. We lasted five years but it wasn't going anywhere. We called it quits. No kids and no hard feelings. I've been bumming around since then. The last four years, more or less. Europe mostly. Did the Eurorail-pass-youth-hostel thing. Studied old churches. Art. Languages. Helped out with some tour groups. I worked in a vineyard for a couple of months," she said with an enigmatic smile. "I finally got a job in a travel office in Paris. It was OK and I loved Paris, so I took an apartment and started to settle in."

Their waiter, a lanky young man with red hair, brought the wine and offered the label for McCall's inspection. After they went through the ritual of approving it, the waiter poured. McCall noticed that Paralee didn't take a demure little sip like most women did. She held the glass at its base, breathed in the aroma, put her nose down into the glass. She swirled the wine expertly, inspected the color against the light. It was all quite natural and unaffected.

McCall watched her drink from the glass, a generous amount, and discretely swish it around in her mouth. "How's the wine?" he asked at last.

"Oh. Fine," she said with wide-eyed innocence, as if nothing out of the ordinary had occurred.

He thought about pursuing the subject but decided it must have been something she picked up working in the vineyard or in Paris.

"So you took a pass on Paris and came back to school."

"Yes," she said, tilting her head slightly. "After Ethiopia, it didn't make any sense to pick up where I left off as if nothing had happened."

"I can imagine," McCall said and paused before going on. "You think you'll find out how to make sense of it all at Georgetown?"

"Probably not," she said, laughing softly, setting her wine glass to one side and picking up her spoon, tapping it nervously against the back of her hand and her fingernails. "It sounds a little silly, doesn't it? I just couldn't think of anything else. I needed to go back to Square One and start over. Georgetown was as good a Square One as I could think of."

"Where'd you grow up?"

"All over. But, hey! Are you going to want my blood type, too?" she asked, smiling. "I might have to call around."

"No," he said, embarrassed. "Sorry. I didn't realize I was grilling you . . ."

"It's OK," she said, wishing she hadn't chided him. "I don't mind, really. I'm an Air Force brat. I was born at Carswell Air Force Base in Ft. Worth and grew up all over—Texas, Nebraska, Puerto Rico. Virginia more than anywhere else when Dad was at the Pentagon."

The waiter returned with their entree and a basket of fresh French bread. Paralee again sampled the aroma before tasting the dish.

"Ummm. That's heavenly. Reminds me of Paris."

When they'd taken the edge off their appetite, McCall asked again, "So where are your folks now?"

"Dad's retired. They live out in the mountains, in Winchester."

"Winchester?" McCall interrupted. "Really? I just named a company after Winchester. Wellington, Winchester, Limited."

"What made you think of Winchester?"

"I grew up in Mt. Jackson," he said. "Just down the road."

"I don't believe it! I wondered if that was Piedmont in your accent."

"Guilty as charged," he said, grinning.

"Do you have family out there?"

"My parents are gone. My grandfather's still alive and kicking, though. He lives on a little farm outside Mt. Jackson. He's in his 80s. Of course, he doesn't work the farm anymore. He rents out the land, but he still drives his pickup, does his own cooking and mostly takes care of himself."

McCall marveled at the coincidence and wanted to know more. "So Winchester's home for you?"

"It's home to Mom and Dad. The house isn't fancy, but they like it. They're happy as can be, except for worrying about a wayward daughter."

"And that would be you?" he asked, arching his eyebrows.

"Yeah. They love me, but they're completely mystified by what I'm doing with my life. So am I," she added, laughing.

The waiter cleared their plates and they ordered coffee.

"Brothers and sisters?" McCall continued.

A cloud passed over her face and he almost felt her flinch. "Two younger brothers," she said at last. "They're at Virginia Tech." For a moment, he thought she was going to say something more, but her bright smile returned and she said. "Enough now. Please."

McCall shook his head.

"I've done it again," he said. "Sorry." "I've still got the job haven't I?"

"Absolutely. I know I haven't given you much chance to think about it, but have you got a work plan?" he asked.

She shrugged. "Hit the stacks at the library. Georgetown first, then the Library of Congress. I'm clear after ten, so I can give it pretty much all day tomorrow."

"Will you call and give me a progress report?"

"You bet. I might even go by the library tonight and see if I can get a start."

"Can I drop you off?"

"No. I've got my bike. It's not far."

"It's dark already," he said. "I could tie it on the luggage rack and drive you over."

She shook her head. "I'll be fine. Thanks for dinner. The veal was magnificent."

"And the wine?"

She didn't answer right away. Then she smiled and said, "A good choice. Nice finish."

He nodded, pleased she'd enjoyed it, but suspecting she'd held something back--something about her family and something about the wine.

Alexandria, Virginia

McCall was surprised to hear from Paralee two days later. He hadn't expected anything for at least a week, given her class schedules.

"Dr. McCall? It's Paralee Campbell. I thought I might give you a progress report."

He smiled at the sound of her voice and the eagerness behind her soft contralto. He'd be happy to listen to her read her grocery list. "Sure," he said. "Where are you?"

"I'm at school."

"Suppose I pick you up, then? We'll go for lunch and you can tell me what you've got."

There was a moment's pause. "I've got a class at two. I thought maybe I could just tell you over the phone."

McCall was disappointed. "No problem. I've got some calls to make this afternoon anyway. Shoot." He settled back in his chair and propped his feet in an open desk drawer.

"I found this great old book published back in 1930 by the Council on Foreign Relations called *Europe: The World's Banker*. And I found a book on scripophily that's helpful."

"Scripophily?"

"That's what they call collecting old stocks and bonds—stocks of companies that are out of business and bonds that have defaulted or been canceled. It's like collecting coins or stamps."

"Oh, yeah," he said, nodding. "I knew there were collectors. I didn't know what they were called." "Scripophilists. Like numismatists for coins and philatelists for stamps. Scripophily is new, though. It didn't get organized until 1976. Maybe that's one reason why it's so hard to find much written on these old bonds. That's not the issue, though."

He heard a shuffling of papers and visualized her flipping through her notes.

"OK. Here we go. According to the book on European banking, about six-hundred million pounds worth of Russian debt was held by foreigners in 1914. The Germans used to be the Russians' main creditors, but they started playing political games around the turn of the century and the Tsar went shopping for other friends. I guess you know the Russians and the Germans turned up on opposite sides in World War I?"

"I took history," McCall said.

"OK," she said, plowing ahead. "I can't track it yet, but it looks like the Russians raised a net four-hundred million pounds in Britain between 1914 and 1917. At least they had a billion pounds outstanding in 1917 when the Russian Revolution started. That's as far as I've gotten with the outstandings, but that should give you some idea of how much is out there."

"Beautiful," he said, impressed. "Well done, my dear. A billion pounds, huh? And I suppose that would be at exchange rates at the time of issuance?"

That stumped her for a moment. When she replied, she wasn't as certain as she'd been before. "I need to check on that. The source is 1930, so they might have adjusted to exchange rates of that year. I don't remember seeing any footnotes that said that, though."

"I'm just trying to get it into current dollars," McCall said. "Like as not, the bonds are denominated in the currency of the lending country. Pounds for Britain, francs for France, marks for Germany. Like that."

"I'll see if I can run that down," she said, sounding embarrassed that she hadn't known that.

"Focus on the British issues. See what you can dig up there. Anything else?"

"Well, I came across something that mentioned gold shipments from Russia to England during the First World War."

"Gold shipments?"

"Um hmm," she said. "Maybe it doesn't have anything to do with the bonds, but some of them are gold backed, so I guess it could."

"Let me know as soon as you get something more on the gold shipments," McCall said slowly.

They rang off and McCall leaned back and stared at the ceiling. What if the Brits had required a compensating balance in gold as security for the bonds? Could the gold have been frozen in the UK all these years? If so, it could be on the table when the Brits and the Soviets settle. Interesting. Very interesting.

He went into the kitchen, made a ham and cheese sandwich and sat down at the little breakfast table. He ate the sandwich slowly, nibbling on potato chips, thinking. By late afternoon, he was ready to talk to Javier. He had just enough time for a conversation before the Fitzgeralds' dinner party.

Back in the small bedroom he'd converted into an office, he punched up the number of Banco Dorado but Javier was out of the office and wasn't expected back that afternoon. He left a message for him to call, then tried his apartment and got no answer there, either. Disappointed, McCall headed for the shower.

Alexandria, Virginia

Barbara Fitzgerald was the only child of a Rear Admiral. The trust fund and the house she inherited from him and her mother perched on a rare plot of ground overlooking the Potomac just above Alexandria. The inheritance allowed Kevin and Barbara to live far above the standard of his university salary and made possible their membership in a minor group of think-tank professionals, rotating foreign service officers, Congressional committee staff and journalists covering foreign affairs. Before he left for Texas, Mack, by virtue of his long-standing friendship with Kevin, was often invited to these small get-togethers.

Knowing the party would begin on the deck that cantilevered over the slope of the ridge, McCall bypassed the house and took the brick walk bordering the azalea beds. Japanese lanterns had been strung above the railings and cast a soft glow over the deck. It was a perfect fall evening, the air crisp and scented with the fragrance of fallen leaves. A pair of mammoth scarlet oaks whose leaves had reached peak color sheltered the deck and its surrounding landscaping. Their limbs had been trimmed to afford a view of the Potomac River and in the distance McCall saw the lights of a cabin cruiser marking a languid passage toward Chesapeake Bay.

Kevin was arranging glasses at the portable bar. He looked up at the sound of McCall's approach. "Ah, there you are. Welcome back. Where was it this time? I can't keep track."

"Vienna. A conference on bank management. Like I'm an expert on the subject."

"At least you might say what not to do," Kevin offered.

McCall ignored this good-natured jibe and moved around behind the bar to ice the gin and vermouth and make sure there were olives.

"Who's coming tonight?" McCall asked.

"The star attractions are Dixie Davenport, Select Committee on Intelligence, and her 'significant other,' Kurt Sorensen, who rides around in George Shultz's vest pocket. Then there's Andre Yanov, a colleague of mine at Georgetown. A *refusnik* who used to pass for what the Soviets call economists. He was in the Trade Ministry. He's supposed to come, but you can never tell about him. Let's see, who else? An AID type named Brad Blackbridge. He's just come out of Honduras, and he seems to be a true believer, so I guess you know what that means."

"I guess I don't," McCall replied absently, his attention given over to swishing vermouth around in several Martini glasses. "I wish you'd remember to do this the day before and stuff them in the freezer overnight," McCall told him.

"Hey, my philosophy is pour 'em a stiff one of the good stuff when they walk through the door and give 'em rot gut the rest of the way."

"You're a Barbarian," McCall told him, setting the glasses on a tray and heading for the kitchen. "I'm going to put these in the freezer. Maybe they'll frost up before any discerning people arrive."

Barbara Fitzgerald, leggy in a long skirt and trim in spite of three children, emerged from the house when he was halfway across the terrace. "Mack," she called. "You came! I'm delighted. I see you've taken charge of the Martinis." She put her cheek next to his and air kissed him. "You're a love. Thirsty ones will be here any minute."

"I aim to please," McCall told her.

"I'll bet you do, you rascal," Barbara whispered in a low, husky voice, her gown rustling as she moved past him.

McCall went into the house and deposited the Martini glasses, then returned to the terrace. "You were telling me who's coming. Something about this foreign service type from Honduras."

"He's not in Honduras anymore. He's posted back here to the Latin America Bureau, which probably means the powers that be appreciated his work. I'll bet he can tell some stories about the Contras and that whole mess down there. It'll be interesting to see if he and Yanov mix it up. And there'll be Dixie looking and listening."

"You're not just a Barbarian. You're a devious Barbarian. Who else?"

"Wives, of course. Yanov doesn't have one. A couple of profs from Georgetown and their ladies. A fellow from Brookings who used to be somewhere in Treasury." Kevin paused, making sure McCall was listening. "And Angela's coming."

"Angela Collins? Really? That's terrific." He'd thought about her a few times since he'd been back, but hadn't tried to track her down.

Angela belonged to his international days in that curious way that travelers see more of each other on assignment than they do at home base. Doubly so in this case because they were in different professions--McCall an economist, Angela a freelance journalist with a penchant for international stories.

They'd met the first time in the *altiplano* of the Peruvian Andes when Angela's bus broke down, leaving her and about twenty Quechuas stranded on the side of a mountain road. McCall and two members of his survey team came across them and loaded as many as they could into their camioneta. Angela wound up sitting on McCall's lap for the thirty miles into the next little market town where they dropped the Quechuas. Angela had come on into Lima with the team and, by way of thanks, invited them all to dinner the next night at the Hotel Bolívar. McCall had been the only one free to accept and they'd fallen into an easy companionship that lasted a couple of days before Angela flew back to the States. They'd come across one another twice more_once in Jamaica and again in Perú. Their relationship had been friendly, but arm's length.

It didn't stay that way.

He'd been on a short-term consulting job in Panamá and took a few extra days to spend some time with Javier. Soaking up the sun beside the pool at the Panamá Hilton, swilling vodka tonics, he found her standing beside him, a beach towel draped over her shoulder but little else concealing her well-oiled, honey colored skin. She was coming off a heart-breaking love affair with some Chilean and McCall was the friend she needed. Whether it was rebound or the culmination of their long pent-up feelings for one another, they wound up in her room and stayed there for three days, slaking their lust and loneliness and living off room service. Then Angela had had to leave to do a story in Venezuela. It had gone that way for a year or so, their running into one another unexpectedly in faraway places, picking up where they'd left off until one or the other had to move on. Then McCall bought the bank in Texas.

The kaleidoscope of remembered images raced through his brain and brought a silly smile to his face. He was happy he'd see her again, hoping that she was still fond of him.

"I didn't know you knew Angela," McCall said.

"I don't. Barbara does, though. I'm not sure how. One of those National Press Club things, maybe. Anyway, she found out you two were friends. I think I was supposed to have left it as a surprise. Don't blow my cover with Babs, will you?"

"It's already a surprise," McCall said. "I haven't seen her in years."

"So. Old home week," Kevin said, turning to see Dixie Davenport appear on the terrace. She was handsome, a well-preserved forty-five or fifty, dressed off Woodward and Lothrop's rack, but she had an aura about her, something that commanded attention when she entered a room.

Kevin immediately moved to greet her. "Dixie, it's great to see you. I'm glad you could make it."

"Hello, Kevin. It's Friday. Why haven't you offered me a drink?"

"Dixie, do you know Jack McCall?" Kevin asked, grinning as he presented Mack. "He's your man if you want a world class Martini."

"In that case I'm delighted," she said, offering her hand.

"The glasses are in the freezer. I'll be back in a minute," McCall told her and excused himself.

"He your bartender for the evening?" Dixie asked when McCall was safely out of earshot.

"He's an old friend. In real life, he's a top gun international consultant. World Bank and AID mostly. He's been running a bank down in Texas for the last few years, but he's back in the international game now."

"Not one of your know-it-all theorists, then. That'll be refreshing," Dixie said and watched McCall returning across the terrace with a tray of frosty Martini glasses.

"Gin or vodka?" he asked Dixie from behind the bar, lining up three glasses and dropping a pair of olives in each. "Gin, maestro," she told him.

He took a shaker from beneath the bar, filled it quickly with cracked ice and emptied half a bottle of Bombay Sapphire into it, swirled the ice and watched the shaker frost up. He filled each glass to the rim.

"No vermouth?" Dixie asked, eyes slightly widened.

"It's in the frost," McCall told her and raised his glass. "Cheers."

Kevin watched with amusement as Dixie brought the glass to her lips carefully. "I'll be damned," she said, following her first cautious sip with a generous swallow and saluting McCall with her glass.

Kevin grinned and said, "I see some of the others coming in. I'd better give Barbara a hand. Watch yourself, Dixie."

Over Dixie's shoulder, McCall saw a great bear of a man lumber onto the terrace, Yanov, he guessed. And behind him, a carefully groomed, tall fellow with ramrod posture accompanied by a slender woman wearing a tight-fitting long gown and a white bolero jacket. She had long, dark hair that cascaded over her shoulders. Since he didn't look professorial in the least, McCall guessed they were the Blackbridges.

Dixie leaned toward McCall and asked, "Do you know this fellow, Blackbridge?"

McCall shook his head. "No, but I think he just came in."

"Don't tell him who I am," she whispered. "Kevin said he was just back from Honduras and his boss is testifying before our committee next week on the Contras. I'd like to get some of the straight skinny from this little foot soldier if I can."

While Kevin was welcoming Yanov, Barbara pointed the Blackbridges in the direction of the bar.

"Hello," McCall greeted them. "I'm Jack McCall and this is my aunt Dixie."

Dixie was caught off guard and almost laughed, but kept her composure and smiled graciously.

"Brad Blackbridge. My wife, Betty. Nice to meet you."

"What can I get you to drink?" McCall asked.   "He makes a wicked

Martini," Dixie said.

"That's great," Blackbridge said, appraising Dixie, who had already taken a light hold on his arm. "Betty, what about you?"

McCall poured a Martini for Blackbridge and watched Dixie draw him away for some private conversation. Betty Blackbridge hadn't taken her eyes off McCall and she paid no attention to her husband or his departure. McCall immediately pegged them as the kind of couple who part company upon arrival and don't hook up again until they leave. They covered more ground that way. In spite of lacking any special beauty, Betty Blackbridge had flawless, tanned skin and nice eyes. She obviously took good care of herself. A lot of tennis, he thought. Probably a swimmer, too. "Do you have white wine?" she asked McCall.

"Chablis?"

"*Won-der-ful*," she said, making it three, breathy words. "What do you do besides make wicked Martinis?"

"Invest," McCall said, working the cork out of a bottle of chilled Chablis in pouring for her. "Stocks, bonds, that sort of thing."

"Mmmmm," she said. "Do you make a lot of money?"

McCall poured the wine and passed it to her. She took the glass from him with long, carefully manicured fingers.

"Once in awhile," he replied, smiling. He was relieved when Barbara Fitzgerald joined them and took Mrs. Blackbridge away to meet a tweedy couple who appeared to qualify as 'lesser lights' of Georgetown University. Kevin and Yanov filled the vacancy at the bar.

"Mack, this is Andre Yanov. Andre, Jack McCall." Kevin had an arm wrapped around Yanov's massive shoulders and was speaking softly while Yanov stared at McCall. "Mack's doing some research on Russian bonds. I told him you might have some thoughts for him."

Yanov grunted in reply.

"Actually, it's not really about bonds," McCall said. "I was lecturing on global finance in Vienna recently and got a question about how we were going to have a global financial system without the Soviet Union. I thought that was a good question and I didn't have a good answer for it. I'm interested in what you think Gorbachev might actually do to make a closer connection between the Soviet Union and Western capital markets. That said, I know it's impossible to answer a question like that without a drink. What'll it be?"

Yanov pointed to McCall's Martini glass. "I drink what you drink."

"Let's start fresh, then. Just you and me." McCall grinned, liking Yanov instinctively. He gave Kevin what was left in the shaker and refilled it with cracked ice and the rest of the bottle of Bombay. Yanov watched in silence. When the shaker frosted, McCall poured two glasses and handed one to Yanov. Yanov saluted with his glass and took it down with one long swallow.

"Come on," McCall said, moving away from the bar and bringing the shaker with him, leaving Kevin to tend his own bar. "Let's get out of the line of fire." McCall led Yanov to the corner of the terrace with the best view of the Potomac and poured the big Russian another Martini.

"So what do you think of Mr. Gorbachev?" McCall asked.

"He has new ideas. *Glasnost. Perestroika.* Not slogans for him, I think. Some close to him are modern thinkers, too. Rhyzkov, Aganbegian, Tatyana Zaslavskaya, Abalkin. There are many ways to step wrong, though. The Old Guard will be threatened by what he is thinking. And they will not always be sleeping. Your Mr. Reagan frightens the old men, too, with his talk about Evil Empires and Strategic Defense Initiatives." Yanov paused and drank his second Martini. McCall poured another. "I do not think you can build missile defense that works, but who knows? Be Russian for a minute. Imagine America protected from attack and Russia not protected. One day the American generals decide to flex their missiles and boom, boom, boom. No more Soviet Union. That is why they are afraid." Yanov cleared his throat and spat over the railing into the underbrush. "Reagan is like wolf, stalking a wounded bear. He wishes to defeat Soviet Union, to humble it and feed upon it." Yanov shook his head and held out his glass.

"Are you saying Russia's like a wounded bear today?"

"Worse," Yanov replied. "Soviet economy is falling apart. Crazy war in Afghanistan is bleeding whole country to death--young men dying for a pile of rocks. This makes US policy dangerous. Wounded animal does not reason. It fights to death. Now is very dangerous time."

"What if the Soviets could raise capital in the West?" McCall asked.

Yanov stared at McCall. "For what this capital? For arms race or *perestroika?*"

"Put Star Wars to one side and suppose the arms race doesn't heat up. How would it be then?"

Yanov shrugged. "First, Gorbachev must hold power. Then he thinks about fixing oil industry. Refineries, pipelines. Billions and billions. Cost a lot. Maybe he makes joint venture with Western oil companies. If you think he can borrow and buy Western expertise . . . That can only be if West would trust him. Is it not so?" Yanov turned away from McCall and gazed out at the Potomac, an inky ribbon running between the trees. Then he turned back. "These bonds you talk about. What? Eurobonds?"

"No. Actually they're bonds of the last Tsar, Nicholas II."

Yanov looked puzzled. "I do not understand. What have bonds of old tsar to do with anything?"

"When the Soviets took power from Tsar Nicholas, they assumed the country's obligations--at least in the eyes of the creditors. A lot of the claims were settled a long time ago, but there are still bonds outstanding on which no settlement has been reached. That damages the Soviet credit rating. Gorbachev needs to reach some kind of agreement with the bond holders before he can take the Soviet Union into global capital markets with an unblemished credit rating."

Yanov grunted. "Soviet Union will never pay debts of old Tsar."

"The Soviet Union settled with the US a long time ago. In 1933."

"Oh? I did not know that. But 1933. Different world then." Yanov turned away and walked toward the bar, leaving McCall standing alone.

Barbara Fitzgerald called them to dinner and slowly, in small conversational knots, they trooped toward the dining room where the buffet was laid out. That was when McCall saw Angela Collins. She was wearing a short leather coat, fitted gabardine slacks and a white silk blouse. She was thinner than he remembered and her mane of wild dark hair gave her the look of a young hawk intent on its prey. She and McCall arrived at the dining room door at the same time.

"Hello, Angie," he said.

"You know I hate to be called Angie," she replied, but her smile said she was glad to see him. "Do it again and I'll call you Johnny."

"A truce, then," he said, grinning. "You're looking great."

She slipped her hand into the crook of his arm and smiled up at him, a broader, warmer, mischievous smile. "You're looking gray and gaunt, old man."

"And you could stand to gain a pound or two. Where've you been? Somewhere in the Sahel?"

"Seriously," she said. "I'm sorry about your troubles."

"Barbara told you?"

She nodded. "But I also hear that you're back in the game, so maybe we'll see one another from time to time."

"Are you still working Latin America?"

"Of course. There are more ugly stories than ever. I've been doing a series for the Post on the Contras. Very bloody. I'm hurt you haven't seen my byline."

McCall gave her a puzzled look and was about to draw her out, but the early diners were drifting back onto the terrace, juggling plates and drinks. Angela took his elbow and steered him toward the dining room.

"I haven't been reading much the last few months," he said. "And I've been on the road a lot since I've been back. Europe and Middle East."

"How fun," she said, releasing him and taking a plate. "Better accommodations than I've been getting lately."

"You haven't been out in the bush with the guerrillas, have you?"

"Not quite. But you can't report this mess from the Hilton. I've seen some nasty things out in the countryside. But I'm shifting away from the village massacres and death-squad atrocities now. I want to try to put the bigger picture together. It hasn't been done yet--Chile, Argentina, now Central America. It's World War III, one country at a time, and the media and the academics must not understand it because they sure as hell aren't making the connection."

"I guess I don't either," McCall said, spearing several steak cubes and spooning a dollop of horseradish onto his plate.

She turned to him, suddenly serious, two lines forming between her eyebrows. "You *do* know about the Contras, don't you? They're what's left of Somoza's fascists, trying to overthrow the duly-elected government of Nicaragua to get back in power."

"Is that what you're working on?" McCall asked, swabbing a steak cube with horseradish and popping it into his mouth.

"There's a thing called the Boland Amendment that Congress attached to an appropriations bill that expressly prohibits the CIA or any other Agency of the US government from supporting the Contras directly or indirectly. That's the law. But I just got back from Honduras and I promise you, somebody is financing the Contras and it's not the Red Cross or the Salvation Army."

McCall shrugged, amused by her intensity. "I'm guessing you think it's the Reagan Administration."

She patted his arm with her free hand and said sweetly, "You've always been so clever. Who else would it be? I just can't prove it. There are a couple of people here I think do know. I'm going to try to get something unguarded out of them tonight." She paused and looked at him, wistfully now. "Think we could get together afterward and catch up?"

"Go get your work done. Look me up when you're ready to go."

McCall watched her turn purposefully and head toward the terrace, his spirits rising like a kite in a strong wind. He wondered why he hadn't thought of her more during his long sojourn in Texas or in the dark days after First Mission went down. Tonight, there was a thrill like you get when you meet someone for the first time, but with clairvoyant understanding of who she is and what it will be like to spend time with her.

****

Brad Blackbridge, looking as if he'd lost the war of wits, moved away from Dixie with grudging apologies before Angela could close on her quarry. In several long strides, he hove up beside McCall at the buffet table and began loading his plate.

"Hi," McCall greeted him.

"Your Aunt Dixie is a piece of work," Blackbridge growled. "She's not really your aunt, is she?"

"What did *she say?*"

"She said she wasn't your aunt."

"Sorry about that. She asked me not to blow her cover. It was the first thing I could think of."

"I don't get it," Blackbridge said, looking directly at McCall. "We have a coordinated Communist assault on every government in South America and people like your friend, Dixie Davenport, want to pamper these pinkos in the name of 'human rights.' Once the Commies had Cuba, the Russians put ballistic missiles in there, didn't they? How'd you like to have them in Mexico? That'll be next if we let them have Nicaragua."

"Sorry. I just met Dixie. I don't know what her angle is on the subject. You work for AID, though, don't you?"

"Yeah. I'm doing a little time Stateside. LA Bureau."

"And after that?"

"Back overseas as fast as I can. I'm due a mission director's slot. Here you're just another strap hanger in a cocksucker suit. Like being a colonel at the Pentagon. Dime a dozen. What do you do, by the way? You're not another Congressional type, are you?"

"I'm more in your line of work. I'm an economist. I consult for AID and the World Bank. Short-term mostly."

"Beltway bandit, huh?"

"I don't sell hammers or toilet seats to the Pentagon," McCall shot back.

"Well, good luck," Blackbridge said without sincerity. "Maybe we'll run into each other down the road," he added and turned away.

"Yeah, maybe," McCall told him, hoping that would never happen, but fearing that it might. He took his plate and wandered back onto the terrace, taking up station alone. Feeling left out and ragged after his confrontation with Blackbridge, he looked over the scene. It was a soirée like hundreds of others going on that night around the nation's capital. Suburban dinner parties, little receptions downtown, the social side of the conferences that drew people from thirty different countries. They all used to be standard fare for him. Those days had been exciting, electric somehow.

Blackbridge was nothing new. There had always been jerks like him and there always would be. Maybe there had always been women like Angela, too. It was still a mystery to him how international travelers could pick up friendships where they left off, even if there were years in between meetings. Of course, there were the immediate conversation openers that broke the ice: 'Where've you been? What are you working on?' And all the mutual friends and acquaintances to catch up on. It was like they grew and changed at the same speed, while people who stayed put in different places changed at different rates and if they didn't see each other for several years, couldn't imagine what they'd ever found interesting about one another.

With Angela, of course, there was more. They'd be able to talk--not just talk, but communicate--right away. And unless she had someone she was serious about, he felt pretty sure they'd wind up in his bed or hers before the night was over. As he watched her across the terrace, talking intently with Dixie, he found her more attractive than any one he remembered from the last five years. Certainly more substantive than the Texas women he'd kept company with. Now that he was back, she excited him because she was savvy, in the game, high on adrenalin, determined to make a difference. Probably smarter than he was. She had a really nice ass, too.

Kurt Sorensen joined him. "McCall, isn't it?" he asked, offering his hand.

"Yes," McCall replied, smiling, feeling the gloom lift a little. "I'm surprised you remember me."

"To be honest, Dixie mentioned you and that jogged my memory. The last time was that conference on financial sector development, wasn't it? You gave a paper and we talked afterward. Right?"

"Exactly," McCall said, flattered.

"Where've you been since then? I don't think I've seen you in quite some time."

"I bought a bank down in Texas. It turned out to be a marvelous way to lose your shirt. And your shorts and your shoes. I came away barefooted and bare-assed."

Sorensen laughed, showing gleaming white teeth. Half a head taller than McCall, lean and well-tailored, he was close to sixty, but his hair was still thick and he kept it a little shaggy, a contrived affectation. Otherwise, he would have been altogether too handsome to be taken seriously.

"You're back for a fresh wardrobe, then?"

"Something like that. I'm consulting again. Not entirely starting over, but it takes a while to fill up the pipeline. You're still at State, I understand."

"Yes. They've pitched me upstairs. Special counselor to the Secretary. Shultz is a good fellow. I like working for him. Unfortunately, we don't always have our way these days."

"Isn't that par for the course?"

"Absolutely. But patience wears thin in one's old age. Well, hope to see you again soon. Dixie says you make a wicked Martini. Sorry I missed that."

McCall watched Sorensen amble away toward where Dixie was now sitting with Kevin. Just beyond, Angela Collins stood alone against the rail. Their eyes locked and some invisible energy put his legs in motion. He was standing beside her in three easy strides.

"Get what you wanted?"

"No," she replied. "Dixie Davenport isn't going public with anything. She wants to know everything I know, but she isn't willing to share anything with me, even off the record. That ass, Bradbrook--no, Blackbridge--was completely buttoned up. Dixie got to him before I did and she must have worked him over pretty good. Nothing there." She paused and looked at him with frank appraisal and a smile. "So that leaves you."

"Save the best for last," he said, smiling back. "Can I get you a drink?"

"Not here. Let's go somewhere I can take my shoes off."

"I know the way out of here if you're ready," he said.

"I need to make my manners to the host and hostess. Meet you in front?"

McCall nodded and headed for the walk that ran beside the house, the way he'd come in.

"McCall," Dixie Davenport said, breaking away from a small knot of people to block his way. "I want a word with you. Two even. About this 'auntie' business. Clever, but not complimentary." She grinned.

"Sorry about that. Did it accomplish the purpose?"

"Not for long, but long enough. Thanks."

"It didn't help Ms. Collins much," Mack chided.

"So you're going to make it up to her, huh?" Dixie smiled knowingly.

"We're old friends," he said, deadpan.

"She's a nice girl, McCall. Wants to do the right thing, not just make a name for herself. Keep that in mind, won't you? I'll help her when the time comes."

"I'll remember that. Nice to meet you, Aunt Dixie," McCall said, disappearing into the darkness.

Alexandria, Virginia

The insistent ringing of the phone roused McCall. His next conscious sensation was a lush natural fragrance. Lying on her side, turned away from him, Angela's dark hair spread across the pillow, one bare shoulder and arm clutching the comforter. McCall ignored the phone a few minutes longer, taking in the vision and the aroma and the warmth of her body.

"Damn," he muttered and eased back the covers, padding naked down the hall to his makeshift office.

"McCall," he growled into the receiver.

"*¿Como te va, 'mano?*" Javier's gravelly voice came through the receiver loud and clear. "I tried to call last night but there was no answer."

"Do you know what time it is?"

"Sorry, Mack. My secretary thought it was important."

McCall tried to clear his head. "Yeah. Maybe it is. We need to talk and I'm not sure we ought to discuss it on the phone. When are you coming this way again?"

"Not soon," Javier said.

"I'm off to Cairo next week for a job. Think you could meet me in Miami first of the week?"

"What about today? The Admiral's Club?"

McCall groaned. He and Angela hadn't made plans, but there was an unspoken agreement that they'd spend the day together. "Ay," he said. "Sure. I guess so. When can you be there?"

"Six this evening. I can fly back at ten. Will that work for you?"

"Yeah. There's an Air Florida flight out of National at eleven or so I think. If they're booked, I can try Eastern or Delta. They have a zillion flights a day. Or at least they used to."

"*Perfecto. Nos vemos entonces,*" Javier said.

McCall hung up the phone and padded back toward the bedroom.

The bathroom door was closed and he could hear the shower running. He opened the door to a cloud of warm, moist steam and stepped into the shower.

Angela shrieked in surprise and then laughed as he put his arms around her and stuck his head under the water streaming from the shower head.

* * * * * * * * * * *

"That smells delicious," she called from the hall.

"You said over easy, right?"

Angela poured coffee in two mugs and carried them into the tiny breakfast area off McCall's kitchen.

"Can you get the toast?" he asked, sliding the eggs onto a plate next to three slices of bacon and a wedge of orange.

"How's that?" he said, joining her at the breakfast table.

"You're a man of many charms," she said, her dark eyes sparkling. "You ought to keep a spare toothbrush, though."

"It just went to the top of my shopping list."

She smiled, dabbing egg yolk from her lips with a napkin. "Leave the wrapper on. I'm going to be out of the country for awhile."

"Where to?" McCall asked, tearing his toast in two and mopping egg yolk from his plate.

"I've got a line on a story about a major arms conduit running through Buenos Aires."

McCall frowned. "You do realize that gun runners are a violent breed, don't you?"

"I've been able to stay arm's length so far." She looked at McCall, brow slightly knit. "It's important, Mack. You haven't seen what those thugs do with AK-47s and RPGs. It's butchery. And our government is aiding and abetting. We're in it up to our bloody armpits. It's got to be exposed."

"What's our government got to do with all this gun running and such that you're trying to stop?"

She sipped her coffee and took a breath. "Here's the deal. The Reagan Administration is getting around the Boland Amendment by raising private funds to buy arms and train the Contras. There seem to be a bunch of CIA fronts . . . no, that's not exactly right. Soldier-of-fortune outfits is more like it. A lot of ex-CIA involved. After the Bay of Pigs, the CIA shut down a lot of covert ops and fired most of the people who ran them. It left one hell of a disposal problem--what to do with all those human lethal weapons. The situation in Nicaragua is tailor-made for putting them back in action."

"You mentioned the Boland Amendment last night. What is it again?"

"It's an amendment to the 1983 Defense Appropriations Act. It forbids the US Government from funding the Contras. But they're doing it anyway. The White House is raising money from wacko patriots all around the country, and pouring it into supplying arms to the Contras and who knows what else. They're breaking the law. I'll concede that there's wiggle room in the statute, but the Amendment clearly states that its purpose is to prevent the US Government from providing military support for the purpose of overthrowing the Nicaraguan government."

McCall leaned back in his chair, suddenly interested. "How's the money moving? Do you know?"

"Well, not by Western Union. Black bags, I guess, or sleazy banks. Maybe they use Swiss banks or those brass-plate outfits in the Caymans. I haven't focused on that yet."

Angela was tipping the scales toward arms dealing as the motive for Ryder's interest in Banco Dorado. He was ex-CIA, so maybe he was backstopping a soldier-of-fortune outfit. A Panamanian bank was every bit as good as Swiss one for moving money and a hell of a lot closer to the action just up the Panamerican Highway.

"What's the matter, Mack?"

He almost told her the story, but stopped himself. The only way to keep a secret is not to tell it, particularly not to a reporter.

"Nothing," he said. "I was just thinking about what you said."

"Who was on the phone?" she asked, approaching from a different angle.

"I've got to meet somebody in Miami this evening. Spoils our day."

She took his plate and carried it to the sink. He pushed back from the table and followed her.

She turned toward him, her arms outstretched, coming to rest on his shoulders. "I want to do this again when I get back," she whispered, touching her lips to his with feather lightness.

His hands fell to the small of her back to draw her against him. He let his hands slip lower to cup the buns he had admired from the first time he saw her. "We'll do dinner first. Meantime, keep your head down. Make sure you get back with all your precious parts in the proper places."

Miami International Airport

McCall flashed his membership card at the well-groomed receptionist at the desk of the Admiral's Club and received a quick smile in return, all white teeth and immaculate makeup. "Meeting someone," he told her, to avoid further conversation. In the corner of his eye, he saw Javier rise and come toward him. Miami was the primary East Coast hub for Latin American traffic, so scarcely anyone noticed when they gave each other a back-slapping *abrazo*.

The club was an island of tranquility in a sea of sound and light and movement that typifies the common areas of the world's major airports. In contrast to the garish neon and glass of the concourse shops, the club's walls were paneled in polished wood, the lighting soft and indirect, the carpet deep and quiet. No backpacks strewn across the floor, no baseball caps worn backwards, no cranky children demanding to be changed or fed or reassured. Here, passengers between flights were tucked into comfortable chairs, the men with ties in place, the women chic in tailored traveling clothes.

McCall wrapped an arm around Javier's shoulder and steered him toward an alcove stocked with fruit juice, coffee and an array of bottles that ran the gamut from rum and vodka to Scotch and bourbon. McCall plucked a tumbler from the glass shelves, scooped a handful of ice cubes into it, twisted the top from a bottle of Johnny Walker Black Label and poured the tumbler half full. He tipped the glass toward Javier, a question.

Javier shook his head. "I'm fine."

"How long have you been waiting?"

"Half an hour. I have a quiet corner." Javier pointed across the room to a table with a phone and a lamp between two overstuffed lounge chairs sat near tall windows looking out on the tarmac.

McCall sank into the deep upholstery, stirred the ice in his Scotch with a forefinger and took a long swallow. "Anything different since the last time we talked?"

Javier's bushy eyebrows rose and fell. "Not anything good. I talked to several of the small shareholders. Without telling them there might be an offer for their stock, it was clear they'd sell. They won't stand with us if we try to fight."

"No surprise there," McCall said, taking a sip of Scotch, looking at Javier over the rim of the glass. "So have you and Don Francisco made a decision?"

"Not yet. I haven't told him about the other shareholders. It will hurt him when I do and I've been putting it off."

"Any luck finding out who Ryder's clients are?"

"I went to see Morales. I told him we thought he was bluffing, that he didn't really have an offer for his stock. He was offended because I questioned his honor." Javier grinned. "He went off like a cannon, told me about his friends and how powerful they were--or had been. According to Morales, Ryder is just a middleman."

"So what have we got here?" McCall said. "A bunch of peacock generals want a bank?"

"I know," Javier said. "I think Ryder wants the bank and the generals are letting him invest their money. By the way, they call themselves *Las Águilas*--the eagles."

"Well, if Ryder has his hand in some deep pockets, we're toast. It's just a matter of time. They'll take Morales' twenty-five percent, buy out the minority shareholders--what's that? Thirty percent? And then they'll tell us what they're willing to pay for the rest. They can steal the damned bank right out from under us."

Javier took McCall's words like a punch to the gut. He fell back in the chair, his dark brown eyes as sad as a Spaniel's. It was several moments before he could speak.

"What can we do?"

"Sell. Make it easy for Ryder and get the best deal we can. Leave the minority shareholders twisting in the wind. Did you get any sense of how fast they want to move?"

"I think they're in a hurry. Morales didn't say so, but he talked about the powerful friends *Las Águilas* have in the United States and I got the feeling that there's some kind of partnership there."

"I think so, too," McCall said. "Along with what I learned about Ryder--that he's ex-CIA, for one thing--I was told that there was a third party that might be interested in having access to the kind of services Banco Dorado could provide if it were in the right hands. When I put it together with some information I got the other night, I think that third party is the US government--part of the government, at least. They're using back channels to circumvent a law against providing aid to the Contras. We've just become collateral damage in a dirty little war."

"*Dios mio*," Javier said. "*No puedo creerlo.* It can't be . . . Can it?"

McCall nodded. "Oh, yes. It can. I think we ought to take the initiative on this. And there's more than one reason why we should. I'll get into that in a minute. But first things first. Why don't you get hold of Ryder and ask for a face-to-face? Take his measure. See what he's offering. They might be generous if we save them the time and effort of negotiating with all those minority shareholders."

Javier's tan turned two more shades of pale and beads of sweat popped out on his forehead. He leaned forward with his elbows on his knees, hands clasped.

"What about Don Francisco? . . . And Carlotta?"

"You'll just have to make the case for moving quickly. Get them to agree to a meeting to see what Ryder has to say. If you tell Don Francisco about the minority shareholders' eagerness to sell, I don't know how he can object. Ryder and these other guys--*Las Águilas*--have got us by the short hairs."

"*Madre de Dios*," Javier muttered.

"Let's hope he hasn't already scouted the minority shareholders and knows what you know about their willingness to sell. We need to be out ahead of him on that."

"Yes, yes, I see," Javier said numbly.

"Now here's the second thing," McCall said, taking a sip of his Scotch. "I've got a once-in-a-lifetime investment opportunity that could take us past anything I had at First Mission or that we have at Banco Dorado."

Javier's eyes were staring straight ahead, unblinking, a thousand-yard stare. He was still in shock and wasn't focused on what McCall was saying.

"Javier. Listen to me," McCall said, snapping his fingers, forcing Javier to shake his head and look McCall in the eyes.

"I said I have a once-in-a-lifetime investment opportunity. We need to seize the moment. I have inside information on a settlement of old claims between the Soviet Union and the British government. The claims I'm talking about are gold bonds of the last tsar and for openers, we have a chance of making a four hundred or five hundred percent profit on all the bonds we can acquire now, before the settlement is announced."

"How much?"

"The bonds are selling for ten, even less. But use ten as a benchmark. If they settle at fifty, we'll make a killing. The more we can buy now, the bigger the nut we'll come away with. And listen, there's a chance they'll settle in gold. I can't even guess what the return would be then."

Javier frowned. Mack had spoken quickly, excitedly. Javier's English was excellent, practically flawless, but he wasn't sure he understood what Mack was saying and he was still trying to absorb the inevitability of selling the bank.

"These bonds are from before the Russian Revolution? The bonds of the Tsar?"

McCall nodded, grinning.

"And they are selling at a price--ten, you think? That is what the paper costs, no? So you want to sell our shares in Banco Dorado and buy these things? If this is what you are saying, this Russian paper makes junk bonds look respectable."

"It isn't crazy, Javier. I've got the information straight from the office of the British Prime Minister. The settlement is going to happen. We just don't know when. And you're forgetting about the gold."

They argued back and forth, Javier skeptical, punching holes in McCall's enthusiasm, playing the prudent banker. Finally, McCall fell back in his chair.

"OK. OK. One thing at a time. We can keep the two things separate. We know where we stand on Banco Dorado. We're up against a wall and Ryder and his buddies are offering us a blindfold and a last cigarette. The Russian bonds are something else. I believe in the deal. You don't. So make me a loan, as much as you can break loose. If I default, it'll be a poke in the eye for Ryder after he takes over the bank. I'll worry about staying out of their way if they try to kneecap me. If the settlement goes the way I think it will, I'll be able to repay the loan and they won't be any the wiser. You don't have to put any of your own money in the deal, but the offer of a partnership still stands once we've sold our share of the bank. What could be more fair than that?"

Javier shook his head. "Mack, I couldn't present a loan like that to the board of directors. You've never seen such a bunch of old pelicanos. One or two would have a heart attack if I even proposed it. Half of them are on oxygen as it is. Once in awhile, we take a piece of a shopping center or an office building. And they think that's deep water. Defaulted Russian bonds? *¡Imposible!*"

"Don't take it to them. You have a discretionary fund, don't you? Something you can commit on your own authority? Use that and don't take the bonds as collateral. Make me an unsecured loan."

"You're asking a lot, Mack."

"Not anymore than you asked me back when I emptied my bank account to help you buy into Banco Dorado. I gave you all I had. And kept giving. I sent you money every quarter to buy stock in Banco Dorado. You haven't forgotten that have you?" He hadn't wanted to put it on that basis, but he had no place to go if Javier didn't come through with the capital he needed to buy the bonds. The opportunity of a lifetime would go a glimmering. Javier needed a push to get him off his banker's butt.

Javier looked away, stung. When he met McCall's eyes, he said, "If you put it that way . . . I'll make the loan, but as much as I can give on my own authority is a hundred thousand."

"That's better than nothing," McCall said. "Thanks, *compadre.*"

They stared at each other, McCall trying to make his eyes speak a silent apology, Javier trying to conceal his confusion and fear.

"There's one other thing," McCall said. "I need a bond trader in London. Do you have a dealer there? I don't want to start crashing around on my own asking questions about Russian bonds."

Javier thought for a long moment, taking inventory. "I deal with several companies in the City, but the one I trust most is Foster and Son. It's a small house, but very good with transactions that are out of the ordinary. What do you need to know?"

"Pricing and availability of the Russian bonds. I'm told they trade on the London exchange, maybe in Paris, too."

The hostess of the Admiral's Club, trim and business-like in her blue sheath skirt and white silk blouse with a bow, came toward them. Javier snapped his notebook closed and slipped it back into his coat.

"Mr. Banderas," she said with sweet efficiency. "They'll be calling your flight in about five minutes." She waited for a moment, tilting her head to inquire. "Is there anything I can get for you?"

"No," he said. "Thank you. I'm fine."

She smiled again, turned on her high heels and retreated. McCall and Javier looked at each other and stood up.

McCall said, "Fax me the quote sheets on the bonds when you get them from Foster. I'd like to meet him when I'm through London next week. Can you set that up?"

They looked at each other for a long moment. It was an unlikely friendship that had reached a crossroads. McCall could see the questions, the uncertainty, in Javier's dark brown eyes and wondered what Javier saw in his--determination or desperation?.

They shook hands, turned it into an abrazo and walked shoulder to shoulder through the heavy glass doors of the Admiral's Club. Javier was heading down Concourse E to security, passport control and his gate. McCall's Delta flight was in the opposite direction. They paused again outside the Club.

"How will you want the loan?"

"I'll set up an account with Foster if we can come to terms. You could remit directly to him for my account, couldn't you?"

"I can do it that way. Where will you be in Cairo if I need to get in touch?"

"The Meridien in Garden City. I don't know the number."

"I can find it. *Nos vemos, 'mano,*" he added, waved sadly and turned away.

The shops were closing as McCall watched Javier head down toward passport control. No point, he thought, in trying to fly back tonight.

Angela had deprived him of sleep the night before and the energy he'd burned pitching Javier on his plan had left him drained. He veered off toward the hotel instead of his gate, hoping they'd have a toothbrush and a razor. A good night's sleep and an early morning flight would have him back home by mid-morning. He needed to get Paralee Campbell moving. He'd let Javier think he knew a hell of a lot more about the bonds than he actually did.

He called her from the hotel.

"Do you have anything more on the bonds?" he asked.

"No," she said. "But I'm going to the Library of Congress on Monday. I'll get whatever they've got there."

"OK," McCall said. "Things are moving a little faster than I expected. I'm going to see somebody in London at the end of the week and I really need to know a lot more than what we've got now."

"I'll do my best," she said.

Panamá City

Pacing back and forth behind his mammoth desk, his mane of silver hair disheveled, Don Francisco Benedetti was in a state of high agitation. Javier had been relating to him what McCall had learned from his sources in the United States and his own conversations with Morales and the minority shareholders. Don Francisco was not prepared for the dark canvas these facts painted.

"Morales! How could he betray me this way? He is Brutus. With his own knife he has stabbed me in the back. To think he would give Banco Dorado to these scoundrels. They will rape her and ravage her, leave her sitting in their filth like a toothless old puta when they are finished with her. I can't believe it!"

Watching the agony of the old man who meant so much to him, Javier's heart ached. He hated his feeling of impotence, unable to think of any way to fight off the takeover. Mack was right that the odds were against them, but Mack was too eager to sell, too anxious to gamble on some crazy scheme to strike it rich with those Russian bonds. Surely there was some other way.

Don Francisco had questioned Javier over and over about what Morales had said and about what he had learned from McCall about the other parties to the takeover. He was uncomfortable with so much second-hand information. Morales was the known among a crowd of unknowns and that was why he was railing at his old ally. The others--well, he had no direct knowledge of them. That was what finally tipped the scales toward his deciding to invite Ryder to discuss his plans to buy Morales' shares.

Don Francisco stopped pacing and slumped in his big chair. "Very well," he said. "We should go as far as asking this Ryder to meet with us. Perhaps better, to meet first with you, then with me if he is open to reason. We need to know what his intentions are in buying Morales' shares. Of course, he will lie to us about some things, but we cannot make a decision on assumptions."

"What about Carlotta?" Javier asked.

"When we know more and I have made a decision about what to do, I will tell her. Now, get on with this ugly business. To force the issue, I will tell Morales that we are denying his loan request. If he wants to sell his shares, he should sell them, and may he burn in hell for betraying our friendship."

Javier went back to his office and asked his secretary to place a call to

Charles Foster in London. He would deal with that first to clear his desk and his mind for the best way to approach Robert Ryder. Then he would call Ryder and invite him to Panamá to talk business.

Washington

McCall was doing laundry, getting his clothes ready for Egypt, when the fax came in. Two pages. It was on Foster and Son letterhead and it offered a long list. There were several entries for Imperial Bonds, including the best of Audrey's, the issue of 1909. It was priced at seven percent of face value. Better than he'd hoped. The others ranged in price from three to eleven. How could you go wrong with bargains like that? You could frame them and sell them at the flea market and make a profit. The frames would be the most expensive part of the package.

He propped his feet in an open desk drawer and looked at the list more carefully. Audrey's Imperials of 1909 had the greatest availability. Other issues in Audrey's collection were there, too. City of St. Petersburg, 1913, the 1908 City of Moscow and the Armavir-Touapse Railway bond of 1909. Audrey didn't have any of the 1912 Kahetian Railway bonds, but there were a lot of them available. The list said nothing about which bonds were gold-backed and which weren't. Odds were, though, that the Imperials were and the others weren't. It would be something for Charles Foster to figure out if they got that far.

The phone rang next to his ear, startling him. It was Paralee Campbell. She barely gave him time to say hello before she started talking, her voice excited and eager. "Mack, I've got something really terrific. I'm in the Main Reading Room of the Library of Congress."

"Give me an hour," McCall said and rang off. He threw on a shirt and slacks, grabbed a leather jacket from the hall closet and headed out the door without shaving or showering.

****

McCall had been in a few handsome university libraries but he had never stood in the Main Reading Room of the Library of Congress. Tranquil, golden light fell on polished mahogany tables radiating from a central core like the circular pews of a cathedral in the round.

The room rose like the layers of a cake. At the base, eight alcoves were enclosed by arches of veined marble the color of camel bone and old ivory. Next came eight arcades screened by seven smaller arches. The arches supported eight galleries with polished, spooled stone railings. There, statues of great scholars stood vigil over the room below. Eight magnificent windows, capped by a baroque dome, vaulted above the outer walls of the galleries.

Awestruck, he at last accepted the room's elegance and began to search for a head capped by Paralee's tousled, sun-streaked hair. He found her at a table near the librarian's station, bent over an outsized book with an old-fashioned hard leather binding. A yellow ruled pad with a sheaf of pages rolled back rested under her right fist. The top page was written half-way down with notes. He pulled a chair up beside her. "You wear glasses," he whispered.

"Oh," she said, startled, the library lamp with the green glass shade dappling her face with light and shadow.

"What've you got?" he asked, still whispering.

"Let me turn this stuff in," she said, indicating a foot-high pile of books and reports. "Then we can go where we can talk."

"Want to do it over lunch at the Hyatt? We could spread out downstairs if they don't have a convention going. Or we could try Union Station. Or sit on the grass and eat a hot dog. It's a great day outside."

"Let's do the Hyatt," she said, replacing her reading glasses with a pair of pale amber sunglasses.

****

"Now, here's the good part. The Tsar was sending gold to London. It had to be as security for the bonds he was issuing there. The British Navy sent ships to Russia and brought the Tsar's gold--or some of it--to London. But I'm a little puzzled why they were actually moving the gold. Isn't that usually just a transfer on the books?"

"Yeah, but not in those days," McCall said. "Europe was on the gold standard then and gold might have been flowing from the ruble to the pound to maintain the exchange rate. The war was probably a more compelling reason, though. Quite aside from the possibility that the gold was being used as collateral, Britain probably looked like a safer place to keep it than Russia or France. It is an island, after all. And it might have been in payment for war matériel, too. Probably all of the above."

"Look at this," Paralee said, her dark blue eyes bright with excitement. "These are my notes from the memoirs of a British captain when he was a lieutenant on the cruiser, HMS *Drake*. The interesting part is that on October 7, 1914, his ship and the transport HMS *Mantois* were anchored at sea outside the port of Archangel--that's practically the Arctic Ocean up there. They took on two million ounces of gold from Russian barges and lighters. The gold was worth eight million pounds then. They loaded at night and the whole thing was supposed to be really secret, but the Germans found out about it and sent U-boats after them. The ships had to fight their way through to get back to Britain. This eight million wound up in the Bank of England's vaults in London. But it was only the beginning of gold shipments from Russia. I've been digging through copies of what our library has from the Bank of England archives and Canadian railroad records and it looks like Britain got about £60 million worth of Russian gold between 1914 and 1917."

"You're kidding."

"No. After the close call in the Arctic Ocean, they didn't send any more that way. Instead, they started shipping it to Vladivostok on the Trans-Siberian Railway. The Japanese navy hauled it from there to Vancouver, then it went by train cross-country to the Bank of England's branch in Ottawa. Altogether, £52 million worth of Russian gold wound up in Canada."

McCall took a calculator from his briefcase. "How many ounces of gold is that? You said the Royal Navy took two million ounces worth eight million pounds, so an ounce of gold back then was worth four pounds an ounce?"

"Sounds right," she said.

"So there's fifty-two million pounds worth in Ottawa and eight million in London. That's fifteen million ounces. Gold's somewhere around three-hundred dollars an ounce in today's market, which makes that gold worth about four-point-five billion dollars. Didn't you say the other day that the Russians owed foreigners, mostly Brits and French, about a billion dollars in bonded debt?"

"No. A billion pounds. We're dealing with different exchange rates, but if we use four-fifty to the pound, the Tsar owed about four and a half billion dollars--the same as the gold's worth now." She sat back, grinning triumphantly the way star pupils do when they've leaped ahead of the professor.

"That's got to be a wild coincidence. The Russians didn't owe all of that to the British. So if the Tsar sent fifteen million ounces of gold to England and only owed the Brits . . . What'd you say? Fourteen percent of six-hundred million pounds?" McCall punched numbers into his calculator. "That's eighty-four million. Then they borrowed another four-hundred million, so five-hundred million in round terms. The pound is worth about a dollar and a quarter these days, which puts gold at . . ." McCall punched his calculator again. "Two-hundred-forty pounds an ounce. In pounds sterling, the market value of the gold then, is three-point-six billion. The Soviets could pay the full face amount of all the gold-denominated bonds and there'd still be a lot of gold left over."

They looked at each other in silence for several long moments. "It gets better," Paralee said, barely able to contain her excitement. "There was an earlier settlement," she said and waited for that to register with McCall.

He knitted his brow and looked at her. *"A what?"*

"Look at this," she said, pushing a photocopy of several printed pages and a sheaf of notes across the table to him. "The Brits did a settlement with the Baltic States in 1969 that used gold they'd deposited with the Bank of England."

McCall scanned the short description of the settlement. After World War I, Latvia, Lithuania and Estonia deposited gold worth £5.7 million in the Bank of England. "Looks like they just made a deposit. There's nothing to suggest it was used as collateral," he said.

"I know, but keep going."

"OK," he said and began to summarize the photocopy aloud. "In World War II, the Germans invade Poland, conquer the Baltic States. . . . The Brits impound the gold under the 'Trading with the Enemy Act.'. . . After World War II, the Sovs absorb Latvia, Lithuania and Estonia . . . The Sovs claim the gold and want the Brits to give it back. . . . The Brits file a counterclaim for payment of bonds sold to British nationals by the three countries. . . . The Soviets cut a deal to pay off the bonds with the gold." McCall looked up, thoughtful.

Her eyes flashed with excitement. "Your Russian bonds are as good as gold."

"Wait a sec. Let's not get ahead of ourselves," McCall said. "This doesn't say the deal was for full payment. The Baltic bonds were issued after World War I, when the gold standard was in shambles. And it doesn't say they were collateralized in any way, much less by gold. We don't know whether they were bonds of the State with sovereign guarantees or issues of the Vilnius Waterworks."

"Exactly," she whispered, her enthusiasm rising. "The Soviets agreed to give up some of the gold to redeem the bonds! That's the important part. They didn't have to be gold-backed. Don't you think they'd do it again? We've already figured out that the Brits--all by themselves--have enough of the Tsar's gold to let the Soviets pay off all the foreign-held Russian debt at face value. The gold's there. They just have to agree to swap it. And if it's like the Baltic deal, there'll be gold left over after the bonds are paid off."

She stabbed the page with her forefinger. "Look. In the Baltic Settlement only half the outstanding bonds were submitted for redemption. The others were probably lost or destroyed some way. Just think. The Germans blitzkrieged Poland and the Baltic states on the way to Moscow in World

War II and the Russians probably blew them up again when they were going the other way, toward Berlin. Between the Huns and the Mongol Horde, a lot of stuff went up in smoke."

"These are bearer bonds," he added, catching her excitement. "They're like currency. They can't be replaced if they're lost, stolen or destroyed. The same thing had to have happened in France and England during the war. And a lot more in England than in France. The Germans bombed London for months and months. The Soviets are probably figuring it'll work the same way it did in 1969. It could be that simple."

"Mack, I want to see the bonds," she said suddenly.

Alexandria

Paralee walked into the center of the large living room and looked around her. A single rattan chair with print covered cushions sat forlorn against a barren wall, a pile of newspapers scattered beside it. McCall stood by the door, watching her.

"I forgot to warn you," he said. "I haven't gotten around to buying much more than the bare necessities."

She moved through the living room to the glass doors opening onto the balcony and spied the breakfast nook, which contained a round, formica-topped table, two castoff straight chairs and a pathetic bookshelf that doubled as a table for a small black and white television. She walked into the kitchen, opened the refrigerator and noted its contents--a quart of milk, two oranges, a half carton of eggs and a sleeve of bacon. A few dishes reposed in the sink, but the counter was clean. McCall watched her in amused dismay from the kitchen archway.

"Come on," he said. "Now that you've seen the refrigerator, there's nothing sacred left. You might as well see the rest of it." He took her down the short hall to the bedroom/office and flicked on the light.

"Well," she said. "Somebody lives here. Desk, a real chair, fax, computer, phone. This is the office, right?"

"Good guess. Executive washroom's across the hall. Next stop's the master suite." She saw an unmade king-size bed without a headboard, a rattan chest of drawers and night stand with a lamp and an alarm clock. Like the living room, no pictures graced the walls, not even a bull fight poster. The master bath had clean towels and his shaving gear was neatly arrayed on the counter.

"It's . . . uh . . . pretty Spartan," she stammered. "I don't know why, but I wouldn't have thought . . . you know . . . that this was your style."

"It isn't," he said sadly. "I still have some stuff in storage that I picked up over the years, but the good pieces went under the auctioneer's hammer, as the saying goes. I really hated to sell the carpets. I got them in Iran, before the Ayatollah. They were gorgeous, but unfortunately also about the most valuable thing I had left. I was lucky to sell the house for enough to cover the mortgage. I had some prints and a little original art, mostly Southwestern--Gorman, Amado Peña, some Carol Grigg. Those names probably don't mean anything to you, but I liked them."

"You sold everything?" "I needed the money. Pretty much everything I had was invested in the bank. I've been thinking about selling this place, too. I bought it back in the '70s as a rental property. Just now, I'm traveling all the time and I don't really need this much space. No point dressing it up if I'm going to sell it." He shrugged.

"Maybe you can sell the bonds instead."

McCall looked at her closely, smiling. "Maybe so. And that's what you came to see, isn't it? The bonds. Come on. I'll give you a drink first. What'll you have?" "What've you got? I didn't see any beer in the fridge."

"I'm out. But there's some decent Scotch. How do you take it? On the rocks or neat?"

"On the rocks, I guess, with a lot of soda."

"Sorry, no soda. I never put soda in good Scotch. How about a splash of water?"

"I'll just take it however you do," she said. "It's time I learned about the taste of peat smoke and the difference between a blend and a single-malt. You can hold forth on those subjects, can't you?"

"Not really," he said, shaking his head. "I like the taste and the effect. I don't need to understand it. But I thought you said your name was 'Campbell.' Scots whiskey ought to run in your veins." He poured Cardhu into two tumblers, and gave one to her.

"What can I say? I've just never been one for the hard stuff. I like wine, so a Frenchman must have climbed into my family tree when the Scots weren't looking. After all, Mary Queen of Scots had a squadron of French cadets in her court. They carried her clubs when she went golfing."

"Really?"

"Really. Where do you think "caddy" comes from? It's the way the French pronounce "cadet." You know, cad-dey."

"You're amazing." He raised his glass. "Cheers."

"Cheers," she replied and took a cautious sip. She made a face and asked, "Is this a single malt or a blend?"

"Single malt."

"It must be an acquired taste."

"You'll learn to respect it," he told her. "Now, about those bonds." He put his drink down and disappeared, returning a moment later with a large envelope. He removed the bonds one-by-one and laid them out on the kitchen counter.

"Oh, my," she exclaimed, letting her eyes move from one elaborately-engraved, richly-colored certificate to the next. "Aren't these gorgeous? Check that shade of green. And that's the Tsar's eagle, isn't it?" she asked, pointing to the double-headed, wings-spread symbol at the top center of one of the bonds.

"Right on. That's an issue of Imperial Russia, a state loan, denominated in gold rubles.”

“And look at this red and gold one. City of St. Petersburg. It’s in four languages and shows the exchange rates. I wonder what it cost to engrave these things? They really went all out, didn’t they?”

“Makes you wonder why there weren’t collectors before 1976. They’re really something to look at, aren’t they?”

“Yes, they are.”

“Had enough?” he asked. “I’ll put them away.”

“I guess so. Thanks for letting me see them. Makes it all more real somehow.”

McCall put the bonds back in their envelope, tucked them away in his office and returned to the kitchen. He found her looking out through the sliding glass doors leading to the balcony.

“Have I worked myself out of a job now?” she asked when he joined her.

“I hadn’t even thought about that. There’s more to be done. A little different from library research, but I’ll bet you could do it.”

“What?” she asked.

“I’m going to need a prospectus. I don’t know quite how I’ll use it yet or even if I will, but it needs to be swotted up just in case. Interested?”

“Sure,” she said. “What’s a prospectus and how soon do you need it?”

McCall laughed. “I’ll show you. But why don’t you catch up on your studies while I’m in Egypt. A couple of weeks. I don’t want you flunking out because you’re spending too much time on Russian bonds.”

“I don’t think that’s a problem. Nobody’s blowing anything by me yet.”

“Why am I not surprised?” he said. “And now, since you’re practically staff, would you mind running me out to Dulles tomorrow? You can keep the car while I’m gone.”

“Your little Benz? No problem,” she said, grinning.

“I’m due back two weeks from Friday.” He scribbled a flight number and the ETA on a slip of paper and gave it to her. “Taking me out there also means picking me up. That OK with you?”

“Sure, why not?” she told him with a crooked smile. “You don’t mind if I take the car out to Winchester to see my folks, do you?”

“Feel free.”

“Thanks,” she said. Turning toward the balcony, she pointed and asked, “Can you see the sunsets from here?”

“Such as they are,” he replied, pulling back the sliding glass door to let her go out ahead of him. “Nothing like the sunsets in Texas. Or twilight, for that matter. The light is different almost everywhere, but in South Texas, twilight is a long, drawn-out affair. One of the few things about the place I still like.”

"Maybe Virginia's not like that, but we have beautiful fall color, as good as New England." She leaned against the railing, gazing toward another high rise condominium to the west.

"I know," McCall said, thinking about the farm and the warm colors of the Valley's fall foliage.

He put his back against the side railing and examined her in profile. She was too bright to be the girl next door. She wasn't built for speed the way Angela was. She wasn't Cat Mercer, either, but there was a lot about her that reminded him of Cat.

Cat was a tomboy and a true child of the Valley. The red blood of pioneers ran in her veins and she had a toughness born of the hard scrabble and heartache of generations of Mercers. Back then, people probably thought she and Mack would get married and take over the farm, but for Mack, there was always a horizon beyond the Valley. He could never have imagined Cat in his grandfather's library, turning the pages of Darwin's *Voyage of the Beagle* or even Graham Greene's *Quiet American*. If Cat had time on her hands, she'd scrub floors or chop wood. It had been no surprise to Mack as they grew up and drifted apart, that Cat had happily become pregnant by the time she was sixteen, dropped out of school, married old Woody Coleman and moved in with Woody's folks. She'd never leave the Valley. Never wanted to.

That wasn't Paralee. She'd grown up all over, gone seeking when her marriage went off the rails, reached out to the starving children of Ethiopia and faced down the pain and panic. She'd done good work on the bonds. She surely didn't want the same things Cat did, but she had the same kind of certainty about her that said she would know what she wanted when she saw it. He decided that she was someone who deserved to be taken seriously.

London

McCall's flight touched down at Heathrow in bright morning sunlight and he passed through customs feeling gritty and sleep-deprived. His head was full of Russian bonds and he'd missed several of those precious few hours of sleep on the night flight to London. He tried to doze in the cab on the way into the city, but failed. Chilty was tied up in meetings until that evening. McCall arranged to meet Charles Foster at his office that afternoon. Then he showered, pulled the heavy drapes, hung the "Privacy, Please" tag on his door and went to bed.

****

Charles Foster's polished pedestal desk was framed by a large Palladian window several stories above Lombard Street. Beyond lay the Thames and London Bridge. It didn't look much like the offices of bond traders McCall knew in the States. It felt more like the lair of a rich lawyer—paneled walls, antique furniture, a large Shiraz carpet on a gleaming parquet floor. Charles Foster didn't look much like a bond trader, either.

For a start, he wore a conservative, three-piece suit, not the red suspenders favored by New York's Masters of the Universe. He was a tall, slender man who projected gentility with a benign smile rather than the arrogant swagger of Wall Street. The skin of his face was tight and wind-burned, as if he'd spent the weekend shooting grouse in Scotland or sailing the Irish Sea. He had to be well into his sixties.

Foster came around the desk and stretched out a hand, palm down, to McCall. His grip was bony and firm and his blue eyes were direct.

"Mr. McCall. Delighted to meet you. Mr. Banderas told me to expect you. Some interest you might have in Russian bonds." Foster's voice was clear and well-modulated, engaging without being eager.

"I appreciate your taking the time."

"Not at all. Tea? I've just received some Melfort BOP from Sri Lanka that's quite nice." Without waiting for McCall to reply, Foster opened a panel door at one side of the small office and spoke briefly with someone in an adjacent space.

As McCall's eyes followed Foster, his attention was drawn first to a colorful document encased in an elaborate frame and then to others around the room.

Foster turned back to McCall, noticing that McCall was staring at his wall decorations.

"Difficult to miss that one, isn't it? A 1908 bond of the Chinese Imperial Railway. My favorite is this one, though," he said, directing McCall's attention to an elaborately engraved bond embellished with exotic animals. "An issue of the Brussels Zoo."

"You're a scripophilist?" McCall asked, moving from one framed certificate to another, hands clasped behind his back as if he were in a museum.

"Actually not," Foster assured him. "My brother is, however. I have mixed emotions about hanging them. They're handsome, but in default. What message does such a display of failure convey to my clients?" Foster didn't laugh, but his smile was wide and his eyes twinkled with good humor. "Sit here won't you?" he added, indicating an antique settee with legs and arms so spindly that McCall was afraid it might break under his weight.

A plain, middle-aged woman in low-heel oxford shoes and a tailored tweed suit over a beige silk blouse brought the tea and poured it into translucent china cups as delicate as the settee. McCall was impressed with the rich flavor and found himself charmed by Foster's discourse on Broken Orange Pekoe, its aging and grading.

The tea finished, Foster sat back and laced his long, bony fingers in his lap and asked, "Now. How may I be of service?"

"I've come into some bonds of Nicholas II." McCall paused, watching Foster's face for any reaction. "Presently, I'm using them as capital for an investment company I'm forming in the Bahamas. I might want to acquire some more of them."

"I gathered that from Mr. Banderas' earlier inquiry. How fortunate he should have come to me, inasmuch as my brother is such an expert. I must say, however, that it isn't an investment I would advise. Again, because of my brother, I stand ready when called on to make a market in the Tsar's bonds as well as some Chinese issues traded on the exchange. In fact, I'm one of the few brokers in London who will make a market in these issues. I can assure you that it's a very quiet affair. There was a flurry after the formation of the Bond and Share Society, but since then . . . Of course, if something were afoot . . ." Now Foster watched McCall's expression carefully.

"I don't know exactly what you mean by something 'afoot.' I like them because they make cheap capital. I can carry them on the books at face value, not market value." McCall hoped Foster didn't see the flicker in his eyes when he plunged ahead. "However, looking to the longer term, there's glasnost and the Soviet opening to the West. Sooner or later, Gorbachev will have to put things right with world capital markets if the Soviet Union is going to be a player in the global economy."

Charles Foster made a steeple of his fingers, his elbows resting on the delicate arms of his side chair. He smiled knowingly at McCall.

"Mr. McCall," Foster began, his head tipped to one side. "I've traded securities all my life. Rather successfully, I might say. I don't take much of an active part in it now. I leave that to my son and his crew of young tigers. But I haven't lost my nose, as it were. And, frankly, I find the prospect of glasnost restoring value to Tsar Nicholas' bonds quite unlikely unless one knew something no one else knew."

McCall shrugged, knowing there was no point in trying to bluff Charles Foster.

"You're free to infer whatever you like, Mr. Foster. I can't prevent that. But the unvarnished facts are these. I presently hold some of the Tsar's bonds. I'm interested in buying more for my own account. I'm here because Javier Banderas and I are old friends and because he trusts you. If he trusts you, I trust you. We're friends of that sort. I'm also here because the bonds trade on the London exchange. So an English dealer makes more sense than an American one. And that's about the size of it."

"I see," Foster said. "And fair enough. A word about our policy, though. Our standard lot is five-hundred thousand pounds. I appreciate, however, that with the Russian bonds, we have a situation somewhat out of the ordinary. Perhaps we could set a minimum trade of, say, a hundred thousand? Actually, it's best to deal in small volume here. It's primarily a collector's market, you see. A purchase of a hundred thousand pounds or so might not make too many ripples, but even so, the price might well advance. I've told you the market's still as a mill pond. But if you buy in any sort of volume, you'll attract attention, no matter what kind of story you concoct to explain it. The market simply has no breadth or depth, therefore no resiliency."

"So, round numbers, lots of a hundred and fifty thousand US?"

"Just so."

"I'm not prepared to invest that much in these issues, Mr. Foster," McCall said. "I *am* prepared to go as high as a hundred thousand dollars. My company is Bahamian, however, and I'd expect to be doing a fair amount of business on the London exchange. If you could accommodate me on these Russian bonds, I'd consider it a favor. I'm not one to let a favor go unrewarded and naturally, I'd look to you in the future."

"How soon do you expect to begin operating?"

"I can't be sure about that," McCall said. "We're only setting up at the moment. But as far as the Russian bonds are concerned, you could proceed more or less right away. If you'd open an account for me today, I can put a hundred thousand US at your disposal within a day or two."

Foster nodded. "Very well. I think we can manage that. Are there any particular issues you're interested in?"

"I want to concentrate on the Imperial of 1909 and any others like it that are gold backed or denominated. The 1909 issue was large, so perhaps you'll be able to buy that one without creating too much furor."

"Will the account be in your name or that of your company?" Foster asked, withdrawing a bulbous Mont Blanc fountain pen from his coat pocket and extracting a leather-bound folio from the center drawer of his desk.

"In the company's name. Wellington, Winchester. Nassau, Bahamas. My bank there is Bahamas International Trust--BITCO. I'm also associated with Banco Dorado in Panamá City."

Foster made the notes and replaced the cap on his fountain pen.

****

When the door closed behind McCall, Foster went to his window and looked out on the Thames. Momentarily, the October sky was clear and the sun was bright on the water. He thought for a few moments, letting his famous nose speak to him. Finally, he turned to his desk, picked up the telephone and called his chief trader, his only son.

"Roddy, I'd like you to buy a hundred thousand of the Russian State Loan of 1909 for my personal account. Let me know how the market reacts. . . . Yes, that's correct. The State Loan of 1909. One hundred thousand pounds. And confirm for me that they're gold-redeemable, would you? . . . Yes, I know. But humor me please, Roddy."

When he put down the phone, he took a deep breath. It wasn't often he plunged in a market, but he felt this might be his last good chance.

****

"I'm glad I could give you a proper meal this time, Mack," Chilty said as they relaxed in soft leather wing chairs in the venerable Travellers Club, secluded from the bustle of commuters making their way home in the damp, chill gloom of an October evening. A barman brought the two large whiskies and the pitcher of water Chilty ordered on the way in and they raised their glasses.

"Where are you off to this time?" Chilty asked, adding water and stirring the whiskey with his forefinger.

"Egypt, but I laid over here to see you."

"Well, that's flattering."

"Frankly, I wanted to find out how the Russian bond deal was going. I've been doing some research and these bonds could be worth a lot. Audrey's don't amount to much but I'm thinking of buying some more."

"Why?" Chilty asked, his smile fading to puzzled concern. "I told you the settlement would be for British holders only." His eyes widened in comprehension. "Oh, no. You've found a British citizen to front the bonds. Which means you've revealed the settlement. Mack, how could you do this? It puts me at great risk. And Mum wouldn't have wanted her dowry treated this way. Damn it all, Mack. You promised," Chilty hissed, his face flushed.

McCall grinned and held up his hand, palm outward. "Whoa, pardner. Don't get your knickers in a twist. Listen to me a minute. You said British and Commonwealth holders. Audrey's bonds are now held by a Bahamian corporation called Wellington, Winchester. That's British Commonwealth. It's quite beside the point that I control the corporation because that's a state secret of the Bahamian government. And how do you know Audrey wouldn't have wanted to make the most of her dowry? I never noticed her being overly sentimental where money was concerned. And if she's watching us now, she's probably laughing her ass off thinking how clever I am to have found a way around that British holders business. I can cut you back in on the deal."

"Not a bit of it. I want a clear conscience on this," Chilty huffed, his cheeks flushing. "Those bonds are yours. I don't see how you can reconcile this skullduggery with Mum's memory, but go right ahead. If word gets out, you can be sure I will hold you accountable."

McCall fell silent and Chilty glared at him for some moments, his jaw set, his eyes glittering with subdued anger.

"This is unfair, Mack, and you know it," Chilty complained, shaking his head. He tried to scowl, but broke into a grin instead. "You scoundrel," he muttered. "You bloody scoundrel! You're right about Mum. That must be why you two got on so famously. She probably *is* laughing right now. She surely thinks I'm the cloddish one not to have known you'd find a way."

"So," McCall said, grinning. "What can you tell me?"

"Look here, old chum. I still have a shred or two of conscience. It must come from my father's side. In any event, I'm not going to give you the keys to the kingdom. And you have to promise me, Mack. I mean it. If this leak is traced to me, I'm finished."

"I promise," McCall said without hesitation. "And if it all goes in the toilet, I'll help you and that old Irishman sweep up at the Four Horsemen."

Chilty forced a laugh, not entirely mollified. After a moment's reflection, he said, "I'll give you this. The settlement will almost certainly take place. The PM wants it and so does Gorbachev. There's nothing I can see stopping it. It's difficult to tell about the timing, but I believe we'll have Council Orders and Statutory Instruments in place by the end of the year. I will also tell you for your fiendish calculations that we're going to accept applications for loss-of-property claims as well as bond redemption, so the fund isn't exclusively for bonds. We're thinking of paying an installment on the bond claims, but the property claims are hugely complicated and they have to be finalized before the settlement can be concluded. This might take years, Mack. "

"Maybe the property claims are complicated, but the bonds are straightforward," McCall said. "They're bearer bonds, Chilty. A lot of them will have been destroyed and lost one way or another. And you've got all that gold to cover what's left."

"What gold?" Chilty asked, a puzzled frown clouding his face.

"The Tsar's gold, old chum. From what we've been able to dig up, the Russians had about a billion pounds worth of bonds outstanding in 1917, just before the Revolution. And about a billion in direct foreign investment. This is supposed to be all foreign-held claims, not just British. So if you restrict the settlement to British nationals and Commonwealth— even throwing in the property claims—the Russian gold in the Bank of England should still return full face value to everybody, particularly the bondholders. I don't suppose the interest arrearage is on the table, but there are fifteen million ounces of Tsarist gold there, which at the current market price is worth more than four-point-five billion US. What if there are some bonds denominated in gold? Won't you have to settle in gold?"

Chilty laughed quietly and shook his head. "You've must have been reading a fable concocted by those Anastasia people. I haven't heard a word about gold, Mack. As far as I know, the Tsar doesn't even have a gold filling on deposit with the Bank of England or any place else in the UK. And if there was gold collateral, don't you think the bond holders would have gone to court, declared the bonds in default and taken the gold?"

"We got the information from Bank of England documentary sources, Chilty, not some tabloid."

"Well, I'm not working on the financial side of things, so perhaps it's true, but I haven't heard a thing about gold being part of the settlement. Not a whisper, Mack. What I have heard about is a piddling sum on deposit at Baring's Bank--something left over from one of the last underwritings. Forty-six million pounds, and it's that much only because of the accumulation of seventy years of compound interest. Moreover, the Sovs aren't adding a single ruble to the Settlement Fund. That deposit at Baring's is all there is, Mack."

"Remember the Baltic States settlement in 1969?" McCall persisted.

"Of course. I looked at it as precedent, but in that case, the Bank of England clearly did have the gold reserves of Latvia, Lithuania and Estonia. I'm not aware that the Bank of England ever held the Imperial Russian gold reserves."

"Something's screwy here, Chilty. If it's going to take years to settle this thing, it hardly serves the Soviet's purpose of regaining credibility in the international capital markets and if there's not a pot of gold involved, why are the Russians fooling around with some penny-ante settlement? Why are you, for that matter?"

"It's diplomacy at the highest and the lowest levels, Mack. It's a grand gesture of goodwill on the one hand and on the other, it's two old pols trading favors. Mrs. Thatcher will get the credit here for cleaning up a problem that's endured for seventy years. Mr. Gorbachev hopes--hopes, mind you--that the PM will intercede with her good friend, Mr. Reagan, to ask you Yanks to stop rattling your sabers. Gorbi's petrified of your Star Wars thing and he'd like it stopped. The settlement won't cost him a single kopek and Mrs. Thatcher's efforts on behalf of ending the arms race will save him billions and billions of rubles. We won't say it out loud, Mack, but we Europeans aren't all that keen on your Star Wars initiative either. It's fine for you to imagine exploding Russian rockets in space before they reach New York, but we'd be beneath the explosions. The fallout would rain down on us. Don't guess you Yanks thought about that."

"OK. Maybe that's the whole deal. Just politics and grand diplomatic doings. But I wouldn't be surprised if you bloody Brits weren't getting ready to steal a lot of Russian gold. That's why the sun never set on the British Empire, you know--God didn't trust you in the dark." They both laughed and rose to go in to dinner.

Devon, the West Country

Charles and William Foster sat in matching wing chairs in front of the fireplace at Northcutt Cottage, smoking Cuban Cohiba cigars and sipping a rare Armagnac brandy that had been laid down by their father before World War II. Except for their wardrobe and their barbering, they could have been taken for twins. Only a year younger, William devoted himself to managing the family farm and looked the country squire--tweeds and brogans, a wild reddish mustache and defiant eyebrows. Scripophily was his mocking tribute to the trade that created the family's modest fortune.

"William," Charles began, clearing his throat. "That business about a museum for your old bonds . . . perhaps it's time to act on that."

"Really? What's changed your mind?"

"It's just that we aren't getting any younger, are we? Having the firm associated with the British Museum of Scripophily might give Roddy a boost when his time comes to manage Foster's."

"Do you mean you're actually thinking of letting him take the helm?" William asked, his massive, untrimmed eyebrows rising halfway up his forehead.

"Why not? The lad will be forty next year. Perhaps that's rushing things a bit, but isn't it time for him to settle down?"

"I agree, of course. The boy's competent. Give him his head. How long has he been chief trader?"

"Six years in January," Charles conceded.

"That would seem sufficient seasoning, don't you think?" William asked with heavy sarcasm. "After all, bond trading isn't as complicated as agronomy."

"Easy for you to be the indulgent uncle who spoils him and takes his side. But Roddy's not the issue tonight. The museum is. I'd like to do something about it now."

"Of course. How stupid of me. After all these years, I wasn't sure I'd heard you correctly."

"Don't be an ass, William. Do you want the museum or not?"

"Of course I do. But I have no first born to pledge as collateral. What would you have me do?"

Charles drew on his cigar and savored its rich taste, releasing the smoke slowly into the firelit room. He had William where he wanted him and he took his time responding, surveying the spines of the books that comprised the family's venerable library and letting his mind drift away to a time when his father was still alive.

As a boy, he'd spent his winters in London at school and in the trading rooms of Foster's, being groomed for a life in The City. Although he had an inherited talent for trading, his heart and soul belonged to the sea. Summers at Northcutt cottage, which lay near Buck's Mill in the West Country, gave him Bideford Bay and the Bristol Channel beyond. He lived for the pull of the sail, the crash of the bow as it cut through the waves, the salt spray against his cheeks and the cold sea breeze in his hair. A bond deal was mechanical, but the struggle with a challenging sea was life itself to Charles.

William thrived on the beautiful country around Northcutt Cottage and had an affinity for farming equal to his brother's for the sea. After a few feeble attempts, their father scarcely troubled to teach William bond trading. Consequently, the mantle of succession to the helm of Foster's fell uncontested to the elder Charles and the farm came to William. Charles had been the obedient and dutiful son, managed the business his great grandfather had established, married his father's choice and provided an heir to carry on. For their father, William was the second son, of whom little was expected. This gave William a freedom Charles had long envied.

Now, Charles thought, if he did it exactly right, he could have what was left of his life to do with as he had wanted so long ago. Elizabeth was gone, a victim of cancer the year before. His period of mourning had expired on Tuesday. He could walk away tomorrow, but Roddy would expect him to keep his capital in the firm. William would never agree to selling Northcutt Cottage to give him his share, so he needed a killing, a bloody, obscenely rich killing to let him sail off to the Caribbean, bake in the tropical sun and the salty air, to besot himself if he chose, be lulled into dreamless sleep by the gentle surf and wakened by the breeze jingling the rigging. With an effort, he forced his thoughts back to the business at hand. William was waiting.

"Well, the thing is we need to assemble a collection of these bonds in advance. If we announce the museum before we have the collection, who knows what the cost might be? Now that we've decided, I feel we mustn't delay. If you'll give me a list, I'll start buying. I wouldn't expect to fund the whole collection, so perhaps your friends will donate some to the museum when we announce its formation. You could be thinking about a proper time and place."

"Did something happen in The City today?" William asked. "Eclipse of the sun or something like that?"

Charles pushed on doggedly in the deception. "No. I'm just feeling . . . Elizabeth's gone. I could go under a bus tomorrow. Time to stop postponing things," he declared impatiently. "I know you want the museum and I feel badly that I've dragged my feet on it all these years. Humor me now, will you? It's time to move things along."

Panamá City

Carlotta came up to the main house from her casita for coffee and a croissant in the kitchen. Vittorio had served her but was now changing into his chauffeur's uniform. He'd been morose and distant, banging pots and pans and ignoring Carlotta's chipper conversation. It was unlike him to be rude to Carlotta because he'd doted on her since she was a little girl. She noticed.

"Vittorio," she said when he returned to the kitchen. "What's the matter? You're so growly this morning."

"We have a guest this evening. I'm going to the airport to collect him in a few minutes. And it would be best if you remained in your casita tonight."

Carlotta frowned. "Who, *padrino?*"

Vittorio wouldn't meet her eyes. He busied himself putting away clean dishes and kept his back to her when he answered. "A gringo named Robert Ryder. To see your father."

Carlotta's face flushed. *Ryder! The one who wants to buy Morales' stock. Papá is negotiating with him behind my back.* She barely contained her anger. She was being treated like a child. Go to your room. *The grownups have business to attend to. They would deal with this Ryder and tell her later, when she could do nothing to change it.*

Carlotta left her coffee on the table, ran down the steps to the pool patio and along the path to her cottage.

****

Even if he hadn't been the only passenger who arrived by Lear jet at the General Aviation terminal that afternoon, Vittorio would have known Robert Ryder in any crowd of people arriving at Tocumen Airport. While the white Guayabera shirt, khaki slacks and aviator sunglasses were almost a uniform for Yankee visitors to Panamá, this one was different. His hard jaw line and the way he carried himself told Vittorio this was a man accustomed to walking with danger. Anyone less observant would have taken the carefully-barbered blond hair and skin as pink as the inside of a conch shell as marks of the pampered American aristocracy. Two more things about this warrior confirmed that conclusion. He wore shoes hand-crafted on British lasts and carried a thin attaché case whose leather was too soft to belong to anyone who worked or fought for a living.

Vittorio took Ryder's hanging bag from the pilot, guided him to the big

Lincoln and poured a glass of fresh orange juice from the built-in bar. As he negotiated the late afternoon traffic, he occasionally checked his passenger in the rear view mirror. Ryder seemed outwardly calm and meditative as he observed the sights passing along their route, but to Vittorio's eyes, he seemed coiled and ready for action should the need arise.

The Lincoln eased through the great iron gates of the Guest House grounds, drove up the curving drive and stopped before the low-lying entry. Vittorio got out and opened the door for Ryder. "If you will follow me, Señor," the wiry old man said. "I will show you to your quarters."

Vittorio led him past the entry down a mahogany-paneled hall softly lit by tiny spotlights focused on impressionist paintings lining the walls to a pair of heavy, carved doors. Beyond lay a guest suite of imperial proportions with a large, round bed, a sunken tub and a balcony overlooking the gardens and the Pacific Ocean in the distance.

"I hope you will be comfortable here, Señor."

Ryder saw the luxurious accommodations with two minds. One was the charade he performed to keep up appearances as head of Ryder and Company--expensive suits, the Lear jet and five-star hotels. The other was his own tough persona, the one that wore camouflage fatigues and belonged to the Laotian highlands. He wasn't entirely averse to opulence, but it offered no more than a pleasant, sensual diversion. He was a patriot, not a dilettante. The core of his ambition centered on redressing the wrongs that weak political leaders had committed, leaving his America exposed to destructive forces. Supplying the Contras was a catch-as-catch-can operation. They'd be forgotten again once the crisis had passed. They needed a permanent organization and getting control of this little bank was one more step in that direction.

Reconnoitering, he spied a small bar at one end of a wall of glass doors opening onto the balcony. He was exploring it when Vittorio returned with his hanging bag and attaché case.

"May I prepare something for you, Señor?" Vittorio asked when he saw Ryder at the bar.

"Something tall, cold and very wet."

"Planters' Punch?"

"Perfect," Ryder replied, turning toward the view of the sea. The water was still bright blue, but twilight was settling over the lush greenery of the garden below. He took the frosty glass Vittorio offered him.

"Would you like dinner at eight, Señor? I would be happy to serve you here, in your suite."

"That will be fine," Ryder told him, peeved that the chairman of the bank apparently wasn't joining him for dinner.

Ryder walked out onto the wide balcony, sipped the Planter's Punch and leaned against the railing. He saw a large terrace vaulting from the center of the house into the garden, spread beneath a canopy of tall tropical trees. Stone steps wound their way down from the terrace to a patio where the slanting rays of the setting sun struck the waters of a primeval pool. A path led away from the pool through a wild profusion of lacy ferns, glossy-leafed banana palms, bougainvillea and fragrant plumeria. Beyond the garden, the shaggy tendrils of a high wall of banyan trees guarded some hidden destination.

Ryder watched the shadows deepen and listened to the insects tuning up for the evening's symphony until the dark blanket of night fell over the garden. Then he went back into the suite and began running water in the large, sunken tub. He had an hour to relax before dinner.

****

Vittorio brought a selection of cigars when he came to clear the table. Ryder took a Larranagas and Vittorio trimmed it for him. Ryder touched it to the flame of the match Vittorio held and drew on it appreciatively.

"That was a superb dinner," Ryder said. "The picante sauce on the lobster was terrific."

"Thank you, Señor. Is there anything else I can get for you? There's cognac in the bar."

"I'll help myself later."

Ryder thought about turning in, but felt too restless to sleep. He poured a little Courvoisier into a balloon snifter and swirled it to bring up the fumes. Opening the drapes that covered the glass wall overlooking the garden, he switched off the lights and let moonlight spill into the room. Then he took his brandy and cigar onto the balcony.

Outside, it was warm and humid, though with sunset, the air had cooled. Moonlight dappled the garden below while the lights beneath the water of the pool made it a shimmering, pale blue diamond in the center of the garden. Night birds called softly to one another and the growing chorus of tropical insects chirped and hummed. A movement caught Ryder's eye and he was surprised to see a figure in a white robe on the path, walking toward the patio--a woman by the supple way she moved. She emerged into a circle of moonlight, the underwater lights of the pool casting an eerie glow on her face. She turned toward the house and looked up to the balcony where Ryder stood. Slowly, she stepped out of her clogs, opened her robe and removed it.

Ryder caught his breath.

The moon was to her back and she was in shadow, but he was certain she wore nothing beneath the robe. When she turned to face the pool, the moonlight first glinted briefly off her breasts and then her buttocks as she arched into the water with scarcely a ripple. Three strong strokes took her the length of the pool and she made ten laps before she rolled over onto her back beneath the silhouetted mosaic of leaves dappling the moonlit sky.

Ryder watched her stroke up and down the pool and float in the aqua-tinted waters, her body illuminated--seemingly levitated--by the moonlight. Blood surged into his loins as he began to imagine her smooth, slick skin warming to his touch. He wondered how long she would taunt him before she climbed the stairs at the end of the balcony and came to his suite.

The girl's moonlit water ballet was delightful evidence of the bank's hospitality, more exotic, more Asian than Latin American. Never in his experience in South America had he been hosted this way. His resentment of the chairman faded, replaced by a new respect. The young woman in the pool below was a *pièce de résistance* for an evening that would not be lonely after all.

He watched her surface dive and reappear at the opposite end of the pool like a frolicking seal. She made several laps backstroking through the water and the moonlight, driving his desire to the point that, even though he had seen her only from a distance, his breath was coming in quick, short bursts and the ache in his loins was acute. She came to the side of the pool and lifted herself to the stone patio in one swift movement. She stood in profile, with the moon bright upon her breasts, a dark patch developing around her feet as the water drained from her body.

She looked up at the balcony again, saw the glow of Ryder's cigar, caught its distinctive aroma, then picked up her robe, draped it around her shoulders without tying the belt and disappeared down the path that had brought her.

"No," Ryder muttered. "Wait!" Realizing then that she must expect him to follow her, he bolted down the stairs at the end of the balcony into the garden, stumbled on the last step and nearly fell. In the darkness, he trampled through the tangle of low undergrowth until he found the path she'd taken. He tried to calm himself before he began walking through the tall trees, but his heart beat even faster. The banyans enfolded him like giant octopi, the moonlight casting eerie shadows through their dangling tentacles. Then he saw a soft light. A cottage. A fairy-tale cottage in the midst of the tropical forest.

****

From just outside the circle of light cast by a table lamp, Ryder watched Carlotta vigorously toweling her long dark hair. He moved toward the screen door that separated them and she looked up, sensing his presence.

"Good evening," he said, gripping the curved handle, opening the door and entering the room. "I'm the guest," he said, grinning as he advanced on her, finding her unbelted robe an erotic invitation.

She let him come close enough for him to take its lapels in his hands. He spread the robe and stood feasting on the vision of her nakedness. She slapped him—hard--the imprint of her hand a bright red welt against his cheek.

It shocked him. "What . . . ?" he said, stepping back, his hand to his face. He started to speak, but she slapped him again, harder, stepping into it with her right hand. This one hurt him and reflexively, he slapped her back, a bruising blow. Even against the copper of her skin, his hand made a red imprint. He seized her wrists and held them. "Stop it," he commanded. "I don't like it rough."

She struggled and they fell to the floor together, Ryder on top. He pinned one of her arms, but she struck out at him with the other.

He laughed. "*You are* a wildcat, aren't you?" She was surprisingly strong and he had difficulty getting a grip on her free arm. Finally, he sat astride her, her arms spread-eagle beneath his hands. He locked his legs around her thighs to keep her from kicking him and bent slowly toward her.

She swallowed her anger and let him kiss her. It wasn't unpleasant. He tasted of cognac and tobacco and he knew how to kiss a woman. She choked back her fear and pretended to give herself to the sensations he wanted her to feel, long enough for him to relax his grip. When she felt him release her wrists, she coiled all her strength and twisted out from under him, spilling him onto his side on the floor. Off balance, Ryder clutched at her robe. She slipped free of it, rolled away on all fours, scrambled to her feet and ran naked through the screen door into the night.

Ryder sat up, feeling foolish and angry. "*¡Putita!*" he muttered to himself. He'd never find her in that jungle outside. He stood up, holding the terry cloth robe in one hand. He balled it up and threw it into a chair, looked around the room for a moment and tucked in his shirt. Angry and humiliated, he stormed out of the cottage. He felt her watching him, laughing at him, as he turned away and began walking back through the banyan forest toward the garden and the main house.

As his heart rate slowed and he cooled off, two thoughts came to him. Perhaps he'd misunderstood. If he had, it was certainly an honest mistake. Why would a beautiful young woman swim naked in plain sight if she didn't intend to invite him? He didn't think he was wrong about that, so perhaps she was playing an elaborate game. He imagined then that she might now come to his room in the main house, contrite and eager to please.

Nothing could have been farther from Carlotta's mind as she crouched in the jungle, watching Ryder walk away. The flesh around her left eye was swelling and she felt the glow of satisfaction. She had what she wanted. She'd have gone to his room if she'd had to, but he'd made it easy by following her to her casita. "*¡Maricón!*" she muttered "Did you think I'd allow you to buy my bank?"

Ryder climbed the stairs to his suite and slipped through the glass door, making sure to leave it unlocked. He splashed cold water on his face, poured another cognac and undressed. Naked, he slipped between crisp, clean sheets and turned out the bedside light. Waiting, his senses attuned to every sound, he lay for almost an hour expecting to hear her footsteps and feel her presence in the room. But there was only the sound of the insects and at last, he slept fitfully for a few hours, waking at first light feeling ragged and cross.

Panamá City

In his ill-temper, Ryder insisted on eating on the patio beside the pool and Vittorio was forced to make several trips carrying trays down the long flight of stone steps. A few sips of strong coffee, the soft tropical air and the calm of the garden improved Ryder's mood. He scooped the flesh of a ripe papaya into his mouth and when Vittorio lifted the silver cover from a dish, releasing the aroma of eggs Benedict, the unsettling events of the previous evening gave way to the bright chatter of the birds.

Carlotta slipped into the garden and, comfortably concealed where she once played as a child, she watched Ryder as patiently as a cat watches a lizard before striking.

A doorbell chimed up at the house and nearby, a myna bird screeched its reply. Ryder turned his attention to the house and saw Vittorio leading a young man wearing a light gray suit onto the terrace and down the winding stone steps to the poolside patio where Ryder sat. This was not Francisco Benedetti and Ryder felt a flush begin to rise in his cheeks.

"Good morning," Javier said, holding out his hand. "I am Javier Banderas, Senior Vice President for Operations. We spoke on the phone. I hope you slept well."

Ryder shook hands without getting up.

Vittorio pulled back a chair for Javier, set a china cup beside his place mat and filled it from a silver service.

"What will you have for breakfast, Señor Banderas? I will prepare whatever you like," Vittorio asked, ignoring Ryder.

"That papaya looks very good, Vittorio. And a croissant with butter and marmalade. That will be enough for me."

Vittorio turned to the serving cart, put half a ripe papaya on a plate and set it before Javier, then turned back for the croissant.

Before Javier could speak, Ryder interjected. "I expected to meet with the chairman. Is he en route?"

"I'm sorry," Javier said, spooning a sliver of papaya into his mouth to conceal his nervousness. "The chairman asked me to give you his deepest apologies--a family emergency. I've been authorized to meet with you regarding your interest in our bank." Javier swallowed the papaya and took a sip of coffee, watching Ryder over the rim of the cup.

"I see," Ryder replied, looking down at his plate for a moment before fixing his cold blue eyes on Javier. "I understood that General Noriega himself sent a letter of introduction. Is that correct?"

"Not that I am aware," Javier said.

"I have been assured that he did. So your chairman's absence now is rude and insulting. I only deal with principals."

Javier flushed beneath his copper skin and an anger he had not expected to feel replaced his uncertainty about meeting with Rob Ryder. He opened his mouth to speak, but no words came to him.

"Look, Banderas, I am already completing arrangements for the purchase of Rodrigo Morales' shares of Banco Dorado stock. That represents a twenty-five percent interest in the company. It's my intention to acquire a controlling interest as quickly as possible. Your chairman can make that easy or difficult, but he cannot change the outcome. Is that understood? Thirty percent of your company is held by minority shareholders whose names I already have. None of them holds more than three percent, so the time and expense of acquiring their shares is a bother. If your chairman is prepared to yield to me, I will take that into consideration in my offering price. I take it the bank is in no position to match my offer to Colonel Morales or to bid for the minority shares?"

Javier was reeling from this verbal assault and he felt his cheeks flushing. He tried to gather himself for a counterattack. "That remains to be seen," he said. "What is your offer for Morales' shares?"

"Two million US," Ryder said, taking a sip of coffee.

"I take it you would be prepared to offer proportionately more for the controlling interest that Señor Benedetti's shares would represent?"

"Not necessarily. If he tries to block me, I will offer proportionately less. The same is true for your shares, Señor Banderas."

"I trust you understand that Banco Dorado was founded by the Benedetti family more than one hundred years ago and has enjoyed a sterling reputation in Panamá throughout that period. Señor Benedetti is naturally concerned about what your plans for the bank might be if you were to gain control."

"When I own the bank, what I do with it will no longer be the concern of the Benedetti family," Ryder said, dabbing at his mouth with the napkin. "Are we clear on this?"

"I have heard what you have said. That does not mean the bank agrees with it or accepts it." The edge in Javier's voice betrayed his growing anger at the man's arrogance. He took a deep breath to control his emotions and pressed ahead. "We can conclude this interview if you will state your offer for the Chairman's shares. And for mine. That will give us some basis for our decision."

Ryder grunted. "Very well. For the chairman's thirty-five percent, I will pay two million, which is more than the book value. For yours--I'm not really interested in your shares. With the chairman's shares, I will have control and you will either work for me or take what I feel like offering for your inconsequential ten percent. Half a million would be generous and I might be persuaded to offer that much if you are helpful in moving this acquisition along. You are quite welcome to resign, keep your shares and receive whatever dividends my board of directors sees fit to distribute. Or burn them in your barbeque pit. They're worthless to me. Now, we're through here, are we not?" Ryder put down his fork and straightened in his chair. "Why don't you just saddle your pony and ride back to town? I'll wait here until noon for your chairman's answer." Ryder pointed his chin toward Vittorio. "Otherwise, I trust this old boy here can drive me back to the airport."

Carlotta heard it all. Ryder's arrogance redoubled her anger. She wanted to rake her fingernails across his face, make bloody furrows down his fancy cheeks to give him scars he would bear for the rest of his life. He deserved whatever she could imagine doing to him.

****

Javier burst into Don Francisco's office without knocking. The old man looked up from a stack of papers he'd been reading, his half-glasses down on his nose.

"Eh?" he grunted, surprised by Javier's sudden appearance.

"The man is the most . . . *bastardo, maricón, hijo de puta* . . . He thinks he can steal the bank!"

Don Francisco slowly removed his glasses and sat up straighter in his chair. "Calm yourself, my boy. You're out of breath. Tell me what he said."

Standing in the center of the room, his arms rigid at his sides, Javier took a deep breath and exhaled. "Did you receive a letter from General Noriega?"

Don Francisco frowned. "Yes. My nephew, Carlos Sosa, brought it to me. Only a letter of introduction. Something anyone can buy from Noriega. I threw it away."

"He offers only two million for your shares, the same as Morales. And even less for mine. Only half a million.

The color drained from Don Francisco's cheeks. "Let him leave. I have nothing to say to him. I will sit here and think. There must be a way to stop this," he said, making a steeple of his fingers and turning slowly in his big chair to stare out at the Bahía de Panamá.

Javier brought his '65 Mustang to a squealing halt at the entrance to the Guest House, leaped out and slammed the car door. He had instructed the driver of the most disreputable taxi cab he could find to follow him and after wheezing up the long drive, the cab sat parked beside the Mustang, its engine grumbling, a wisp of noxious, oily black exhaust seeping from beneath the engine and escaping under the grill and the front tires.

Javier threw open the front door of the Guest House and crossed the upper foyer to the stairs. One hand on the railing, he took them two at a time to the main level, sweeping past a bewildered Vittorio and striding directly to the sofa on which Ryder was casually turning the pages of a day-old copy of the *New York Times*.

"I have an answer for you," Javier said, his hands balled into fists.

Ryder looked up from the newspaper, stared at Javier and raised his eyebrows.

"The bank is not for sale."

Ryder folded the newspaper slowly and got up. His cold blue eyes bored into Javier and he said, "Your chairman has made a mistake. So have you." Ryder looked over Javier's shoulder at Vittorio.

"Bring the car around, will you? I'll be leaving now."

"Vittorio isn't available," Javier said, his fists clenched even tighter, his anger barely contained. "A taxi is waiting outside. His meter's running, so I wouldn't waste any time if I were you."

Ryder flushed, his composure finally shaken. He pointed a manicured finger at Javier and said, "I *will* own this bank, Banderas. This little bungalow, too. And you'll be lucky to find a teller's job in a credit union in Guyana. I'll see to that. Now get out of my way."

Ryder picked up his hanging bag and briefcase and climbed the stairs. Outside, he pushed past the cab driver, threw his luggage onto the cracked plastic upholstery of the back seat, got in and slammed the door. The rancid smell of countless unwashed bodies that preceded him assailed his nostrils as the driver ground the gears and pulled away from the Guest House in a billow of black smoke.

The old taxi rattled down the hill from the ridge on which the Guest House sat, heat and humidity bathing Ryder's anger in a clammy emulsion. By the time they reached Tocumen, his clothes hung on his body like a sour dish cloth and his ill temper had twisted his guts into a knot.

****

In the Lear's toilet, he stripped down, mopped the drying sweat from his body and changed into fresh clothes. He slipped into his seat and told Tommy Mason, his chief pilot, to wind it up. As they gathered speed down the runway, he took a deep breath, exhaled and consciously brought his anger under control. It was just a hurdle he hadn't expected. His contact on Noriega's staff had told him the bank was in trouble and the chairman an aging old don who would be eager to sell. So the intel was wrong and precious time and effort was going to be wasted bringing the bank down. His knew his anger was a weakness and he fought it. He let his chin fall to his chest, closed his eyes and struggled to clear his mind.

They were well out over the Caribbean before Ryder opened his eyes, refreshed and assured once more. Morales would have to use his contacts to bring the minority shareholders into the fold and he'd have to deal with Las Águilas' carping about putting up the money. The conduit was worth all the trouble, though. He wondered if he'd played Noriega properly. His contact on Noriega's staff had hinted that Noriega would require a share of the bank, but that would be like going to bed with a cobra. He knew he might have made an enemy of Noriega, not paying the General's price, operating on his turf without proper clearance, but it was a calculated risk he was prepared to take. After all, he was holding the ace of trumps, not Noriega.

Once he had the bank, he could organize his private army. They were coming together now, but they still weren't an independent force, just a bunch of too-brave-for-their-own-good outcasts the Agency threw crumbs to when it pleased them. He'd add ex-military as the book of business grew. The bank was what he needed to make them into a fist. He could cut out the Swiss and get control of the cash flow from the Agency's covert enterprises, make sure the troops got their share of the spoils and their insurance and retirement funds in the bargain. He'd call it Blackstone or something like that. He'd make sure his troops couldn't be disposed of by the vagaries of the political winds in Washington. Let the black ops generals take the credit. He'd be the one pulling the strings. And he sure as hell wouldn't let it be like the Hmong in Laos. Once the war was over, nobody gave a shit what happened to them. Nobody cared about the cadres who got RIFed out of the Agency, either--not until it was time to fight again. All that was going to change.

Panama City

"Don Francisco," Vittorio said, surprised to see the old man appear at the Guest House at twilight. "I didn't know you were coming."

"It's all right, Vittorio. I just need a little time to myself. It's been a difficult day."

"May I bring you a cigar and a brandy? I can prepare dinner, but it will take a little time."

"Bring a fresh Macanudo, Vittorio, and a very large Martini. Make it the way I like it. Very, very cold. Never mind about dinner. I have no appetite. Our guest has departed, has he?"

"Yes, Don Francisco. Señor Banderas sent him to the airport in an old taxicab_one without air conditioning." Vittorio cackled softly. "Señor Banderas was very firm, Don Francisco."

"Good. I'm going down to the patio by the pool. It's peaceful there. Where is Carlotta?"

"I spoke with her this morning, Don Francisco, after Señor Banderas left. I will call the cottage and tell her you are here."

"Yes, Vittorio. Please do that."

****

Carlotta smelled the sweet aroma of the cigar before she saw the curl of light gray smoke hanging like a halo around the old man's head. He was stretched out on a chaise longue beside the pool, staring into space, thinking his own thoughts.

"Papá," she greeted him, her voice a caress.

Benedetti looked through the dusk at a vision of young beauty. Her dark, lustrous hair was pulled straight back and tied with a white ribbon. She wore a sleeveless white cotton blouse with a round neck and a long, brightly-colored sarong wrapped around her waist. He could just see the tips of her toes in leather sandals beneath its hem.

"My dear Carlotta. You are so lovely. Come, sit with me."

She glided to his side in three languorous strides, sat down in a single graceful motion and touched his temple with the tips of her fingers.

He looked at her and his eyes widened. "What happened to your face? Is it bruised?"

She burst into tears and threw herself into his arms. "Oh, Papá! I'm so ashamed," she wailed against his chest. His arms went around her to

118

comfort her.

"Now, now, my love," he said. "What's happened?" She sobbed even harder and he held her tightly, waiting for her to gain control.

Finally, snuffling and dabbing at her eyes, she said, "The man who stayed here last night. He came to my cottage . . ." "

What?" Don Francisco said, sitting straight up. He held her at arms' length, his fingertips circling the discoloration at the corner of her eye. He didn't touch her as he strained in the half light to inspect the bruise. "He did this to you?" he asked, his voice hard and sharp.

"Yes, Papá," she whimpered.

"Did he . . .? Were you . . .?"

She broke into a fresh shower of tears and fell into his arms again. "I fought him, Papá, but he was so strong."

"Hush, now, my dear Carlotta. He'll pay for this," Don Francisco growled, holding both her shoulders and setting her to one side. He started to rise, but halfway to his feet, he was convulsed with excruciating pain. "Oh," he grunted, his hands clutching his chest.

Carlotta pulled back, her eyes widening as she saw his face contorted in pain.

"Vittorio!" she screamed at the top of her voice. "Call the doctor! Papá's having a heart attack." Don Francisco groaned and slumped back against the chaise longue, beads of perspiration suddenly popping out on his forehead. Carlotta, shocked into action, loosened his tie and began massaging his chest. She heard Vittorio clattering down the stone steps from the terrace.

"Papá," she said urgently. "Do you have medicine? Pills? Where are they?"

"Coat," he gasped.

She looked around frantically, found his coat thrown across the back of one of the wrought iron chairs and scrambled to it. She patted the pockets until she found a small pill case and hurried back to him. "Here," she said, putting a pill to his lips. "Take this, Papá." She forced it between his lips and with an effort, he used his tongue to position it. Then his head fell back against the cushion and his eyes closed.

****

Javier had just finished telling a sleepy McCall in Cairo about the disaster with Ryder and Don Francisco's refusal to sell when his phone rang.

"Señor Banderas," he heard Vittorio say breathlessly. "Don Francisco has had a heart attack. The ambulance is coming now. Can you please meet us at the hospital? Señorita Carlotta insists on going with him, but I must tell Doña Isabella and bring her to the hospital. Would you please look after Señorita Carlotta?"

"I'm on the way," he said, hanging up the phone and scrambling for his shoes beneath the coffee table. *'Dios mio, what more could happen today?'*

He found Carlotta pacing the floor outside the Emergency Room. She was pale and her features were drawn.

"How is he?" Javier asked, panting. He'd sprinted from the spot where he'd left his car and was out of breath. She threw herself into his arms when she saw him.

"Oh, Javier. Thank God you're here! I'm so worried about Papá."

"What do the doctors say?" Javier asked, inhaling the scent of her hair, turning her so that he could watch the entrance for the arrival of Vittorio and Doña Isabella. Carlotta kept her arms around him, but leaned away and looked into his eyes.

Javier noticed the bruise on her face, but said nothing.

"It is bad. They had to shock him in the ambulance to start his heart again. The doctors are still with him."

As she spoke, a green-gowned doctor appeared at the Emergency Room doors and spoke briefly to the admitting nurse. The nurse pointed toward Carlotta and Javier and he came toward them.

"Señorita Benedetti?"

"Yes," Carlotta replied, her face a mask of concern. "How is he?"

"He is stable now. We're moving him to a private room. We want him to rest tonight. Tomorrow we'll do more tests to decide on his treatment."

Carlotta fell back against Javier, almost fainting with relief. "Oh, thank you, doctor. Thank you so much. Can we see him?"

"He's sleeping now. Don't worry. A nurse will be with him at all times. Go home and rest. There's nothing you can do here tonight."

As the doctor patted Carlotta's arm and prepared to return to the emergency room, Javier saw a black Lincoln Town Car pull up to the entrance. The driver's door swung open and Vittorio got out.

"Carlotta," Javier whispered urgently. "It's your mother.

Doña Isabella is here." Doña Isabella made a grand entrance worthy of Spanish royalty. Twenty years younger than her husband, she courted a more mature image with perfectly coifed silver hair and an ebony and ivory cane used more for dramatic effect than support.

Carlotta ran toward her. "Mamá!" she called out, tears streaming down her face.

Doña Isabella stopped and scowled at her daughter with a withering look that brought Carlotta up short several paces from her haughty parent.

"Mamá?" Carlotta asked timidly.

"You are to blame for this," Doña Isabella hissed at her daughter. "You and your silly ideas. Get away from me." She waved a jeweled hand at Carlotta and resumed her regal progress toward the Emergency Room, Vittorio by her side. Over the mother's shoulder, Vittorio saw Carlotta's bewildered face and gave her a silent, sympathetic look.

Javier came to Carlotta and put his arm around her shoulders. At his touch, she threw up both hands to cover her face and turned into his shoulder, sobbing. Javier held her close and murmured a prayer. "*Dios mío, por favor. Esta noche, toca Su mano a mi patrón, Don Francisco. Guarda su vida, por favor. En el nombre de nuestro Salvador, Jesucristo. Amén.*" He crossed himself and whispered to Carlotta, "Come. I'll take you home."

The first heavy drops of rain pelted them as they left the shelter of the hospital entrance. Javier, his arm around her, pointed toward the car parked at the far curb, out of the way of arriving ambulances. "There," he said. "Hurry!"

"The little Mustang?" she asked, her voice still quavering.

"Yes," he replied. They sprinted across the pavement and Javier opened the door for her just as the rain began to come down in earnest.

She collapsed into the leather bucket seat and let her head fall back as Javier ripped open the driver's door and slipped behind the wheel, dripping.

She turned to him, watching him sponge his face and hands with a handkerchief. "I was so afraid," she whimpered. "I was there. Right beside him when it happened."

Javier brought the engine to life, switched on the headlights and the windshield wipers and pulled away from the curb. The rain beat an insistent tattoo on the body of the car and ran in swift rivulets up the hood while the powerful engine whined through each gear change, then settled into a deeper, throaty rhythm.

The soft, rich texture of the leather seats and the smell of the man beside her wove a cocoon around Carlotta. She closed her eyes and said nothing as Javier drove toward the Guest House. A terrible gloom fell around her. Her mother was right. It was her fault that her precious Papá was in the hospital. All the more reason why she had to save the bank.

****

Francisco Benedetti's eyes opened in the middle of the night and he looked around him. He was in a strange bed and the room was cold. Beside him, a woman in white dozed in a straight chair. '*Oh, yes. Carlotta. Then the pain in my chest. Yes, I remember.*'

"Nurse," he said. In the stillness, his voice seemed loud.

121

She came awake with a start and stood up. "Yes? Are you in pain?" She checked the green-screened monitor above his head. The blips were steady.

"No," he whispered, making an effort to modulate his voice. "But I must see a man. Now. Tonight."

"I'm sorry, Señor Benedetti. No visitors until tomorrow. Doctor's orders."

He seized her wrist and pulled her toward him.

"Stop, Señor. You're hurting me. Stop," the nurse whined, her face twisted in pain.

"Bring him," Benedetti hissed. "Major Carlos Sosa."

"I don't . . . ," the nurse wailed, trying to free herself from his grasp. "Please. Let me go."

"Call *Guardia Nacional*. Tell them. Send Carlos. At once." He relaxed his grip then and with the blips on the monitor showing an acceleration of his pulse, she was torn between calling the *Guardia Nacional* and the doctor on duty. She decided to do both.

****

Carlos Sosa's large frame loomed out of the dim-lit hallway and moved toward the nurses' station. The nurse on duty looked up in surprise and alarm. In the eerie silence of the ward, Sosa's dark eyes and scimitar-shaped scar were menacing.

"I am Major Sosa. Take me to Don Francisco Benedetti," he commanded.

The nurse hurried from behind the counter. "This way, please."

Major Sosa followed her to Benedetti's room, halfway down the hall. A nurse and a doctor were standing over the old man. The doctor looked up and scowled.

"How is he?" Sosa asked.

"He's on the verge of another attack," the doctor said. "The nurse says he insists on seeing you. Don't excite him or you'll kill him."

Sosa moved beside the bed and leaned down. In his years of service to the *Guardia Nacional* and the *Fuerza Ocho* he'd seen dead men and dying men and he'd inflicted more than his share of pain, but a chill went through him at the sight of the old man in the bed. The skin on his face was pulled tight and Sosa could almost smell death in the room. He swallowed and spoke tenderly. "Tío Pancho, I'm here."

Don Francisco's eyes flickered and opened. "Ah, Carlito. A man . . . Robert Ryder . . . dishonored Carlotta. I need your help. Promise me."

"*¡Dios mío!*" the big man growled. "He raped her?"

Don Francisco nodded and gasped, "Family . . . not politics. Understand?"

"I understand, *Tío Pancho*," Sosa muttered, leaning down to the old man,

122

his lips close to his ear.

Don Francisco's eyes closed for a moment before he fixed them on Sosa. "Promise," he whispered through dry lips.

"That's enough," the doctor said, noting the erratic blips on the monitor. "Get out of the way. He's going back to emergency. Stat!"

Sosa stepped back to allow the nurses to wheel the old man out of the room. As he watched them, he considered his options. He had been with Noriega a long time. Would the general sanction this?

****

The next day, Major Carlos Sosa stood on the balcony of a private dining room at the Officers Club of the Panamanian National Guard. Beyond the half wall of that balcony, a long line of ships lay patiently waiting their turn to enter the locks of the Canal and a departing trail of West-bound vessels was strung out alongside them. The day was clear and Sosa thought he could see five miles into the Pacific. A strong breeze was coming off the sea, fluttering the starched white tablecloth, bringing tears to his eyes behind the large sunglasses. Above him, the wind snapping the Panamanian flag sounded like gunfire.

He turned when he heard the scrape of the sliding glass door behind him and looked into the pale blue eyes of a middle-aged gringo in khaki pants and a white guayabera shirt. The wind caught the wisps of his thin blond hair and flayed them about his face.

"*Hola, Julian,*" Carlos said. He didn't like Julian Pressman, his CIA counterpart for Contra arms shipments, but he needed a favor and Pressman was the best one he could think of to provide it.

"Carlos," Julian answered, hurriedly withdrawing his fleshy hand from Sosa's powerful grip. Julian backed against the wall that divided this balcony from the next, seeking shelter from the stiff ocean breeze. "We weren't scheduled to meet until next week," Julian said. "Anything wrong?"

"Not with the shipment. I need a personal favor."

"Oh?" Julian asked, placing a hand on his head to keep the strands of his hair from whipping his face.

"I wouldn't need your help if that *maricón* in Miami had not issued a warrant for me. You were supposed to do something about that, Julian, but my people tell me that the warrant has not been withdrawn. Why do you Americans think you can arrest anyone anywhere in the world? I can't go to the US. It's giving me a problem with Noriega, too. He wonders why the US Attorney in Miami wants to question me. It makes him suspicious and it is not good to have Manuel Noriega suspect you."

123

"I'm sorry, Carlos," Julian said. "These things take time and the US Attorney in Miami is a genuine hard ass. We'll get it done, don't worry. Is that the favor?"

"No. I need surveillance on a target."

"A target?"

"Yes," Sosa replied, setting his jaw and fixing Julian with a hard stare. "It's personal. He lives in New York and I cannot go there--as you know."

"What do you want, then?"

"I want to know when the man is going to leave the United States and where he is going—with as much advance warning as possible."

"Who is it?"

"A man named Robert Ryder. An investment banker in New York. He will not be difficult to find."

"All right," Julian said, moving toward the sliding glass door. "I'll call you when we have something."

The Shenandoah Valley

A cold front swept through Northern Virginia on Friday, bringing thunderstorms and heavy rain. In its wake, Saturday's dawn came with brilliant sunshine and uncommonly clear skies. When Paralee rose and looked out the window of her rented room, she knew it would be a fantastic day in the mountains. Usually dimmed by haze, the Shenandoah Valley was at its most beautiful after the passage of a storm. She showered quickly, threw on jeans, her old hiking boots and a heavy, Irish wool sweater. She packed a bag for overnight and dashed downstairs to the Mercedes, parked at the curb several doors away. Mom and Dad would be surprised to see her.

She drove down Wisconsin and turned onto 'M' Street, crossed the Key Bridge into Arlington and worked her way onto Interstate 66. She left the Interstate in Fairfax to pick up coffee and half a dozen hot doughnuts at a Krispy Kreme and almost took the scenic route through Middleburg. But it had been so long since she'd driven that she decided to get back on I-66 and put the car through its paces.

The Mercedes ran west across Northern Virginia like a young stallion and in less than an hour, Paralee found herself approaching the exits for Interstate 81, the north-south artery of the Shenandoah Valley. Winchester and her parents' home lay fifteen miles to the north, but on impulse, she took the exit that would lead her to Mt. Jackson, thirty miles to the south. She told herself that her parents didn't know she was coming and it was only a small detour. She could easily be in Winchester for lunch.

****

"Yes, ma'am. Can I help you?" the Sheriff asked her. He was a large man with close-cropped hair, a ruddy complexion and a prodigious amount of equipment attached to his wide, polished belt. The brass plate on his uniform shirt said 'Templeton.'

"I'm looking for a Mr. McCall who owns a farm around Mt. Jackson. He's about 85 years old and I think the family's been here quite a while. Would you know where he lives or how I might find him?"

Sheriff Templeton shook his head and replied, "I don't know any McCall who fits that description. I went to high school with a McCall, but he doesn't live around here anymore."

Paralee judged the man to be in his late thirties and took a chance. "It wasn't Jack McCall, was it?" she asked.

"Yes, it was," he answered, breaking into a wide smile. "Jack McCall." He continued grinning until something clicked in his memory. "Oh, yeah," he said. "Jack lived with the Coopers—his grandparents. We all called him Jack Mack, Jack Mack McCall. He was a year ahead of me in school, but we played on the same football team. His senior year we won the district and bi-district championships and almost won regional. Yeah. We had quite a team that year." Templeton shook his head and smiled, unable to avoid remembering that the regional championship game had been lost when Jack failed to catch a last-play desperation pass in the end zone that would have given Mt. Jackson the victory. He remembered McCall's leaping attempt, the ball skittering off his fingertips. Then he said, "You're looking for Josh Cooper. Jack McCall's grandfather—his mother's father, you know. He lives out forty-two way."

"How do I get there?"

"Go down to two-thirty-six and turn west," he said, waving his arm in a westerly direction. "You'll hit forty-two going north and south pretty quick and you want to turn north at the junction. The sign says Columbia Furnace. You can't miss that. Then Old Josh lives, oh, four or five miles north of the junction. You'll see the house. Sits up on a ridge, back from the road. He's got a hundred and twenty acres up there, probably fifty acres in corn, an apple orchard and the rest in pasture and woods. Nice old fellow. You'll like him. And what's your name, ma'am? I didn't hear you say."

"I'm Paralee Campbell. From Winchester." She flashed him a radiant smile and called over her shoulder, "Thanks a million."

Sheriff Templeton's directions were spot on. She spotted the house on the ridge four and a half miles from the junction, slowed and then stopped on the shoulder of the main road to study the fieldstone house. It stood like a stately sentinel over the field below, fallow now with corn stubble. Beyond the corn field she could see an apple orchard rising up the slope. The approaches to the house were dotted with sheep, fluffy with wool. At the top of the ridge, tall pines sheltered the house and its outbuildings. A deep porch with white banisters spanned the width of the main house and the steep roof of the second story was punctuated by four dormer windows. A sun room extended from one end of the house and a dog trot connected the garage at the other. Someone was home because gray smoke curled from a chimney that scaled the wall between the main house and the sun room. Paralee set her inhibitions aside, put the little Mercedes in gear and turned into the black gravel drive to make the crunching climb to the house.

She parked in the circular drive and noticed that the flower beds on either side of the steps leading to the porch had been tilled and mulched. They held no blooms this late in the season, but they were ready for planting in the spring. The porch steps were solid and the door she faced when she pressed the bell was a recently varnished cut-glass antique that might have welcomed Stonewall Jackson or Robert E. Lee. She pressed the bell a second time and heard movement within the house. The shadow of a figure appeared in the opaque window of the door and a moment later she was face to face with Joshua Cooper.

He was tall and straight, but he couldn't have weighed as much as a hundred and fifty pounds. Piercing brown eyes stared at her from deep sockets beneath bushy white eyebrows and a sturdy shock of iron gray hair.

"Mr. Cooper?" she asked.

"Yessss?" he answered, half a smile playing around the edges of his mouth.

"My name's Paralee Campbell. I know your grandson, Jack McCall, and I was in Mt. Jackson and . . ."

The old man waited for her to finish, then saw she was embarrassed and moved back from the door, opening it wider to allow her to enter. "Come on in. You can tell me about him. I haven't seen him in a while."

Paralee stepped across the threshold onto a multicolored hooked rug and a wide-planked, pegged hardwood floor that defined a spacious living room bathed in sunlight from a bank of tall windows that ran the length of the porch. Joshua Cooper herded her to her right and shuffled slowly toward the sun room. At the archway entrance, she caught the sweet aroma of pipe tobacco mixed with the scent of an oak fire crackling in the fireplace. He welcomed her with an open-palm sweep of his left arm.

"This is one of my lairs," he said. "I spend my mornings where I can see the fields and tend to my birds." He pointed a gnarled forefinger toward an array of feeders hanging from the trees beside one battery of windows. A male cardinal flashed his scarlet plumage at one of them, enjoying a brunch of sunflower seeds. "I have a fine time keeping the squirrels out of the feeders, but to tell the truth, I admire their ingenuity. They'll do most anything to get at bird seed—fly through the air, hang by their tails, whatever it takes."

"It's marvelous," she exclaimed, looking up to the four sky lights spilling brilliance into a room already suffused with light from three walls of windows. Two oval hooked rugs covered the stone floor and a stone hearth and mantle blended with what must once have been an exterior wall.

He smiled at her awed appreciation of the space and eased himself into a well-worn maple rocking chair, picking up the pipe from which a wisp of smoke curled. A book lay face down on the table beside his chair, the pages open to mark his place. "Paralee," he mused.

"Paralee. Never knew a girl named Paralee. Interesting name. How do you come by it?"

She forced herself to stop exploring the room and its furnishings to answer him. "My grandmother," she said.

"Well, it's a beautiful name and you're a beautiful young lady." Josh appraised her frankly, with the forthright self-confidence that comes with age. "Mack grew up in this house, you know."

"I didn't. He hasn't said much about himself, but he told me a little about you. Just enough to make me curious." She smiled so engagingly that Josh barely suppressed an urge to laugh.

"How do you know Mack?"

"I work for him, sort of," she began and sketched how she'd met him. The old man smoked quietly, rocking slowly, enjoying the lively way she spoke and moved her hands, fascinated by her facial expressions and unusual blue eyes. He was sorry when she said, "And that's about it. He let me keep his car while he's in Egypt. I was on my way to my parents' house in Winchester when I got the urge to meet you." She laughed self-consciously.

"Well, I'm delighted you gave in to impulse. You've brightened my day." Josh looked at her closely, thinking she wasn't that much different from the little girls who used to come visiting when Mack was in high school. The old house fairly sparkled when one or another of them was in it and he missed that. "I suppose you want to know something about Mack."

Paralee blushed, finding herself on uneven ground, unsure of her continued welcome. "I meant it when I said I came on impulse, but I guess I did want to see where he grew up and . . . Well, I'm just nosy, I guess."

Josh thought about those high school girls, hanging around Missy, hoping to see Mack when he came in from the orchard. Guess this one wasn't much different. Just older. But having her here was a darn sight more pleasant than sitting around the house by himself.

"There's coffee on the counter in the kitchen," Josh said at last. "Maybe you'd be kind enough to bring me a cup?" He held out a heavy mug to her. "The kitchen's back there. You'll find it."

"How do you take your coffee?"

"Black with two spoons of brown sugar. You'll find yourself a cup in the cabinet to the right of the sink."

The sun room had two entrances. One opened into the living room, the one she'd come through. The other was toward the back of the house, beside the French doors that led into the garden where the bird feeders were. Paralee now passed through that doorway into a roomy country kitchen. The orange light of an electric coffee maker guided her to a long counter against the back wall of the house. The two windows over the sink were the source of the natural light in the room, but it was filtered through tall pines and the kitchen seemed somber after the brilliance of the sun room. She poured coffee into two heavy mugs, sugared them from a canister on the counter and brought them back to the sun room.

Josh Cooper was standing at the front windows, smoking and gazing out over the pastures where the sheep were grazing. She handed him one of the mugs and stood beside him.

"Mack used to come up that drive after the school bus let him off," Josh said, pointing down the hill with the stem of his pipe, remembering him as a gangly youngster. "His dad was a fine man and a brave soldier. But Mack never knew him because his daddy got killed in World War Two. His daddy's name was Jack, too, so when Mack came along, we needed to call him something different. That's why he's always been Mack to us." Josh pulled on his pipe for a moment to keep it smoking, then went on with his story.

"His daddy and my Cassie married in 1940 after they both finished college. Cassie was ready to quit school and get married before then but I wouldn't let her. Made 'em wait. Mack's dad got himself a job teaching school down in Harrisonburg while he was waiting for Cassie to finish. Sixth grade, I think it was. When Cassie graduated, I let 'em get married. They rented a little house down there and they were happy as could be. Those were still hard times--the Depression, you know--and they weren't making any money teaching school. Of course, it was a steady job and that was something. Better'n what a lot of men around here had. Cassie was happy just taking care of that little house. She wanted a family. That was her goal. But she couldn't seem to get pregnant. Then the war came along."

Josh turned and pointed to the mantle over the fireplace. "There," he said. "Go get that picture of Mack's dad and Cassie. That was taken right after he got his wings and came home on furlough. Late '43, I think it was. There's another one of him up there alongside his P-51. I guess that's the one he died in, or one like it. Normandy. The invasion. They said he was flying close support for our infantry, strafing Germans at fifty feet off the ground when his plane got hit. No way for him to get high enough to bail out, so . . . Fellow came to see us after the war. He was there that day and he said the plane just cart wheeled and exploded. He said that pilot--Mack's dad--saved the lives of the men in his platoon because they were pinned down when Jack started strafing the Germans, so he made it a point to find out who the flier was and tracked us down somehow. Don't really know how he did it and I never asked. Maybe it was on some form Jack filled out when he went into the service. Jack grew up down in Harrisonburg, but both his folks died while Jack was in college and he didn't have any kin at all left. Just Cassie and us."

She held the silver-framed photograph in both hands, her eyes going first to Cassie, Mack's mother. Pretty, but not a fluttery Southern belle. The slender lines of her face and figure testified to her descent from strong pioneer women. It was only a snapshot, but Paralee found something in Cassie's eyes and in her smile that was warm and welcoming. When she shifted her attention to his father, a replica of Mack in uniform stared back. The hair came up on the back of her neck. "I'm sorry . . ." she said. "I . . . If you'd rather not talk about this . . ."

Josh smiled at her, seeing her concern. "No. We cried all our tears a long time ago. And don't you cry for us, honey. We weren't totally snake-bit by war. Mack flew in Vietnam and he came home safe. We don't know much about it. When he got back he just said he lost some good friends out there and that's all he'd say. I think he took losing pretty hard. He never liked to lose. His pictures are in the library. I'll show you later. After Mack's daddy got killed, Cassie came home to live and just stayed on. And that's how it was that Mack grew up here."

"Your daughter never married again?"

"No. She and I and her mother raised Mack, at least up to a point. Cassie died when Mack was in junior high school. So raising him up the rest of the way was left to me and Missy--that's what we called my wife. Her name was Melissa." Josh puffed on his pipe and tamped the tobacco with a brass implement before he went on. "Now you might think that being an only child, raised by his grandparents, Mack would have been pretty spoiled, but he wasn't. He was a fine athlete. Never satisfied, always working on it. Wanted to be the best. He didn't care much for farming, but he'd grit his teeth and do whatever he had to. He was good with the apples--picking them and making juice for cider--but Missy kept chickens for the eggs and such. Mack hated those chickens for some reason, but it fell to him to feed 'em and bring in the eggs and he buckled down and did it. It was like that with the war. Mack didn't agree with it, but he put his country first and went on and did his duty. I've always been proud of him for being able to make the hard choices. That's a good measure of a man, you know." Josh fell silent then and relit his pipe.

"Do you see him often?" Paralee asked.

"Not so much. He writes and calls. I think he'd come more often if things were going better for him. Like I told you, he doesn't like to lose and lately he's lost his business. Maybe you know that. He's back up here now. I guess he'll be travelling a lot again. Didn't you say he was in Egypt?

He always did have the wanderlust. Surprises me that he can make a living at it, though. I keep hoping he'll settle down to something steady and I thought maybe this bank would be the answer, but I guess it wasn't."

Josh laid his pipe in the ashtray and stood up. "That's enough about Mack. I want to hear something more about you, Miss Paralee Campbell. Let's go in the kitchen and see what we can rustle up for lunch. Then I'll show you my library."

****

"Mom? Dad?" Paralee called, flinging open the front door and bursting into the living room. "I've had the most fabulous day!"

"Lee! What a wonderful surprise," Laura Campbell said, coming out of her chair by the fireplace to greet her daughter. "Why didn't you call us? How'd you get here? Have you had anything to eat? I'll heat up what's left from dinner."

Paralee's father, stretched out on the sofa, lowered the book he was reading and inspected his daughter's face, flushed with excitement from a source he couldn't imagine, and waited for her to stop bouncing around and come down to earth.

"I'm not hungry," she said, hugging her mother. "Hi, Dad," she called over her mother's shoulder and gave him a little wave. A look passed between father and daughter that caused him to prepare for something unexpected, which, with Paralee, had been the norm for as long as he could remember.

"Hi, Baby," he said, acknowledging her greeting without taking his eyes from hers.

Paralee's mother held her shoulders and pushed her away to take a good look. "You look wonderful. You're finally putting on some weight. Now, what's all this about?"

"I spent the day with Mack's grandfather. He's a wonderful old man and I learned so much about Mack."

"Who's Mack?" her father asked in a monotone voice as a smile spread slowly across her mother's face.

Alexandria: November

Paralee was waiting at the gate when McCall's connecting flight from New York arrived and she watched him being carried along by the stream of passengers straggling through the jet bridge.

"Hi there," he said to her as they spilled into the concourse of Dulles' Midfield terminal.

"Hi, yourself," she told him, matching his stride and offering what she hoped was her best smile. "You look a little frazzled around the edges."

"I came straight through from Cairo. Really stupid. I forgot what clearing Customs at JFK was like. And it was choppy on the way down. There's a storm coming in off the Atlantic. Thunder and lightning all over. Let's grab my stuff and get out of here."

McCall claimed his baggage on the ground level and was waiting at the curb when Paralee brought the car up. She popped the trunk and got out, expecting that he'd want to drive. Instead, he waved her back to the driver's side, threw his bags into the trunk and slipped into the passenger seat.

"Boy, that air feels good," he said, running the window down and filling his lungs.

"It's been a nice fall so far," she said, easing into the traffic heading for the airport exit. "How was Cairo?"

"Too many people. Too many cars. Too much dust and dirt. Hopeless job. I'm glad to be back."

She paid the toll at the exit booth, accelerated onto the Dulles road and looked over at McCall. He was sound asleep. She pressed one of the buttons on the console to put his window up and smiled to herself. With Mack beside her, the Mercedes flying through the golden rays of a late afternoon sun and dark, blue-gray storm clouds filling the eastern sky, she felt an unfamiliar, vibrant pulse of new life.

****

McCall woke up enough to get his baggage into the elevator and she helped him through the door of the condo.

"I'm out of it," he told her. "I'm going to get a shower and hit the sack. Thanks for picking me up. I won't need the car if you don't mind bringing it over tomorrow."

"No problem," she said. "But have you got anything to eat? The last time I was here, there wasn't much in your fridge."

"Never mind about that. I don't want to put you to any trouble."

"It's no trouble. I'll just get you some eggs and stuff."

"You're a champ," he said, smiling sleepily and handing her his money clip. "There ought to be some dollars mixed up in there with the Egyptian pounds. Here's my billfold if you need some more. I'm heading for the shower. Make yourself at home."

She checked the refrigerator, found the milk curdled and the eggs ready to hatch. The bacon was hard at the edges and there was no cereal anywhere. When she took inventory of the drawers and cabinets, she found no canned goods, only salt and pepper, a small bag of sugar and a can of coffee. Nothing else. '*How does the man live like this?*' She started making a shopping list.

She made two trips up from the garage with four bags of groceries--milk, eggs, bacon, corn flakes, apples, tomatoes, Bermuda onions, New York strip steaks, lettuce, bleu cheese dressing, fresh French bread, butter, a dozen doughnuts, half a gallon of vanilla ice cream and a six-pack of Corona.

She put things away in the refrigerator and stacked the rest on the counter where he would see it. '*That's more like it. At least he won't starve when he wakes up.*' Satisfied, she opened a bottle of Corona and went through the glass doors onto the balcony. She took a long swallow and stared out at a curtain of dark clouds. Thunder rumbled through the damp air and a crack of lightning split the night just before the rain began pelting down. Her head and shoulders were drenched before she could open the glass doors and escape into the living room. Using a towel from the guest bathroom, she dried her hair and watched the storm raging outside. With the rain still pouring down, she paced the empty living room, studying the barren walls, wondering about McCall's taste in art. He'd mentioned some Southwestern painters. She'd have to look them up. Then she noticed he'd left the light on in the master bathroom and went to turn it off.

She shook her head, seeing the disarray he'd left. His clothes were in a heap and a large, damp towel was draped half on the floor, half in the tub. She set the Corona on the counter by the sink and hung the towel on its rack to dry, picked up his clothes and took them into the bedroom. In the flickering light of the storm, she saw him sprawled on the king-size bed, tangled in the comforter, an arm, a shoulder and one bare leg showing. His breathing was deep and regular. She put his clothes on top of the hamper and cautiously approached where he lay. His face was turned away from her and she had to walk around the bed to see his expression.

She tilted her head to see his face straight on, letting her eyes drift away to the hairy, muscled leg lying free of covers, thrilling to her secret invasion of his privacy.

****

Around midnight, McCall awoke on Cairo time and found Paralee curled into a ball on top of the covers, a corner of the comforter drawn over her legs. As in a dream, he put an arm around her and drew her to him. Still sleeping, she nuzzled into the circle of his arm.

"Ummm," she muttered.

"Why don't you get under the covers?" he asked, his voice thick with sleep. "You're freezing."

A bolt of lightning lit up the room and a clap of thunder shook the windows. Paralee awoke with a start then, rising on one elbow. "Oh! Mack! I'm sorry. The storm. I just laid down for a minute."

"Hush up, Paralee, and get under the covers," he mumbled.

Completely awake, every nerve tingling, her heart hammering, she lifted the hem of the sheet and inhaled the aromatic warmth rising from his body. She turned her back and eased down beside him, trembling, touching his skin for the first time as another shaft of lightning shattered the night. His arm went around her, drawing her to him. He settled her against his body and was still. For a moment, she thought he'd gone back to sleep, but then she felt his hand slip under her blouse and touch her skin, moving in wider circles, idly caressing her. Deftly, he freed her breasts from her brassiere, cupped them and explored their shape and texture. Then one by one, the buttons of her blouse flew open, deserting her, leaving her panting and defenseless. He found the top button of her jeans and popped it loose as easily as if it had been his own. The palm of his hand pressed against the flat of her belly and her chills disappeared as his touch suffused her loins with a spreading warmth. "Ohhhh," she murmured, taking a deep, nervous breath, pressing his hand down with both of hers, arching herself toward the pressure of his fingers.

****

Mack awoke for good at four in the morning, savoring the warmth and weight of the woman beside him. Still asleep, Paralee tried to hold him, but he eased out of her grasp and left the bed. He found his heavy robe on the floor, slipped it on and padded into the bathroom. He came back to check on her and found her still sleeping peacefully, both arms clutching a pillow, the curve of her shoulder revealed in the light from the other room. He almost touched her then, but instead, he smiled and went into the kitchen. Light rain was still splatting against the sliding glass doors but the front had moved through and the thunder and lightning had passed.

He discovered the doughnuts and wolfed two of them while the coffee was brewing. When the coffee finished, he poured a cup and took it back to the bathroom, careful not to wake Paralee. He brushed his teeth and sponged off, then went into his office to check the messages and fax mail.

He found Charles Foster's confirmation of a purchase for his account of US eight-hundred-thousand dollars--face amount--of the 1909 Imperials at an average price of US eight and three-quarters, leaving a small balance after paying Foster's commission. Even without a gold settlement, if the bonds brought a price of twenty-five, he was going to double his money. The cloud over that was his potential loss on Banco Dorado. He'd had that cryptic telephone conversation with Javier the day he met with Ryder. McCall had been half asleep and with Javier talking in code, the only thing he was sure of was that Don Francisco had dug in his heels and was going to war. He'd heard nothing from Javier since.

There were no offers of consulting assignments in his incoming fax mail. Not that he wanted to be out of the country just now. He didn't know what more he could have done if he hadn't been in Egypt, but he had a feeling that he was going to have to jump into the Banco Dorado deal to keep it from blowing up. Damned hot Latin temperaments.

The answering machine clicked and whirred as he rewound the tape of the messages received. "Mack," he heard Sam Tate's Texas twang say. "Call me at the office when you get a chance. The Feds are into your wire transfer records and they've got a lot of questions. You know, why a little bank like yours was wiring money all over the world. I told them it was the game ranch, buying exotics, but they're not satisfied yet."

"Bastards!" McCall snorted. They had no right to do that. It was too early to call Sam, so he scooped up a bundle of back issues of the *Wall Street Journal* that had come while he was away, picked up another doughnut and sank into the lone chair in the living room. He tried to focus on developments in the financial markets, but Paralee's musky scent, still clinging to his body, drifted to him every time he moved and the memory of the satin of her skin lingered on his fingertips. He dropped the papers and went back to bed. She awoke when he took the pillow away and slipped in beside her.

"Ummmm," she purred, wrapping one leg around him and pulling him to her. He found her lips and kissed her gently.

"You taste like doughnuts," she said in a sleepy, throaty voice.

"I taste that way all the time," he said, stroking her back, drawing her against him with growing urgency.

"Oh, Lordy, I'm lost then," she whispered and kissed him long and fully, melting around him, suddenly on fire again.

****

"You have one of the most ill-equipped households in all Creation," Paralee said, standing in the kitchen door, tousle-haired, wearing nothing but one of his white shirts. "Shall I use your toothbrush?"

He winced, remembering that he'd promised Angela to buy one. "Sorry about that. By the way, you look a lot better in that shirt than I do," he said.

She waggled her hips at him.

"You really don't have a spare toothbrush?" she asked, tilting her head and giving him an exasperated expression.

"No. I've been meaning to get one," he said. "Look in my carryon bag. I think I took it into the bedroom. There ought to be one of those complimentary things they give you in first class."

When she returned half an hour later, she was dressed, her hair combed, jacket slung over her shoulders.

"Breakfast?" he asked. "Bacon and eggs? Toast? I didn't find any jelly, but there's butter."

"I want a doughnut."

"I'm your man," he said, coming to her, kissing her playfully.

"I've got to go home, Mack," she said, leaning back in his loose embrace, a serious look on her face.

"It's cold and rainy outside," he said, frowning. "Stay here. We'll play gin rummy or . . . something."

"Mack," she said. "It's been a long time for me. Maybe you noticed?" She smiled shyly and went on. "How can I say this? I don't sleep around. I don't treat making love like . . . I don't know . . . And right now all you have to do is touch me and I get all . . . you know . . . ," she moaned, pulling away from him. "Listen, staying is definitely not a good idea. Really. I need to go center myself."

"OK," he said, grinning. He knew he could change her mind, but he let her back away. "What am I going to do with all that beer?" he quipped to lighten the moment.

"It'll keep. But the doughnuts won't," she said, taking one in each hand.

Alexandria

When McCall reached Sam Tate, he got a tense, terse response. "Go to a pay phone and call me at this number: 210.698.3645. Have you got that?"

"I've got it," McCall said, his heart suddenly pounding. "Give me twenty minutes."

He hung up and leaned against the edge of the desk. *What the hell? Couldn't be anything good with the pay-phone hocus-pocus. He must think the Feds are running a tap on my phone.*

He found an outside booth at the little shopping center down Duke Street from the condo. Miraculously, it hadn't been vandalized and the dial tone came through loud and clear.

"What's up?" McCall asked when Sam answered.

"There's a bit of a problem here, podnah. I told you these guys were raising questions about the salary you drew from First Mission. They think it was excessive and then they started digging into your international wire transfers, looking for a smoking gun."

"Screw them!" McCall howled. "My board approved that salary and I paid tax on every penny of it. It's none of their business what I did with it. As for the wire transfers, hell's bells, the bank records ought to be clear on that. The game ranch bought exotics all over the place--Africa, India, I don't know where all. Completely legitimate."

"They still think you've got an offshore account somewhere, Mack. Listen, podnah, you assured me there wasn't one and I'm startin' to smell a little bit ripe here. You want to tell me again there's no Swiss account?"

"There's no Swiss account," McCall said, still steaming. Knowing he was telling his good friend a lie, he pulled back, got control of himself. "My grandfather gave me two hundred thousand dollars to buy First Mission. You know that. I sent him money. I don't remember right now how much altogether, but a fair amount. I had a nice house and nice things in it. I entertained. You know all this, Sam."

"The thing is, Mack, it doesn't all quite add up. I didn't know about what you sent your grandfather, so I can use that, but I happen to know that the house was mostly mortgage and you weren't driving a new Maserati, just some five-year old toy car from Germany that needs a wash and a wax. Aside from your liquor bill, which I'll agree must have been prodigious, it looks like something on the order of twenty thousand a year leaked out of your account. You didn't send your grandfather that much did you?"

"It might have been more than that. We didn't have a formal agreement.

It wasn't like he had stock in the bank, so it wasn't dividends, but I sent him money every few months. I wired it so he wouldn't have to mess with all the check clearing business."

There was silence on Sam Tate's end of the line. The operator broke in and asked for more money. McCall poured quarters into the slot, his mind racing as every coin rang a tiny bell. *Damn! The Feds have the scent. Is there any way they can trace those investments in Banco Dorado? I made deposits in Javier's account at Riggs Bank and he bought the stock. Lucky Pa kept an account there, too. I didn't think I was doing anything illegal, so I didn't do anything to hide the transfers. I guess they can dig it out if they look hard enough.*

"Mack?" Sam said. "You still there?"

"I'm here."

"You got any other documentation besides your tax returns-- some little notebook you wrote this stuff down in? Anything like that?"

"No. And if I did, I'd burn it. They'd find some way to hang me with it."

"Well," Sam said. "You're not entirely wrong there. Just watch your back, buddy. They smell something."

****

McCall didn't want to sit around the apartment and stew over the Feds or worry about what was going on in Panamá. He decided to call Paralee and ask her to dinner.

"Are you centered yet?" he asked when she answered the phone.

"That depends," she said.

"I just thought you might like to go to dinner. Why don't I pick you up around seven? I was thinking Lion d'Or."

"I haven't got a thing to wear to Lion d'Or, but I'll do my best."

****

McCall wasn't prepared for the Paralee who greeted him at the door of her Civil War-era rooming house. Her blonde hair was tossed about in its familiar fashion but her cheeks were now smoothed by an invisible coat of makeup. The faintest touch of gloss brightened her lips and he'd never before seen a trace of eye shadow around her eyes. The effect was electric.

In spite of her earlier protests about having nothing to wear to Lion d'Or, she knew immediately what she'd wear_a sleeveless black sheath with an oval neckline and a single strand of pearls. She didn't remember where she'd learned it, but she'd been told that if you wore basic black and string of pearls you could meet the Queen of England. To dress up the ensemble, she draped over one shoulder a black Persian lamb jacket, a treasure she'd bought in Paris second-hand. Now she watched McCall to gauge the effect. He was frowning.

"Well?" she asked, waiting for the compliment while she appraised his dark blue suit, burgundy tie and white shirt.

"I thought you said you didn't have anything to wear."

"Women always say that. It lowers expectations."

"You look fabulous," he said, breaking into a broad smile. "Fantastic even."

"How *gallant*," she said, blushing in spite of herself. "Thank you." She took his arm and whispered in his ear. "Let me hold on to you. I haven't worn heels in so long I may have forgotten how to walk." McCall put her hand in the crook of his arm, walked her carefully down the steps to the curb and helped her into the Mercedes.

"So is there an occasion?" she asked when he slipped behind the wheel.

"Probably several. But the biggy is that I got the money to buy a lot of Russian bonds," he said, pulling away from the curb and heading toward Wisconsin Avenue.

"Outstanding! So I can order anything I want tonight?"

"Well, some restraint is in order. I didn't earn a hundred thousand dollars . I *borrowed* a hundred thousand. And the news out of London wasn't as lovely as I would have liked."

"Oh?"

"It'll keep."

****

McCall left the Mercedes with the valet and they passed through the glass doors into Le Lion d'Or, one of Washington's finest French restaurants.

"Mmmmm," Paralee murmured, admiring the room's muted red and gold decor as the *maitre d'* led them to a banquette in a quiet corner of the room. Almost immediately, a waiter appeared to explain Chef Jean-Pierre's specialties of the evening. McCall ordered squab and wild mushrooms and asked the waiter to send the wine steward. When the *sommelier* came, McCall told him what they'd ordered and asked if he'd recommend a Montrachet.

"Monsieur, that would be an excellent choice. May I recommend the 1979 Puligny-Montrachet?"

McCall was about to nod his approval when Paralee spoke up. "Is it the Premier Cru or the Grand Cru? And which vineyard?"

139

"The Premier Cru, Mademoiselle. From Champ Canet."

"Do you have a Chevalier Montrachet Grand Cru from Leflaive? A 1978?" she asked in perfectly accented French.

"Mademoiselle?" the sommelier said, lifting his eyebrows. They launched into an animated conversation in French that McCall witnessed but scarcely understood.

"Monsieur, the lady is quite knowledgeable," the sommelier said to McCall. "With your permission, I will bring the 1978 Leflaive Grand Cru."

McCall yearned to know its price, but this was no time to hesitate and he bravely forged ahead. "Of course."

"With great pleasure, Monsieur." He bowed to Paralee and took his leave. McCall glared at her, a poorly suppressed smile taking away the sting.

"Why do I have the feeling that you just spent a couple hundred dollars, Paralee?"

"*You* chose Montrachet," she said, almost giggling. "And it's a celebration, isn't it? So you deserve a really, really fine wine. Something extra special. You were so awfully close to the best. I thought you ought to go the extra centimeter. If you like Montrachet--and who doesn't?--you'll love this wine. I promise."

The *sommelier* returned cradling a bottle in the crook of one arm and bearing a silver ice bucket in the other. He set the ice bucket beside McCall, showed the label to each of them in turn and placed the bottle in the ice bucket.

"We must allow it to cool for just a few moments to reach exactly the right temperature."

When the *sommelier* left, McCall looked at Paralee and said, "Thanks for coming tonight."

She covered his hand with hers and leaned toward him. "Mack, I'm thrilled you asked me. I mean, you could have asked Dr. Fitzgerald and his wife." She stopped suddenly. "Oh. Maybe you did and they couldn't make it."

"No. You were the only one I thought of."

"Ahhh. That's very nice," she said and gave him a broad, bright smile.

The *sommelier* returned, extracted the bottle of Montrachet from the ice bucket and uncorked it with a flourish. He poured a small amount into his tasting cup and inhaled it. Making a show of it, he waited a long moment before taking McCall's glass and pouring a little of the Montrachet into it. McCall passed it over to Paralee, who put her nose into the glass to inhale the bouquet, swirled it, held it to the light, then took a swallow, discreetly swished it over her taste buds and waited a few moments for the after-taste.

She smiled at the sommelier and announced her approval with an appreciative "*C'est magnifique!*"

The *sommelier* beamed and poured the pale yellow wine into their glasses.

When the *sommelier* left, McCall raised his glass and said, "To the good stuff." He took the smallest sip of the Montrachet and smiled in amazement. "That's incredible." "It's better than that. The '78 Leflaive is the greatest Montrachet in years, maybe in a generation."

"I'm a little puzzled, Paralee. You told me you worked a little while in a winery or a vineyard in France, but I think you need to elaborate on that."

"I told you I worked tour groups, too, didn't I?"

"Yeah, I guess so."

"Well, some of them were tours of the wine country, mostly Burgundy, so I picked up the patois. Even better, I got to taste a lot of really good wine. Not that the tourists ever got a free taste of a '78 Leflaive, but sometimes the vintners were generous with the tour guides."

"But you drink Mexican beer."

"I can't afford good wine," she explained. "And after you've had the best, the stuff you get in the grocery store just doesn't quite make the grade."

"I hear that," McCall said. "Peruvian avocados. West Bank oranges. Uruguayan beef. I've got a long list of things that are so good where they come from it's hard to settle for anything less."

They chatted amiably through the meal, marveled at the way the chef had prepared the *paté*, savored the squab and wild mushrooms, fell willing victims to the wine and a new-found intimacy they owed to an unspoken remembrance of the stormy night before.

Over a dessert of raspberries coated with brown sugar and a dollop of whipped cream, McCall asked, "You've been working on the Russian bonds for a couple of months now. What do you think?"

"It's a fascinating story. I guess the gold is the most interesting part. I'd like to use some of the research for a master's thesis. You wouldn't mind would you?"

"Not as long as you don't say anything about any of this to your faculty adviser, or anybody else, for that matter. Not until the settlement's been announced."

"Of course not," she said. "But it'll be soon, won't it?" She paused, waiting for an answer, and then added, "Oh, no. Does the not-so-lovely news from London have something to do with that?"

"Not with the settlement. With the gold. My man doesn't know about any gold."

"No gold?" she asked, her spoon poised in mid-air.

"He doesn't say definitely, but he thinks it's the kind of thing he'd have heard about. They're working on the assumption that the only funds available for settlement are in some piddling deposit at Baring's Bank that amounts to about forty-six million pounds, which is one hell of a long way from four and a half billion dollars worth of gold."

"I can't believe that," she said. "I've never seen a reference to the Tsar spending the gold that came to England. He borrowed four-hundred million pounds, remember? It must have been secured by something and I can't find any accounting for the gold. He was a first cousin of George V, but I don't think the King of England had all that much to do with underwriting bond issues. Of course, an accounting of the gold was probably out of the question. They were having a civil war. Chaos." Paralee paused for a moment, thinking. "There is the story about Admiral Kolchak's White Russians and a Czech outfit getting hold of some of the central bank's gold reserves and using it to buy guns and ammunition to fight the Bolsheviks. But that was after the Tsar was dead, so the gold in London wasn't available to either the White Russians or the Reds." She put the waiting raspberries into her mouth and chewed slowly. "But hey!" she said, her hand flying to her lips to contain the raspberries. "What about Lili Dehn's affidavit?"

"Lili Dehn?"

"You were in Cairo when I came across it, so I haven't had a chance to tell you. She was a really close friend of the Tsarina's. Darling Lili left Russia one step ahead of the Reds and migrated to Venezuela, but she gave an affidavit in Caracas that said she remembered Alexandra telling her after Nicholas abdicated that they had a fortune in the Bank of England. It was in gold and it was in the millions, she said. Doesn't really matter much if she meant pounds or rubles. Millions of gold somethings. I haven't seen a thing that says it isn't still there."

McCall smiled indulgently, amused by her intensity and her enthusiasm. But when he didn't respond, she pulled up short, unsure where to go next.

"The news isn't all bad," he said. "Even if the bondholders only get twenty-five percent of face in the settlement, I could still double my money buying now just under ten. The trouble is, I don't have that much to put at risk."

"What do you mean?" she asked.

"I've borrowed up to my limit. It drives me crazy that I can't capitalize on this information and make a fortune."

"So you've borrowed a hundred thousand and you're going to get back two hundred thousand?"

"Exactly."

"What's wrong with that?" she asked, eyes wide.

"It's great as far as it goes. But it could be so much more. I'd like to be able to pay back my investors. Particularly my grandfather. He put two hundred thousand into my bank and he won't get back a nickel unless I can pull off something with these bonds."

"Mack," Paralee said, her hand covering his. "I'm so sorry. Does your grandfather need the money?"

"Probably not. Paying him back is symbolic, I guess. I'm his only heir, so whatever sugar bowl he pulled that two hundred thousand out of will still be mine after he's gone. I hate letting him down, though."

"Then let's not talk about it tonight. Let tomorrow take care of itself." She squeezed his hand, pressed her thigh against his and commanded her dark blue eyes to promise something beyond the raspberries.

The Shenandoah Valley

Beyond Fairfax, driving west on US 50, McCall dropped the top on the Mercedes to take in the crisp fragrance of fall in Northern Virginia. His mood was bittersweet. This was football weather and it took him back to his youth, when so much seemed possible and within his grasp. He filled his lungs and tried to recapture that bullet-proof feeling that he carried onto the football field and put swagger in his walk. From then on, it seemed like he'd been collecting more demerits than gold stars--the reprimand in Viet Nam, now the bank and his betrayal of the trust of so many friends. The cloud of his family's disappointment was still following him around.

US 50 became two lanes not far from the western suburbs of Fairfax and he was quickly running through the rolling hills of the Virginia hunt country toward its unofficial capital, Middleburg. The two-hundred-year old stone fences marking the fields passed in a swirl of fallen oak leaves. Beyond, the estate houses that presided over these ancient acres could occasionally be spied atop a rise. On the outskirts of Middleburg, the venerable old homes that had been extended by succeeding generations clustered closer to the road. They were far grander than his own home place out in the Shenandoah, but they still bore the stamp of families who traced their blood lines back to colonial days and the Revolutionary War. Recently, Middleburg had attracted some of the glitterati of Hollywood and New York, the obscenely rich trying to buy bona fides that were buried beyond their reach in the soil of this land. The local gentry whose ancestors had first cleared it and fought for it stayed out of their way and bore with stoic aplomb the transformation of the town and the neighboring farms that, for one reason and another, had passed out of family hands.

A few miles further west, Upperville remained a more quietly authentic settlement, farther removed from the power magnet of Washington and closer to the eastern slopes of the ridge of Appalachian Mountains that formed the Shenandoah Valley.

Once in the Valley, speeding south along Interstate 81, the character of the land changed. Gone were the picturesque old pubs and the quaint bed and breakfast places that drew weekenders out of Washington. In their place were working farms, and in the little towns, garages and grocery stores and home-owned cafés.

McCall turned off at Woodstock and navigated the well-remembered streets that led him to Highway 42. In minutes, he'd be at the farm and a ripple of anticipation swept over him. It had really been too long since he'd seen Pa. He didn't like coming home with another sad tale to tell, but he smiled to himself, remembering that home was where they had to let you in, no matter what.

The house was as he'd seen it from the road back in August, though the corn was in and the leaves of the ancient trees that sheltered the cemetery had changed color and fallen, drawing a multi-colored quilt over the graves on the hill behind the house. As he came up the driveway, he spotted Josh outside the sun room, filling the bird feeders. Most of the migrating birds had long since passed through, but Josh took good care of the cardinals, his cherished year-round companions. To McCall, he looked as he always had, a little thinner perhaps, but straight and strong. The weathered leather of his face broke into a grin when he saw Mack get out of the Mercedes.

"Did you bring lunch?" he asked.

"No, I didn't. I thought I'd take you to Molly's and let her feed you something good. I'll bet you're living on peanut butter sandwiches and macaroni and cheese out here."

"No, I'm not," Josh retorted, setting the bird feed on the ground and grinning as he watched his grandson cross the dormant lawn toward him. "But I sure won't turn down Molly's."

Eyeball to eyeball, Josh held out his hand and McCall shook it, his left hand on the old man's shoulder. He was wearing the three-quarter length leather coat McCall brought him from Spain on one of his last trips before he went to Texas. Josh's hand was cold and bony to the touch and the chill air had brought a ruddy glow to his cheeks.

"Want some coffee?" Josh asked.

"Sure. That'll hit the spot. It's still a long drive out here."

"Then let's get on in the house. Feels like winter's just on the other side of the ridge." Josh picked up the bird seed container, put a hand on McCall's shoulder and walked him toward the French doors at the back of the sun room.

They hung their coats on pegs inside the kitchen door and Josh took another mug from the cabinet above the sink for McCall. He poured coffee in both cups, spooned brown sugar into them and handed one to McCall.

"It's good to see you, son," Josh said when they were seated in the sun room. "How long are you going to stay?" he asked with studied casualness, tamping tobacco into the bowl of his pipe.

Watching Josh fill and light his pipe brought a quiet smile to McCall's face, remembering that when he was a child, Josh would let him blow out the match when the pipe was going good. "Can you put up with me for the weekend?"

"Be more than happy to. I haven't checked on your room in a while, though. Might want to air it out. Those ladies from the church come by now and then to make sure I haven't died or burned the house down, but I don't think they bother much with the upstairs."

****

McCall finished his coffee and took his small duffel up to his old room. The air upstairs was stale, so he opened the upper casement of the windows in his room and the bathroom to create a draft of fresh air. He found a dust cloth in the linen closet, wiped down the furniture and the windowsills and changed the sheets. When he finished, he looked in on his mother's room and the guest room. They were in need of refreshing, too, and he gave them a quick swipe with the dust cloth before he returned downstairs to see if Josh were ready to go for lunch.

Molly's served hearty fare, family style--roast pork, black-eyed peas, fried okra, corn bread and steaming apple cobbler for dessert. Josh ate with gusto, as if he had been living on peanut butter and macaroni and cheese. As for Mack, the only other person he knew who could cook like Molly was his grandmother, Missy.

When they arrived back at the farm, Josh turned to McCall and said, "Come walk with me." They took their time climbing the hill behind the house, but Josh was still out of breath when they reached the family cemetery. McCall hadn't climbed the hill in years and the mantle of time hung heavy over him as he looked on the stones. Had it been so long since he'd thought about his mother? Or his grandmother? Their souls were somewhere else, but their markers were here, on top of this hill. With all the other Coopers.

The family cemetery was a familiar place to McCall because he'd been responsible for its care when he was a boy. He'd been away too long. The plots needed weeding and the black paint on the wrought-iron fence was chipped and rust was showing through. He made up his mind to tend to it tomorrow.

"You remember all these folks?" Josh asked when he had his breath back.

"Pretty much," McCall said, easily returning to the litany. "There's your dad, Jubal Cooper, named for General Jubal Early, and your mom, Julia Ann Valentine. And there's my great-great grandfather, Thomas, and great-great-grandmother Nancy Pritchard. The ones who rebuilt the place after the Civil War, after Sheridan's boys set fire to the house and the fields and the barns and everything else that'd burn. There's one of your namesakes, Pa—Joshua the second, lieutenant in Jubal Early's cavalry. Killed at the battle of Cedar Creek, just up the road. And his wife, Martha.

His father, Samuel, and his mother, Elizabeth Brewster. And over there's Philip Cooper and Marcy Boyd. And the grand old man himself, the first Joshua Cooper, our Revolutionary warrior. And here's Mom and Dad and Grandma," he concluded, walking to the markers for Missy and Cassie and Jack McCall. "Forty-five graves altogether, Pa. There's even a marker for Gentleman Jack."

"Elijah Jackson Cooper," Josh said. "There's a stone alright, but Jack's out there in the Atlantic chasing mermaids. I guess his brother, Thomas, thought putting up a marker for him was the only way to get him to stay put."

"Do you ever think about what would have happened if the ship hadn't sunk and he'd come home with all that gold?"

"Not much way of knowing," Josh said. "There were letters, but they went up with everything else when old Sherman burned us out. The legend is that Jack wanted to buy up half the Shenandoah Valley and settle down. He even had a girl picked out. Can't remember her name right off, but it seemed like he had good intentions. Jack's track record wasn't such that you'd want to bet a lot on it happening, though. Hard to imagine him settling down with just one lady."

Josh watched Mack out of the corner of his eye, wondering if he was cutting a little close to the bone for Mack's comfort. But Mack was just looking out to the ridge line and the mountains over in West Virginia. Probably thinking how Gentleman Jack would have changed everything if he hadn't drowned in that storm.

They'd seen Jack's genes in Mack for a long time. It didn't stop them loving him. Mack was a charmer like Old Jack. Half the girls in the Valley were breathing heavy before Old Jack ran off to California. Josh and Missy had prayed that Mack would break the pattern, find a sweet girl and settle down on the farm, but that hadn't happened and there was a real danger that the line would run out before Mack found the right girl. The Coopers had never been a prolific clan.

Josh pointed the stem of his pipe toward the cemetery and changed the subject. "Eight generations of Coopers--one generation of McCalls. Your dad's bones aren't here, but his spirit is. I'm the last of the Coopers who belong to this place, son. You're going to be digging me a hole there next to Missy pretty soon. And I want you to know I'm ready. I've been real lonesome for her lately," he said, bracing himself against the fence with an outstretched hand. "Just look out there," he said, sweeping his free hand across the panorama of the farm below. "Hard to imagine a better place to leave your bones."

Half a dozen sheep had followed them up and grazed quietly a few yards away. "Pretty peaceful, Pa."

"I hope you won't sell the farm when I'm gone," the old man said and McCall saw the tears in his eyes when he turned to look at him. "Someday--I don't know when--but someday when you're through wandering, this will be where you belong. You were born here. Hell's bells, you were even conceived here. The dirt of this place is in your veins. Your family's here," Josh told him, waving a hand at the little graveyard. "Meantime, Malcolm Birney's a real good tenant and he'd rent the house if you gave him half a chance. The farm's share more than pays the property tax and . . ."

A spear pierced McCall's heart and he gathered the old man to him in both arms. "Pa, I'd never sell it. Never."

Josh pulled a handkerchief from his hip pocket and wiped his eyes. Quickly back in control, he looked at McCall with a firm jaw and said, "If you mean that, I'm pleased and I thank you, son. All your ancestors here thank you, too. I know you have doubts about it, but we were always proud of you."

A wisp of smoke curled from the library's chimney and the late afternoon breeze brought its aroma up the ridge to them.

"Are the apples all in?" McCall asked, squinting to see the distant orchard.

"Not quite," Josh answered. "The Pippins and the Jonathans are but Malcolm's boys are taking their time with the Yorks and the Arkansas Blacks. Lot of cider yet to make. The fruit looks good. We'll make a piece of change out of the crop this year. Seems like more tourists up this way now. Skiers, too. I don't know where they all come from, but Malcolm's got a deal with a couple of these roadside places and he gets a good price for our cider. They sell out most every weekend."

Josh took hold of McCall's arm for extra support and started back down the hill, his pipe clenched between his teeth, the aromatic smoke mixing with the fragrance of the fallen leaves.

They walked in silence for awhile, Josh paying attention to where he stepped, steadying himself against McCall's arm. When they reached the house, Josh steered them into the library and took a place beside the fireplace, tapping the ash out of his pipe and catching his breath. McCall stirred up the fire and added two logs to the grate. "You still chopping your own wood, Pa?"

"I don't do much chopping anymore. Got me one of those chain saws and Mike, Malcolm's youngest, trims the winter wood out of the pines and the oak trees up on the ridge. He does the splitting and hauling for me. A good boy. Reminds me of you." Josh hunched his shoulders and folded his arms across his chest. "Listen, son, I got a bit chilled up at the graveyard. Why don't you go in the kitchen and look on the top shelf of the pantry. If those church ladies ain't run off with it, there ought to be a bottle of bourbon up there and I wouldn't mind a sip of it. Maybe you'd have one, too."

McCall found a bottle of Maker's Mark, a fine layer of dust covering its neck and shoulders. He brought it and two shot glasses back to the library. "I can see you're not doing a lot of drinking out of this bottle," he said, making a line in the dust with his finger before pouring for them both.

"I never was much of a drinker," Josh said. "A drop now and then is good for you, though." He lifted the glass to his lips and took a sip. "Mmmm. That's just fine. Knocks the chill right off."

Josh took another sip, put the glass on the table beside his chair and lit his pipe. The fire lapped and crackled around the new logs McCall added and the fragrance of the seasoned oak, the pipe tobacco and the whiskey wafted around them like country incense.

McCall slipped into the maple rocker that was once his grandmother's and wondered why he didn't own one. The gentle back and forth was relaxing. McCall noticed Josh's lever-action 30-30 resting in the corner beside the front door. "You ever shoot that thing anymore?" he asked.

"Not in a long time. I used to like tramping around in the woods and taking some venison, but not anymore. And it's no sport putting up a feeder and shootin' them in your front yard, like some people I know. You miss your hunting in Texas? You used to write me about those hunts you went on."

"I miss it some. I miss Sam more," McCall said. "We had good times together. Hunting was just a part of it. I don't suppose there's anybody around here that I have much in common with any more. I've still got friends I run into traveling, but that's just a sometime thing." Angela's face flashed before his mind's eye. "I didn't mind being in one place down in Texas, getting to know people. Guess that surprises you." A grin turned up the corners of McCall's mouth.

Josh raised his brushy eyebrows and his brown eyes twinkled. "Not much surprises me anymore, Mack, but I'm glad to hear it. To belong to somebody and some place . . . that's a all those foreign places?" Josh asked.

"I was in Vienna--Austria--a few weeks ago and I just got back from Egypt. Seems like it's all I know, or at least the only thing anybody will pay me to do. I must be a lot better at telling others how to run their business than I am at running my own. I'm making a little out of the market, but it sure isn't much." McCall laughed ruefully.

"You're making a living, though?"

"I won't go hungry. The FDIC is still hounding me, though. Sam's trying to keep them out of my pocket, but we're not clear with them yet."

"I don't guess I understand about this, son," Josh said, puffing at his pipe. "You gave them the bank, didn't you? I thought they'd be paying you something for it, but you're saying you have to *pay them* to take it? Doesn't seem right somehow."

"It isn't right, Pa. It's . . . it's damned criminal is what it is. But there's not much public sympathy for bankers these days--if there ever was--and Sam tells me that even if we fought and won, there's nothing to win and I'd lose what's left of my shirt over the legal fees. It's better to just cut my losses and move on,"

"I see," Josh said, a small frown showing on his forehead. "I hate to mention it, son, but I wonder how we're going to handle the loan now. Bob Fitch down at the bank called me the other day, wanting to know when I was planning to pay the balance. I've just been paying the interest, you know, and until things went sour for you down there in Texas, you always sent me enough to cover it and some left over. In fact, that leftover is what I used to pay the last installment. There's another one due middle of next month."

McCall stopped rocking, both feet went flat on the floor and he leaned forward in the chair. "What are you talking about, Pa? A loan? What loan?"

"Where'd you think I'd get two hundred thousand dollars, son?" Josh laughed. "I put a mortgage on this place. Wasn't any other way to raise the money."

"Pa . . ." McCall stammered, scarcely able to believe what he was hearing. "You never said anything about borrowing that money. I thought . . . When I asked you, you said 'just never mind' like . . . I thought it was money you'd saved up. I would never have let you mortgage the farm."

"Well, maybe I didn't tell you, son. I don't remember just now. It didn't seem to matter at the time. I figured you'd pay it back when the bank was going good and as long as we kept the interest payments up, we'd be all right. Bob Fitch gave me the money without much bother. He's Tom Fitch's son, you know. Tom's dad, Henry, and I were lifelong friends and you couldn't ask to know a finer man. Tom wasn't so bad, either. I can't say much for young Bob. Guess he takes after his mother, who never was what she made herself out to be. I wouldn't be surprised if young Bob wasn't hoping I couldn't pay the loan so he'd be able to buy me out at a sacrifice price."

McCall's throat went dry. He gulped the whiskey in his glass and poured another. "How much is the interest, Pa?" he asked quietly, dreading the answer.

"Fifteen thousand every six months," Josh replied matter-of-factly.

"Seemed kinda high--fifteen per cent--but Bob assured me he wasn't charging any more than anybody else would." Josh sat back and took a long look at his grandson. He frowned and added, "From the look on your face, I'm guessing maybe this is a problem."

"It's a surprise," McCall answered, a wave of nausea suddenly welling up in his stomach. "Pa, excuse me a minute. I'll be right back." He got out of the rocking chair, fought the bitter saliva surging in his throat and took the stairs two at a time to reach the bathroom.

The racking heaves that put him on the floor with his face in the toilet bowl temporarily overcame his panic. When the nausea passed, he struggled to his feet and flushed the toilet. One wobbly step carried him to the basin. He used both hands to brace himself against the counter. As his equilibrium returned, he twisted the cold water tap and rinsed his face, over and over. He thought he'd been so generous with Josh, sending him quarterly dividends that amounted to nine or ten thousand dollars, sometimes more. Consulting wouldn't pay thirty-thousand dollars interest every year. Finally, he looked at his face in the mirror and thought, '*What the hell do I do now?*'

Josh was still sitting in the library, smoking peacefully. He looked up when McCall returned.

"You all right, son? You look a little peaked."

"No. I'm OK," McCall lied. "Just had to go to the john. A little Pharaoh's revenge."

"Maybe you're not used to Molly's good cooking," Josh said. He waited until McCall was settled again in the rocker, then picked up where the conversation had left off. "Son, I don't know what it's going to take, but we can't lose this farm."

"I know, Pa. I know," McCall said, the queasiness in his stomach returning. "Don't worry. It'll be all right. I promise."

＊＊＊＊＊＊＊＊＊＊＊

McCall lay in his bed in the room upstairs that had been his as a boy. Smoky blue moonlight poured through the windows, bathing the dresser and bookshelves against the wall opposite the foot of his bed. All his things from high school and college were still there_books he'd read in childhood and in his teens, the individual football trophies from his high school years, bookends he made in woodshop. His deer rifle, the stock in need of oiling. The framed diplomas. His letter jackets still hung in the closet. How uncomplicated it had all been then, when he knew all the moves and he only had to think it to make it happen. He sweated through two-a-day football practices in August like everybody else and Friday night lights held nothing but success--on the football field and in the back seat of his '56 Monte Carlo. College was the same. He lived in a dorm at JMU, but he could be home at the farm, forty miles away, anytime he wanted to be. Pizza and beer never came close to his grandmother's cooking and the familiar stones and trees and furrows of the fields were a soothing balm for the hectic days and wild party nights of campus life.

He wanted to drop off to sleep with those nostalgic images in his mind, but sleep wouldn't come. Idyllic memories were no match for the oppressive guilt that lay upon him. He'd been stupid and selfish. He should have known Josh didn't have two hundred thousand bucks tucked away in a shoe box somewhere. It didn't matter that Josh hadn't told him. It didn't matter that Josh hadn't paid down some of the principal out of what he'd sent him. He still should have known. There had been a couple of years in the beginning when the bank was doing so well he could have paid it all back and never felt it. Instead he threw it away on that house and a lot of fancy stuff he didn't need. Now the moment had passed. He'd lost the bank and the farm was at risk, the Cooper family farm that had been hacked from the wilderness by the first Joshua Cooper, rebuilt by Thomas Cooper, preserved by four generations right down to him, the one who was about to piss it all away.

****

Frost was in the air the next morning when McCall climbed the hill to the cemetery. He carried a rake to clear the leaves from the plots and several black plastic bags to gather them up in. He wanted to chip the flaking paint from the iron fence and give it a heavy coat of rust proofing before he repainted it. That would have to wait for the next time he came.

Anger toward Bob Fitch gnawed at him. Josh didn't have the income to warrant a two hundred thousand dollar loan--worse than that, neither did he, not these days. But being mad at Bob Fitch wasn't going to get him anywhere. He could sell the condo, but it wouldn't net more than sixty or seventy thousand after paying the balance of the mortgage. Throwing all of Audrey's inheritance into the pot would still leave him short of two hundred thousand. The net on the Russian bonds would close the gap, but who knew when the settlement would come. At a minimum, he had to make the interest payment coming due in December and persuade Bob Fitch to extend the loan for another six months while he put the condo up for sale. He could see the burgeoning interest charges chewing up his cash balances like a shredder. A worse thought struck him. 'What if the condo

152

doesn't sell in six months?'

He moved the rake back and forth, pulled the brown, red and yellow scraps of nature's parchment into crackling piles and mechanically filled the bags. The work drew a merciful curtain over his despair. Suddenly, a bright ray of sunshine broke through the clouds and a vagrant breeze swirled the leaves around his feet into a blaze of color. Magically, they became the colors of foreign currency notes, complete with distinctive portraits, scripted denominations and stylized engravers' art. He stopped raking. As quickly as it had come, the sun retreated and there was no more currency, only nature's bounty of leaves, looking back at him innocently. The real world returned, but with it came an idea.

He thanked his ancestors for their inspiration, quickly finished raking and took the bags down the hill.

Alexandria

"Where have you been? I've been trying to get you all weekend," Javier said when McCall picked up the phone Sunday evening.

"At my grandfather's farm. I'm glad you called. I need to talk to you."

"You'd better let me tell you why I called first."

"Watch what you say."

Javier didn't acknowledge McCall's warning. He plowed ahead. "Don Francisco had a heart attack. Ryder tried to rape Carlotta and . . . well, it's an ugly scene. There's no way we can sell now."

"OK, OK. Don't say anymore," McCall said, afraid Javier would blurt out what the FDIC listeners, if any, were aching to hear. "I get the picture. I'm going to call you back in about an hour. Are you at your apartment?"

"Yes. I'll be here."

****

McCall had to stop at three drugstores before he found one that sold prepaid phone cards. He bought a hundred dollars worth and drove back to the pay phone in Magruder's parking lot and placed the call to Javier. Javier answered on the first ring.

"I'm sorry to hear about Don Francisco," McCall said. "Is he going to be OK?"

"I don't know. He's an old man, you know. He's still in the hospital and not yet stable. He might die at any time."

"Then what? Carlotta inherits the bank?"

"Maybe not. His wife, Isabella, has to be taken care of. She and Carlotta are barely speaking because Isabella wants Carlotta to marry and make a family. If Don Francisco dies, Isabella might claim the bank and who knows what would happen then."

"Well, that is a tangle. Guess we'd better pray that Don Francisco pulls through. Meantime, the situation makes what I'm going to suggest even more relevant than I thought. But first, I got some bad news of my own. My grandfather borrowed the money to help me buy First Mission. He put a mortgage on the farm. You know the place. I used to take you up there on weekends."

"Of course," Javier replied. "I remember. And your grandfather, too. How big a loan?"

"I need to come up with two-hundred thousand to retire the note. It's all

I've been thinking about for the last twenty-four hours and here's what I've come up with. I'm going to syndicate the Russian bonds." McCall waited for Javier's reply. There was a long silence.

"How big a syndicate?"

"I'm thinking five million. But I've got another idea to go with it."

"Five million is a lot, Mack. Who are you going to invite? You said your Texas oil men were broke and when we looked for a white knight for Banco Dorado on Wall Street, we got a black knight--Ryder."

"Forget them. I've got something else in mind. For starters, can you give me the name of another bank in Panamá like Banco Dorado?"

"What do you mean, like Banco Dorado? Small? Consumer-oriented?"

"Yeah, but more important, one that's on the edge. One that's eager to sell."

There was a long silence on Javier's end of the line. At last he said, "Comercio de Colón, maybe. I heard their chairman is retiring."

"They're in Colón? Not Panamá City?"

"Right."

"Any idea what they're worth?"

"Their book value is probably less than ours. Three and a half, maybe four million. Where are you going with this?"

"I'm thinking about pitching this bunch of militares who are backing Ryder's play, offering them participation in a syndicate to buy the Russian bonds if they'll leave Banco Dorado alone. I need to give them another bank in Panamá. I just have to figure out how to get in touch with them."

Javier laughed. "Mack, what an imagination. It's a great idea. If you got Las Águilas to switch targets and go after Comercio de Colón, Morales wouldn't get his two million dollars. What sweet revenge it would be after the way he betrayed Don Francisco."

Across the miles and through the phone lines, McCall and Javier grinned at each other for a long moment, then Javier said, "We still have to get in touch with them. Do you have any contacts who might be able to help?"

"One in Perú. He used to be in the Banco Central. He ran the foreign exchange desk. I imagine he used to know to the last centavo how much every one of the Hundred Families had and probably where they kept it. He might have heard of this bunch. Or even know some of the partners. Perú was under military rule for a good part of the sixties and seventies. They didn't have an elected government until Belaúnde came back in 1980. Surely there was one or two who might have wound up with Las Águilas."

"That doesn't mean he'd be the one to introduce you to them."

"True, but he'd be a good place to start. Guess I'd better get on an airplane and go talk to him."

"Is there anything I can do to help?"

"You said you could do an overdraft for me based on that escrow account. I'm going to need some traveling money. Five or six thousand. Something like that. How would you do that so the FDIC wouldn't find out about it?"

"I'll phone Winston Peterson at Riggs Bank and tell him to give you a cash advance against Banco Dorado. Six thousand?"

"Make it ten as long as you're at it. I have a research assistant to pay. I'm going to book a flight to Perú for tomorrow."

"Let me know how it turns out." Javier said. "*Cuídate, hermano. Cuídate.*"

"I'll be careful," McCall said. "*Ciao, compadre.*"

After Javier hung up, McCall held the receiver in his hand for a few seconds, thinking. Then he dropped a quarter in the slot and dialed Paralee's number.

"You're back?"

"A little while ago. I'm getting ready to have a drink and hit the sack. I didn't sleep much last night."

"Out there in the Valley? I thought the lights went out at sundown."

"There's a new twist on the bonds. What if I pick you up in the morning and give you a ride to school?"

"Can't you tell me on the phone? Now I won't sleep."

"I'm too tired to go into it now. See you in the morning."

****

McCall waited until Paralee had settled into the passenger seat and was staring at him expectantly before he began.

"My grandfather mortgaged the farm that's been in our family for two hundred years and gave the money to me to buy that bank down in Texas," he said. "The one that went broke."

Paralee's hand shot up to her mouth and her eyes widened. "Oh, my."

McCall shook his head. "I should have known there was no way for him to come up with that much money. He didn't tell me he borrowed it. I just assumed he pulled it out of his hip pocket. Anyway, we owe two-hundred thousand and I don't have it or anything close."

Snapshot visions of the farm and Josh Cooper flashed through Paralee's mind. She had a sudden urge to tell McCall she'd been there and barely resisted the temptation. "Two hundred thousand. Golly, that's a lot." She sat silent for a moment, then asked, "What are you going to do?"

"I've got to find a way to pay it off and I don't have a lot of wiggle room to work with. There's an interest payment due the middle of next month."

"How much?"

"Fifteen thousand. I can handle that one. It's afterward that's the problem. The Russian bonds are my only hope. So I'm going to syndicate them," McCall said, watching her carefully, the Mercedes' engine turning over quietly while he waited for her reaction.

"Syndicate them? I don't understand," Paralee said, blue eyes wide and questioning.

"The inside information on the settlement is worth a lot. I just need to bring in some other investors--form a limited partnership to buy ahead of the announcement. I'll manage the deal and the partners will put up the money, pay my expenses and a percent of the profits. It's done all the time. It's called syndication. If we can keep the price from going through the roof when we start to buy, a five million dollar investment could control fifty million of face value and if the settlement came in at twenty percent of face, the partnership would produce ten million--a five million dollar profit. If my share of the profits were ten percent, I'd make half a million. And if you're right about the gold, it could be a lot more. At the low end, it would be enough to pay off Pa's loan and leave something for me."

Paralee perched on the edge of the seat and turned her whole body to face him. "Let me get this straight. You're going to get a bunch of guys to invest five million dollars in the defaulted bonds of a dead Russian Tsar and they're going to pay you half a million dollars to manage the deal for them. Is that it?" she asked, shaking her head in amused disbelief.

"That's about it," he said, his eyes twinkling. He gave his head a cocky half shake to emphasize the point.

Paralee's sarcasm faded. "You're serious."

"Quite," he said, dropping the gear lever into drive and pulling away from the curb.

"Like where are you going to find people like this?"

"Unfortunately, most of the people I know in Texas--some oil men and a cattle baron or two--are as broke as I am. And right offhand, I don't know anybody else in this country who'd let me invest five million for them in this kind of a deal. My best bet is South America."

"South America?" she asked, a frown drawing two lines between her eyebrows. "From drug lords?"

"Of course not," he said. "The old money in South America has always been invested offshore. That's how they survive hyperinflations and revolutions. Now may be an especially good time. There's a roaring debt crisis going on in South America--all over the Third World for that matter, at least in every country that's not an oil exporter," he told her as they inched toward Georgetown in the clogged early morning traffic on Wisconsin Avenue.

"After the oil price shocks of the 70s, some of these countries are ready to crack. The new president of Perú has just defaulted on a big chunk of foreign debt and thumbed his nose at the International Monetary Fund. If they start running the central bank's printing presses to keep the economy going, there'll be an inflationary conflagration. Nobody's going to want their money around for that. So the demand for hard currency investment ought to be really strong. Longer term, if we pull off the Russian bond deal, I could have a shot at managing the profits out of Wellington, Winchester. Maybe it wouldn't be just a once-off deal. It could be a whole new career."

Paralee looked away, seeming not to have heard him, her face clouded.

"What is it?" he asked, looking at her, ignoring the passing storefronts and the pedestrians, who were moving as quickly as the Mercedes.

At last, Paralee turned to him. "I can't be a part of this."

He frowned. "Why not? It's just business."

"I won't be part of anything that has to do with drugs."

"I just told you . . ." "Let me out, Mack."

"No, damn it!" he shouted. "Didn't you hear what I said? I'm not going after any drug money. I wouldn't want to be in bed with those people. Do you think I'm nuts?"

"One way or another, it will be drug money if it comes from there," she shot back, her mouth a hard line, her eyes dull and distant.

Mack looked for a place to pull to the curb and park, but he was locked into the compressed traffic stream and had no escape.

"Have I ever lied to you?" Mack argued. "Can you tell me any time I have?"

She sighed, gripping the door latch and reaching for her books. Looking at him sadly, she said, "No, but this is different. You don't understand."

"Then make me understand," he growled. "We're not going anywhere in this damned traffic anyway."

"All right," she said, her deep sigh of sadness seeming to take all the air out of her. "I told you I have two brothers. I used to have three. He was fourteen when he died."

Mack looked at her, his brow furrowed. "What happened?"

"An overdose. He . . . crack cocaine. We don't think he'd been addicted long. It's such evil stuff. And the people who make it and sell it . . . you can't imagine what I'd like to do to them. That's why I can't be a part of anything that helps them."

"Aaaahhh, that's awful," he said. "But you've got my word that I'm not taking any drug money. I swear. Trust me on this, will you? A syndication is all I've got and it has to work for me. I need a big score. If I lose my family's farm now . . . I'll have screwed up everything."

Paralee looked at him from a long distance, as if she were fixing his face in her memory, opened the door, the car still creeping down Wisconsin Avenue.

"Paralee," Mack said, reaching out to stop her. "The damned car is still rolling!"

She slipped from his grasp and glared at him, a withering look that showed him a depth of bitter feeling he had never seen in her before. In that one look, she made him feel a stranger, worse, an enemy. He stopped the car and she got out. Horns began honking at him immediately.

She skipped between parked cars and was gone, leaving him stranded in the traffic.

McCall watched her round a corner and disappear from sight. "Shit," he muttered to himself. He couldn't track her down and argue with her. He had seats on a noon flight to Miami and a connecting flight to Lima. And anyway, if she didn't want to believe him, then to hell with her.

He hadn't told her about Banco Dorado or Las Águilas. But he hadn't lied to her, either. If she was going to walk out on him so easily, it was just as well she didn't know any more than she did.

Lima, Perú

Jorge Chavez International Airport was the same as he remembered, just older and more littered. It had been five years since he'd been to Perú, a short trip to celebrate Audrey's birthday with Chilty and he'd done little more than fly in and fly out. He'd been told that the modern business center had shifted from downtown out to Miraflores, but nostalgia took him back to the old Gran Hotel Bolivar on the Plaza San Martín. In his experience, it had always lived in the shadow of some former elegance, but he loved the faded glory of the domed lobby and they still made the best pisco sours in Perú.

He felt the familiar warmth of homecoming as he walked through the main entrance into the lobby, diffused sunlight filtering softly down through the cupola. An ancient bellman carried his bag to the registration desk and waited patiently while McCall took a single room on the quiet side of the hotel, away from the Plaza. Upstairs, he tipped the bellman generously and closed the massive door, smiling at the old-fashioned open transom. The temperature in the room was pleasant and he doubted he'd need the fan suspended from the high ceiling. The seasons were reversed in Lima and an early spring had cleared the air of Perú's chilling *neblina* while the heat of summer had not yet arrived. Unless the din of the traffic proved too much, he could sleep comfortably with open windows.

He unpacked his shaving gear and laid out a change of clothes, coaxed an uneven spray of water from the shower, shaved and lay down on the bed, damp and naked. The beds in the Bolivar still sagged like hammocks, but he slipped easily into slumber.

Below his window was the little jewelry shop of Luis Bermúdez de las Casas, known to his friends as Lucho. When Mack knew him at the Banco Central, Lucho controlled Perú's foreign exchange transactions and kept track of the government's debt position. Now close to seventy, Lucho had retired from government service and had a small shop on the ground floor of the Hotel Bolívar where he bought and sold antique jewelry, gold and silver and rare coins.

McCall dozed for an hour, then got up and dressed. He wanted to catch Lucho before he left his shop.

A bell tinkled over the door as he went in. Lucho was helping a matronly customer sort through a tray of inexpensive rings. McCall caught his eye and smiled. Lucho's mouth fell open in surprise and he left his customer, bringing the tray of rings with him, out of her reach.

"McCall!" he cried. "*¿Eres tú?*"

"*Sí, ya estoy. ¿Como te va, Lucho?*" The heavy-set man with the lively, large brown eyes and bushy eyebrows came around the counter to give McCall a back-pounding *abrazo*. The woman who'd been looking at rings fidgeted impatiently for a few moments, scowled at the two men and left.

When Lucho saw the woman leave, he went to the door, locked it and turned the sign to say '*Cerrado*.' "Now," he said. "We will not be disturbed. Come into the back. I'll give you a pisco and we can talk."

Concealed from the sales area of the shop, Lucho's office held a cluttered antique desk, two wooden file cabinets, a hot plate, a coffee pot and an ancient Mosler safe that a quart of nitro wouldn't crack. From one of the file drawers, he brought a bottle of *pisco añejo* and two small glasses. He poured them to the rim and raised his glass.

"*¡Salud!*" he toasted and McCall replied, "*¡Salud!*" "Ah. That's the good stuff, Lucho. It's been a while since I had any of that."

"Too long, my friend."

McCall and Lucho talked through three more tiny glasses of *pisco añejo* about old friends and the times they shared in the days when McCall was consulting for the Ministry of Economics and Finance. "And what brings you to Lima now?" Lucho asked. "To be honest, my friend. I need your help." "I am flattered that you would come so far. What can I do?"

"Lucho, I've got some information that can be turned into a very substantial profit for investors. What makes this information so valuable is that it's very secret. Because so few people know, we can buy some obscure financial securities at an extremely low price today. In a few months there will be an announcement that will let holders of these securities cash them in at a substantial increase in value. There is a very good chance they will quadruple." McCall held up four fingers, wiggled them and paused, enjoying the sight of Lucho blinking in surprise.

"The downside risk is very little. If there's no announcement, the securities can be sold back into the market at more or less the price we paid for them. I don't personally have the money to capitalize on this information so I want to form an investment syndicate. I'm willing to open it up to a very select group of people and manage the deal for them. Obviously, I want a commission and longer term, I'd like to manage the profits for the investors offshore. I have a company in Nassau that will keep the ongoing transactions confidential. My question to you is, do you know anyone here who would be interested and whom I could trust to keep quiet about the deal?"

"How much money are you looking for, Mack?"

"Five million US. It's not worth it for less and I'm not sure we could manage more. This is a very thin market and if we tried to push more than that, it would create a ripple big enough to invite questions. You understand."

Lucho nodded and made a steeple of his fingers. "There are several families who might be interested. But let me think about it over dinner. I always think best on a full stomach."

McCall's spirits rose and he grinned, content to let Lucho tease him with the bait of some promising names. He'd get around to asking about retired generals later. "Then we have to go to *Trece Monedas*."

"*Si. ¿Como no?*" Lucho said, gathering up the tiny glasses and stoppering the bottle of *pisco añejo*. "I'll call the driver and have him bring the car to the Plaza."

****

Twilight was on the Plaza San Martín when Lucho and McCall left the shop and stepped into the bustle of off-work pedestrians hurrying to busses that belched oily exhaust and colectivos that staggered on their weary springs. The light was that special iridescent blue that heralds the changing tempo of the day. The heavy air of the sea, only a few miles away, reflected the raucous blare of car horns. Mack let it swirl around him, bombard his senses, smiling at the recollection of days past when Lima had been the center of his universe.

As he stood there watching the passing parade, a dark green Land Rover popped out of the mouth of *Avenida Nicolas de Piérola*, its boxy profile standing out among the minivans, shiny Japanese sedans and battered taxis negotiating their way around the Plaza.

"There he is," Lucho said, pointing to the Land Rover.

Unconcerned that he was clogging the traffic lanes, the driver stopped in the street, forcing cars and cabs to flow around the Rover as if it were a boulder in a stream.

"We will be early," Lucho said as they clambered into the back seat. "I will ask the *maitre d'* to give us a quiet table where we won't be bothered."

"This is great," McCall said. "My mouth has been watering for ceviche and mariscos and ripe palta ever since the plane landed."

****

The *maitre d'* led them through the dark colonial splendor of the venerable restaurant to a table in an alcove away from the main dining room and assigned a waiter to give them continuous attention. Lucho called for a bottle of pisco añejo and asked for a plate of mariscos, tiny shellfish drawn from the cold currents of the Pacific.

From the opposite corner of the dining room, a guitarist coaxed the chords into a melody that bespoke a memory of the sweet pangs of unrequited love. With romantic guitar music floating around him in an old and familiar setting, McCall felt suspended in time, almost as if it were fifteen years ago and all that had happened since then had been compressed in his memory as if they were distant, long-ago events.

When the pisco añejo arrived, Lucho poured two crystal thimbles to the rim and pushed one toward McCall. "Salud, mi compañero," he said, raising his glass and holding it level, his old eyes dark but nearly luminous even in the low light. Seeing McCall return his salute, he brought the tiny glass to his lips and drank.

They had two more with the mariscos while Lucho ran through a detailed chronicle of the political and economic currents swirling about Perú--the new president, the debt crisis, the troubled economy, the rising tide of terrorism that Sendero Luminoso was bringing to the countryside.

Lucho ate the last of the mariscos, wiped his mouth on the heavy napkin and called the waiter. Without consulting McCall, he ordered ceviche as a second course and corvina a la Florentina for their entrée. When the waiter had gone, he turned back to McCall.

"And now, amigo mio, tell me about this proposition of yours."

McCall was frank with Lucho as he explained how his bank had gone down in the wake of the collapse of oil prices and that he'd lost just about everything. "I'm starting something different now. An offshore investment company. Wellington, Winchester. I'm still working out of Washington, but the company is in Nassau for business reasons. I'm going to use it for investment management. And now I've come across this fabulous opportunity to kick it off. God never closes a door without opening a window, they say."

The *ceviche* arrived, distracting Lucho for a moment. He looked at the plate and asked McCall, "Would you like some wine? They keep a good sauvignon blanc from Casa Lapostolle. It will go well with the corvina."

"Sure. That'll be great," McCall replied. "Is it Peruvian?"

"Unfortunately, it is Chileno," he replied, smiling. "But we can make an exception this time, don't you think?" Lucho turned away to instruct the waiter about the wine.

McCall tucked his chin against his chest, exhaling discreetly to blow off the tension of explaining the deal to Lucho. He let his mind relax for a moment, focusing on the guitarist, who had been joined by a percussionist. Soft fingers on a pair of bongo drums rounded the guitar's sharp notes and gave the music richer body. The guitarist left his melancholy chords behind and moved on to brighter tones. McCall took new energy from the music and was ready when Lucho turned back to him.

"That God opens a window," Lucho said. "Yes, it is a good saying. Go on."

"Well, as I told you at the shop, what I came to talk to you about are investors in a syndicate. Do you want to be the first?"

Lucho smiled and shook his head, squaring his shoulders against the high-backed Spanish colonial chair. "I have a comfortable life, Mack. I sleep well at night and every morning is a new miracle for me. If I had money in this venture of yours, I would worry all the time. No, my friend. It's not for me and I have no children to leave it to, so it's better that I enjoy the life I have. But I have been thinking about who you might contact and I can think of two families who would be good prospects. Can you tell me something more?"

"The five million I've mentioned already. I'll want reasonable expenses to manage the syndicate and ten percent of the profit. Considering that I'm providing the opportunity as well as managing it, ten percent is surely reasonable."

"Oh, yes. Very reasonable."

"I'd rather have one partner with five million, but I'd take five with a million dollars each. The information is sensitive and I don't want to risk it leaking out," Mack added.

Lucho speared a morsel of ceviche on his fork and chewed it thoughtfully.

"Eduardo del Valle? They were in copper long ago. His family has a fortune offshore. They saw the writing on the wall before the mines were nationalized. José Miramonte might be another possibility. The family had great estates along the coast. Velasco took care of those when the *Junta* came to power. I see José at the *hipódromo* in Monterrico from time to time. I still love the horses," Lucho said. "I like the racing and I only bet a little." He held up his thumb and forefinger half an inch apart. "If you talk to Miramontes, don't mention that you worked for *Economía y Finanzas* during Velasco's time. He might kill you on the spot. The Miramontes are oligarchistas of the first order."

"I've heard of them. Is José the one to see?"

"He would be a place to start. He's your age and you could try to see him here in Lima, but the decision would be up to old Jorge, his father. He lives on what's left of the family estate in Paracas. José would have to invite you to stay for a few days. Do you know anything about horses? All the Miramontes are crazy about them. You lived in Texas, yes? So perhaps that would be a way."

"I don't know anything about horses, Lucho. Living in Texas doesn't make you a cowboy."

"It was just a thought. Actually, I think you and José would like each other, even if you don't know anything about horses. In a week or two, you could get around to talking to old Jorge about the business."

"*¡Ay!*" McCall exclaimed, shaking his head. "I don't have a week or two to cultivate a possible investor. The opportunity is right now and if I miss it, it will be gone forever. I need to meet people who can make a decision quickly."

Lucho shook his head and frowned. "The old families don't operate that way. A business like this is . . . well, there's trust involved. They have to know you."

"It would be the same with del Valle?" McCall asked.

"Of course."

"I see," McCall said, nodding sadly, knowing in advance it would be this way. He watched Lucho attacking his ceviche, leaving the silence between them to be filled by the guitarist, the drummer and the muted conversation of the growing number of diners in the main dining room. In his mind, he reviewed the pitch he would make to Lucho for an introduction to *Las Águilas.*

"Lucho," he said at last. "I have heard of a group of *militares*, veterans of the *juntas* of the seventies and early eighties, who might be interested in such an opportunity. You must know some of them. Could you possibly introduce me, vouch for me with them? I would consider it a great favor."

Lucho laid down his knife and fork and, chin up, looked at McCall. "I know some people like that. And they might be willing to make a quick decision to give you five million for the kind of return you describe. I did not mention them, *amigo mío*, because I have always known you as a man of honor and high principles. I did not think you would want to deal with them."

"Thank you, Lucho. I appreciate that, but I don't know how much time I have before an announcement is made and the opportunity is gone."

"I will warn you in advance that they are not trustworthy individuals," Lucho said. "They may betray you. They will almost certainly try to cheat you. You may not know how to protect yourself from these men, Mack. You could lose everything. After what I have just told you, would you still want to talk to them?"

"I understand what you're saying, Lucho, and I appreciate the warning. There's only one thing that would stop me at this point, though. I won't have anything to do with drug money. That's not what it is, is it?"

Lucho shook his head slowly. "It is corruption money. Bribes and kickbacks, money earned through the betrayal of the public trust. It is nothing compared to the drug lords, but these men still delude themselves about their honor. Most of them are military officers who once held political positions. You may even know some of them. By name, at least. The general who speaks for them is a Bolivian. We are distant relatives and I know him personally. If you want me to talk to him about you and this proposition, though, I will have to know more than you have told me so far."

McCall caught his breath. This is the tricky part. He didn't want to violate Chilty's trust, but this might be his only chance. He leaned closer to Lucho and lowered his voice. "I have a friend close to the decision-makers. I can't say more than that--and certainly not in a restaurant--but he's given me information about a settlement of old claims between Britain and the Soviet Union. I can buy the securities at very deep discounts before the announcement of the settlement." McCall stopped for dramatic effect, watching as the impact of the information slowly crept across Lucho's face, trying to time the moment when he could sink the hook. When he thought he had Lucho's full attention, he added, "And the payment could be in gold."

"Gold?" Lucho asked, his eyes widening. "Would that change the profit estimates?"

McCall nodded, keeping his serious expression. "Of course."

"Where will you be for the next few days?"

"I'm at the Bolivar now. If you can arrange a meeting in the next couple of days, I'll stay. If it can't be done, I'll have to go somewhere else. This is too important to me to let it get bogged down. What I've got to sell could be worthless in a few weeks."

The *corvina a la Florentina* and the sauvignon blanc arrived and Lucho and McCall finished the meal talking about some recent discoveries of Moche ruins along the northern coast. When the plates had been cleared, Lucho offered McCall a cigar.

McCall shook his head and watched the ritual as Lucho clipped the end, licked the wrapper, warmed it with the flame from a wooden match and lit it.

****

McCall awoke the next morning to bright sunshine, showered, slipped on gabardine slacks, a cotton shirt and a pullover sweater. Downstairs, he ordered café completo and read the morning edition of El Comercio while he smeared butter and orange marmalade on flaky croissants and sipped the Bolivar's dark, rich coffee.

Sitting in the elegant dining room beside one of the tall windows, he watched an assortment of tourists and Limeños come and go. After breakfast, he walked out into Plaza San Martín to have his shoes shined. He chatted with the shoe shine boy while a brilliant luster grew on the tough leather of his half-boots with each snapping pass of the shine rag. He paid the boy, flagged down a taxi and asked for the hourly rate.

"*Quiero alquilar su taxi por la hora. ¿Cuanto cuesta?*"

"*Cincuenta mil Soles cada hora, Señor, o cinquenta Intis. La moneda nueva,*" the driver told McCall with a cynical expression that was meant as a comment on the new currency.

"OK. Esta bién," McCall agreed, checked his watch, got in and told the driver, "*Vamos a San Isidro. Los Libertadores, ciento sesenticinco.*"

He knew it was a mistake as soon as he saw that Audrey's pensión had been converted back into a private home--recognizable, but clearly not the same. And the guitar makers had abandoned the little park across the street. He sat looking at the sprawling house for a few minutes, trying to decide what to do. Finally, he remembered the beach Audrey liked--La Herradura. Maybe it had changed too, but maybe not.

"*¿Conoces la playa Herradura?*" he asked the taxi driver.

"*Sí, Señor. ¿Como no? ¿Quiere ir a la playa? No hay nadie alla. Está muy tranquilo, Seño*r," the driver cautioned.

"*No me importa. Adelante.*"

The driver wasn't entirely correct in saying that no one was at the beach.

A few sunbathers were stretched out on the sand. And half a dozen surfers in shiny black wet suits were lazing on their boards in the distant swells where the sea struck the southern end of the horseshoe that gave the beach its name. Sitting up a little from the beach, the weather-worn, ramshackle café that Audrey favored was open for business. McCall told the driver to come in if he liked, but that he had to wait. The driver turned off the engine, put his head back and covered his face with the battered brown fedora he wore.

Inside the café, McCall took a seat on the open porch where he could watch the sea, the way they had the last time he'd come here with Audrey seven or eight years before. An ancient *Peruano* brought him coffee and when McCall took the first sip, that long-ago day came back to him. It had been early in the *Limeño* spring, a day like today.

****

The sea breeze was fresh and cold and the smell of salt invigorating. He was returning to the States the next day and the outing was Audrey's way of having him to herself for an hour or two before he left.

That day, the beach below them was deserted except for an old beachcomber shuffling along the sand at the high-water mark of the previous tide, gathering shells and hoping for a random bit of treasure. The waves were tall and heavy and they broke with dangerous force, like the outriders of an approaching storm.

"Do you come here often?" McCall asked her.

"Not in summer, dear boy. I've never had the complexion for sunbathing in these latitudes. But I love the sea. That's why I come at this time of year and in the winter." Her tinkling falsetto voice was almost carried away by the wind and the crashing surf below.

"I like the sea," he said. "But I've learned to give it a wide berth. I've sailed with people on the Chesapeake and it's wonderful, but I have to confess it scares the bejabbers out of me. You must have to learn as a kid."

"I had a friend when I was young," she said, looking wistful for a moment. "He and I often sailed in Bideford Bay. He always spoke of pointing the boat into the Bristol Channel and just sailing right into the North Atlantic and never coming back. It was quite a romantic notion for a young girl and I loved it. Poor fellow. He was destined to be trapped in his family's business in London. I think of him sometimes when I come here."

"Did you love him?"

"I was sixteen," she said, laughing. "Of course I loved him. Perhaps not desperately, but passionately. At that age, I thought about everything passionately."

He remembered looking at her then, her blue eyes as bright as a schoolgirl's, as if she were back there on Bideford Bay sailing with her young love, the mainsail and the jib tight and straining, the salt spray in her hair. He imagined the bitter tears when her mother packed her off to Perú.

"It must have been hard to leave," he offered, inviting her to talk about that time.

She smiled at him, a gentle smile. "Of course it was. I thought it was the end of my world and I hated my mother for it, but those were the days when proper young girls didn't disobey their parents or run away. I got my grand voyage on an ocean liner--not what I'd dreamed about, of course, because every turn of the screw took me farther and farther away from my bonny lad. It was a cruel twist, to be at sea then. But after a few days sailing, I resolved that I wouldn't let it ruin my life. I resolved to do my best to be happy no matter what. I've done that and it hasn't been a bad life at all. Harold was kind and gentle and he loved me much more than I deserved. I have Chilty and I have you and my beautiful Pacific," she added, smiling and waving a hand across the horizon.

"Did you ever see him again? Or write?"

"No. I wrote him one last letter to say goodbye. Later I heard from friends that he'd married. He was older than I and I never really knew if he loved me. I was afraid to put it to the test and it was a memory too sweet . . . Better to just tie it with a ribbon and put it away."

A squadron of seagulls made a swooping, raucous reconnaissance over them, was disappointed and flew away down the beach. Audrey ignored them and reached across the rough table to take one of his hands in both of hers.

"And what about you, dear boy?"

He didn't remember exactly what he'd answered. Something about his struggle to exorcise the demons he'd brought back from Vietnam. The nightmares seldom came anymore, but some confused, deep-seated, unpleasant feeling remained--some mixture of regret, guilt and futility.

He watched the sea for a long time, the rollers forming far out and building toward a foamy collision with the shore. At last, the vision of Audrey across that rough table snapped back into focus. They'd stayed most of the afternoon and he remembered so well that handsome face, the waves crashing against the sand, the seagulls squawking and wheeling around them. He remembered what she'd said, too, especially the part about resolving to be happy, even as a ship was taking her away from the guy she loved, her homeland and everything she'd ever known. He smiled, thinking she'd always been both wiser and more courageous than he was.

He drew strength from that memory. With the sea breeze ruffling his hair, he stood up and looked across the infinite expanse of blue water--and blew her a kiss.

He had what he'd come for at *La Herradura*, so he laid a wad of Soles on the table and set the cup and saucer on top of them.

The driver, his mouth open, the brown fedora still propped over his eyes, was sleeping. McCall woke him and told him to drive back to the Hotel Bolivar.

****

Lucho met McCall in the lobby and they ordered cafécito and pastries brought to them there.

"General Tovolaro, huh?" McCall asked, frowning.

"The son of my mother's older brother," Lucho said, taking a bite of one of the flaky pastries. "He's involved in something else, but he said he would meet you at *Isla de la Luna* day after tomorrow."

"*Isla de la Luna?*" McCall asked, leaning forward and lowering his voice. "Where the hell is that?" "In Lake Titicaca. Not an easy place to go, but you want five million dollars quickly. Is it too much to ask?"

"No. I'm game to go. You said these guys had a peculiar sense of honor, though, and I've been wondering about that. Could you tell me a little more about them, how it is that you think they have five million to invest in something like I'm offering?"

"Of course," Lucho said. "But it wounds my national pride to speak about it. You are an old friend and you know our world. I will trust you to understand."

McCall nodded and waited for Lucho to go on. "My cousin and his associates have made their profits in many ways. I could make a list, but you would not be surprised. They have worked with your CIA to fight revolution in Latin America--or whatever they were asked to do. The man you are to meet--Raul Tovolaro--helped track down Che Guevara and kill him. And there are those in his group who were part of Videla's "dirty war" in Argentina. Most of these men think fighting communism is a noble cause, even if people are tortured and executed without a trial. Noriega in Panamá is paid by the CIA. Somoza's dead now, *gracias a Dios*. I do not know how anyone can excuse what he did to his own people in Nicaragua. I'm sure you know that the Contras that your country supports are Somoza's. I do not think any of his money is in this fund, but relatives are represented and Somoza had many, so . . . who knows? If Somoza money is in the fund, somehow it will be used to overturn the Sandinistas. Maybe you think what

169

your Contras are doing is national defense because if they didn't fight, the Sandinistas would give the Russians a base to launch missiles at the United States. If you believe that, dealing with these people will not bother your conscience. You know I'm not a socialist or a communist, Mack. But I am not proud of what these men have done. I would not have called my cousin except as a favor to you."

"I'm sorry, Lucho," McCall said. "I'm not real proud of where I am in this deal either. Maybe it will help if I tell you that what's at stake for me isn't just the money. It's . . . it's a matter of family honor, I guess you'd say. My grandfather borrowed money to help me buy the bank I lost. If I don't pay back that money, we're going to lose a farm that's been in my family since the American Revolution. It just isn't the time for me to be too squeamish about how I get that done."

****

That afternoon, McCall boarded a Lloyd Aero Boliviano 737 and settled back for a spectacular flight through the snow-capped Andes. He'd overnight at the Sucre Palace Hotel in La Paz and spend most of Tuesday on a bus to a remote town with the unlikely name of Copacabana. On Wednesday, about noon, he'd meet General Raul Tovolaro on *Isla de la Luna*--a fly-speck of an island in the Bolivian waters of Lake Titicaca, 13,000 feet above sea level.

Buenos Aires, Argentina

Eduardo Rivadavia had given Angela three rendezvous points. She was at the first one, sitting at a small table in the lobby bar of the Alvear Palace in Buenos Aires, feeling like a high-priced hooker. She didn't know the person she was to meet, only a recognition sign and it was early to be sitting in a bar. Perhaps Rivadavia had chosen it for that reason. Besides herself, the only occupants of the bar were the bartender and four men having a spirited discussion at a table across the room.

She'd been nursing a glass of malbec, twisting its stem for half an hour, wishing she'd brought a book or a magazine. She checked her watch for the hundredth time. The contact was now fifteen minutes late and she decided to give it up.

She drew the saucer toward her, inspected the bill and counted out enough pesos to cover it with a generous tip. As she rose, conversation at the table across the room stopped and all four men appraised her openly, eight dark eyes undressing her as she made her way through the bar into the lobby. Once the elevator doors closed and she was alone and out of sight, she breathed a heavy sigh of relief while the cage lifted her toward her room on the fourth floor.

Inside, the maid had opened the drapes to fill the room with sunshine. Angela quickly closed them and retraced her steps to the closet. The next rendezvous point was in Recoleta Cemetery, in two hours, beside the mausoleum of the Urquizas. She had an hour to wash her face and change into something dark, something befitting a mourner, before going downstairs and taking a taxi to the famous cemetery.

She kicked off her high heels, shrugged out of the bolero jacket that covered her bare shoulders, lay down on the bed and closed her eyes. 'Damn,' she thought, frustrated that the first rendezvous had proved sterile. She had wound herself up for an encounter with a man who could tell her about the ship lying in Montevideo harbor and the captain who talked too much about what was keeping him in port. Rivadavia had told her that her contact might want to look her over before he approached and that she shouldn't be upset if there were no meeting at the first rendezvous or even the second. But only the four men and the barkeep had been in the lobby bar. Was her contact one of the four? Or was it the barman?

She tried to project their faces, one by one, against the inside of her eyelids. She remembered the barman best, perhaps because his head was as bald as an ivory doorknob and he had a bushy mustache. The other men were dark-haired, clean-shaven, in dark suits. Her eyes still closed, she concentrated, squinting, her body tense and straining. One man stood out . . . older than the others . . . gray at the temples . . . a square face with fleshy jowls and heavy-lidded eyes. She had seen him best because he had been seated facing her along a direct line and she had caught him looking at her more than once. She saw two others only in profile and one she saw not at all because his back had been turned to her. She had only a glimpse of him when he watched her leave the bar.

She relaxed then, believing she had seen her contact and that she would recognize him again at the second rendezvous, in Recoleta cemetery. The thought of it brought her straight up in the bed, wide awake, heart pumping with panic. She had no idea where the mausoleum of the Urquizas was. Was there a map?

Time suddenly compressed, she flung herself out of bed and began tearing off her cotton sun dress. She slipped her feet into flats and drew the black dress from the closet.

Both hands awkwardly behind her in the familiar contortion women required to fasten a zipper perversely stitched up the back of the dress, she walked into the bathroom and stared at herself in the mirror. Grieving widow? 'No," she thought. *'Too young for that. Better a faithful daughter mourning a dear departed father. That's what I'll be.'* She changed her lipstick to a darker shade and bore down with her eyebrow pencil to darken her eyebrows and make them heavier.

Satisfied, she emptied the clutch purse she'd carried downstairs and sorted through its contents. Lipstick, tissues, sunglasses, wallet overflowing with pesos, pad and pencil, microcassette recorder. She swapped out the lipsticks and then, one by one, placed each item in a black leather purse that matched her dress, picked up the room key and went back downstairs.

Angela had noticed the Alvear's concierge at his desk in the lobby before. He was immaculate, but in her experience, much too young, lean and good-looking to be a concierge. He must have graduated first in his class, because the Alvear Palace was arguably Buenos Aires' finest. He greeted her in English and she was surprised that he knew her name.

"Good afternoon, Señorita Collins. May I be of assistance?"

Her eyes flicked over his coat and found 'Arturo Vargas' engraved on a polished brass badge. She gave him her brightest smile and was gratified to see it had a warming effect on him. "Thank you, Señor Vargas. Yes, I have a small problem. I want to visit the Urquizas' crypt in La Recoleta Cemetery, but I'm not sure how to find it. Is there an office or an attendant at the cemetery who would show me the way?"

"There are guides, Señorita. Most are honest, but they will try to take you to Evita's tomb and expect a large gratuity even for taking you where you do not want to go . . . I can give you a map of La Recoleta and mark the Urquizas for you. You will have no difficulty." His eyebrows rose slightly and he smiled politely through white even teeth.

"Perfect," she said, a quiet sigh escaping her lips.

He opened one of the drawers of his desk and withdrew a small map. He spread it out and bent over it for a moment. "Yes. Here it is," he said, drawing a circle around the Urquizas' plot with a gold pen. "You can enter at the Cemetery gates, but the mausoleum of the Urquizas is near the Basilica de La Nuestra Señora del Pilar and perhaps you would prefer to enter there."

Angela bent over the map to see Vargas' directions. "And we are here?" she asked, pointing to a block near the intersection of Avenida del Libertador and Avenida Callao. "It doesn't look far. Could I walk?"

The concierge shrugged. "Of course. Avenida Alvear will take you directly to the Plaza Alvear and the Basilica is just to the left. Recoleta is a pleasant neighborhood."

"Then I'll walk. Oh, is there a shop along the way where I might buy a hat? It's so difficult to travel with hats, you know."

"Of course, Señorita. There are many fine shops in the Recoleta district. May I suggest Iliana's? It is a small boutique on Avenida Alvear, just before you cross Calle Ayacucho." Vargas put a manicured finger on a spot on the map.

"Perfect. Thank you so much for your help, Señor Vargas," Angela told him, leaving a large denomination bill, folded in thirds, next to Vargas' hand.

He covered it quickly and tucked it into one of the small pockets of his vest. He bowed his head and said, "You are very gracious, Señorita. I am happy to be of service."

The uniformed doorman swung wide the front door of the Alvear Palace and Angela stepped out into the afternoon sunlight. She hoped Iliana's would have something wide brimmed. Beneath a hat and behind sunglasses, she would feel less conspicuous, less exposed than she had felt in the lobby bar.

She allowed herself to be taken by the flow of late afternoon shoppers and homeward-bound office workers and found her spirits lifted by the soft spring air. Along the way, she passed sidewalk cafes beginning to fill with customers taking an aperitif or a *cortado*, the *Porteño* version of espresso.

At Iliana's she found exactly the hat she was looking for--a black straw with a wide brim that shielded her face and the back of her neck. She wore it out of the shop, leaving the hat box behind.

Ahead, she could see what must be the Basilica de La Nuestra Señora del Pilar through trees whose branches were bursting with new buds. Beyond the Plaza Alvear, the tombs of La Recoleta came into view--an ornate, stately city of the dead. Acres of marble domes and columns and crosses, statues and spires. At the entrance to the first of the narrow avenues she encountered, she stood stock still, imprinting it on her mind. She checked her watch and saw that she was ten minutes early, so she strolled slowly past the crypts, noting the names. On some, glass doors revealed interiors like doll-house palaces--chandeliers, silk hangings, polished marble floors, even sofas and armchairs. Others were more sedate, less pretentious. The display of neo-Baroque statuary was impressive, but her mind was focused on the task and her eyes darted frequently to the path ahead, where just beyond the first turning, she was to look for a bench beneath the overhanging branches of a tree. The Urquizas' tomb would be nearby. She was to sit there and wait.

She turned the corner and saw the bench. A man was there, the torso of his body stretched out on the slats, feet still on the ground. Cautiously, she moved closer. It was then that she saw the dark pool of blood oozing away toward the center of the paving.

Her hand flew to her mouth. "Oh, my God!" she said aloud to the deserted lane. The man didn't move and she took several tentative steps closer to the body. A black fedora had fallen away from his dark hair, graying at the temples. She saw the wicked red gash across his throat, purpling now from coagulation. While she gaped at the body, a single, heavy strand of dark red blood stretched from his neck, hung suspended for a moment, then spattered into the pool below. Heart pounding, she looked at his face--square with fleshy jowls, the heavy-lidded eyes closed.

The man from the lobby bar.

Panic seized her and she ran back the way she came, turning the corner into the wider corridor. Ahead, a tour group ambled toward her like a gaggle of geese, the tour guide talking quietly and gesturing. She forced herself to stop. With more composure than she felt, she opened her purse and took out a tissue, holding it to her face, dabbing at her eyes. Then she walked steadily toward the tour group, turning away as she passed them.

Back in her room at the Alvear Palace, she closed the door and fell against it, heart still pounding, her breath coming in gasps, a montage of snapshots flickering through her memory--her passage through the lobby, collecting her key, the concerned look of the concierge. '*My God,*' she thought when she began to feel herself under control again. '*They cut his throat. In that . . . that . . .*' she struggled to find words to describe so peaceful a place--a park bench in the silence and solitude of the cemetery, the branches of a tree hanging over his body, budding incongruously with new life. *'And they left him there for me to see . . .'*

At last she pushed herself away from the door and walked slowly into the room. Hands trembling, she opened the minibar and took two miniatures of Johnny Walker Black Label from it, twisted open the caps and poured the whiskey into a tumbler without ice. Holding the glass with both hands, she brought it to her lips and swallowed half the amber liquid. She coughed and choked back the tears as the whiskey burned her throat, its heat spreading quickly across her abdomen.

'He was my contact,' she thought. *'Somebody killed him to keep him from talking to me.'* Then a more dreadful thought struck her. *'How do they know he didn't talk to me?'* She went to the phone, pressed the key for an outside line and rang the emergency number she had for Eduardo Rivadavia.

"Our business, not your business," Rivadavia told her when she described the man. "If you want the story, do as you have been told. Go to the third rendezvous point tonight. And do not call me again. I can do nothing more for you." Rivadavia broke the connection and she was left alone in the darkened room again.

She stared at the dead instrument in her hand, feeling utterly out of her element. A dull panic rose in her chest and she found herself wanting to forget it all, throw her things in a bag, grab a taxi to the airport and catch the next flight back to New York. She took down the rest of the Scotch in the glass and tried to focus. She forced herself to think about all the work she had done, about the career breakthrough she was sure the story would bring. Woodward and Bernstein had Watergate. Why couldn't her story be just as big? If Reagan knew . . . Even if Bush knew . . . It could mean a Pulitzer.

She closed her eyes and let the Scotch numb her senses. Slowly she moved toward the bathroom, letting her clothes fall to the floor along the way. Naked, smelling rank with fear, she bent over the round marble tub and ran the water, decided she would have another drink and went back to the minibar. She set the drink on the edge of the tub and sprinkled bath salts into the water. When the tub was half full, she eased her body into it and sank back, letting the steam rise around her and the warm water wash away her fear. As she floated, drowsing just short of sleep, Jack McCall slipped unbidden into her mind and she smiled, remembering their last night together. The memory was suddenly so vivid she could smell his body, feel the hair matting his chest and arms and the deep, smooth valley between the hard muscles of his back. Why was she so far away from him now, chasing a story that could get her killed?

The taxi dropped her in San Telmo and she went on foot, looking for the *parrilla* that would mark the narrow, nameless street she was seeking. She found it quickly enough, the rich aroma of beef broiling on the grill floating in the still chill air. Everyone ate late in Buenos Aires but she didn't think she would have the appetite later so she ordered a brochette of *bife de lomo* and ate it on the sidewalk with the smoke of the grill swirling around her head.

She was surprised that the meat settled so well on her nervous stomach and that the food gave her a new resolve. With the faint chords of tango music drifting toward her from the mouth of the alley, she squared her shoulders and set off down the narrow sidewalk, her shoulder brushing the plastered walls of the buildings. Ahead, a cat scolded her with a rasping cry and scampered away.

Two blocks from the main street, beneath a single bulb, hung a weathered plaque announcing the establishment as Casa de Mi Bandoneon. A wall of faded blue French doors facing the street was closed to the night air and she entered through a single open door. Tables sat in semi-shadow around a polished dance floor. A small orchestra--violin, bandoneon, guitar, flute and piano--inspired four couples. Angela found a table near the back of the room, away from the floor, and slipped into a bent wood chair. She was immediately drawn to the distinctive, exaggerated movements of the tangueros as they slashed through the smoky light spilling onto the dance floor. One couple dominated the floor, the woman quite young, her glossy black hair severely swept back, the man much older, but lithe, with a sharp-featured, tanned leather face, pomaded dark hair and a graceful precision born of years of tango.

Then from the darkness, a hand gripped her shoulder and she jumped, hot prickles of electricity sizzling through her body. She jerked her head around and looked up into the face of middle-aged man with a long, thin nose, large dark eyes and hair combed straight back.

He had the lean, slender look of a dancer or a swordsman.

"*¿Quieres bailar, Señorita?*" he asked in a deep, gravelly voice.

It took her a moment to translate the obvious. He was asking her to dance. That wasn't part of the recognition code and, still quivering, she replied, "*No, gracias. Espero un amigo.*"

"*Yo estoy un amigo,*" the dancer replied, his hand still gripping her shoulder, his fingers as strong as steel cables.

A yawning pocket of fear opened in Angela's stomach and her heart began to pound. She tried to shrug away from his hand, but it gripped her even more tightly. '*Oh, my God,*' she thought. She looked around her for help, but so early in the evening, the only tables that were occupied were at the edge of the dance floor.

"*¡Señor! Por favor. ¡No me molesta! No quiero bailar,*" she begged.

The dancer smiled, moved to her side, pulled out a chair and sat down.

"Do not be afraid of me, Señorita," he said in accented English. "Crossed keys will open two doors."

Almost fainting with relief, she took a moment to catch her breath and then replied, "But only one can be entered."

"I have what you are seeking," he said, smiling wickedly, taking her hand as it rested on top of the table and pressing his knee against her thigh.

Copacabana, Bolivia

Standing beneath the cross at the top of the ridge of Isla de la Luna, McCall heard the chopper's distinctive whock-whock-whock-whock before he saw it. He turned toward the sound and picked it up skimming the electric blue water of the enormous lake, an old bug-eyed UH-1 Huey rigged with pontoons and painted olive drab. The chopper came abreast of the tiny island but stood well out over the lake while a pair of large black binoculars focused on him. After no more than a minute's inspection, the helicopter moved slowly around the island, continuing its reconnaissance, a trooper sitting in the door sweeping everything with binoculars. The chopper came back to its original position and hovered at the shore line near the boat dock. Three men in camouflage fatigues slid down lines from the helicopter and covered the boatman with their assault rifles while they searched him and the boat before taking up positions around the dock. The chopper veered off when they were satisfied, crossed over the island and let down three more troopers on the other side near the ruins of an Inca wall. When they were in position, the chopper lifted up to the ridge.

McCall took shelter behind a scraggly tree as the chopper hovered just beyond the cross, its blades churning up a small tornado of dust, twigs and dead grass. Shielding his eyes, he watched the man he presumed was General Raul Tovolaro step from the cabin onto one of the pontoons and vault the last three feet to the ground. The chopper quickly bore off and set down on the lake near the boat dock.

The General straightened his uniform--polished knee-high brown boots, riding breeches, a gabardine jacket and leather gloves, accented by a red beret and a short holster affixed to a wide leather belt. McCall did not fail to notice that the holster's flap was unfastened. He looked McCall over and strode briskly toward him, a riding crop tucked under his left arm.

"General Tovolaro?"

"Señor McCall?"

"Correct," McCall said, resisting a reflex temptation to salute.

"So you are a friend of Lucho's?"

"Yes. We're old friends."

"Lucho said you were a banker." "

I'm an economist by training and an investment banker by trade. I can make a lot more money that way. That's what I came to talk to you about."

The two men stood face to face, each taking the measure of the other.

The General was shorter than McCall, with a firm, powerful build, a square jaw and a bristling black mustache. McCall saw himself reflected in the General's sunglasses--khaki pants rolled up to reveal rough hiking boots and a leather flight jacket over a natural wool turtleneck. Without a hat, his hair fluttered in the wind.

"Bueno. Talk to me."

"Perhaps Lucho told you that I'm seeking to syndicate five million dollars for a special investment opportunity and because of the need for confidentiality I want as few investors as possible. May I ask you to treat all that I tell you in the strictest confidence?"

The General didn't answer McCall's question right away and an eerie silence settled over the ridge. The General's helicopter had shut down and the only sound came from a cold breeze off Lake Titicaca that rattled the brittle leaves of the tree behind McCall.

"My associates and I are men of honor who know how to keep confidences."

McCall stared at him and nodded. "I understand, General. But I ask for this explicit assurance for two reasons. The first is to protect something valuable that I alone hold at the moment and the second is that I will be asking something of you in exchange for my offering you this opportunity to participate in the syndicate"

"Very well," Tovolaro said, taking the riding crop from beneath his arm and swatting it against the calf of one of his riding boots. "Lucho said nothing about a quid pro quo. What is it?"

"I didn't tell Lucho about the quid pro quo. And it's simply this. In exchange for giving you the opportunity to double your money--and possibly more--you must abandon your efforts to buy Banco Dorado. I can give you the name of another bank in Panamá that will serve your purposes just as well--whatever they are. But I require your assurance that you will stop trying to acquire Banco Dorado."

Tovolaro paced back and forth in front of McCall, swatting his boot with his riding crop, the crack of leather against leather like a gunshot that flew from the top of the ridge out over the water. After every stroke, he gave McCall an appraising look.

Finally, he drew himself up to his full height and faced McCall. "I could have you killed for even knowing of our interest in Banco Dorado."

McCall swallowed hard, sensing the malevolence in the man and acutely aware of the commandos surrounding them. His heart pounded in his chest and an uneasy thought passed through his mind. Would they let the boatman live?

McCall held Tovolaro's gaze, demanding his body to show no fear, to play his own cards and, if possible, make Tovolaro blink. "You certainly have me at a disadvantage, General. But you claim to be an honorable man and before you decide to kill me, you ought to know that your agent, Robert Ryder, tried to rape the young daughter of the chairman of Banco Dorado. The chairman, who is not a young man, was so upset that he had a heart attack. He may not live. Through your agent, you are indirectly responsible for this. The only honorable thing--the very least you can do--is leave this poor man alone. Although it is not a condition of any arrangement you and I reach, you should also consider disassociating yourself from Robert Ryder. You should find someone honorable to represent you."

Tovolaro's eyes were hidden behind the sunglasses, but McCall felt he'd made a telling thrust and had the General back on his heels, if only for a moment.

"Is this true?" Tovolaro asked at last. "Roberto did this thing?"

"Yes."

"Very well," Tovolaro said. "I give you my personal word I will not reveal what you say to me in confidence and I will consider withdrawing our support for the acquisition of Banco Dorado. Now, what is this investment opportunity?"

McCall swallowed again, feeling his knees weaken with relief. Tovolaro hadn't promised, but McCall thought he'd cleared a critical hurdle. Now for the pitch. McCall sketched the parameters of his proposal and the prospective returns to the investors. And he told Tovolaro about the gold.

For my part, my company, Wellington, Winchester-, will act as general partner and receive ten percent of the net profit, plus reasonable expenses, for bringing the opportunity to the investors and for managing the fund from inception to final liquidation. I know you need more information to make a final decision, but I need a good faith commitment from you also. I've made arrangements for an escrow account to be held by Bahamas International Trust in Nassau. When the funds are fully subscribed, I'll release a prospectus with further details of the investment and legal documents for each participant to execute. You'll have a little time--very little--to decide whether to go forward or not. Each partner who decides to go ahead will instruct Bahamas International Trust to release his escrowed funds to Wellington, Winchester. Any partner who doesn't go forward must leave those funds on deposit until the escrow account expires, which will occur six months after the funds are deposited. When the escrow expires, BITCO will return each nonparticipating partner's investment intact, plus interest at the Bahamas bank rate, less a small service charge. I hope you find that fair all the way around, General."

"Señor McCall, please," Tovolaro said, the suggestion of a smile working around the edges of his mouth. "I have come here at some inconvenience--

on the spoken word of my cousin--to meet a stranger. Perhaps we can take a little time to know one another."

General Tovolaro put his hand in the air and waved to his troops at the boat dock. He made the motions of pouring something into a cup and then walked to the low wall near the tree where McCall was standing.

"One of my men will bring coffee," he said, removing his sunglasses to reveal large brown eyes and a much older man than McCall had imagined from the General's muscular build and the athletic way he moved. The General slipped the swagger stick under his arm and clasped his hands behind his back, at parade rest, and stared across the great vacant expanse of Lake Titicaca. "It is a beautiful lake, is it not, Señor McCall?"

****

McCall remained on the ridge watching the General recover his troops. The chopper made a final pass and Tovolaro flashed a toothy smile from the pilot's seat and threw him a salute. McCall waved and waited until the helicopter was only a speck in the distance before he sat down heavily on the stone wall at the base of the cross and released a long breath. He sat there in the rarefied atmosphere for twenty minutes, collecting himself. He'd gone so far as to tell the General he had inside information and that the project involved Russian bonds. He hoped his allusion to the possibility of a settlement in gold was enough to excite the General's appetite for the deal. At least the General had promised an answer in three days. McCall had given him the name of Comercio de Colón as an alternative to Banco Dorado.

He had no illusions about the trustworthiness of General Tovolaro or Las Águilas, but for the first time since he learned that Josh had mortgaged the farm, his spirits lifted a little. Maybe he'd been able to steer Banco Dorado into safe harbor, which left him with a couple of hundred thousand locked up in the stock of a troubled Panamanian bank, but at least it wasn't going to be lost. It would be there for another day.

He stretched and began his descent along a winding footpath to the little boat dock beside a cluster of rude houses. The children who'd been fascinated by the helicopter and seen the assault rifles of the General's sentries were curious about the Norteamericano now. They shadowed him silently from a distance and were disappointed when he paid them no attention and went directly to the boat.

Anaya, the boatman, was waiting stoically in the stern of his seventeen-foot power launch. He brought the big outboard engine to life while McCall was still walking down the narrow dock, the weathered planks rattling as he came. McCall let go the bow line and brought it aboard as he stepped off the dock onto the launch, steadying himself as it rocked in the water. Anaya's face was as expressionless as a stone mask, but the dispatch with which he cleared the stern line and backed the boat away from the dock, barely giving McCall time to settle, made it clear he was eager to be away from men with assault rifles. McCall resolved to tip him generously when they reached Copacabana.

At Lake Titicaca's altitude, the air was thin and frigid, even past midday, and once they'd come about and roared away from Isla de la Luna, Anaya, standing in the stern with his hand on the tiller, buttoned his old Army field jacket up to the throat. McCall followed his example, zipping up his leather flight jacket. The adrenalin flow had mercifully suspended his altitude-induced headache while he was treating with General Tovolaro, but now the sorojchi returned. He unwrapped a Snicker's bar to combat it and offered another one to Anaya, who took it with a stained, broken-toothed smile. Seeing the smile, McCall wondered how Anaya would tell the story of the day's adventure once they were back in port. He threw him a salute and retreated into the cuddy cabin to stretch out on the wooden-slatted bench for the two-hour run to Copacabana.

****

General Tovolaro's helicopter put down on a hardened pad at the Hacienda Tovolaro near the little town of Coroico, tucked away in a valley northeast of La Paz. Coroico was only six thousand feet above sea level--a comfortable altitude compared to La Paz's twelve thousand--and the General was conveniently out of sight whenever he chose to be. La Paz was scarcely a hundred kilometers away--an arduous drive over narrow mountain roads, but a short flight for the chopper.

The General shut down the engine, left the post-flight checklist to the pilot and strode purposefully to the rambling hacienda. It took an hour to arrange the conference call with the Council of Las Águilas. McCall was still on Lake Titicaca when the meeting began.

****

The bus for La Paz had long since gone by the time Anaya docked on the stony shores of Copacabana and McCall was forced to stay another night in the frigid embrace of the Hotel Ambassador. He used the toilet in his room, splashed ice cold water from the tap on his face and walked up the hill toward the main square until he found a one-room café, dimly-lit by a single sixty-watt bulb hanging by a wire from the high ceiling.

Against all advice of mixing alcohol with the high altitude of the Andes, he took a shot of singani to celebrate the day, wolfed a meal of tasteless chuño--dried potatoes, Inca style--and pejerrey, a sweet fish from the frigid waters of the lake, washing it down with two bottles of Paceña beer. The proprietor was friendly enough, but the other patrons--three grizzled fishermen wearing several layers of hand-knitted, llama-wool sweaters-- ignored him. As soon as he finished eating, he pushed away from the rickety table and left. He was ready to fall asleep, but strolling back toward the hotel, he was drawn to the blooming of an extraordinary sunset and continued down the hill to the waterfront.

A few people sat at tables on the packed dirt outside a tumbledown café, drinking mate and talking softly in the luminous twilight. McCall took a table facing the water and ordered a Paceña from the tiny waitress--an Aymara Indian girl who looked no more than twelve. She took his order wordlessly and went away. Watching the sunset's vivid green, gold and purple pastels tint the languid waters lapping against the rocky shore, the tension of the day flowed out of him. When the Indian girl brought the beer, McCall gave her a large bill and held up the palm of his hand to indicate she was to keep it all. Her large, passive eyes stared at him, her mouth clamped shut. Then she snatched the bill, turned and ran back into the café.

McCall hunched his shoulders against the night air and took a sip of Paceña. A thought struck him suddenly and he almost choked. He sat up and sputtered the beer out of his mouth, laughing to himself. He imagined the ghosts of his Cooper ancestors standing around the rocky shore of Lake Titicaca, watching him and shaking their heads. Each had defended the farm in his own way after the first Joshua hacked it out of the wilderness. Joshua had held out against the Indians with a combination of diplomacy and determination. Thomas had stood off a company of Yankee soldiers, lost his arm and then rebuilt the farm almost from scratch. Whatever crises they'd faced, they faced them on the land within a few miles of the farm. Now here was the latest in their long line mounting a defense from some God-forsaken place in South America. They had to be wondering about fate's capriciousness in putting their legacy in his hands. McCall smiled at the irony. If he pulled it off, it would mark a new paradigm in defending the old homestead. Maybe, too, it would put an end to the nagging of his ancestors.

The air grew swiftly colder when the sun dropped below the horizon and McCall finished the beer and got up. Night came absolutely with the disappearance of the sun and he marveled at the crystal clear air and diamond brilliance of the first stars of the evening as he trudged up the hill to the hotel.

Inside his white-washed, sparsely furnished room beside the narrow courtyard, he pulled off his jacket and was assailed by the rank odor of fear and stale perspiration. He'd sponge off in the morning and load up on deodorant. A shower was out of the question. There was no hot water and the window in the bathroom was broken. The air in the room would be below freezing by morning, so he unlaced his boots, peeled off his sweater, got into bed and wrapped the alpaca blankets around him tightly. With the light out, the room was as dark as a coal mine.

He closed his eyes and thought of the long bus ride back--across the Straits of Tiquina by ferry to San Pablo, through barren high country and on into La Paz. A hot bath and a steak at the Sucre Palace, then the dawn flight to Miami, Customs and a connecting flight to Washington.

La Paz, Bolivia

Toweling off from the shower, his mouth watering with the vision of a thick slab of Argentinean beef, he dressed carelessly and hurried downstairs to the dining room.

It was early and only a few tables were occupied, leaving the dark wood of the high-backed chairs in sharp contrast with the sparkling silver table settings and bright white table cloths. Near the glassed-in Spanish colonial balcony that overhung the sidewalk below, the blind piano player who was a fixture at the Sucre Palace had begun his evening serenade.

A soft rendition of Wave, a Brazilian favorite of McCall's, wafted from the keys. It wasn't quite music for dining, but it was relaxing and energizing at the same time.

McCall stood a few feet from the maitre d', taking a moment to imprint his experience of the last twenty-four hours. Had he really stood atop a tiny island in a deserted lake as large as an ocean, cutting a deal with a Bolivian general who'd made a name for himself tracking down Che Guevara? Had he really eaten sweet pejerrey and greasy chuño with sullen Aymara fishermen in a one-room hole in the wall lit by a 60-watt bulb? Had he really burrowed under alpaca blankets to sleep in a pitch black, frigid room with a broken window on the ragged roof of the world? The Sucre Palace might not be The Four Seasons, but there was hot water and a bed with crisp, clean sheets and he was standing in a glittering dining room already filled with savory aromas and the lush melodies of a blind pianist. Had he really been so far away from civilization yesterday?

The tuxedo-clad maitre d' approached McCall with a welcoming bow and a wide smile and led him to a table for two beside the windows on the balcony. He offered McCall a large menu and motioned to a painfully thin, white-jacketed waiter to bring rolls and butter.

McCall found the steak he wanted on the menu and looked up to see if anyone were nearby to take his order. No one was, but three unoccupied tables away, a woman sat alone against the wall. He watched her lower her dark glasses with a forefinger and saw a smile spread slowly across her lips.

His mouth must have fallen open. "Angela?" he said, not sure if he'd said it out loud. He began to rise from his chair, the napkin falling to the floor, the menu set aside on the table.

She was already coming to join him, a large handbag slung over her shoulder and a slender attaché case partially concealed beneath it.

"I can't believe my luck," she whispered, pulling back the chair across from him and slipping into it. "God, how I've been thinking about you."

McCall was sure he was grinning stupidly, unable to believe she was sitting across from him. He could smell her scent, something subtle and rich with a touch of musk. "What are you doing in La Paz?" he asked, unable to take his eyes from her face. She looked under stress, her cheek bones more prominent, her dark eyes deeper in their sockets.

McCall was sure he was grinning stupidly, unable to believe she was sitting across from him. He could smell her scent, something subtle and rich with a touch of musk. "What are you doing in La Paz?" he asked, unable to take his eyes from her face. She looked under stress, her cheek bones more prominent, her dark eyes deeper in their sockets.

"I've got a load of notes and tapes in my attaché case. Right here in my lap." She leaned toward him, her voice dropping several more decibels. "They're building a conduit for Contra arms from Cape Town through Buenos Aires. What I've got will blow the whole deal wide open and maybe send some people to jail. I'm afraid they know I've got it and if they do, I won't be able to get it out of the country. Will you take it? Give it to Dixie Davenport? She'll know what to do with it."

The waiter rushed over and retrieved McCall's napkin from the floor where it had fallen when he stood up. Then he addressed Angela, flustered because she'd changed tables. "Disculpame, Señorita. ¿Quiere algo mas?"

"No, gracias. Estoy terminada y me voy en seguida. La cuenta, por favor."

"Muy bien, Señorita," he replied with a bow and went away to find her check.

McCall leaned toward Angela. "How'd you know I'd be here?" Angela's eyes widened and bored into him and McCall felt something press against his leg.

"Dixie tracked you down, but never mind that. Be quiet and listen. My attaché case is under the table on the floor. I just pushed it over to your side. I want you to take it," she whispered and got up.

"Whoa, whoa, whoa," McCall protested, rising. "You're not leaving?" She rose from her chair and came around the table, pressed against him, one hand on his shoulder, kissing him on the cheek, the other plucking his room key from the table. "I'll wait for you in your room," she whispered, kissed his other cheek, flashed a brilliant smile, then walked quickly through the dining room to the stairs.

McCall started to follow her, but her act stopped him. Was someone watching? He held on to her promise to meet him in his room and sat back down. The waiter appeared and, seeing that Angela had disappeared, handed McCall a slip of paper. "La cuenta de la Señorita, Señor."

"Esta bien," McCall said. "Incluye con la de mio."

McCall picked up the menu, trying to decide whether to follow Angela's lead and eat as if nothing had happened or skip dinner and go to the room. His stomach made the decision.

He pointed to a steak on the menu and told the waiter. "Traigame este bistek, medio crudo, con papas fritas, un botella de vino tinto de la casa y un de agua sin gas. De prisa, por favor. Tengo mucho hambre." To emphasize his impatience, McCall held up a ten-dollar bill.

The waiter took it quickly and smiled. "Sí, sí, Señor. Inmediatamente. Gracias, Señor." He hurried away, still scribbling on his pad.

****

McCall found the door ajar and pushed it open slowly, holding the bottle of vino tinto by the neck in one hand and her attaché case in the other. The drapes were open and she was sitting in the big chair by the window in the soft light of the city, wrapped in one of the hotel's big terrycloth robes. He could smell cigarette smoke mingled with bath salts.

"What took you so long?" she asked softly.

He picked his way across the room until he stood in front of her. He held out his hands to help her up and she grasped them, letting him take her weight. He drew her up slowly, his eyes fixed on her distant smile in the half-light, letting her arms coil around his neck and her body press against him. When she trembled, he pulled her closer.

"What are you doing here?" he asked, his mouth brushing hers.

"I missed you," she said, barely touching her lips to his but moving her hips slowly back and forth against him, loosening the tie that held her robe closed.

Kissing her, his hands slipping beneath her open robe to touch her silky skin, he forgot all his questions.

****

She was gone when he awoke and the sheets where she had lain were cold. For a long moment, he wondered if he had dreamed it all. Then he saw her attaché case on the coffee table and knew that he hadn't.

He called down to the desk and asked for her room. The clerk told him she was not registered at the Sucre Palace. There was no message for him, either.

He replaced the receiver and checked his watch. He was booked on the dawn flight out of La Paz. Just time for a shower. No time to track her down.

He found her note on the little shelf above the sink in the bath.

Mi amor, You can't imagine how I hate leaving you. I never could have if you'd awakened and asked me to stay. Fair warning for next time.

He went through the routine of packing and checking out, trying to put her out of his mind, but she wouldn't go away. Her scent and her touch were imprinted on him, even as he stood on the sidewalk in the pre-dawn cold watching the porter load his baggage into a weary, faded green taxi.

McCall left the window open, gulping the thin, icy air as the taxi bounced through the sloping streets of La Paz on exhausted shock absorbers, skirting clots of men in shaggy sweaters and rough trousers and women in odd hats and colorful, billowing skirts as they piled out of busses and milled around colectivos in the gray dawn. The vision of Angela lingered as they cleared the city and rattled upward through the tall eucalyptus forest toward El Alto. He felt her breath against his neck and heard her murmured words, but what haunted him was the way she clung to him as if he were life itself and the desperate, urgent way she made love. Staring into the wispy fog shrouding the mountain, his heart ached a little. They hadn't had enough time. Why were they always being pulled apart?

Alexandria

The flight from Miami was late and McCall was in a foul mood by the time he struggled through the door of the condo with his bags draped on both shoulders. He dropped them in a pile beside the entry and trudged down the hall to the bathroom, stripping off his clothes as he went.

He let the shower pound the stress and fatigue of travel out of him and thought seriously about having a large Scotch, tucking into bed and letting it all wait until tomorrow. But the sooner he put the prospectus in Tovolaro's hands, the sooner he'd get a final decision from Las Águilas. After his shower, McCall thought he could at least make a start on it.

He toweled off, pulled on shorts and a T-shirt and padded into his office. There were no messages on his answering machine and no evidence that anyone had missed him. He switched on his computer, booted up Telerate, checked the action in the day's markets and read the significant developments. He'd collect the accumulated mail and newspapers from downstairs tomorrow and bring his portfolio up to date. The prospectus was the first order of business right now. He opened the word processor to a new document and stared at the blank screen.

He began crafting some boilerplate about the company, doing his best to overcome its recent vintage by puffing up its banking relationship with Barclays and the venerable law firm that took the company off the shelf and supplied his This-Vote-For-Hire board of directors.

Then he took a stab at the history of the Tsar's bonds, working from his memory of Paralee's research, but the details wouldn't come and the piece sounded vague without them. Reluctantly, he realized he wasn't going to be able to do this part without her notes.

He sat back and thought about that for a minute. *'Damn it. I paid for the research and the notes are mine, whatever she thinks about me or the people I'm dealing with. They may not be the old families of Perú, but even with old money, there was always a pirate or a slave trader if you went back far enough. She owes me the notes.'*

He picked up the phone and dialed her number.

"It's Mack," he said when she answered with a wan 'hello.'

"You're back," she said and he thought her tone sounded cautious, tentative.

"A little while ago. Look, I need your research notes on the bonds. I'm bushed now, but I wondered if I could come over and pick them up in the morning."

"I don't know if you can decipher them," she said. "I don't spell everything out."

"Well, I'd ask you to help, but you made it pretty plain that you weren't interested in continuing with the project."

"I guess I could help you with the notes."

"OK. I'd like to make an early start. Seven o'clock?"

"I'll be ready," she said, unable to resist the temptation to ask, "Did you get the money?"

"I'm writing a prospectus. That's why I need the notes. They're not coughing up five million bucks because they like the color of my eyes."

"No," she said, hurt. "I guess not."

McCall softened his tone. "Look, I didn't mean to be sharp with you. I'm sorry. It's just that the damned plane was late and I'm under the gun here."

"No. It's OK."

He could almost see her chin come up, stiff upper lip and all that. There was a long silence.

"See you in the morning then," he said and rang off.

Risking a call from his own phone, he reached Javier at his apartment. "I think we're off the hook," he said.

"You made a deal?" Javier asked, excited.

"I think so. I can't tell you about it right now. I'm calling from home and I'm dead tired. Just got in. But sleep well, 'mano. I'll call you tomorrow and give you the whole story."

****

McCall and Paralee kept their distance on the way to the condo, an invisible wall between them, their conversation polite but superficial, as if they were casual acquaintances.

As soon as McCall opened the door, he saw Angela's attaché case, resting at a slant among the other bags he'd dumped beside the door the night before.

"Shit! Angela's stuff. I promised to take it to Dixie."

"Who's Angela?" Paralee asked, following him through the door.

He ignored her question and said, "Look, you know where everything is. I've got to make a phone call."

McCall took a chance that Dixie Davenport was one of those people who showed up for work at the crack of dawn and tried her Capitol Hill number. She answered.

"Aunt Dixie," he said. "This is Jack McCall. From Kevin Fitzgerald's a couple of weeks ago."

"Ah, yes. My quick-witted friend. How are you?"

"I'm good. You surely remember Angela Collins from that party. You ought to since you gave her my address."

"Of course I do," Dixie answered, her tone more alert.

"She asked me to bring you some stuff. All pretty mysterious, but I got the impression that there was some urgency. Any chance I could stop by your office this morning and drop it off? I don't think this should wait."

your office this morning and drop it off? I don't think this should wait."
"Come as quick as you can," she said. "I'll make sure nobody slows you down at this end." The quicker tempo of Dixie's voice told McCall he now had her full attention and that she was sitting up straight in her chair.

"I've got to go up to the Hill," he told Paralee. "I won't be long. Coffee's hot and I won't be around to pester you--at least not for an hour or so."

"Yeah, but . . ." she protested. "What do you want me to do, write out all my notes? I can't do that in an hour."

"Just do an executive summary of it. The story of the bonds, the gold and all that. Be brief, but make sure you lay out the critical details. I'll shape it up when I get back," he said as he went through the door.

* * * * * * * * * * *

Dixie met him in the foyer, took him by the arm, led him into her small, cluttered office and closed the door. A thin haze of cigarette smoke hung in the air and a smoldering stench rose from a large, overflowing ashtray. "Sit down, my friend, and tell me about Angela Collins."

"Sit down, my friend, and tell me about Angela Collins."

"I ran into her in La Paz. Total surprise to me, but apparently not to you. Anyway, there she was, three tables away from me in the dining room, looking like a Hollywood starlet trying hard not to be recognized. Dark glasses and all that. She stopped by my table, asked me if I'd bring this stuff to you." McCall held up Angela's slender attaché case and passed it across the desk to Dixie.

"What did she tell you?" Dixie asked, popping the latches on the attaché case, but keeping her eyes on McCall.

"Something about a conduit for Contra arms and that what she had in that case would blow the deal apart and put some people in jail. When I asked her what it was all about, she told me it was better I didn't know."

Dixie nodded, her eyes dropping to the material she was taking from the case. "She told you too much as it is."

McCall waited while she looked through Angela's papers, the lines on her face hardening. Finally, she lit another cigarette and sat down.

"You're an Air Force officer, aren't you?"

"Was. What's that got to do with anything?"

"Still on reserve status?"

"No," he said slowly. "I resigned my commission."

"They can still bring you back, pal. I don't think your oath of allegiance to defend and protect has a time limit on it. Even if it does, I can promise you I'll see to it that your ass hangs from the Washington Monument if any of this leaks out to the press or to anyone else. Do I make myself clear?"

Dixie, his palms flat on her desk and his chin jutting toward her. "Look, I don't know what's in that stuff, so I can't very well talk about it. And as far as your hanging my ass from anywhere, you just ain't tall enough, lady." He glared at her for a moment and was about to turn and leave.

McCall continued glaring at Dixie, but his anger subsided. After several tense moments, he scratched his chin and said, "Yeah, OK. But so you know--I don't like to be pushed around."

Dixie held up her hand in a gesture of apology. "Sorry, sorry. I didn't mean to come on so strong. It's been a ragged twenty-four hours. I still have to ask--and I'll ask politely. Can I count on your keeping all this to yourself?"

McCall eased back into the chair and crossed his legs. "No. She said something about their never letting her out of the country with what she had. I thought she meant customs or . . . I don't know. As far as being afraid, it was more like she was pumped up, excited."

"That's all you remember?" Dixie asked, drawing deeply on her cigarette, tapping the ash away nervously and exhaling.

"She mentioned Cape Town and Buenos Aires," he added, thought further and then shook his head. "That's all."

"Did anyone see you together?"

"The waiter. She wasn't at my table more than a couple of minutes, less maybe. Other than the waiter, I didn't notice anyone watching us. It was early, there weren't many people in the dining room and the piano player was blind. What's going on?" he asked, beginning to feel a gnawing anxiety. "Is she in some kind of trouble?"

"You caught an early flight out of La Paz?"

"Yeah. The dawn patrol."

"Maybe that's how you got through. They couldn't get on you in time. Look. The thing is that Angela's gone missing. She was coming out by train, through Arica, but we think she must have been picked up in La Paz before she got on board. The embassy hasn't had any kind of word that she's been detained and no hospital admission, either. It definitely doesn't look good. Consider yourself lucky. My guess is they'd have reeled you in, too, if they'd known you had this," Dixie held up a fistful of paper.

"What do you mean 'picked up' in La Paz? The cops? Secret police? What? Look, Angela . . . well, she's more than a casual acquaintance."

Dixie raised her eyebrows and gave him an exasperated shake of her head. "Was she with you somewhere besides that restaurant?" "None of your business, Dixie."

"None of your business, Dixie."

"That's a 'yes,'" she snorted. "I don't care about that, but I really need to know if there's anything else you haven't told me--anything at all that has to do with what's in this attaché case?"

"No. I want to know what you know about Angela."

"I've told you all I can. Are you going somewhere for the Thanksgiving holiday?"

"Yeah. My grandfather's place. In the Shenandoah Valley."

"Good," Dixie said. "It won't hurt for you to be out of sight for awhile. In the meantime, don't take any candy from strangers, OK? By the way, what were you doing in Bolivia?"

"Personal business," McCall replied. "And by the way, I don't appreciate your tracking me all over the world. What gives you the right . . .?"

Dixie's eyes narrowed. "Trust me, this is important. And I'd feel better knowing what you were doing there. It might help Angela," she said, getting up and coming around her desk.

"You have secrets, Dixie, and so do I. So you trust me--what I was doing in Bolivia has nothing to do with Angela. But I'll make a deal with you. You let me know the minute you hear that Angela's OK and I'll tell you everything I know, starting with my sock size." He pulled an old First Mission National business card from his wallet and wrote two telephone numbers on the back. He handed the card to Dixie. "The top one is my local number. The other one's the farm." McCall locked his eyes on Dixie's, demanding with a look that she promise him.

Dixie nodded and held out her hand. "I'll call you."

As he walked toward the Mercedes, parked several blocks away, Angela Collins' face swam into his memory and the cold hand of dread gripped his heart as he thought about what might be happening to her at the hands of Bolivia's Security Service--or whoever it was that might have picked her up. Why hadn't she been afraid? Maybe she had been. Now he was.

****

The phone rang as soon as he opened the door at the condo and he heard

Paralee answer it. She looked up when he appeared in the doorway of the office.

"He just walked in. Can you hold, please?" She covered the mouthpiece with her hand. "London calling," she said, raising her eyebrows and handing him the phone.

"Charles Foster here," the voice with the British accent told him.

"Nice to hear from you, Mr. Foster. How're we doing?"

"Quite well, actually. I was able to invest the hundred thousand US Mr. Banderas sent to your account. Not all in the gold ruble bonds of 1909, I'm afraid. I've put it about that we're assembling a collection for a museum my brother's been keen on forming. That seems to be giving the rumor mongers enough to chew on. Accordingly, I had to buy issues other than the 1909 Imperials. However, the Imperials do represent about eighty percent of the portfolio."

"That's a great idea about the museum. How much did we have to pay? Were you able to hold the price under ten?"

"No. Please remember I told you this market would be sensitive to activity even of this small magnitude." Foster paused for a moment to let McCall prepare himself for the pricing. "The average price worked out to eleven point two, so at today's dollar exchange rate, less commissions, Wellington, Winchester now controls eight hundred three thousand five hundred and seventy one dollars of the bonds of Tsar Nicholas II and other assorted Russian entities."

"That's not much of a bump. What's going to happen to the price if I bring five million dollars to the table?"

"Five million? You'll have to expect a more significant advance, probably across the board, but certainly on the gold ruble bonds if you persist in buying them."

"How much of an advance?"

"Impossible to tell."

"I understand," McCall said. "Look, I'll be out of touch for a few days--our Thanksgiving holiday over here--but I'll call you when I get back in town."

McCall said a silent prayer that his phone wasn't being tapped. What could the FDIC make of his conversation with Charles Foster? At a minimum, that he was connected to an offshore operation in the Bahamas, that he might have undeclared money in play. How rich could their imaginations be?

The phone rang again as soon as he hung up. McCall picked up the receiver.

"Hello," McCall said. It was Kevin Fitzgerald and a picture of Angela

Collins by the buffet table at Fitzgerald's popped into focus. He took a moment to answer Kevin. "Thanksgiving? No. Sorry. I'm going to spend the holiday with my grandfather. I've been neglecting him lately. . . . OK. After the first of the year, when you get back from Colorado. . . . Millard Fillmore's birthday? You bet. . . . Love to Barbara."

The phone rang again.

Christian, James. Audrey's Bonds . James Christian. Kindle Edition.

"What is this?" McCall asked. "Has the phone been going off like this all morning?" He picked up the receiver.

"McCall," he answered.

"Señor McCall? This is Raul Tovolaro. We have decided to take the first step."

"I'm delighted to hear that, General. I've just been on the phone with my broker and he tells me that the prices of the issues in question are firming. We need to move quickly."

"Someone else is buying?" Tovolaro asked, a touch of anxiety in his voice.

"Why, I am, General. For my personal account."

"I see," Tovolaro said. "Thank you for telling me. If you will give me the escrow account number, I will have five million dollars wired to the Bahamas International Trust."

McCall read off the number of the Wellington, Winchester account. "When may we expect to learn the details?"

"I'm finalizing the prospectus now, General. I'll send it Federal Express to Philip Gerard in Nassau and instruct him to send you the prospectus as soon as your money goes into escrow. Agreed? Don't be concerned if you can't reach me for a few days. I'm leaving town, but I expect to return by the first of December. Where shall I tell him to send the prospectus?"

"To Jorge Villanueva in Miami Beach. The address is Collins Avenue, 1165. I will call you after we have examined it."

For a split second, McCall thought of asking Tovolaro to intervene for Angela, at least to see if she were being held by the Bolivian Security Police. Instinct and logic smothered the impulse--he'd promised Dixie to keep his mouth shut and some inner voice told him Tovolaro wasn't the right man to talk to about missing gringas. He said his goodbyes to Tovolaro, put down the phone and turned to Paralee.

"Guess who that was."

"The money, I guess," she said. "You called him General. . ."

"I told you I wasn't going to have anything to do with drug lords."

"Being a general doesn't mean you don't deal drugs," she snapped and regretted it instantly. "I'm sorry, Mack. That was tacky. Is he from one of the old families who made their millions in copper mines and sugar cane?"

McCall stared at her, returning the flash of fire in her eyes with a stern look of his own. He didn't have to explain anything to her and resented her making him feel guilty.

"They're not old money," McCall said at last. "But they're not drug lords, either. The General manages money for retired military. They're soldiers, not drug lords."

"Are you saying he runs the Army's retirement fund?"

"No," he replied, wishing he'd never started with her, but realizing that if he stopped now, she'd think the worst. "It's their own funds."

"Boy, that's interesting," she said sarcastically. "My dad's retired military and he doesn't have five million bucks to invest. I guess he was in the wrong army."

McCall glared at her, his jaw clenched.

"If it's not drugs and it's not the government, where does the money come from, Mack?" she asked, holding herself in, watching him carefully. "Unless you know where it does come from, you don't know it doesn't come from drugs."

"I'm not Price-Waterhouse, either. I didn't do an audit on them." His language and his tone stung her and shamed him at the same time. "Sorry, sorry," he added. "Look, it's not pristine. What I know from a man I trust is that it mainly comes from bribes they took when they were in political office. Stuff like kickbacks on loan agreements, which they probably called 'commissions' or 'consultant fees.' And 'favors' of a million different kinds. I don't know. I'm not condoning what they did or what they do, Paralee, but I was firmly assured that they weren't into drugs. Think about it. A drug lord wouldn't give me five minutes of his time to talk about a measly five million dollars."

"Yeah," she said, looking down, her anger subsiding. "Well, maybe it isn't dope . . . But these people don't sound much better to me. In Ethiopia, one army or another stole our food and medical supplies and sold them on the black market whenever they took a notion. Nothing we could do about it." She saw again the vacant eyes and distended bellies of the children of Tigray Province.

She put the faces from her mind and looked at McCall. "I've been reading up on Latin America. The "dirty war" in Argentina, the death squads and all the desaparecidos. You know about this, don't you?" She waited a moment for McCall to register something, but he only stared back at her.

"I can't believe you don't know," she said. "People who were suspected--just suspected--of anything that was anti-government, just disappeared. Nuns, priests, children, whole families, were picked up and never heard from again. They even gave away the children of parents who became desaparecidos. Mack, it's unimaginable." She stopped for a moment, her mouth a grim, angry line.

"In Buenos Aires, mothers of desaparecidos still march in the Plaza de Mayo every Thursday because, even after all these years, the government hasn't told them what happened to their sons and daughters. No one knows for sure, but more than ten thousand people disappeared. It's been like that in Chile and El Salvador and Nicaragua and Guatemala, too. We think of Hitler as such a monster and here we have people running around in South America who are just like him--Somoza, Videla, Galtieri, Pinochet, d'Aubuisson, Noriega, I don't know who all. They're right at our doorstep and we're not doing anything about it. We're even helping them." Her breath was coming in short bursts, her cheeks flushed.

"Did you know we were still supporting that regime in Argentina until the Falklands War? The only reason we broke off with them was because we had to side with Britain in the war, not because of their hideous death squads." Paralee stopped, out of breath, quivering.

"I'm not sleeping with these guys," McCall said, avoiding her eyes and thinking that Angela and Paralee and Dixie, each in their own way, probably weren't too far apart in what they thought about what was going on in Latin America. "I'm just using their money. And it's a long way from being a corrupt politician to running a 'dirty war' and torturing civilians and dissidents."

"They have blood on their hands, Mack," she replied, the fiery edge clinging to her voice. "In some ways, they're worse than Nazis. They're doing it to their own people, just like in Ethiopia."

McCall looked into her honest blue eyes and knew the truth of what she was saying. He answered her charge patiently. "Paralee, neither of us knows that the people I'm dealing with have anything at all to do with that. Can you give me any proof that they do?" He paused to let her answer, knowing she couldn't. "There's corruption in every country and you're dreaming if you think the world will ever be free of it. It doesn't always come to butchery. Look, that said, I don't disagree with you. But I'm not the World Court and the stakes are different for me. I can stand up all by myself for what's right and good and pure and lose my family's farm, land my ancestors cleared and fought for and cared for. Or I can hold my nose for just a little while and save it. I can do what's right for my family." He shook his head and looked at her with anguished eyes.

"What punishment do you think I could possibly lay on Tovolaro and his buddies to make it come out at least even? Nothing. Not a damned thing. I can't stop them. I can't even hurt them. I can only hurt myself and my family. It's like fighting the FDIC. What they're doing to me is wrong, but

I can't win by fighting them. I just can't. I don't like doing this, but I'm between a rock and a hard place, Paralee."

"OK," she said. "I'm not a little girl wearing rose colored glasses. I see the point, but I don't like it, Mack. I really, really don't like it." She looked at him with older eyes then, seeing him in a different light, hoping that the General and Las Águilas were just thieves, not murderers.

They fell silent, Paralee sitting at the computer, McCall leaning against the door frame. They stared into space, both drained by their emotional outbursts.

Finally, Paralee flicked some keys and McCall heard the printer engage. She took the pages from the printer one by one and handed them to him.

"This is what I did while you were gone," she said. "See what you think."

"This is what I did while you were gone," she said. "See what you think." "It's good," he said when he finished reading. "There's a lot we can leave out for the prospectus, but now that it's all here, that's not a problem." He looked at her, sitting in the chair behind the computer, her hands in her lap, looking small and deflated. "Thanks," he said. "I appreciate it. And I'm sorry about . . . well, everything."

"It's OK. I understand. But I think I'd like to go home now." "Sure. I'll take you, but wait a sec," he said. "What about Thanksgiving? I'm going out to the farm to spend it with my grandfather. You could drop me off and take the car on up to Winchester, pick me up after Thanksgiving. Why not?"

Paralee searched his eyes. "My brothers are probably already home from Tech. I haven't actually told them I'm coming."

"You ought to meet my grandfather," McCall said, hoping to lift the ugly cloud that had fallen over them. "He's a treasure. You'll like him." He took her silence as consent and said, "Take the car back to your place, pack what you need for the holidays and come back here. I'll have the prospectus finished by then. We'll drop it off at FedEx on our way to the Valley."

New York

Chanille was awakened at four o'clock by a call from Colonel Guillermo "Willy" Leuders in Bolivia.

"Señorita, there is something you should know. Two nights ago, our people took into custody a gringa at the train station. She said she was a free-lance writer doing a story on General Garcia Meza's government. All that is ancient history. But she talked to one of Garcia Meza's generals--Hugo Velasco y Llosa--and he asked our people to check her out. Just routine. She had nothing suspicious in her possession, not even notes or tape recordings. The muchachos were about to let her go when the Argentinos came in, you know, the ones who have been helping us. This gringa was very pretty, so they decided to play with her. They all took a turn, then they decided to really interrogate her, just to stay in practice. She talked a lot."

Chanille was awake now and alert. She lit a cigarette and coughed. "OK. Go on."

"OK. Go on."

"Somehow she charmed Velasco y Llosa into telling her about his connections in the United States and how close he was to people in the White House. He even showed her copies of the Condor communications that talked about the arms conduit. Once she started talking, she told them she had also seen documents showing who owned the ship in the harbor at Montevideo. Ryder's name was on the ship's papers."

"Oh, my God."

"She knew about people in Argentina and Bolivia and Panamá and El Salvador and the United States, too."

"What did you do with her, Willy?" Chanille asked.

"After El Gaucho and his young bulls finished with her, they threw her in a cell and drank some more. The day shift found them all borrachos and sound asleep. The gringa was gone. They only called to tell me about this an hour ago."

Chanille lit another Marlboro. She hated the filthy things, but under stress, she just couldn't do without them. "You said she had no notes or tapes. Writers always take notes. I mean always. You'll have to find them. Didn't they ask her what she did with them?"

Leuders' heavily accented voice echoed over the phone. "They found her tape recorder. A little one. There were tapes but no voices. She was seen with a man at the Sucre Palace. Only for a moment, but if she did have notes or documents, she could have passed them off to him."

"Shit, Willy," Chanille said, exasperated. "Have you got a track on him?"

"Another Norteamericano. He was in the country for a very short time and was away from La Paz for two nights. We do not know yet where he went, but we know his name and his address."

"Well, what the hell is it?" Chanille asked, her voice rising angrily. She threw off the covers and sat up. With smoke curling into her eyes and the phone cradled between her shoulder and cheek, she took a pad and pen from her bedside table and prepared to take notes.

"John Cooper McCall. Of course, his passport could be false. He was registered at the Sucre Palace the night he met the woman. He did not have dinner with her, but he paid her check, so there must be a link. He flew from La Paz to Miami on the first flight the next morning. We picked her up yesterday, but I didn't know about him until a few hours ago. I called you as soon as I finished questioning our people."

Chanille scribbled McCall's name on the notepad and took a long drag on her cigarette. "And you put all this out on the SouthCom net? So everybody in the whole damned system knows?"

"Those are our standing orders, Señorita. You know that."

"Yeah, yeah. OK, Willy," she said, sighing. "What else?"

"Nothing else. I will call you if we learn anything new."

Chanille hung up the phone and walked slowly into the bath, trying to find a positive aspect to this bad news. She let her robe slide to the floor and examined her tall, slender body in the wall of mirrors above the two sinks. She cupped her breasts to check their firmness and held in her stomach with the palms of both hands, turning from side to side. She wasn't that scrawny, too-tall girl named Tammy Sue anymore and she was a long way from where she grew up, in the adobe wasteland of Albuquerque where the horizon never went past a new pickup every two years, where life was a case of beer on the weekend and a house trailer full of dirty kids. Smiling in spite of the complications with the conduit, she opened the glass shower door and twisted the taps to release a gush of water from the double nozzles.

****

The sign on the door of the rented offices across the Potomac from Washington said Costa Linda Corp. There was a desk for a receptionist, but it was much too early for her. It was not too early for Sandy Hammond, a veteran of the CIA's war in Laos and a host of other covert ops. He'd done counter-terrorism training in Uruguay and Chile in the 1970s before the massive Reductions-in-Force hit the CIA in the middle and late '70s. A thousand guys like him were whacked in '73 by Jim Schlesinger, Nixon's DCI. Sandy had hung on until the second wave of cuts in 1977 when Carter's DCI, Stansfield Turner, sent another eight hundred covert operatives into the cold, reducing the clandestine service to an ineffectual four hundred. At forty-five, with a wife and two kids in high school, finding work wasn't easy for Sandy Hammond. When the Sandinistas kicked Somoza out of Nicaragua, the old boy network helped him get contract work running arms into Honduras through Secord's pipeline. He moved quickly up the ranks of the CIA's 'secret army' of RIFed veterans of covert ops and his project for the past several months had been laying out an alternate route for weapons shipments to take some strain off the Secord logistics system.

He'd recruited his old buddy from Laos, Rob Ryder, to help. Now the shit had hit the fan before he'd even pulled the switch on the new pipeline. When he saw the SouthCom flash from Bolivia, he knew it was trouble. He got the details that weren't in the flash from Willy Leuders, then woke Danielo Martinez and put him to work checking out John Cooper McCall.

"See if there really is such a guy and if he lives in Alexandria. If he does, see where he goes, what he does and who he does it with," Sandy told Martinez, his feet propped on the desk, a steaming mug of coffee in his fist. "We're looking for documents, Danielo. Notes, tapes, the kind of stuff a journalist would have. ¿Entiendes, compadre? And be quick about it. ¡Rapido! Got it?"

"*Entiendo, Sandy. ¿Es importante, no?*" Martinez answered.

"Bet your ass it's importante. Call me with anything you get. Top priority."

****

While she was waiting for Ryder to arrive, Chanille made half a dozen calls to Washington from the office in the World Trade Center in downtown New York City. Before the close of business, messengers would deliver to her the essential details of John Cooper McCall's life since birth and she could begin to evaluate the possibility that he'd been Angela Collins' drop.

The door of the executive suite flew open, startling her. Ryder, pale and sleek in a camel's hair coat, stormed past her desk.

"Get in here," he commanded, heading directly for his corner office without breaking stride.

He began talking while he was taking off his coat, throwing it carelessly on one of the overstuffed, black leather chairs. "I got a call from Sandy this morning. There's a problem."

"I know. Leuders called me from Bolivia."

Ryder looked up, his patrician face a tight, angry mask. "You first, then."

"According to Leuders, they picked up a woman in La Paz who knew a lot about the conduit. The bad news is that they didn't find any of her notes or tapes or documents. Reporters always have notes but those damned goons didn't know enough to ask her what she did with them." Chanille went on to fill in Ryder about the interrogation and the woman's escape. Then she added, "When they finally got around to calling Willy, he found out that she'd been seen with another American in one of the hotels. She was only with him for a minute, but that's all it takes for a brush pass, you know. He paid her check, so they must have known each other."

"The next thing you're going to tell me is that the guy got away," Ryder said through clenched teeth.

Chanille nodded. "Afraid so. First flight out to Miami. They got a name and address, though. I'm checking it out now. I should have some stuff up from Washington by close of business. That's all I've got. Oh, no. One other thing. Leuders said they passed their info through the SouthCom net."

"That's what Sandy called about. He told us to put the project on hold while he does damage assessment. He's got somebody on McCall, too," Ryder said, his blue eyes spitting icy fire.

A heavy silence fell over the room. Finally, Chanille shrugged. "Should we let the General know?"

Ryder shook his head. "Not yet. We don't know much. Wait until your stuff comes up from Washington."

"What if he already knows? This happened on his turf. I think we ought to touch base," Chanille said. Ryder sighed. "OK. I'll call him. See if you can track down Captain Adamantiades in Montevideo and let him know his sailing orders are going to be on hold a little longer."

****

"Hammond told you to stop?" Tovolaro asked.

"We're just on hold while they evaluate. We're not cancelled. They know we've got six months work in this and a lot of our own money . . ."

"*Las Águilas*' money, Roberto," Tovolaro corrected him.

"Mine, too, General. And my time," Ryder shot back. "I'm not exactly a disinterested party here. I've got expenses, you know, and I'm not doing any loans in Latin America these days with everybody defaulting. If this deal doesn't go, I'm up shit creek without a paddle."

"*Las Águilas* pay you commissions every month, Roberto."

"It doesn't cover my costs, General. Not by a long shot."

Tovolaro didn't continue, but Ryder knew he hadn't hung up because the empty echo of the open line was still there. Finally, Tovolaro spoke again. "There's another matter, Roberto. I have learned that your negotiations in Panamá did not go well. Is that true?"

Ryder was surprised. *'How the hell did Tovolaro know that?'* "Temporary setback. The old man won't sell, so I have to buy up the minority shares and throw the old bastard out."

"I understand there is a reason for his attitude. You raped his daughter. Is that true?"

"I . . . I . . . She was his daughter? Look, General, a woman came on to me," Ryder stammered. "Swimming naked in the pool right under my window. I thought she was part of the hospitality. And for the record, I didn't rape her!"

"She says you did and her father believes her. Roberto, understand that you are our agent and you have not only dishonored us but made acquiring the bank more difficult. I'm very disappointed in you."

"It wasn't my fault, General. Maybe it was even a set-up. Anybody would have thought she was saying 'come and get it.' Look, it won't matter in another month. They'll all be out of there and we'll be in control of the bank."

"Why not forget this bank? I have been told of another that can be acquired for less money and without the kind of difficulty you have made for us with Banco Dorado."

Ryder was pacing around the office, the long phone cord trailing after him. A vein pulsed in his temple as he tried to keep his voice under control. "We can't do that, General. Part of our deal on the arms is to provide banking facilities to support the operation. We promised to be up and running by the end December. We're running out of time. And what would we do about Morales? I've already got his twenty-five percent of Banco Dorado in my pocket."

"No money has changed hands. Let Morales twist in the wind. You can acquire Comercio de Colón in less time for less money--if you can keep your *pico* in your pants."

Ryder swallowed hard and his face turned scarlet with humiliation. "Comercio de Colón?" he choked out.

"It has the same powers and authorities as any Panamanian bank and it is out of the capital city where it will attract less attention."

Ryder ground his teeth and fumed. *One day I'll put a garrote around your neck and cut your head off with it, you little bastard.*

"Roberto?"

"I'm here," Ryder answered, frost on every word. "I don't think you understand, General. I'll have control of Banco Dorado in thirty days. We don't know anything about this other bank. It'll mean starting over."

"Perhaps," Tovolaro said. "But if I let you go ahead with Banco Dorado, there is another matter you will have to handle for us."

"What's that?" Ryder said, his knees going rubbery with relief. Banco Dorado was personal now and he was going to enjoy ripping it up, particularly that smartass Banderas.

"I have obtained information about a settlement of cross-claims between the Russians and the British. We are considering taking a position in the instruments at issue--up to five million dollars."

"Five million," Ryder scoffed. "At what return? Ten percent? Fifteen?"

"Our return on the investment in the Russian opportunity could be fifty million," Tovolaro replied calmly.

"Fifty? Did you say fifty? That's ten times. How can that be?"

"The assets the Soviets will redeem when the settlement occurs can be purchased today for ten percent of their face value. If the settlement is for full face value, that's ten times the current price."

Ryder stared out the window into space, the wheels of his mind turning rapidly. "When is this settlement supposed to take place? And what kind of instruments are you talking about?"

"Soon, we understand. We have been promised a prospectus when we escrow our funds. We will read it and decide whether to release the funds or not. It's a very safe arrangement."

"Who holds the escrow?" Ryder asked, skeptical.

"Bahamas International Trust in Nassau," Tovolaro replied.

"You're sure it's Bahamas International Trust, not some outfit whose name just sounds like that?"

"We aren't children, Roberto."

"Where did you get hold of this?"

"I told you. An old friend."

"You didn't say what kind of claims these are that are being settled."

"Bearer bonds. Gold bearer bonds of the last Tsar."

"The Tsar?" Ryder couldn't suppress a laugh. "Are you kidding? He's been dead for seventy years. His bonds have got to have been in default for . . . well, hell, ever since the Soviets took over."

"Why do you think they are selling for ten instead of ninety-five?" Tovolaro shot back. "It is the inside information that a settlement will take place that makes them a highly profitable investment. Can you imagine their value if the settlement is in gold? The return will be much more than fifty million."

Ryder sighed. 'If these people were left on their own, they'd be broke in a year.' "General, we have an agreement that I advise you on all investments over a million dollars. And my advice to you right now is don't come within a hundred yards of these things. This sounds like a replay of all the old petro-dollar scams. Forget about it. Let's concentrate on the arms deal I have lined up. We've got a twenty-five percent commission on the gross value of the arms, General. Sandy told me to figure on twenty million moving in the next six months. That's five million for us. Meantime I've got a ship sitting in Montevideo harbor with the meter running. Those damned harbor fees are eating me up. I have to pay the crew, too, you know. And the damned Honduran end-user certificates didn't come for free," Ryder added, his voice rising.

"Yes, yes. But your Mr. Hammond has put a cork in your bottle, has he not? Do you think he will take it out this afternoon?"

"There wouldn't have been a cork if your people had the sense to pick up that bimbo in La Paz before she unloaded her information. I understand why Sandy doesn't want the conduit exposed, but what the hell, they keep running stuff through Secord and everybody knows about him. I'm going to talk to Sandy again today and try to get us going."

"In my experience, these things take more than a few hours to start again once they have been stopped," Tovolaro said. "In all the years *Las Águilas* worked with your father, Roberto, we never exposed our fund to these soldier-of-fortune ventures you're so fond of. They make me uncomfortable. You say you want to continue with the acquisition of Banco Dorado. I want to pursue the Russian bonds. If you're not interested in handling them, I may lose interest in arms shipments to Contras and I will have even less interest in owning a Panamanian bank. Do I make myself clear?"

"I didn't say I wouldn't do the bonds, General," Ryder said, rivulets of sweat trickling down his sides, feeling the whole enchilada of the arms deal at risk unless he played this exactly right. "But can't we please hold the decision until we see the prospectus?"

"Very well, Roberto."

****

Sandy Hammond snatched the phone from its cradle before it could ring a second time.

"Hammond," he barked.

"It's Danielo. A person named John Cooper McCall lives at the Alexandria address you gave me. We have it under surveillance. The desk clerk told us what kind of car he drives and I have stationed a man across from the driveway. We will follow him when he leaves."

"Is he in the apartment now?"

"We do not know. The elevator goes directly from the garage to the apartments. I have a man on the roof of the next building with a camera and a long lens. He will tell me if he sees anyone in the windows or on the balcony."

"OK. But you're going to have to get in there. I want those notes and tapes he brought out of La Paz."

"Should we go in now and take the chance?"

"I'd rather you do it nice and neat when nobody's home," Hammond said. "Fewer complications, but I don't want him to get out of there with the stuff. What about hitting him in the parking garage?"

"Are you certain this is the man who was in La Paz?" Martinez asked.

"No. But same name and address, right? You'd think if he had a phony passport it wouldn't check out."

"You are my best client, Sandy, but I don't want to lose my PI license and I don't want to go to jail. If you know for sure, all you have to do is say so. We can take him out. But what if this guy just lost his passport and the one you want is John Doe . . ."

"Yeah, yeah. I hear you. OK. Keep the surveillance on. And get a phone tap working. Go in when he leaves and check it out. Might as well bug the whole damn place while you're at it. I'll see if I can nail down the identification." He smashed the receiver back onto its cradle, but kept his hand on it, deciding whether to call the Project Director or not. If this is the guy and he unloads the information that broad in La Paz got hold of, they might cancel the deal and not a single *pistola* would go through that conduit. Shit! All their work down the tubes and no return on the investment.

Thirty Four
Alexandria

Danielo Martínez posted men at National Airport and BWI and took the watch at Dulles himself. On his earpiece, he was in direct contact with the other members of the team, including Sandy Hammond. There had been some confusion at first about the car because only a woman seemed to drive it. Danielo's source in the Virginia DMV confirmed that the yellow Mercedes was McCall's, but the woman hadn't yet been identified. Her face in the surveillance photographs had so far been obscured by the sunglasses she wore or by reflections off the windshield. And because the elevator provided direct access from the garage to the condominiums, the desk clerk in McCall's building had never seen her and knew nothing about her. Gonzales, Danielo's sentry waiting outside to follow, remained in place because he saw only the woman.

In the crush of passengers arriving and departing for the Thanksgiving holiday, Martínez sat in the waiting area with a picture of John Cooper McCall concealed in a copy of the *Washington Post* and scanned the passengers clearing security in the main terminal. A practiced 'watcher' who enjoyed the game, he visualized McCall's face in all the likely configurations--with a hat, without a hat, with glasses, without glasses, in sports clothes, in coat and tie. He even imagined him in disguise, with a mustache and cotton balls in his cheeks. He was sure he'd spot him, no matter what McCall tried.

Suddenly, Gonzalez' voice crackled in the earpiece, startling him. "They're moving. The guy's wearing a leather jacket and the woman is with him."

Martinez whispered into his lapel microphone, "OK. Stay with them, Gonzalez. Ricardo, you and Flaco hit the apartment. Remember what you're looking for."

A few minutes later, Gonzalez came on the air again. "They're stopping at the Federal Express."

"Send Paco after him. Get the package from the clerk if you can. At least get the address. We can lay on an intercept."

****

McCall jumped out at the Alexandria Federal Express office, addressed and marked the forms for next day delivery, inserted the prospectus into a stiff FedEx envelope, sealed it and gave it to the clerk. He didn't notice the burly Hispanic who followed him in and stayed behind after he left. When he came out, he found Paralee behind the wheel and was amused.

"What's this?" he asked, sliding into the passenger seat. "You getting proprietary about my car?"

"No," she said, frowning. "But I want you to look. Mack, I think somebody's following us. It's one of those new Fords--the ones that look like big jelly beans. The blue one that's double-parked across the street. I saw it at the condo when we left. There were two guys, but one of them followed you into the Federal Express."

McCall turned sideways in the passenger seat to make it appear that he was talking to her while he watched the Ford Taurus from the corner of his eye. He hadn't told Paralee about his meeting with Dixie, so it couldn't be her imagination. The man in the Taurus was holding something to his face, like a microphone. In McCall's opinion, that wasn't a good sign.

"Drive," he said, sensing her tension as she pulled into the street and accelerated away from the Federal Express office. The Taurus waited until they had committed to the right turn lane before it began to move.

Paralee took a slow right then a quick left. Brakes squealed and a horn blasted angrily behind them when the Taurus cut across the oncoming traffic to follow them.

"Shit," McCall said. "Not much doubt about that. Stay on the Beltway until you hit the Dulles road. Maybe he thinks we haven't spotted him. He's still juking and jiving back there, trying to hide in the traffic. There's no place to hide on the Dulles road."

"Why would he care? If you're on the Dulles Road, he knows where you're going," Paralee said, a nervous edge to her voice.

"What's our choice? We could keep driving around the Beltway and hope he runs out of gas before we do. I'll see if I can lose him in the airport. It's not much out of the way to the Valley. Drop me off at the departures level, I'll go through the main terminal security, change clothes in the men's room and slip back out. If this guy really is following us, I don't think he'll expect that."

"What are you going to do with your baggage?"

"Take it with me. All I've got is my small duffel and a hanging bag. It'll look like carryon stuff."

"What do I do about the guy in the Ford?"

"Maybe he'll drop off once we're on the Dulles Road. If he does, just come around the loop and pick me up again on the lower level. If he sticks with you, go back to the condo and barricade the door. I'll hide out in the Clipper Club and call you in a couple of hours. Maybe I'll have an idea by then."

"Why are we being followed, Mack?" Paralee asked, her eyes flicking nervously between the traffic ahead and the mirror.

"Probably the General checking me out. I don't know why, but they sure got organized awfully fast. I am asking them to trust me with five million bucks."

They rode in silence for another twenty minutes before Paralee moved into the left lane to exit onto the Dulles Road.

"Mack," she said. "He didn't follow us. What do you think?"

"It means they've got the airport covered and he's just radioed in that we're on the way."

****

Fifteen minutes after being notified that McCall and the woman had turned onto the Dulles Road, Martinez spotted McCall in the line to pass through security. It wasn't good that he'd stopped at Federal Express. The notes might already be on their way to press if Paco wasn't able to bribe or bully the clerk into giving him the package.

Martinez whispered into his lapel microphone. "Patch me through to Hammond." He waited anxiously, watching the line with McCall in it inch forward. Finally, Hammond answered. "Sandy," Martinez said. "He's at the airport. We're going to lose him."

"It's the right guy, Danielo," Hammond replied. "We got the stubs from the plane tickets. He was in La Paz. But the apartment's clean and the stuff he dropped off at the FedEx was headed for the Bahamas. Whatever it is, maybe he has it on him."

"Then I'm going to take him here," Martinez said.

"Go for it. But keep it smooth."

Martinez slipped the photo of McCall into his coat pocket, folded the newspaper he'd been reading and dropped it in the seat beside him. He got into line three people behind McCall. He watched McCall put his duffel and hanging bag on the conveyer for the x-ray machine, drop his coins in the plastic container and pass through the scanner. Martinez saw him collect his change and bags and move away toward the transporters that ferried passengers to the mid-field terminal. The man in front of Martinez had boots with metal arch supports in them and the security people made him take them off. In the delay, he lost sight of McCall.

Finally, it was Martinez' turn. He reached behind him to remove the snub-nosed .38 revolver from its holster. He held up his PI credentials in his left hand and slowly laid the pistol on top of the scanner column.

"Gun! Gun!" the young security woman screamed when she saw the weapon. Two massive black security guards seized the diminutive Martinez and slammed him to the floor, jerking his arms up behind him. Someone's enormous knee bored into the base of his spine and a large, meaty hand pressed his face into the hard, cold floor of Dulles International.

****

McCall ducked into a stall in the first men's room he found inside the secure area and exchanged his khakis, turtleneck and leather jacket for gray flannel slacks and a plaid shirt. For good measure, he pulled on an orange and blue stocking cap with a Chicago Bears logo. It wasn't much of a disguise, but he waited for one of the shuttles from the mid-field terminal to disgorge its passengers and blended into the throng. He followed the deplaning passengers down the escalator to the baggage claim level and headed straight for the exit. Outside in the dusk, he found Paralee waiting in the little two-seater Mercedes, three cars down, engine running. He slipped into the passenger seat and told her to go.

She worked her way onto Route 28 and flew south toward I-66. McCall looked through the rear window often to see if they were being followed.

"I'm no expert at this," he said as they approached the on-ramp for I-66. "But I don't think there's anybody behind us. Go onto 66 and air it out. We'll separate the men from the boys or get a very expensive speeding ticket."

"Hang on. Here we go!" Paralee said, the adrenalin surging with the excitement of a chase, real or imagined. She roared onto the Interstate and kept her foot flat on the floor until the speedometer needle moved up to a hundred. Eyes firmly fixed on the road ahead and her knuckles white against the steering wheel, she asked, "Anything keeping up with us?"

"No. You can back off now."

"Do I have to?"

"Yes."

Reluctantly, she brought the Mercedes down to seventy-five and they cruised through the Virginia countryside as the setting sun painted the sky with the blues and purples of late autumn. "Mack, that guy following us. And the business at the airport. Please tell me it's OK."

"It's OK."

"You've got to do better than that," she begged.

"It's creepy."

"Ignore it. At least for the holiday. Whoever it is thinks I'm on my way somewhere. We've lost the tail and I can't believe they'd know about my grandfather's farm."

****

"Where the hell did he go?" Hammond demanded. "You just let him disappear?"

"You promised me US Marshall's credentials a month ago. The damned woman at security freaked out when she saw my pistol. I've got a cut on my cheek and a dislocated shoulder. They were going to throw me in jail."

"I'm sorry, Danielo. I guess we blew it."

"I checked the flights ¾ nothing but international departures. Hes headed out of the country, Martinez said. Maybe thats good.

"Yeah, maybe," Hammond conceded. "At least he's not heading for the *Washington Post*. It's OK, Danielo. Come on in. We bugged the phones and the condo, so maybe we'll get something from the taps."

The Shenandoah Valley: Thanksgiving

Paralee hadn't decided what she'd say if Josh forgot his promise not to tell Mack that she'd been there. For the moment, she'd have faith that her visit would remain a secret, but her heart beat faster when the Mercedes' tires crunched on the gravel drive leading up to the house.

The lights were on in the library and McCall bounded out of the car and up the steps onto the porch. Paralee followed him at a distance, coming up beside him at the door as he was pushing the bell. They saw Josh's silhouette behind the cut glass door a moment before the porch light came on. Paralee held her breath as the door opened.

"Hey, Pa," McCall said, gathering the old man up in his arms and giving him a hug. When Josh looked over Mack's shoulder at her, she put a forefinger to her lips, her eyes pleading, hoping he'd remember.

"Well," Josh said when McCall released him. "This is a surprise. Come in, come in. Who's your friend?" Paralee let her eyelids close for a moment in silent thanks, then put on her brightest face. "This is Paralee Campbell, Pa," McCall said, putting an arm around her shoulders and drawing her into the living room. "Paralee, this is my grandfather, Joshua Cooper. Paralee and I have been working on a project together." "Well, come on in here, Miss Paralee, and let me look at you," Josh said. Paralee separated herself from McCall and gave Josh a shy pirouette. The old man laughed and they laughed with him. "Yessiree!" he said. "You're a pretty woman. Now Miss Paralee, you just make yourself at home. I've had my dinner, but what about you two?" He closed the door and steered them toward the library.

"We stopped at the chicken place in Front Royal, Pa. Not to worry. But I think we could both use a drink."

"Well, you know where it is. Same place as last time." To Paralee, he added, "I keep it for snake bite and special occasions." He called to Mack, already in the kitchen, "I'm going to show Miss Paralee the library. You take your time." He turned to Paralee with a twinkle in his eye. "So . . . nice to see you again."

"Thanks for not saying anything," she told him, taking his arm and finding it surprisingly frail for someone she thought of as so vital.

"That's all right. It won't hurt if you know a little something about him that he might not tell you on his own."

She followed him into the library where they had spent the afternoon before. She took in the books lining the walls from floor to ceiling with fond remembrance. The lamp on Josh's reading table was the only illumination in the room and the volumes, standing like faithful sentinels waiting to be called to duty, were barely visible.

Her eyes drifted around the room, saying hello again to the worn leather sofa and the wing chair, to the spindly, glass-topped display case that held some of the family's memorabilia--a Revolutionary War bayonet, a half-dozen encrusted bullets and several silver buttons from an officer's tunic. Josh had apparently been reading when they came, for a book was open on the table and his pipe smoldered in an ash tray beside it.

She'd never known either of her own grandfathers and Josh filled a space that she'd barely known existed before she met him. Whatever happened between her and Mack, she resolved to keep him as her friend, to drink coffee with him in the sun room and share his thoughts here in this library as often as she could.

McCall returned with three tumblers and a dusty bottle of Maker's Mark.

"Scotch?" Paralee asked, resenting Mack for a moment for intruding.

"Oh, no, my dear," Josh said. "This is Kentucky straight Bourbon sippin' whiskey, a hand-made American confection. Now make sure we don't lose any of that fine whiskey to evaporation, son. I don't drink alone and since I've got company, I want to make the most of it."

Josh sipped one small drink slowly and chatted with Mack and Paralee for almost an hour before he excused himself to retire to the master bedroom adjoining the library.

When Josh's door closed, McCall looked at Paralee and smiled. "He's a treasure, isn't he?"

The warmth of Josh's presence and his obvious pleasure in their company thawed the frostiness that their argument over McCall's investors had created. Relaxed, Paralee sat in an old high-backed leather chair with her legs tucked under her. McCall walked along the bookshelves, running his fingers across the spines of the books. "This isn't a very big library, but Pa seems to have pulled everything into it that really matters. He never went to school either. College, I mean."

"College isn't the answer to everything."

"No," McCall said, appraising her in the soft lamp light. "No, it isn't." They were silent for a moment, looking at each other. "It's getting late. Why don't you stay here tonight and go over to Winchester in the morning?"

"Mack . . . ," she said, lowering her eyes and then meeting his gaze. "A lot's been happening. That night at your place, the storm and all. I wasn't thinking. And now the General . . . and people following us . . ."

He came away from the bookshelves and knelt beside her chair. He put one hand on her knee and looked up into her blue eyes. "Driving up to Winchester in the middle of the night won't change any of that. There are three bedrooms upstairs--mine, my mother's and a guest room--in that order. There are even two baths. Take the guest room. I dusted in there awhile back, but you might want to put on fresh sheets. I know you don't attach much value to my word, but I assure you that your virtue is safe tonight."

"Is your grandfather a light sleeper?" she asked.

"The guest quarters are right over his room. I imagine he'd wake up if you put up a fuss about anything."

She made a show of giving the proposition serious thought, then said, "OK. I'll stay and leave first thing in the morning."

Upstairs in his room, McCall closed the door, undressed and turned off the light. He burrowed into the covers of his boyhood bed, every muscle heavy with sleep. But Angela Collins intruded. If she was still in Bolivia . . . He shouldn't have let her get away like that. Her note all but told him she wanted him to come after her. And he would have if she'd been in the hotel. But she wasn't. *What the hell was I supposed to do?'* he asked himself, trying to push away the guilty feeling.

Georgetown

Beneath the quilts in the four-poster bed, Dixie Davenport stared at the crown molding in the firelight and struggled with the decision. Kurt's breathing had already become regular and she knew he would soon be asleep. If she were going to talk to him, it would have to be now. She moved her hip against him, hard, so that he had to change positions.

"Kurt," she said, louder than for ordinary pillow talk. She wanted his full attention.

"What's the matter, biscuit?" he asked, his voice thick with sleep.

"I need to talk."

He groaned and turned toward her. "Wait until morning?"

Dixie propped herself up on one elbow, pulling the cover away from his shoulder. "It won't wait. Wake up, Kurt. Please." She saw his eyes open and knew she had his attention. "Kurt, we've always kept our promise not to talk shop, but I'm scared and I really need to talk about this."

"OK," he said, now fully awake. "Want me to get the cognac? We could get up and sit by the fire."

"I can think just as well here."

"Then go ahead. I'm listening."

"Something really bad is going on. Something like Watergate. The Administration is lying to us about this Contra business. Every administration lies a little, but this has gone a lot farther than that. I'm pretty sure they're breaking the law in a very big way."

"This isn't about the wine we had for dinner tonight, is it? I'm sure I only gave you two glasses."

"I'm not snockered, Kurt. Do you remember Angela Collins from the Fitzgeralds' party? We met a couple of days later in my office and she told me what she was working on--a story about arms shipments to the Contras."

"There's nothing new in that. We know they're getting weaponry from the Israelis and who knows where else. It's a sorry business, but it's par for the course in guerrilla warfare."

"Kurt, she thinks the arms shipments to the Contras are being coordinated out of the White House--the National Security Council--in direct violation of the Boland Amendment. I didn't take her too seriously at the time. Ever since Watergate, reporters think they have to make their bones by bringing down some icon. She's not like that and I agreed to help her. She went to South America for a couple of weeks but she was finished, leaving

Bolivia to come home with a lot of good stuff. Then she dropped out of sight. Didn't make the train she was supposed to take and didn't show up in Arica. I made some calls, got the embassy working on it. Nothing. We can't find a hotel record for her and she wasn't reported in custody by the Bolivian government. No hospital. No nothing. She just vanished. I hate like hell to use the word, but she's *desaparecida*."

"How do you know she was in Bolivia?"

"I got her stuff this morning, from another guy who was at the Fitzgeralds' party--Jack McCall."

"I know McCall," Kurt said.

"It turned out he was in Bolivia and when Angela called in, I told her where he was. She made contact and was smart enough to pass off her notes and some tapes from her interviews and research in South America to him to bring back. I'm having them translated now. My Spanish isn't good enough to evaluate what's on them. But I know enough to get the general drift. The short and sweet of it is that they're going to start sending guns and ammo through Cape Town to Buenos Aires, more of that stuff the Israelis captured in their invasion of Lebanon, so it's East bloc and not traceable to the US. They've got a ship standing by in Montevideo. I guess they're going to use it to bring cargo from Cape Town. Southern Air Transport, that old CIA airline they spun off a few years ago, is going to fly the cargo from Buenos Aires or Montevideo to Panamá. Another ship is set to take it up the Pacific coast to a port in Honduras."

"Except that they're moving the stuff a different way, what's so special?"

"Angela has a source--a 'Deep Throat'--really, really close to the operation. I don't know if it's White House or CIA, but she says we sold Hawk antiaircraft missiles to Iran this month and I can promise you *that* hasn't been reported to Congress. By law it has to be reported as a sale by the US, if that's what it was. If Israel sold them to Iran--with some under-the-table agreement from us to replace their stocks--it's a violation of the Arms Export Control Act. That hasn't been reported either. But here's the killer. Angela's source says that the Iranians are going to be charged something like nineteen million dollars for Hawks that cost three million. Twelve million is going to be siphoned off to buy arms for the Contras. That's how they're going to circumvent the Boland Amendment. Twelve million, Kurt. The Iranians will pay nineteen million, but the Defense Department will only get three million for the Hawks. Four million is going into people's pockets. It's more illegal than sin and they know it. They're lying to Congress about what they're doing."

"How high do you think it goes?"

"You mean as in 'what did he know and when did he know it?' That kind of high up?”

“That’s what I meant.”

“There’s probably a firewall, but I have the feeling it goes awfully close to the top. Angela’s source says some Marine colonel or major named Oliver North is running the operation out of the National Security Council. The White House! Can you believe it? And Poindexter--Reagan’s National Security Adviser--knows all about it. How close do you want to get?”

A log collapsed into the coals and threw up a shower of sparks.

Kurt didn’t answer and Dixie went on. “I’m afraid Angela’s been killed. If I’m right, her murder will never go to court in this country, but it will be on my conscience, like the ones who are dying in Nicaragua because of what some people in our own government are doing illegally. Kurt, we’ve got to stop this.”

Kurt was silent for a long moment. Finally, he said, “You wouldn’t tell me this if you weren’t pretty sure of your information, right?”

“Do I have to answer that?”

“I’ll pass it on,” Kurt replied. “The Secretary has some suspicions of his own. Maybe this fits. What will happen after that, I don’t know.”

New York

"Who did you say?" Ryder asked, rising from his chair and rounding the desk to come toward Chanille, standing in the center of the large oriental carpet.

"McCall. The guy's name is John Cooper McCall. She flipped through the stack of paper she was holding, found a five-by-eight photograph and passed it to Ryder. "This isn't exactly his college photo, but . . ."

Ryder took the photograph and stared at it. "Hmmm."

"Do you want what I've got?" Chanille asked.

Ryder snapped back into focus and stared at Chanille. "Might as well."

"I've been talking to Sandy Hammond. This could definitely be the guy. They tossed his apartment and found airline ticket stubs. He was in La Paz at the right time. But no notes or documents. Sandy had a tail on him, but he managed to get something into Federal Express and it's gone--to Bahamas International Trust Company in Nassau. Probably the stuff we want. Then they lost him at the airport. Who knows why the Bahamas--maybe he's got a safe deposit box down there. Anyway . . . " Chanille turned the pages of her notebook and looked up at Ryder. "This is the background material I got out of Washington. You interested in that?"

"Go ahead," Ryder said, one leg thrown over the black leather chair. He inspected his fingernails and picked at them idly.

"OK. I'll just hit the high points. Stop me if you want me to elaborate." Ryder nodded and Chanille went on. "Grew up in Mt. Jackson, Virginia. BA from James Madison. Viet vet. Decorated. DFC. A reprimand, too. No court martial, but he resigned his commission. PhD in economics from the University of Texas after he left the service. Freelance consulting. Third World mostly. Divorced. Bought a bank in Texas a few years ago. It just went belly up. He's back in Washington, consulting again. His last three gigs were Jordan, Egypt and Vienna. Jordan and Egypt were for an AID contractor, but the Vienna job was for an outfit that straddles the Iron Curtain, you know, East-West communications, all that *détente* bullshit."

"What's it called?" His interest perking up.

"Magyar Enterprises. They organize conferences." Chanille moved to one of the overstuffed leather chairs and rested her buns against its back. "Those things are just job fairs--spies and spymasters, secrets bought and sold, commercial as well as military."

"Any idea how this guy got hooked up with them?"

"Nope," she said. "He gave a series of lectures on global finance. Everybody got their pictures taken, but nothing special showed up. I mean, what kind of secrets could he have? He gave a couple of late-night tutorials to a very snazzy *fraulein* from the seminar, but she checked out. She wasn't Stasi, KGB, STB or any of the others. Just a grad student at a university in Koblenz. Nobody vetted her, of course, but . . . Want to know about the bank?"

"Why not?"

"First Mission National. A little bank in San Antonio. The guy who'd run it for years died suddenly and McCall took it over himself. He was aggressive in a booming market, but too aggressive, it turns out. The Mexicans devalued, oil prices cratered and so did his bank. Seems to be a common occurrence down there these days. A big shakeout going on. FDIC didn't liquidate. They have some toadstools keeping the doors open. They'll clean up the portfolio as much as they can and then sell it to another bank. That's pretty standard. I mean, McCall didn't do anything criminal. Apparently the bank had good investments. It was the loan portfolio that took it down."

"Wasn't that bank on the RTC list? A lot of international stuff, but Africa and Asia, not Latin America. I think I remember it."

"Want me to get the file? There's a full report from the FDIC if you want to read it."

"No. I'm more interested in his link to that spook fair in Vienna. You think it's a coincidence that he shows up as a cut out for information that'll torpedo our arms deal?"

Chanille shrugged. "Could be, I guess, but the deed's been done. Nothing more we can do but wait for Sandy. And he's waiting to see if there's a story in the *Washington Post*. He figures they're just checking it out before they go into print. If we haven't seen anything in a week or so, he said he might take the hold off."

"A week," Ryder said. "It'll seem like a bloody year and the damned documents will still be out there. You think there's anything in them that would be serious trouble for us?"

"You mean like getting tangled up in Congressional investigations? Like losing your seat on the Exchange? Like criminal charges? Like spending a fortune on lawyers? Like . . . I don't know. Isn't that enough? Yeah, I imagine whatever that gal had could make your life hell for awhile. Might even get you an all-expense trip to that Club Fed over in Allenwood and a long-term lease on one of their condos. Even if Sandy gives us a green light, I'd sure be concerned about those tapes and documents. Whoever has that stuff is holding your balls in his hand. If he squeezes, it'll hurt."

Panamá City

Carlotta stormed past the secretary and threw open the door to Javier's office.

"You told me they were not going to try to buy the bank, that your friend had stopped them."

"That's what he told me," Javier said, looking up from his desk in surprise.

"It isn't true," she said. "Maria Fuentes and Elena Ardita just told me their families have sold their shares."

Javier stared at her, trying to assess what the sale of two small holdings meant. "And you think it was Ryder who bought them?"

"No. It was a lawyer. José Fernandez."

"Then you don't know it was Ryder."

"José Fernandez is Morales' lawyer. Do two and two make four?" Carlotta stood in front of his desk, one fist knotted at her hip. She was dressed in a white suit with a tight skirt and a silk scarf at her throat, her bright red lipstick a grim gash across her mouth, her teeth clenched.

Javier fell back in his chair and stared at her. At last, he said, "I don't understand."

Carlotta's stony stare began to crumble. First, her lower lip trembled. She clenched her jaws, but a tear trickled from one eye, tracing a line of mascara down her cheek. Finally, she burst into tears, throwing both hands over her face.

Javier sprang out of his chair and went to her.

"Now, now, Carlotta. Don't cry." He took her by the shoulders and eased her into one of the leather club chairs in front of his desk. "Let me get you some water. Concepción!" he called out to his secretary. "Bring a glass of water for the *señorita*."

Elbows on her knees, hands covering her face, Carlotta sobbed while Javier knelt beside her, completely at a loss about what to do to comfort her.

Concepción took over, consoling Carlotta with little pats and whispers. "*Ay, pobrecita. No le preocupe. Todo estará bien. Estoy seguro.*"

Slowly Carlotta's sobs subsided and Concepción took her away to the ladies room to repair the damage.

Javier breathed a sigh of relief. Dealing with weeping women was not among his interpersonal skills. The problem she presented was not going to go away so easily, though. Obviously, Mack had failed--*Las Águilas* and Ryder had double-crossed him. Javier didn't doubt Mack's word. Mack believed he had an agreement. They just weren't going to honor it. They were going to buy up Banco Dorado anyway and the Fuentes and Ardita families were the first ripe fruit to fall from the tree. Together, he thought they held perhaps three percent of the shares. So with Morales' shares, Ryder and *Las Águilas* now controlled twenty-eight percent of the bank. How long would it take them to corner another twenty-three percent once the word got out that there was a buyer for Banco Dorado stock?

Still sniffling, her face washed clean of makeup, Carlotta returned to his office and sat down. Concepción closed the door and left them.

Carlotta looked up at Javier, eyes wide and glistening. "What can we do?"

"My friend, McCall, . . ."

"I do not want to hear his name," Carlotta shot back, her cheeks suddenly flushing with anger. "He lied to us."

"No, no. I'm sure he has been betrayed by Ryder and his friends. This isn't his fault."

"You may think that if you want, but he has no stake in what happens to us. We have to defend the bank ourselves."

Javier almost told her about McCall's share in the bank then, that Mack had as much to lose as anyone if the bank were taken over, but he stopped himself. With Carlotta's mind so set against him at the moment, he could wait. But he was reminded of Mack's idea of buying the Russian bonds and hoping that the settlement came in time for them to use their profits to fight the takeover. It was a wild scheme, even now, but it was no longer unthinkable.

"The only way to defend ourselves is to bid for the minority shares ourselves, but we don't have the cash. And I only know of one investment that might give us a high enough return to be competitive. It's risky beyond belief."

"Tell me," Carlotta said, brightening and sitting up straighter in her chair.

"The gold bonds of the last Tsar."

"Gold bonds? The last Tsar? Do you mean the Tsar of Russia?"

Javier nodded, his face a somber mask. Slowly, he told her about the bonds, the settlement with the British that was coming, the chance that the bonds would be redeemed in gold and the ridiculously low price the bonds were selling for on the London exchange.

Carlotta's mouth opened slightly as the tale unfolded and it took her a few moments to digest what Javier had told her when he had finished.

"You said we had no cash. How would you buy these bonds?"

"The only way is to liquidate as much of our investment portfolio as we dare. The bank will lose the income from these securities, but if we lose the bank, that will not be our problem, it will be Ryder's and *Las Águilas'* problem. There's another matter. I don't have the authority to take such actions. I need the approval of our board of directors and pigs will fly before they would approve such a gamble. If we are to do this, we will have to do it quite illegally."

"I am Don Francisco's daughter," Carlotta said, drawing herself up and projecting her chin. "I authorize you to do this."

Javier laughed in spite of himself. "Even Don Francisco himself would not do this without the approval of the board."

Undaunted, her cheeks flushed, Carlotta bristled. "Then we will not tell them."

"If I do this, I will never find another job in banking," Javier said.

"That will not be necessary. I will make you my personal financial adviser," Carlotta said, then softened. "Please, Javier. There is no other way."

They stared at each other for a long moment. Javier felt almost giddy, thinking McCall would be proud of him for even considering such a scheme. Suddenly, Carlotta's expression changed.

"No!" she said. "Wait. There is another way. We can take options on the bonds. It will spread our resources greatly and you won't have to sell the bank's investments."

"Options?"

Carlotta sat forward on the edge of her seat, her eyes flashing. "An option gives you the right to buy or sell something at an agreed price during a period of time, usually six months," she began. "The price of the option is the premium you pay to remove the uncertainty of the future. Like insurance. I had a whole semester on futures and options in Switzerland. There are two kinds of options. You have a 'put' option if you agree with someone to *sell* him a security at a particular price. That is called the 'strike' price. You have a 'call' option if you have the right to *buy* a security at an agreed price. Put to sell, call to buy. We will want call options on the Russian bonds. And maybe only for three months. If the settlement doesn't take place by then, we will be finished anyway."

Javier sat quietly for a few moments, then leaned forward in his chair, elbows on his knees. "Let me see if I understand. We know of securities whose price will rise a great deal in the future. And no one else knows about it. If we had the money, we would buy the security and hold it. But we do not have the money. So are you saying that we can buy a 'call' option to buy the security at the low price, even after the price rises in the future?"

"Exactly," Carlotta said. "And the price of the option will be very much less than the price of the security. That's the beauty of it."

"But we have to buy the security at some point, don't we? And what if we never buy it?"

"Yes, of course, if you exercise the option, you have to buy it, but you have the right to buy it at the low price. Then you can sell it right away for the higher price and pay off the one who sold you the option to buy his securities. Securities dealers take care of such things."

"And if we never buy the securities?"

Carlotta shrugged. "Then we lose what we paid for the options. But it is a very small price."

"How small?" Javier persisted, skeptical, but hopeful that he could avoid liquidating the bank's investment portfolio.

"It depends, but quite small relative to the value of the security."

"Then perhaps we have a way to defend the bank," Javier said, a wide grin emerging from beneath his bushy mustache. He practically leaped from his chair and began to walk around the room. "I know just who to call."

****

Charles Foster was taking his afternoon cup of Broken Orange Pekoe and idly turning the pages of *The Economist* when Margaret appeared in the doorway and cleared her throat. He looked up.

"Yes, Margaret? What is it?"

"A call from Panamá, Mr. Foster. A Mr. Banderas. Would you care to take it?"   Foster nodded and picked up the receiver on his desk.

"Mr. Banderas. How nice to hear from you. . . . Yes. Oh? Ninety-day options? Hmmm. To my knowledge, it's never been done with Russian bonds. And I must say I'd be very cautious here if I were you. You do realize that you're taking a highly speculative position here, don't you? . . . You're sure then? . . . Yes, I understand. I'll let you know."

Foster replaced the receiver and shook his head. '*This will be a challenge.*'

He picked up the telephone again and called his son.

"Roddy, see if you can get a quote on ninety-day options to buy those Russian bonds. . . . Yes. If you can find anyone willing, commit up to one hundred thousand US for Banco Dorado. . . . No, nothing for *my* account at the moment. But let me know how it plays. Thank you, my boy."

The Shenandoah Valley

"Let's go up to the orchard," Josh said after he and McCall had watched Paralee take the little Mercedes down the gravel drive, turn onto the road and disappear beyond the trees. Josh took out his tobacco pouch, tamped a load into the bowl of his pipe and lit it. McCall caught a whiff of the sweet smoke before it drifted away on the wind.

Josh set a leisurely pace, his hands clasped behind him, the pipe clenched in his teeth. "I've been thinking about you a good bit since you were down here a couple of weeks ago," he told Mack. "I know you feel like you're starting over. But you ought to remember it isn't the first time that's ever happened in this family. Can you imagine how Thomas Cooper felt, looking at this place after old Sheridan's boys put the torch to it? That couldn't have been easy. Thomas spent most of the rest of his life rebuilding what it took them about an hour to burn down. Thomas stood his ground and shot a couple of those troopers before that Yankee lieutenant rode him down. It's a miracle he didn't bleed to death on the spot. He would have if his wife, Nancy, hadn't run back in the house and grabbed a hot poker from the kitchen. House burning and everything. She cauterized that arm right there on the spot with the Yankees watching her. Burned her own hand something fierce and set her apron on fire. They were a pair to be proud of."

"I know the story. I used to think it was an act of heroism beyond anything I could imagine," McCall said. "Both of them."

"I guess it was," Josh said.

"Maybe I'd understand it better if I'd done my fighting on the ground. Flying jets . . . it's not personal. But to stand there alone in front of a company of soldiers and attack them . . . They say that great acts of heroism are like out-of-body experiences. Some kind of insanity takes over. I never got that crazy when I was flying in 'Nam. And I don't think my father was crazy when he went down to strafe those Germans. He was just doing his job."

"Well, I don't suppose it was that way with old Thomas," Josh said as they continued toward the apple orchard. Josh puffed on his pipe, leaving a trail of smoke behind him. "You and I and your dad were fighting a long way away from home and the threat to our families was just some intellectual thing. Your dad didn't expect a German tank to pull up in the yard here. And I don't imagine you thought there was much chance of the Viet Cong cooking rice in our kitchen. But for Thomas, those damn Yankees were tromping on his corn field, violating his property . . . no, worse than that. They were profaning what was his. I imagine he had a fury that brought blood to his eyes. I don't think he stood out there intending to die."

"So it *was* a kind of insanity that took hold of him," McCall said. "He could have taken the family up into the woods and let them have the damned place. He was going to have to build it back anyway."

Josh shook his head. "I don't know that he could have run. We don't all of us get the chance to prove to ourselves where it is we draw the line. I never had to face anything like Thomas did. Maybe you never have, either."

"I never had a bunch of Yankees standing in my yard."

Josh laughed. "Me, either. But Thomas standing up to the Yankees in this yard wasn't what took courage. It was rebuilding this place. He didn't have much but the land and the timber and the stones to work with. He had to wake up every morning and face that awesome task. Seems to me there must have been a lot of times when he would have wanted to give up, but he didn't. That's why this place is still here for us. It's been our safe haven from the time the first Joshua Cooper cleared the forest and fought off the Indians. It's your safe haven, too, my boy. And it's not like those corn and wheat farms out West, always blowing away when the rains don't come."

They reached the apple orchard, where McCall could see that the harvest was about half finished.

"Pick a few of those Yorkies," Josh said. "We'll make ourselves a cobbler for Thanksgiving."

"How many will we need?"

"Half a dozen. Ten maybe. We'll put some in the turkey stuffing. Might want to pick a few of those Arkansas Blacks, too. The Pippins and the Jonathans are already up in the barn."

McCall began picking the best of the Yorks, slipping them into the space between his shirt and his leather flight jacket. As he moved among the trees, he mulled over what Josh had said about the farm being a safe haven and it being *his* safe haven.

How could that be, he wondered. He'd never done anything to deserve a place like this. Worse than that, he'd put two hundred years of history in jeopardy by pissing away Josh's money in First Mission. If they lost the farm to that chubby little pissant, Bob Fitch . . . Why the hell did he ever let Sam talk him into buying First Mission in the first place? And Pa approved his moving down to Texas to take it over. Did that mean he *didn't* want him to have the farm and it was just his way of . . .? And now he was saying the farm was McCall's safe haven, just like he was one of the family. It was time to ask.

"Pa," McCall said. "I hope you don't misunderstand this. You put a big mortgage on this farm to help me buy the bank, like you wanted me to move on. You didn't tell me what you were doing at the time, or really why."

"I wanted you to have something of your own. I was thinking about what was best for you at the time, thinking you'd always have the farm. I always wondered how your dad would have felt about it if he'd come back from the war. He was a proud man and he had a touch of wanderlust in him that Cassie never saw," Josh added. "The farm might've been a problem for him when he was trying to be his own man. Maybe it's some kind of problem for you, too. I watched you grow up, and I know you're dead set on proving yourself on your own terms. I didn't think you'd want this farm handed to you on a platter, any more than your dad would have."

Josh shook his head and smiled. "Damn shame it didn't work out better down there in Texas. Now we've both got our tits in a wringer. I know banks failed in the Great Depression in the nineteen-thirties, but I thought we fixed all that and I never imagined if I helped you buy a bank that we'd have to face a problem like this. If things had gone well for you in Texas, you'd have been able to pay off the loan and you could have kept the farm until you needed it. Malcolm Birney would have taken good care of it in the meantime."

McCall reached out for an apple, judging its ripeness by the ease with which it came into his hand. He'd always liked the apple orchard, the picking and the cider pressing. He tossed the apple in the air, caught it, tossed it again and caught it before he spoke. "I'm sorry I didn't pull it off, Pa."

"Well you need to remember that fellow Lindbergh, the first one to fly across the Atlantic Ocean. He said a life without risk wasn't worth the living. Or maybe that was Hemingway. Sounds like Hemingway. You've always had the courage to try. That counts for a lot in a man's life. What counts for more is not giving up. You see this apple orchard here? The first bunch of trees I planted got the fire blight and they all died. I dug 'em up and burned them right where they fell and planted some more. *They* would hardly grow at all and didn't produce any fruit worth picking. So I dug them up, too. I let the land lie fallow for a few years and little by little, started putting in some different varieties. All this was before you were born, so I guess I never told you about all the trouble I had. Well, anyway, I got hold of a Jonathan that did pretty well. Then I tried some Arkansas Blacks and they did fine, too. Had the devil of a time finding any Pippins that would grow, but I finally did. The Yorks came last and I think they're my favorites. This orchard didn't come easy to hand, son. I wanted apples and I wasn't going to give up until I got them. My working up this apple orchard doesn't amount to a hill of beans compared to what old Thomas did, but it's still something I had to stick to. That's what you need to be about, son."

****

Josh had gone to bed and Mack was nursing a tumbler of Maker's Mark by the fire in the library when the phone rang. It was Angela.

"Angela! Where the hell are you?"

"I'm in the airport in São Paulo." "São Paulo? Are you OK? Dixie said . . ."

"It's been a rough go. But I'm OK. I've got a flight to London, boarding in a few minutes. I just wanted to touch base and thank you for getting those documents out for me. I'm sorry if I put you in harm's way."

"What happened?"

"Got picked up by the Security police. They interrogated me, but didn't find anything, thanks to you."

"So they let you go?"

"Yeah. Sort of. I walked out while they were sleeping."

"How'd you get out of La Paz? How'd you get to São Paulo?"

"They left my purse out, so I had money and my passport. I bought a poncho and a hat and bummed a ride in a vegetable truck out of La Paz. Just kept bumming rides all the way across Brazil. Let me tell you there a lot of shitty little towns between San Matías and São Paulo."

"How'd you get across the border?"

"Money, Honey. Almost all I had. Look, they're calling the flight. I just wanted to say thanks--for everything. For being my friend and . . . well, you know. Keep the engine running. I'll see you down the road some day."

"Wait a minute, damn it! Don't just . . . Does Dixie know you're back?"

"I called her. She gave me your number. Where are you anyway? I didn't recognize the area code."

"My grandfather's. In the Shenandoah. Where are you going to be in London? I might be there in a bit."

"Just passing through. Heathrow for a few hours. That's all. The story's in Cape Town. Gotta go. Love you!"

McCall put down the phone and fell back in the chair, swamped by conflicting emotions. She was safe--for the moment. They'd have a contract out on her. She wouldn't be able to walk around Cape Town like some tourist. They'd be looking for her. Maybe he would see her down the road. But maybe not. They had so much history. Would there ever be another chapter?

Winchester

When Paralee pulled into the driveway in Winchester, her dad and two brothers were playing three-cornered catch with a football in the front yard. They stopped and stared when the little Mercedes turned into the drive.

When they saw Paralee get out, they drifted over, admiring the car.

"Where'd this come from?" Eddie said.

Paralee smiled. "Friends in high places."

"Some set of wheels," her younger brother, Frank, said. "Gimme the keys. I want to check it out."

"Dream on," Paralee said. "You're as close to it as you're gonna get."

"Ah, Lee. Come on. At least take me for a ride."

"Later, Squirt," she said, taking her bag from the trunk and heading for the house. Her dad and brothers hung around the car, inspecting it reverently.

"Hey, Mom," she called out, slipping out of her jacket and dropping her bag by the stairs.

"Oh, Lee," her mother said, emerging from the kitchen holding out her arms, flour dust covering her hands. "I didn't even know if you were coming. I'm so glad you did. You've been hard to catch on the phone lately. Why don't you get one of those answering machines?"

"Can I help?"

"The turkey's done and resting," she said, putting the back of one hand to her forehead while she took inventory. "The sweet potatoes are cooking. So's the corn pudding. The light rolls are rising and I'm making pie crust now. You can do the Waldorf salad. I hate all that dicing."

The two women worked together over the next hour to complete the Thanksgiving feast, talking about small things--Paralee's courses at Georgetown, her mother's volunteer work at the new regional hospital, her parents' winter vacation in Florida.

"Oh, Lee. See to the wine, will you? I bought four bottles of Liebfraumilch. I hope that was the right thing."

Paralee found the wine, judged it to be much too cold and took all the bottles into the dining room. The table was beautifully set with heavy silver, crystal and china on a Belgian linen tablecloth that had been in her mother's family for three generations.

"Everything's ready, Mom," Paralee said, returning to the kitchen holding a bottle of Liebfraumilch by the neck. "Why don't I open this and you and

I can have a glass before we call the hogs?"

"That's a wonderful idea," her mother exclaimed, rinsing her hands at the sink.

****

"Mmmm," Paralee's mother said, tasting the wine. "I like that. Don't you?"

"Good choice, Mom," thinking it too fruity, but not wanting to criticize her mother's selection.

"It's wonderful to have everyone home for the holidays," she said, sinking into her favorite chair beside the fireplace in the living room. Neither of them mentioned Harry, but he flashed through their minds. Since Harry died, the table was always a little lopsided. Mom and Dad at the ends, Frank and Eddie on one side and Paralee alone on the other. Harry should have been beside her--oldest and youngest together.

Through the picture window, Paralee could see the men of the family still throwing the football. "How are Frank and Eddie?" she asked.

"They seem fine. Their grades are dismal compared to yours, but they're not in trouble and from the sounds of it, the girls they date are nice and there's nothing serious so far. I don't lose any sleep over them."

"But you do over me," Paralee said.

"Oh, dear, I didn't mean it that way. Don't be so sensitive. You're my first child and you're certainly the most complicated one. Don't mistake my concern for criticism."

"Sorry, Mom. I guess I'm just a little edgy," Paralee apologized, taking a sip of wine.

"What is it, dear?" Laura Campbell asked, leaning forward in her chair.

Paralee sat down on the hearth and rested her elbows on her knees. "Oh . . . ," she began, her head bowed, searching for a place to start. Finding no easy way, she met her mother's eyes and plunged. "It's Mack. I'm so conflicted. He's getting involved with people in South America. He says they're retired military, but I can't believe they don't have something to do with drugs. After Harry, I just couldn't have anything to do with that."

"I see," her mother said. "Did you explain about Harry?"

"Yeah. We had an argument."

"What sort of an argument? Surely he didn't defend drug dealers?"

"We didn't argue about that. He said he wouldn't take drug money and that the people he'd be talking to weren't drug dealers. But I got out of the car anyway and he didn't come after me."

"That doesn't sound like much of an argument. Where were you?"

"In the middle of Georgetown. Actually, he couldn't have followed me because we were stuck in traffic. But still . . ."

"So that's all there was to it?"

"No. We really did have an argument after he got back from South America. He swears the people he's getting to invest their money aren't into drugs, but what they are into isn't much better. I saw what people like that did in Ethiopia and . . . well, I've been reading up on Latin America and you just can't imagine. There are all these military dictatorships who say they're fighting communism, but Mom, what they do is so horrible. They're just Nazis. Maybe worse."

"And these men that Mack's involved with--they're part of that?"

Paralee looked at her mother with pain in her eyes and shook her head slowly. "Mack admits they're corrupt. They took kickbacks and sold favors when they were in power. This money is . . . I don't know . . . it's like it was stolen from the mouths of hungry children. It gives me a terrible feeling and I'm just sick about it, that he'd be a part of that. I know he's in a quandary--his family's farm . . . well, his grandfather, the one I told you about who's such a wonderful old man--he mortgaged it to help Mack buy the bank down in Texas, the one that went broke, and Mack didn't know, but now the loan's due and Mack doesn't have the money . . ."

"Lee, honey, slow down. You're going a little fast for me."

Paralee bowed her head and put a hand to her forehead. She tried to collect her thoughts and finally looked up at her mother. "The thing is that Mack thinks this is the only way he can save the farm. It's been in their family since the Revolutionary War. Can you imagine? Anyway, he says he doesn't want to deal with these people, but he says there's no way he can punish them by *not* dealing with them and if he didn't deal with them, he could lose the farm. Josh--his grandfather--still lives there. What in the world would happen to him? He was born there. It's the only place he's ever lived. I can't imagine him moving into Mack's condo or going to a nursing home."

"I don't understand about the Nazis, but it seems like Mack is putting his family first in this. Don't you think that's a good thing?"

"Of course it is, Mom," Paralee said. "But there's a principle at stake here. If they made money taking bribes and kickbacks . . . like Mack admits . . . then they're the same as the ones in Ethiopia who let their own people starve to death. Actually, they're worse than that. You just haven't read what's been going on in Latin America over the last ten years. Torture and murder and people disappearing without trials or anything."

Paralee got up and stared out the window, absently twirling the stem of the wine glass. She didn't look at her mother, but spoke to the trees beyond.

"What if they made a lot of money out of Mack's project and they just used it to hurt more people? Isn't there something terribly wrong with that? Maybe keeping the farm isn't all *that* important."

Laura looked down at her hands and thought for a time before she answered. "Lee, life presents us with these kinds of conflicts. They aren't easy. I've never had one quite like yours, but let me tell you about one I did have. You know your father was a pilot all those years. He used to fly planes that carried atomic bombs. We always knew that one day he might have to drop those bombs on the Russians and if that happened, there'd be Russian pilots trying to drop bombs on us. It would just be a horrible end of the world. I didn't want him to be an instrument of that destruction. If God wanted to end the world, I thought He could do it with an earthquake or a big meteor. He didn't need to use my husband. There were so many times I begged him to quit and open a hardware store or pump gas, just so I wouldn't think about him being one of the ones who dropped the bombs. Twice, I almost left him. I was going to take you and the boys to Idaho or Saskatchewan, any place where we wouldn't have to face it. Once, I had the car loaded, sitting in the driveway. But in the end, I didn't go. I guess I realized I was weighing my marriage and my family on scales with a kind of abstract principle. It was unfair to your father. And disloyal. So I stayed and I'm not sorry. The danger seems to be passing now and maybe we can live in a world of peace. Your father stood tall and did what he thought he had to do. They had a big name for it. Strategic deterrent. But I guess it worked. The Soviets were scared of us and we were scared of them. It was just a standoff. And the world is still going round and round. I know it's not the same thing, dear, but Mack has to stand up for what he thinks is right and you have to decide whether you're going to stand with him or not."

Paralee stared at her mother, seeing her suddenly as a young woman with four small children, packing them into a five-year old station wagon and driving away from one of the tiny Air Force base houses they lived in. Which was the harder choice, she wondered, leaving or staying?

"Mom," she said. "I never knew . . ."

"Never mind about me," Laura said. "You're the one with the choice to make now. Which one of these things do you feel stronger about--the principle or the man?"

The question threw Paralee off balance. "I . . . I don't think it comes to that, exactly," she stammered. "I don't have a claim on him. I work for him and he's taken me to dinner . . . barely a date." Paralee thought of their lovemaking and knew she wasn't telling her mother the whole truth. She also thought of their being followed when they left Washington and knew she wasn't going to tell her mother about that, even if it would make her case stronger.

Laura Campbell saw through her daughter as clearly as through crystal and for a moment, thought of letting it go. But Paralee wasn't just another grown woman who had the responsibility for making her own decisions. She was Laura's daughter, flesh of her flesh.

"Paralee?" Laura said, her tone saying all she needed to say.

"Well . . . I guess . . . Oh, Mom, I guess I'm in love with him," Paralee blurted, the pose shattered, tears streaming down her face. "It's killing me," she added, looking away and struggling to compose herself.

"Well, that's what I thought the first time you came home full of stories about his grandfather."

"I don't want to lose him . . . but I don't want him involved with these people. There's Harry and every dead person I saw in Ethiopia . . . how can I?"

"That's a different problem, isn't it?" Laura looked at her daughter for a long moment before going on. "You haven't got him yet, but let's talk about the man. Do you think he's fighting to save his family's farm or do you think he's the kind of man who'll spend his life looking for the easy dollar and not being too concerned about where it comes from?"

"I think he's a good man," Paralee said. "I don't know everything about him, but that's what I feel." "And I assume you know the difference between love and lust?" Laura paused for half a second, unsure she wanted an answer. "No, of course you do. Well, if you love this man and you want to have a life with him, and if you think he's a good man down deep, you're going to have to take him warts and all. And don't think you can change him. You can't. Don't try. Another thing. You can't win a man's heart or get through a marriage without trust and commitment. There are too many hard times. It's too easy to walk away if you don't have an irrational, makes-no-sense, can't-live-without-him, loving feeling for the man. He needs to feel that way about you, too. If he does, he'll want your respect as well as your love and he'll want to do the right thing. And if you both don't have that-- the love and the trust and the commitment--it probably won't work out. Maybe that's why you and Cary didn't last. You were both smart people and you made those lists of what you liked and didn't like, discovered that your bio-rhythms were synchronized--or whatever it is that bio-rhythms do-- and said, 'well, we should get married. We're perfect for each other.' You thought you didn't need anything more to live happily ever after."

"Mom," Paralee protested. "It wasn't like that."

"Then tell me you loved him enough to fight and die for him," her mother shot back, sharper than she intended.

"Of course I loved him." She looked at her mother for a long moment, then lowered her eyes and conceded, "But I don't guess I would've died for him. And we didn't do it all wrong, Mom. We had an understanding that I could have my own goals and ambitions. I wasn't Cary's slave. I had a life I could call my own. That's still important to me."

Her mother shrugged and looked down at the hands in her lap. "I know and I suppose that means more to your generation than it does to mine. But I don't see how that won't always be a problem and a source of conflict. If you don't have love, you'll never be able to reconcile the differences. I'm old-fashioned, dear, and I hope you'll think about this. Open your heart and let it speak to you. If Mack's a good man and if he's the man you'll walk through fire for, then maybe you have a chance to discover lasting love and a life you can call your own. I don't know the right and wrong of these people you're so opposed to. I haven't met any of them. Neither have you, for that matter. You're just reading all this in books. Mack seems to have weighed the pros and cons and maybe you ought to trust him in that. As for Harry," Laura stopped and gathered her strength.

"As for Harry," she went on. "Harry's gone. There's nothing you can do about that. We all miss him. I think about him every day and sometimes I still cry for him. But we can't live our lives for Harry. You can remember him for the wonderful brother he was and believe that God chose to take him when he did for God's own reasons. The how of it . . . it could have been anything. He's at peace now and you need to be, too."

She stood up and held out her arms to her daughter. "Now let's get those rascals in here and thank the Lord for all His mighty blessings."

****

Paralee came on Sunday afternoon to pick up McCall and he took her into the sun room to have coffee before they headed back.

"Great room, isn't it?" he said.

"Magnificent. It lets in so much light, you feel like you're floating in the sky. I love it."

"Pa added this room to the house. It's his baby. He went a little crazy with skylights. They're all over now--in his bedroom, in the bathrooms upstairs. They're nice, though," he said, then changed the subject. "How was Thanksgiving?"

"It was good. Mom and I had a little heart-to-heart. I'm still thinking about it."

"You and your mother get along?"

"Oh, yes. But once in awhile she surprises me."

"What did she say to you? She tell you to stay away from dirty old men like me?"

Paralee gave him a crooked smile and her blue eyes caught fire from one of the skylights. "What she said is just between us girls."

He looked at her with puzzled amusement for a moment, gave up and said, "Are you ready to go?"

"Sure. I guess. Do you really want to? It's early yet."

"Pa's seen enough of me. I've done some chores for him, stuff the ladies from the church don't take care of. I chipped and painted the fence around the graveyard. We've talked about everything under the sun. I think he wants his privacy back."

Josh appeared in the doorway.

"Pa," McCall said. "We're going to head back. Anything you need before I go?"

"No, I don't think so. Come back at Christmas. We'll put up a tree. There hasn't been a tree in this house for a long time. Bring Miss Paralee with you and make her stay a few days. I like her smile," he said, speaking directly to her. "And those are the prettiest eyes I think I ever did see."

Paralee smiled and shook her head in embarrassment.

McCall threw an arm around Josh's shoulder. "We'll see."

"I'll walk you out," Josh said, following them through the front door.

McCall and Paralee each gave him a hug on the front porch and he smiled his blessing like a Biblical patriarch as they got into the car. McCall waved once more from behind the wheel and put the car in gear. Paralee looked back halfway down the drive and saw the old man standing as straight as one of the columns of the house. While she watched him growing smaller as they moved away, Josh crumpled and fell.

"Stop! Mack! Stop! Go back!" Her voice broke as she released an agonized cry. "It's Josh! Oh, my God, it's Josh!"

The Shenandoah Valley

The first snow of the season fell the day they buried Josh Cooper--wet, heavy flakes. People came from all over the upper Valley to the little church the Coopers helped found more than a hundred years ago. Most of them followed the hearse to the farm, climbed the hill and stood in the snowy cascade to honor one of their own.

When Paralee saw Josh fall, McCall slammed on the brakes, skidded around in a shower of gravel and raced back up the drive, but the coroner said Josh was probably dead by the time he hit the ground. A powerful heart attack had taken him to be with his Missy.

In the days that followed, McCall made it through the necessary arrangements and was kind to the people who came to pay their respects, but he was distant and often lost the thread of their conversation.

Whether caught up in long-forgotten memories or merely benumbed by events, Paralee couldn't tell, but she knew he needed someone and she put their differences aside and stayed with him, taking phone calls, dealing graciously with a community determined to bring enough food to feed them for weeks. People mistook her for Mack's wife and when she tired of correcting them, she found unexpected pleasure in being treated as 'Mrs. McCall.'

Paralee's parents came to help and McCall met them in a daze. Something about them registered with him--Laura Campbell's warm brown eyes and the Colonel's dark blue ones, the obvious source of Paralee's. He was touched by their concern and by their trust in allowing Paralee to stay.

Now McCall was shaking hands with the last of the mourners, thanking them, watching them off down the hill into their cars and pickups while two men in coveralls and stocking caps filled in the grave. He and Paralee waited until they'd gone and then stood alone staring at the mound of raw earth rapidly being covered with a blanket of new snow, not wanting to let Josh go.

"Come on, Mack," she said at last. "Let's go down. I'll fix you something hot to drink. Josh is already up in Heaven with Missy. They're having a grand old time right about now." Gently, she led him down the snowy slope of the hill.

Inside the house, he shed his coat and slipped off his shoes, now soaked from standing in the snow. He stared vacantly at the living room and drifted into the library. The door to the master bedroom was open and Josh's empty bed stood in the soft light filtering down from the skylights.

McCall first stood transfixed, then took a tentative step . . . and another. The steps kept coming until he stood at the foot of Josh's bed.

Paralee watched him for a few moments through the open door, then went into the kitchen to heat a mug of cider. When she came back he was gone.

"Mack?" she called, but there was no answer. She found him on the bed in his own room, lying on his back, a forearm thrown over his eyes.

"Mack?" she said from the open doorway. "I brought you some hot cider." She didn't wait for his invitation, but came into the room and sat the mug beside his bed. "It smells delicious," she said.

He looked at her then. "Thanks," he said, taking the mug from her. His eyes were red-rimmed and he made no effort to hide them from her.

"Mack . . . is there anything I can do?"

"Stay with me a little while," he said and made room for her on the narrow bed.

She sat down and put her back against the headboard. Her arms went around him naturally and instinctively and brought his head into her lap, the way a mother would cradle a small child. She stroked his shoulders and his hair and gradually she felt him relax. When she was sure he was asleep, she placed his head on the pillow and spread the comforter over him.

She went toward the guest room to change into comfortable clothes but stopped for a moment at the door of Cassie McCall's bedroom. Throughout the week, she'd felt drawn to the room and had looked in many times, but she'd never crossed the threshold. Today, she did.

Cassie's personal items seemed to be just as she'd left them--pictures on the dresser, prints on the wall, a large hooked rug in the center of the wide-plank hardwood floor. A writing desk stocked with stationery sat against the inner wall beside a book shelf crammed with an eclectic array of bindings. These things Paralee saw in the periphery of her vision. It was the bed that drew her, its headboard centered between the two dormer windows beneath a rustic, hand-carved cross. The bed was made up with two large pillows and a star quilt. A comforter was folded across the foot. Paralee walked slowly toward it, rested both hands on the footboard, knowing instinctively that this had been Cassie's and Jack's bed, that this was where they slept before Jack shipped out to England, where Cassie and Jack made love for the last time, where Mack was conceived. Such a short distance between this spot where his life began and the bed down the hall where he now slept.

A vagrant breeze swirled through the room and ruffled the swagged sheers. Paralee no longer felt alone. This new presence didn't alarm her nor was she chilled by it. It was a companionable presence, as though two strangers had come down different paths to journey together along the same road.

Paralee lingered in Cassie's bedroom, trying to draw the presence closer, but she couldn't. Perhaps later, some other time. She went to the guest room then, changed clothes and washed her face, as comforted by Cassie's presence as if she'd found a new friend.

Downstairs, she scanned the cornucopia of covered dishes and pies and hams for something that might appeal to Mack when he awoke. As she did, a vision of the feeding station in Ethiopia fell on her like a hammer. The food in this kitchen would have fed so many. Sad that it would have been far too rich for them to keep down. Then she remembered Josh's twinkling eyes and his warmth and realized how very far away she was in time and space from Tigray Province and how far away she still was from understanding what she'd seen there. Those dark, pleading faces she tried to nourish were as dear to their families as Josh was to his. Josh died so peacefully, so mercifully. She saw it happen. One moment vital, full of life, the next an empty vessel. Not like those in the world of the walking dead she'd seen in Ethiopia.

Turning away from the abundance of the Shenandoah Valley, she found a small jar of beef bouillon cubes in one of Josh's cabinets, heated water and made a cup of broth. She took it into the library, put another log on the fire and coaxed the flames from the embers. When the fire was going well, she settled into the big wing-backed chair and stared out the windows at the snow-covered corn field, letting her mind go blank.

She didn't know how long she had been sitting there when a movement caught her eye and she saw McCall standing at the foot of Josh's bed. She rose and went to stand beside him.

"My great-great grandfather, Thomas Cooper, made this bedstead from trees he felled on this land," McCall told her solemnly. "Every master of this farm since then has slept in it."

"I assume you're going to inherit the farm," Paralee said, standing close to him, breathing the maleness of his skin. "Are you going to be its master now?"

"I don't know," he said. "It's such a lot to be responsible for. And they're all standing around looking at me, watching, waiting to see."

"All who, Mack?"

"All those people up there on the ridge. My ancestors. They're standing up there shaking their heads and muttering about how empty the gene pool is."

****

Early the next morning, Paralee smelled the aroma of coffee drifting through the open door of the guest room and followed it downstairs. The sun was sparkling bright and through the kitchen windows, she saw Mack tramping around in the patches of snow beside the woodpile, stacking logs for the fireplace onto one of his arms. They hadn't eaten the night before, so she began preparing breakfast. By the time he had a blaze going in the sun room fireplace and another in the library, a large slab of ham and a stack of pancakes awaited him at the kitchen table. When he sat down, she fried his eggs and popped two slices of bread into the toaster.

When the dishes had been washed and put away, Paralee came to join Mack in the sun room. "What's next?" she asked, startling him.

He whirled around at the sound of her voice. "What? Sorry, I was somewhere else, I guess. What did you say?"

"I just asked what's next. Are you going to stay here or close it up and go back to town or what?"

"I haven't got to that point yet. I suppose I'd better call Malcolm. He rents the land. I'm sure he'll look after things until I figure out what I'm going to do."

He stood staring out the window, as if he'd gone away again, then he added. "I need to call Sam, too. There'll be some legal stuff to deal with." He looked at her then, seeming to see her for the first time. "What about school? Didn't classes start right after Thanksgiving? What day is it anyway?"

"Wednesday," she said. "It's OK."

"No, no. It isn't. I've got to get you back to school. You've already missed three days. Why don't you get your stuff together and I'll drive you back? It's no trouble. I can come back tonight or tomorrow morning."

"Do you want me to go?"

"I didn't mean that. It's just . . . well, you've already done so much and . . . I feel like I'm taking advantage."

"Another day or two won't matter. Josh meant a lot to me, too, Mack. I don't quite want to leave here yet." She kept her eyes locked on his and watched his expression soften.

"Yeah, I guess you and he had a little secret, didn't you?"

"What do you mean?"

"I figure it was when I was in Egypt. You came up here to see him, didn't you?"

Paralee blushed and stammered, "I . . . I . . . How do you know that? Did Josh tell you?"

"Bobby Templeton's the sheriff in Mt. Jackson. We went to school together. He recognized you at the funeral and mentioned your looking for Josh back a month or so ago. I guess you didn't remember Bobby, but he remembered you."

"I'm sorry I didn't tell you. It was just curiosity. I wanted to see where you grew up. Josh was wonderful. We spent almost the whole day together.

I never knew any of my grandparents and I . . . well, I just sort of adopted him then and there."

McCall nodded. "OK. We'll stay another day or so. I can call Sam from here. Did Pa show you around?"

She shook her head. "Just the house. I've seen a little more these last few days, but of course, I don't understand it all."

"Well, I can do something about that," he said, the pall of his dark mood lifting. "You've seen the cemetery, so there's no need to do that again. The corn field you can see from these windows."

"I stood here with him that first time we met. He was smoking his pipe and drinking coffee I brought him. So I know about the corn field and the apple orchard over there." She pointed toward the leafless trees in the distance.

"Then I imagine he told you about Thomas Cooper standing off a company of Yankees. They weren't impressed with his courage. They took everything they fancied and burned the place down anyway."

She nodded and said, "He showed me the musket balls they took out of him, over in that case in the library."

"There wasn't much left of anything here after the Yankees burned the place down. Those slugs my great-great grandmother dug out of him after the Yankees left, that two-foot bayonet from an old Revolutionary War musket that the first Joshua owned and some buttons from his uniform. Some pots and pans, the things that wouldn't burn. That's about all that was left. Old Thomas had to rebuild the place pretty much from scratch and he had to do it with a crippled arm. He stood right out there in the yard against fifty Yankees in the cornfield. His wife, Nancy, stood right there with him. They put the kids in the root cellar and told the Yankees to get off their property."

"No wonder this farm is so important to you."

"Did Pa take you up to the ridge? Probably not. He was getting a bit old for climbing."

"No," she said. "I didn't see the ridge."

"Get your coat. Maybe a blanket, too. It'll be cold up there. I'll get a tarp out of the barn and we'll go up."

Their breath fogging the cold, clear air, McCall walked Paralee through the fragrant pines to the top of the ridge, to a clearing among the trees where, with a little imagination, you could see the haze-shrouded Appalachians of West Virginia.

"This was always one of my favorite places," he said, spreading the tarp over a deep bed of pine needles covered with snow. They sat down side by side and Mack drew the blanket over their shoulders. "I used to think you could see the rest of the world from here. All those exotic places I used to read about were out there beyond those mountains. All you had to do was follow the sun. One of my great-great uncles did that. Went to California during the gold rush. Made a lot of money selling stuff to the miners. On his way home, though, his ship ran into a hurricane off the Carolina coast and sank. They called him Gentleman Jack because he was sort of a ladies' man. Anyway, Gentleman Jack and his gold went down with the ship and he never got to spend it."

"That's a sad story to tell in such a beautiful spot," she said, sitting beside him, pulling her knees up to her chin and wrapping her arms around her legs.

"I told you because I'm a bit like Gentleman Jack. I used to sit up here and think how I'd take off like he did, see the world and someday bring back the gold. My ship wouldn't sink. As it turns out, I've seen the world, but my damned ships keep sinking."

Somewhere in the tall trees nearby, a rare, pileated woodpecker hammered away, ferreting out insects.

"Is that why you decided to leave here?"

"It was more than that, I guess. Did you look at that graveyard where we buried Pa? It's loaded with Coopers. My dad's not really there--just his marker. And he didn't have a choice in the matter. When I was growing up, one of my chores was taking care of that cemetery, so I came to know them all. The Coopers were big men, and warriors--Revolutionary War, War of 1812, Civil War. Pa was in World War I."

"Your dad fought in World War II. And you were a warrior, too." When McCall didn't respond, Paralee persisted. "You were a flier like your dad. I saw the pictures in the library. Was that big jet yours?"

"I flew F-4s in 'Nam."

"Your Distinguished Flying Cross is up there, too. And I know you don't get those in a box of Cracker Jack. You were a warrior like your dad and all those Coopers."

"So what? Look, I've also got a busted bank to my credit. And whatever you think that DFC means, Vietnam wasn't a bravo performance."

"Maybe the policy was wrong, but that doesn't diminish the courage of the men who fought or the honor they deserve."

"That's not what I meant," he said. "I broke the rules to hit a target that had been giving everybody grief. I was coming out at low altitude to avoid the SAMs, but we got hit by ground fire and I lost a good friend."

"How do you mean?"

"My Wizzo. Weapons Systems Officer. He got hit too bad for him to eject, so I tried to bring us home. I didn't make it. I bellied in on the beach, but he died before the Air-Sea Rescue choppers could get to us. He'd be alive today if it I hadn't been such a damned cowboy."

"You don't know that. And what about the target? Didn't you save lives by knocking it out?"

"Look, you're an Air Force brat so you ought to know that the rules are there for a reason. I broke them. Somebody died who shouldn't have. I crashed an airplane worth a couple of million dollars. I got reprimanded and I deserved it. It was no great loss to the Air Force when I resigned my commission. Now you know, so let it go, will you?"

"OK, but you need to stop beating yourself up. We don't deserve all the bad stuff that happens to us--or the good stuff, either. It just happens. You need to go with it."

He stared at the haze-shrouded mountains in the distance for a long time. "At the end, I was all Pa had. Pa was the last of the Coopers. Now it's up to me. And I just don't know if I can stick it out here or make a go of it if I did. Maybe I don't have the genes. My mother told me my father was a peaceful sort of person, content with teaching school down in Harrisonburg, coming home every night and all. But maybe that's just the way she wanted him to be. It's hard for me to believe the guy she remembered was the same one who put his P-51 up against Focke-Wolfes and Messerschmitts at twenty thousand feet and flew treetops against German tanks and infantry in the Normandy invasion. I know what that's like and he had to have some kind of fire in the belly to do it. I don't know if he'd have been happy teaching sixth grade after that or if he'd have been comfortable on this farm, growing corn and feeding chickens and making apple cider. Maybe. Maybe not. Pa said almost the same thing. He said that was why he put the farm at risk to help me buy the bank. So I'd have a choice."

"You talk about growing up here as if you liked it."

"I did."

"And you promised Josh you wouldn't sell the farm."

"I also promised him I wouldn't lose it. I don't know if I can keep those promises. I'm going to bust my ass to get this loan paid off, one way or another. After that . . . I don't know. Maybe one day I'll come up to the ridge here and just keep going."

The big black woodpecker stopped his racket and flew away, flashing his red crest and white trim. They sat in the vast silence looking out over the Valley.

"Tell me about your mother, Mack. Tell me about Cassie," Paralee said at last.

"She was a beautiful lady," he began and then stopped, staring out toward the mountains. It took him awhile to begin again. "We were close. She did all the usual stuff— reading me stories and tucking me in at night when I was little--but that wasn't all. When I was still in grade school, we used to take long hikes around here and she'd go on and on about the wild flowers and what kind of tree this one or that one was. She could read animal tracks like an Indian and she must have known every bird call in this part of Creation. She was a lot more than my mother. She wasn't just somebody who cooked and washed dishes and kept house. She was . . . she was a real good friend--the best. She got cancer and died. It all happened pretty fast." He slammed the door on the subject by immediately asking Paralee, "Do you miss Paris?"

"Sometimes," she said, not wanting Cassie's story to end so abruptly, but respecting his not wanting to talk about her any more. Maybe there would be another way to get to know Cassie. "School doesn't seem to be the answer, but Paris wasn't either."

"What's the question?"

"What my life's about, I guess. I don't have roots the way you do, even if you're afraid of them. I don't want to relive my mother's life--Air Force bases and wives' clubs. Mom and Dad are happy now. I used to think they'd always been happy, but I found out not so long ago that maybe they weren't. At least not always. Anyway, I just meant to say that their life isn't for me."

"And you know which one is?"

"No," she smiled. "Not yet. But I know I want my own life, not a copy of somebody else's."

A pine cone fell into the snow at their feet and they looked up in time to see a squirrel scampering away in the branches.

"One of Pa's nemesises," McCall remarked. "That's one furry little varmint who'll be doing without birdseed for awhile."

They watched the squirrel for a time, content to leave the worries of the waiting world on hold. Finally, McCall turned to her and said, "That's about all there is to the farm. I'd better go see if I can get hold of my lawyer and get this probate business started."

****

Bitsy Tate answered the phone in San Antonio. "Hello, you scoundrel. Sam's been trying to get hold of you."

"I've been traveling and my grandfather just died, so I've been busy with that."

"Oh, Mack. I'm so sorry," she said and went on to ask all the questions about the circumstances. McCall gave her the particulars and then asked to speak to Sam.

"Hi, podnah," Sam said when he picked up the phone. "Listening to Bitsy's side of the conversation, I figured out that your grandfather died. I'm real sorry to hear that."

"Thanks, Sam. Listen, I was wondering if you'd handle the estate for me. I'm not altogether sure about the legalities, but Pa had a mortgage on the farm, a pretty big one, and I can't pay it off without selling the place, which I promised him I wouldn't do."

"I don't suppose he had credit life insurance," Sam said.

"No. He was eighty-five. Credit life would have been prohibitively expensive. Sam . . . that's how he got the money to help me buy the bank. Can you imagine how I feel?"

"Oh, man," Sam said and there was a long pause. "If there's no insurance and you can't pay off the loan, you're just going to have to refinance. Is there any problem with that?"

"Damn straight there's a problem. I don't have enough income to qualify for a loan that size. I'm working on that, but the bank shouldn't have made a loan like this in the first place. Pa sure as hell didn't have the income to qualify. You know the saying about real estate--the best buys come from death, divorce and default. I think that's what this banker's got in mind. He figured my grandfather would die or default and he'd be able to steal the farm in a sacrifice sale. I need to play for time, Sam. I can cover the interest payment coming due, but I can't get the loan over into my name right away and I don't want to get tripped up by some legal technicality."

"Any other complications? Your grandpa had a will, didn't he?"

"There's a will and everything looks copasetic except this business with the loan."

"Any chance you've got a judge who's related to you?"

"As a matter of fact, I do. Judge Lewis Pritchard. He's a cousin of some sort. He belongs to the family of my great-great grandmother, Nancy Pritchard. He came to the funeral."

"Mack, my calendar's absolutely jammed, but I'll call this judge of yours and we'll get acquainted. We ought to be able to work it out to settle the estate after the first of the year. If that's a problem with the judge, I'll get back to you. Meantime, you might want to see if he won't give this banker a call. You know, just to let him know the judge wouldn't take kindly to somebody screwing around with one of his relatives. I'd guess this will hold while we deal with some other problems. I hate to put them on you right now, but they're not going to wait."

"Ah, shit, Sam. Do we have to do this now?"

"I'm afraid so. I'll make it as quick as I can. They found out you inherited some money. You know they were poking around in all your foreign travels and stumbled over some recent probate records in London. Anyway, they know you got more than fifty thousand dollars from Audrey Chilton Chesley a couple of months ago. Now they're insisting that your inheritance be counted as part of your assets and that's going to raise the ante on what they're willing to settle for. They're not real happy that you didn't disclose this right away, so they're going to be hard-assed about it."

"I don't have constructive receipt of it. If they're so damned smart, why haven't they figured that out?"

"They know some Brit law firm is holding it in escrow, but they figure it's at your request, so you're still up shit creek. Tell you the truth, I'm not too happy about having to find out this way, either. You might have told me what was happening."

"I didn't want you to have to lie about it. If you didn't know about it, you wouldn't have to."

"Lawyers can't pass the bar unless they know how to protect their client's interest."

"Is that the same as being good at lying? If I'd known that, I'd have told you."

"No, damn it. It isn't the same as lying, but I might have figured something to do about it if you'd told me before I got hit between the eyes with it by our adversaries."

"OK, OK, Sam. I'm sorry. What do we do now?"

"Release that money from escrow and take receipt. It has to go on the table. I'll save as much of it as I can, but you can figure they're going to stick it you now. I'm not sure what we're going to do about your real estate. You've declared the condo your homestead, but we may have to switch that around to put the farm out of their reach. Then we'll have to worry about the value of the condo."

＊＊＊＊＊＊＊＊＊＊＊

Mack and Paralee foraged among the many dishes brought by the neighbors and sat for awhile in front of the fire in the library with what was left of Josh's Maker's Mark whiskey. Paralee persisted in drawing Mack out and he told her the story of Josh and the apple orchard. When she begged, he told her several others that he knew second hand about Josh's humorous adventures with the first truck he bought for the farm and a horse named Wanda who was always running away.

Paralee's soft laughter was a healing balm and telling the old stories lifted McCall's spirits. With the whiskey and the crackling fire warming them inside and out, McCall took Paralee's hand and looked into her dark blue eyes. "Thank you," he said. "I didn't really want to talk about Pa, but it was the right thing to do. Now I think I'm going to call it a day. Sam's got the ball on settling the estate and Birney's on board to take care of the place. The FDIC is going to skin me alive, but what the hell. We could leave in the morning."

Paralee nodded. "Thanks for talking about Josh. It helped me, too."

McCall bid her goodnight at the top of the stairs and watched her go down the hall to the guest room. At the door to her room she turned back to look at him, a long, questioning look that seemed to be saying something he couldn't decode. He smiled, gave her a little wave, went into his room, switched on the bedside light and undressed. He pulled on a pair of light-weight sweat pants and a T-shirt and crawled into bed.

She appeared in his doorway in a long, white cotton gown. "I saw your light," she said.

"Are you afraid of the dark?"

"I am tonight."

Alexandria: December 1985

Danielo Martinez was frustrated by the lack of activity on the taps on McCall's condo. In ten days no one had occupied the condo so there were no outgoing calls. Several incoming calls disconnected when the answering machine kicked in. Only one message had been left. It had come from Panamá. The caller had made it sound important, but it was impossible to know what it was about.

With McCall's return in early December, however, the taps came alive.

****

McCall found a message on his answering machine from Javier, sounding excited and secretive. He called him at his apartment but there was no answer. He left a message that he'd returned the call.

McCall's travel alarm nagged him in the dead of night. He flicked it off to keep it from waking Paralee, peeled back the covers and tiptoed out of the bedroom, closing the door behind him. In the bathroom, he checked his watch. It would be eight in the morning in London, time enough to call.

He tried Chilty at his flat, but got no answer. Like people who worked at the White House, McCall supposed the 10 Downing Street gang also arrived early and stayed late. He didn't want to call Chilty at the office, so he decided to wait until evening. It was too early to try Javier again. He would be sound asleep. He made coffee and attacked the accumulated mail in his office.

Time flew by in the early morning stillness. He had finished prioritizing the bills to be paid and was getting drowsy in spite of the coffee when the telephone rang. It startled him, almost sending him through the ceiling. He grabbed the receiver before it could ring again.

"What?" he said, startled, half angry.

"That hurt my ears," he heard Dixie Davenport say. "I take it you're awake. Go to a pay phone and call me back," she said and hung up.

McCall looked at his watch. He'd been awake longer than he thought. It was 6: 30 in the morning. Go to a pay phone? That again? At first, he thought Dixie was taking her job too seriously, then he remembered they'd been followed at least as far as the Dulles road two weeks ago, right after he'd talked to Dixie on the Hill.

****

"Denny's?" Paralee said when McCall pulled into the parking lot beneath the green and yellow sign. The blue Ford Taurus that had followed them from the condo parked on the street, half a block away. "Why don't we ask the guys in the Taurus if they want to join us? Maybe they'll get ptomaine."

"What's wrong with Denny's?"

"I'm not eating any grits," she muttered, getting out of the Mercedes and following him into the restaurant. "I thought we were going for doughnuts at Krispy Kreme."

They sat in a booth near the door and McCall ordered coffee, fried eggs, bacon and pancakes. Paralee asked for orange juice, coffee and whole wheat toast.

"I'll be back," McCall said and headed for the men's room. There were pay phones in the alcove. He dialed Dixie Davenport's direct line.

"What's up, Dixie?" he asked when she came on the line.

"Where are you?"

"Denny's. At a pay phone, like you told me."

"Have you talked to Angela?"

"Yeah. She called me from São Paolo. At my grandfather's. On her way to South Africa. She said you gave her the number. Sorry I didn't close the loop with you, but my grandfather died and I had a lot of stuff to deal with."

"I'm sorry for your loss, McCall," Dixie said. There was a long pause. "What did she tell you about Bolivia?"

"Hardly anything. Just that she'd been picked up, but got away and hitched rides out of Bolivia and across Brazil."

"That's not the whole story. Some Argentines interrogated her . . . the way you might expect some animals to interrogate a good-looking woman."

"Raped her?"

"Afraid so. Beat her up a little in the process, too. But she's OK and broadly pissed. Determined to nail the bastards' hides to the wall. That's why she's going to Africa."

"Why the hell didn't you call me, Dixie? You knew where I was."

"Standard need to know, McCall. But as I thought about it, I figured you might be in some danger yourself. That's why I'm calling now."

A war had begun in McCall between his feelings of anger and outrage and agonizing images of their last hours together in La Paz flashing through his mind.

"She said she told them everything she ever knew about what she found out in Buenos Aires and Bolivia, but nothing about you. That said, they've probably figured out by now that you took her notes and tapes out of La Paz and that she told you to bring them to me. You have to figure that you've come up on their radar screen by now."

He couldn't speak for a few moments. *'Damn it!' he swore to himself. 'Why the hell didn't I wake up when she got out of bed? I could have made her stay. Why did I go on to the airport? Why didn't I hunt her down?'*

"McCall? Are you still there?"

He forced himself to focus.

"I heard you, Dixie. And I know we're under surveillance. I just didn't figure it was about Angela. When we left town a couple of weeks ago--the day I came to see you--we were tailed," he said. "I lost them at Dulles. And before you ask, there's no doubt about it. They're sitting outside now. But I don't know who they are. That is, I didn't know what it was about."

"You can figure they've also searched your house by now--and bugged your phone and probably the walls, too. That's why I told you to call me from a pay phone. What you need to do now is call Stackhouse Exterminators. Use my name and ask for Barney. He'll sweep your house for bugs--the electronic kind. I don't know what kind of security you've got, but it wouldn't hurt to beef it up. And did you say 'we' a minute ago?"

"My research assistant was with me."

"Better put him in the loop, too. They surely know by now that someone besides you and me know about Angela's notes."

"She's a she," McCall said. "But I didn't tell her anything about Angela."

"*They* don't know that. They probably wouldn't take your word for it, either, if you get my meaning. And listen, McCall, don't get any heroic ideas about doing something on your own here. You may be a capable guy, but not against this kind of opposition. You hear me?"

"I hear you." he growled.

"Angela--she's one hell of a lady."

"She is that," McCall said and hung up.

Halfway back to the booth, he turned around and went back to the phones. He found the number for Stackhouse Exterminators in the Yellow Pages and called them. By dropping Dixie's name, he was put through to Barney and got an appointment for eleven o'clock that morning. Then he used his phone card to call Javier at the bank. He was in a meeting so McCall left a message for him not to call. He didn't know what Javier wanted, but he didn't want any details of the Russian bond deal on somebody's tape recording. It was a long shot, but there was also a chance Chilty might call, so he rang him at Number Ten Downing in London.

"Chilty?" McCall said. "I know you're busy, but I wanted to tell you--just in case--not to call my home number. . . . I can't explain right now. I'll call you tonight at your flat if that's OK. . . . Right. Sorry for the bother."

Paralee was standing behind him when he hung up the phone and turned around. "What is it, Mack?" she asked, alarmed by the look on his face.

He shook his head and walked her back to the booth. He sat down and took a sip of coffee, his thoughts still riveted on Angela, on that last night in La Paz.

"Mack," Paralee said. "You look awful. Can't you tell me?"

He sighed deeply, icing his feelings and speaking slowly. "Remember the day we left for Thanksgiving, when I left you at the condo to work on the prospectus? I took some papers up to the Hill to a friend of mine, notes a woman gave me in La Paz to bring out. She got picked up by Bolivian Security and got roughed up. She told them about the papers and that she'd given them to me. She's out now, but I . . . I might have been able to . . . Hell, I don't know."

"I don't understand, Mack."

"I knew she was in danger. I might have been able to help her. She bugged out before I . . . I should have gone after her, but I didn't know where to look or where she was going. La Paz isn't New York, but I still could have made the effort."

"And maybe gotten picked up by the Bolivian cops yourself," Paralee said. Then a new light dawned. "Oh, no! Is this why we're being followed?"

"Maybe. And they've seen you with me, so they have to assume you know about those papers, too. That wasn't true until just now, but they won't believe that. That's what the call was about."

"How well do you know this woman?" she asked.

"We've known each other a long time. We used to run into each other on the road. She's an international correspondent. Journalist. Does a lot of Third World work. She's doing a story on illegal arms shipments to the Contras in Nicaragua."

The look on his face told Paralee there was a lot more to it than his 'running into her' on the road, but Mack wasn't giving her a way to press the case, to make him tell her what the woman in Bolivia meant to him. *'Damn you, Mack. You said you 'flew a little' and it turns out you've got a DFC. Now it's 'we used to run into each other on the road.' It's not a lie, but it's not the truth either.'*

"I see," she said, hiding her curiosity, hating him for dissembling, hating herself for letting him get away with it, hurt that there were other women in his life.

The waitress brought their order, covering the awkward moment. When she left, Mack gave his full attention to the meal, ignoring Paralee.

Paralee fidgeted, waiting for McCall to say anything. Finally, she broke their silence and asked, "Who's Chilty? That last phone call you made."

"Chilty? That's a long story."

"I've got time," she said, fixing her blue eyes on him over the rim of a large orange juice.

"OK," he said. "The short version. Chilty's a friend and the son of one of the best friends I ever had. The Russian bonds were hers. She died recently and Chilty inherited them from her. He passed them on to me."

"Why'd he do that?"

"They were a problem for him. He works for Margaret Thatcher. You know, the Prime Minister."

"Then he's your source, isn't he?" Paralee said, wide-eyed. "Got to be. He couldn't keep the bonds because he's in the middle of the deal. Conflict of interest."

"How'd you figure *that* out?"

"I'm not stupid. But Mack, she died? Chilty's mother? And she was . . . special to you? Why didn't you tell me?"

"I haven't told you about her because . . . I don't know . . . I just haven't felt like talking about it. Damn it, Paralee! Every which way I turn, I'm losing somebody!" He took a deep breath. "Her name was Audrey Chilton Chesley. She died last August. The bonds were her dowry."

"So these are Audrey's bonds,"

"Yeah," he said. "They're Audrey's bonds."

The awkward silence settled on them again. When she had borne it as long as she could, she asked, "What'll happen now?"

When McCall looked up, his eyes were cold and dull. "By now they've searched the condo and bugged it. A sweeper's coming over this morning to clear them out."

"Bugs?"

"Electronic listening devices. Those kind of bugs."

Her eyes widened in horror. "Could they have heard us last night?"

The thought of it broke McCall's somber mood and he smiled in spite of himself. "Every moan, every 'Oh! Oh!', every breathless 'Yes! Yes! Now! Now!' I'll bet they're already selling that tape in every trucker's triple-X joint from here to Pittsburgh."

"Damn it, Mack!" she said, embarrassed and angry at the same time. She blushed and then broke into nervous laughter. "This isn't funny," she chided herself.

"No, it isn't funny," he said, sad and serious again. "And you're staying with me for the duration now. I want you where I can keep an eye on you."

"Oh?"

"I don't think they're going to make a move on us. They probably know I don't have the notes any more, but I don't want to be stupid about that." He could imagine her being taken and tortured like Angela or held hostage, but he didn't want to use that argument to persuade her. It would only scare her.

"I have to go back to school, Mack. I've missed a week of classes and finals are coming up. Commuting from your condo . . . well, it'd be easier if I went back to Dent Place."

"I'll take you to school, walk you to class and wait for you."

"There's no place to park around Georgetown and I don't think I could get you a permit."

"Let me worry about that."

"There's another thing," she said. "What makes you think I'm willing to share your bed and board on more than an episodic basis?"

"Hey, look . . . "

She held up her hand with the palm toward him. "I didn't say I wouldn't. I have some conditions, though."

"Like what?"

"You've gotta have something more than one chair in the living room. And you've gotta put some color in that place. Prints on the wall, a rug or two. It's as dull as Dracula's cave."

****

The Stackhouse technician cleared McCall's condo of the listening devices Martinez' people had installed and spent four hours adding electronic countermeasures and a steel door that looked exactly like the old one except for the coded keypad lock. He told McCall the lock wasn't infallible, but it would significantly raise the bar of sophistication for anyone trying to break in. "The only thing that'll open this baby is an MC-7 or an acetylene torch. They're special order and there aren't many of 'em around. Unless you've got the CIA or the FBI after you, you should be OK. The bugs these guys put in weren't state of the art. Probably just a pretty good private eye outfit."

By the time the Stackhouse tech left, it was ten in the evening in London.

"Chilty? It's Mack. Sorry to have called you at work. My phone was fouled up. The repair people just left."

"Not to worry. Look, I don't want to hurry you, but I'm meeting some people and I'm late already. What's on your mind?"

"I wanted to let you know my grandfather died. It happened right after Thanksgiving. No pain. He went in an instant. Just keeled over."

"I'm so sorry, Mack. Forgive me for rushing you like that. I'm really sorry to hear it. You were close, weren't you?"

"He and my grandmother finished raising me after my mother died. I had a few good days with him before he passed on, so . . ."

"Is there anything I can do?" Chilty asked.

"Actually there is. I know you don't want to talk about it, but you promised to check on the yellow stuff. You know what I mean," Mack said, avoiding a direct mention of the gold.

"I did, didn't I?" Chilty said, obviously sorry McCall had reminded him. "Take a chair then, my friend. There's not a single ounce. All spent on bombs and bullets--and hospital supplies. The Tsarina was quite the Florence Nightingale it seems."

"You're sure about that? We can't find a shred of evidence that the Tsar spent the stuff he sent to the UK. And there's an affidavit that says it ought to still be there."

"We have it from the Bank of England herself. It's official--but damned well not public. All we have is that deposit I told you about. You'll be lucky to get twenty percent, Mack. Sorry." McCall was silent for so long that Chilty thought he'd lost him. "Mack? You still there?"

"Yeah. I'm still here. I think. Thanks, Chilty. I'll let you buy dinner the next time I come through town."

"I'm sorry about your grandfather, Mack. Do please be careful about trading Mum's dowry. Dealers all over Europe have been in a tizzy about something recently. Our people have noticed an advance on prices without a lot of actual transactions, so something's stirring."

"It's not me. I bought a couple of weeks ago and I haven't done anything since. There was a little advance on prices then, but not enough to spark a 'tizzy' in the markets. Could somebody else be in on the story?"

"Of course," Chilty said. "It's possible, but not likely."

"Don't worry about it, Chilty. Markets have hiccups now and then that nobody ever quite understands."

"That's your department, of course, but the hounds seem to have a whiff of the fox and I'd be very disappointed if they should trace the scent to my lair. You understand, don't you?"

New York

Chanille was waiting in Ryder's office when he arrived the next morning. "Sandy called."

"And?" Ryder asked, moving toward his desk.

"He said the phone taps and electronic surveillance had been flushed and he wasn't going to risk sending anybody in again. He doesn't seem as worried as he was. No stories in the newspapers. But he was emphatic about our still being on hold."

"Damn. What about that other thing I asked you to run down? The Russian bond deal. What have you got there?"

Chanille faced Ryder on his side of the desk, resting her buns against the desktop, her arms crossed under her breasts. "I read the prospectus--some brass plate Bahamian outfit. The chairman of the board is a local lawyer named William Weller. That's as far as you get with those things. I made some calls about the substance, but only one of my contacts has heard about anything like it and he won't talk. He's a code-cracker at NSA, so what he knows must have come from an intercept of a Soviet transmission. I don't think I'll get anything more out of him. My CIA buddies aren't so closed-mouth."

Ryder raised his eyebrows and waited for her to go on. "Well?"

"Maybe NSA put them onto it, but you know how fixated London Station is on anything to do with the Soviets. They reported a lot of chatter in the market for those old bonds a few days ago. They started back-tracking and found two small buys earlier this fall--each around a hundred thousand-- and some talk about starting a museum. Both buys were credited to a single London dealer probably acting for this outfit in Nassau. Listen, Robbie, my gut tells me something's going down. I know the arms deal is more important, but I think this is worth some serious attention."

"Maybe there's action on the rumor, but there's no proof there's going to be a settlement. And I wouldn't exactly call a tickle in your tush evidence," Ryder said, wondering, not for the first time, what the Agency had wanted with Chanille d'Orsay when they hired her. Sandy told him she had good French and serviceable Russian and was an excellent pistol shot. Ryder had asked about her record when she'd been offered to him, but her personnel file was Top Secret and they wouldn't tell him a thing about her history.

Her willowy frame made her seem taller than her actual five-ten and she'd have had to wear a chador to hide her Junoesque figure. The only thing she would have been good for was setting honey traps for East Bloc diplomats the Company wanted to turn into double agents.

"I don't think it's just speculation," she continued. "People running around talking about hundred-year-old bonds issued by a government that's as defunct as you can get. . . . Something's cooking."

"Get me some coffee," Ryder said. "I need to think a minute."

When she returned, he motioned her to a chair. He didn't want her leaning against his desk again. Too distracting. He took a sip of coffee and asked, "What do you think would prove a settlement— short of an engraved invitation?"

"It'd be nice to know the source. London Station apparently doesn't have a clue and the Brits aren't sharing. If you can't nail the source, some kind of documentation that the settlement is actually going down would be good."

"Where would we get that?"

"Why not tell Tovolaro to get it? He's the one pushing the deal."

"Exactly. That's the way to do it."

Alexandria

"Señor McCall," Mack heard Tovolaro say when he answered the telephone. "This is Raul Tovolaro. I am in Washington. Would it be possible for you to meet me at the Madison Hotel?"

"Of course, General. When would you like to do this?"

"We are prepared to move forward if a few details can be cleared up. Could you come right away? I'll wait for you in the bar."

McCall hung up the phone and walked into the living room where Paralee was stretched out on the new sofa, wearing a gray Georgetown sweat shirt and tight, low-rider jeans, her glasses down on her nose, reading Hourani's *History of the Arab Peoples*.

The room had been transformed since she'd moved in. Following Sam's instructions, McCall had confessed to the funds in escrow, taken receipt of Audrey's inheritance and spent some of it on the condo's décor. The gray wall-to-wall carpet was now brightened by a vivid red and gold Bedouin rug from Jordan and the walls were alive with an array of prints--mostly Impressionists--in austere, but expensive frames. Paralee had also insisted on a stack of Fisher components with serious speakers. She had something Arabic playing to accompany her reading. Mack turned it down to a whisper.

"Want to go downtown and have a drink with General Tovolaro?"

"Tovolaro? Bet your ass. I've never seen a Nazi up close and personal." She leaped off the sofa and ran past him toward the bedroom to change. "Studying for finals is a drag anyway."

****

"Mack," Paralee said as they crossed the 14th Street bridge entering the District. "They're still following us."

"Are you sure?"

"Pretty sure," she said, looking through the back window. "It's hard to tell at night."

"I won't drive to the Madison then. We'll park at the Capital Hilton and go in, then duck out the back of the garage. We'll have to fight our way through the hookers, but we can walk to the Madison."

It was a slow night. Only three or four hookers were on the block across from the *Washington Post*. They eyed McCall but ignored him because Paralee was walking beside him.

They joined Tovolaro in the Madison at a table away from the windows at the far end of the cocktail lounge.

"*Encantado*, Señorita Campbell," Tovolaro said when McCall introduced her, but he frowned, displeased by the unexpected presence of a third party.

Paralee smiled uncertainly. Tovolaro didn't look like a Nazi. The lines of his face were perhaps too strong to give him a grandfatherly image, but his eyes were warm and expressive, even when he frowned. In spite of his eyes, she felt chilled in his presence, as if the aura surrounding him were five degrees cooler than anywhere else in the room.

"You can talk in front of Miss Campbell, General," McCall said. "She's done most of the research on this project and as far as the history of the bonds is concerned, she's the expert."

"Very well. We have had the historical background checked and while we cannot verify every detail, we have confirmed the basic elements." Tovolaro looked at Paralee. "Well done, Señorita," he told her and turned back to McCall. "And we have asked men we trust about you. Still, there are those who want something more."

"Like what?"

Tovolaro rested his forearms on the table and laced his fingers. "We are satisfied that the prospectus is factually true. Tsar Nicholas borrowed a great deal of money in Europe. A fact not in dispute. The bonds are still outstanding. Some are in gold rubles. A large amount of gold was shipped from Russia to Great Britain. All true, yes? Facts not in dispute. We even have information from a reliable source that the gold is still in the Bank of England. And it is encouraging that the Soviets settled the issue of the gold reserves of the Baltic States in 1969. You think this will be the pattern of the settlement this time. That is reasonable. These are facts, Señor McCall, but you have shown us no fact, not even a small bit of evidence, that says a settlement has been agreed to or that one is even being discussed. Is this not so?"

McCall stared at Tovolaro, unblinking.

Tovolaro plunged ahead. "We would like to know the name of your source or what position he holds that gives him access to such information. And we would like some kind of document that proves the settlement has been agreed to by the two governments. Then we would be prepared to release our funds from the escrow."

Paralee saw a flash of anger in McCall's eyes. Tovolaro saw it, too.

As McCall stared at Tovolaro, Angela Collins' face came to him. The wild mane of dark hair, the nervous, excited smile, the dark glasses defeating their purpose of disguise. He even imagined he could feel the touch of her hand on his shoulder and her breath against his neck. He remembered what Dixie said they'd done to her. He'd never seen a woman who'd been gang-raped and tortured, so he had no reference point, but he could imagine how she had been humiliated and subjected to hideous pain for scraps of information that were not going to stop the death squads or the flood of arms into Central America. A bitter taste flooded his mouth. There wasn't going to be any punishment for the people who hurt her and he, Jack McCall, was sitting here doing his damnedest to make one of them richer. The farm might be at stake but he was beginning to believe there had to be a better way. He choked back the anger, took a deep breath and decided to put the ball in the General's court. He could damn well take it or leave it.

He spoke slowly, the words as hard as flint. "General, I trust my source, but I'm not going to tell you who it is. End of story. Call it a matter of honor if you like. I've invested my own money in these bonds. I can give you proof that I've done so. If that's not enough, we're finished here." McCall pushed back from the table, his legs coiled to stand.

Paralee's eyes widened in surprise. So did Tovolaro's.

"What about a document?" Tovolaro asked. "It might not be necessary to know the man's name or position." When McCall made no further move, Tovolaro relaxed a little and went on. "I admire your loyalty. But surely you understand our concern, Señor McCall. Give us something. At least some document that would confirm the settlement but not make a trail to your source."

McCall kept his eyes fixed on Tovolaro's for several long moments, the outline of an idea forming in his head. "A document," he said at last, sighing. "A document. Maybe we could do that. I'll have to let you know."

****

"Mack, you don't have any proof, do you?" Paralee asked, skipping alongside him to keep up as they made their way back to the Capital Hilton. "Surely you're not going to ask Chilty for something. . . . You're not, are you?"

"Of course not. But I think I can give Tovolaro a document," McCall said, charging down the sidewalk. The population had grown and McCall had to weave between young ladies in leather mini-skirts and knee high boots, some in ski jackets and stocking caps because of the chill evening.

"How?" she asked, hurrying to keep pace.

"Tovolaro needs something he can hold in his hand. It doesn't matter what it is because I've already told him the truth. Something from the *Russian* side ought to do it."

"Russian?"

"There's nothing in the prospectus that says my source is British."

257

"Right. It doesn't say."

"So why can't my source be Russian?"

"Because you don't know any Russians. . . . Do you?"

"*They* don't know that," he said and waited for it to sink in. When she didn't respond, he went on.

"Look. All I'm after is a document that provides tangible evidence that the settlement's being discussed. Right? If I truly, truly believe the settlement is on, I'm not lying if I make up a Russian document and a story to go with it. All I need is a Russian to write it up and make it look legitimate. And it turns out that I *do* know such a Russian. You ought to know him, too. He teaches at Georgetown. His name is Andre Yanov."

"What does he teach . . . forgery?"

****

Sandy Hammond took the call at home, sitting in his lounge chair in front of the television set. "What have you got, Danielo?" he asked.

"He slipped the tail downtown, so he knows he's being followed. We picked him and the girl up at the Madison. They met a man in the bar there. A Latino. Civilian clothes, but my guy said he looked military. They met for about fifteen minutes. My man was inside, watching the meeting, but he couldn't hear what they were saying. It seemed to him, though, that they reached some kind of agreement. They shook hands. Then McCall and the woman left."

"OK, Danielo. Let's think a minute. He's onto the tail. He had his apartment swept. He knows you came calling."

"We're not getting back in, either," Martinez interrupted. "He had a state-of-the-art lock and a steel door installed. You could blow it off the hinges with C4, but that's the only way I know."

"Yeah," Hammond replied absently. "I can't figure out what the deal is. He brought that woman's stuff out of La Paz, but it hasn't surfaced anywhere. That's a funny little mystery, but we're not going to get anything from this guy now. No point in going on with the surveillance. Roll it up, Danielo. Send me a bill. Thanks, *compañero*."

****

When Paralee first saw Andre Yanov, a rumpled bear of a man in a three-day old shirt and a stained tie, with a tangled beard shot through with streaks of gray, he was wedged into a small office that reeked of strong, bitter cigarette smoke and rank body odor. The office was dark except for a desk lamp that left Yanov's face mostly in shadow. The desk was covered with books and papers and he was writing in a cleared space about the size of a ruled pad. He peered at her and McCall through steel-rimmed glasses and broke into a smile when he recognized McCall.

"Mr. Martini," he said, pushing his chair back, rising and extending a very large hand across the cluttered desk. "Good to see you again. Sit," he said, but the two chairs were buried in books and bulging manila file folders.

"That's OK," McCall said. "Looks like you're a little cramped for space here. I just came to ask a favor. It's very important to me and I'm willing to pay for your help."

Yanov sighed and McCall sensed that he was disappointed it wasn't a social call. He leaned back in his chair, folded his hands over his stomach and closed his eyes. When he reopened them, he seemed resigned to hearing them out.

"What is this favor?"

McCall decided to tell him as much of the truth as he required. Yanov listened with growing interest as McCall, prompted occasionally by Paralee, went through the story of the Tsar's bonds and the gold movements. Then McCall explained that a close friend, almost a brother, had given him information that there would be a settlement of claims and that he was trying to capitalize on it, but he wanted to shift attention far away from his source, to actually put it on the other side. McCall told Yanov he wanted a Russian document that would confirm or strongly suggest that a settlement was imminent. He confessed he didn't know what such a document should contain or where it should come from. He was wide open to suggestions.

Yanov sat very still for quite some time before he said anything. Finally, he asked McCall. "Is for CIA?"

McCall gave a short laugh and said, "No. This is just business. No politics."

"Business? OK. I give you what you need."

McCall grinned. "That's great. How much will it cost?"

"Teach me your Martini. Best I ever tasted."

"Fantastic," McCall said, grinning. "No problem. But the document . . . I need it right away. Like tonight."

Yanov shrugged and nodded his great head. "*Da, da.* I can do it. I give you negotiator's travel document. It will say his responsibilities and authorities. I have seen many like it. It is not difficult. My word processor is with Cyrillic characters, but I need European paper--here you say A4. I will write travel authority but you must bring me paper." He tore out the pages he'd been writing on, added them to one of the piles on his desk and began working on a new sheet.

****

"Where the hell am I going to get A4 paper?" McCall asked as they went through the outer doors into Red Square, the affectionate name given to the red brick courtyard of the Intercultural Center, where Georgetown University's School of Foreign Service was headquartered.

"Office supply? One of the embassies?" Paralee asked. "What's it look like?"

"It's measured in millimeters. It's a little bigger than ours. And he's not kidding. It'd be noticeable if we used our stuff."

"Let's try the Georgetown bookstore before we go chasing around. It's practically next door. OK?"

"Why not?"

"What do you think of his idea for the document?" Paralee asked as they hurried through the late afternoon chill, fallen leaves swirling along the bricks of the narrow walkway.

"It's aces. Perfect."

"Are you sure? We just made up a guy who's traveling. He'll have to have a name. What if they check the roster of the Ministry of Finance and don't find him on it?"

"If they look and don't find him, they'll think he's KGB or part of some special group. That'd be even better."

"How are we going to get it to them? You didn't make any arrangements with Tovolaro."

"One step at a time. When we've got the document, I'll call Tovolaro and work it out."

She pulled him to a halt outside the Leavey Center, where the bookstore was located. "There's something else, McCall. If you go anywhere with this, I'm going with you--Perú, Bolivia, Panamá, London, wherever. That's a non-negotiable demand." She tugged at his arm until he looked directly at her.

"Where'd you get this 'non-negotiable demand' thing? I thought that went out with the '60s," he said, hiding his pleasure in looking at her, the high collar of her Navy pea-coat turned up, the cold wind blushing her cheeks, blue eyes hard and bright even in the soft light of late afternoon.

"You do understand what it means, don't you?"

"OK," he said. "You're on the manifest. Now stop being a pain in the ass."

****

Yanov removed his steel-rimmed glasses, rubbed his eyes and grunted when McCall passed him the paper. Yanov inspected it, took several sheets, added another one from his desk and held them out to Paralee. "Copy seal from old paper onto new paper. Hide all what is written on old paper, so is clean paper with seal only. Understand? Then we print new document."

It was after eight o'clock when they left Yanov's office. McCall's inside coat pocket contained two copies of a Soviet travel order for Mikhail Aliyev, deputy assistant minister for finance, authorizing him to fly from Moscow to London to meet with representatives of the British Foreign Ministry to finalize arrangements for a settlement of financial and property claims between the two governments. At least that's what Yanov said it said. It was written in Russian and as far as McCall could tell, it was a love letter from Yanov to an old girl friend. Before they left, McCall wrote down the simple instructions for his Martini and thanked Yanov profusely. "Next time, bring gin." Yanov said and waved them out of his office.

Tonosi, Panamá

Julian Pressman, wearing a bush jacket, khaki trousers and scuffed boots, blended into the tree line at the rude jungle airfield twenty miles from Tonosi. He'd inspected the crates of AK-47s, still in cosmoline, being loaded into an old C-119 under Carlos Sosa's supervision. Julian's sense of smell was assaulted by the fetid rot of the jungle and of Carlos Sosa every time he came near. His camouflage shirt was soaked with rancid sweat that reeked of garlic and stale beer.

Sosa was growing more irritable with each passing moment as the efforts of the men doing the heaving and hauling flagged in the tropical heat. Finally, he called a break. "¡Cinco minutos!" he commanded and, mopping his face and neck with a soggy, stained handkerchief, he joined Julian at the tree line.

"How much longer?" Julian asked, swatting nervously at the mosquitoes feasting on the exposed patches of his skin. "You're cutting it close."

"Before the sun sets," Sosa growled and cast a concerned eye toward the sky, already showing pink streaks against the low clouds.

Sosa stepped away a few paces to where a canvas water bag hung from the limb of a young flame tree, stuck his head under it and let the water cascade over him. When he stood up, the water coursed down his front and back and he shook his head from side to side like a wet dog, flinging spray in all directions. He turned back to Julian.

"What have you learned about this man Ryder?"

"Ryder? Oh, yeah. Him. Sonofabitch owns his own plane--a Lear, no less. We've got a source at his home field keeping tabs on the flight plans his pilot files. Trouble is, he charters it to other people. The plane goes out of country, but that doesn't mean he's on it. We're not going to be able to give you as much lead time as you'd like. Better be ready to go on a moment's notice."

"Can't you do better than that?" Sosa frowned.

"I've got tags on him in New Jersey, where he keeps the plane, and in Miami, Houston and New Orleans. We've got the Caribbean and South America covered unless he gets really cute crossing the border, like flying out of McAllen or El Paso, Texas. And we'll know about that from our watch on New Jersey. You won't need a lot of lead time if he comes this way. He'll be flying right to you."

"And if he goes to Europe?"

"Well, that's another story," Julian conceded, taking a damp pack of cigarettes from his shirt pocket and offering it to Sosa. Sosa plucked one with finger and thumb and returned the pack. Julian lit both cigarettes with an ancient Zippo.

"Does he go there often?" Julian asked.

"Europe? How should I know? I asked you to find out. How difficult can it be?"

"Carlos, your personal vendetta isn't one of the Company's main concerns," Julian snapped. "It's not like we can tell the rest of the world to take time out while we do you a personal favor." The words were out of Julian's mouth before he saw the look in Sosa's eyes and wished he could take them back. He held up his right hand, palm outward, and quickly added, "I'll see what I can do."

Washington

Two days later McCall was sitting across a round table from Raul Tovolaro in a conference room in the Clipper Club at Washington's Dulles International. "Your source is Russian, Señor McCall?"

"We've been through that, General, and I'm getting downright weary of it. You want a document and I'm getting you one. It happens to be in Russian. Don't read anything more than that into it."

"Very well," Tovolaro said, frowning. "How are we to proceed?"

"My guy wants ten thousand pounds for a document that proves the settlement is being actively negotiated--not agreed to, understand--but in the final stages. He'll have it delivered to you or someone you designate. In Paris. And only in Paris. Not in the US. Not in London. Not in Moscow or Geneva or Rome. If you agree, he'll let me know how he wants to handle it from there and then I'll tell you--time, place, the whole routine."

"How will we get the document?"

"By courier. That's as much as I know right now. Are you going to make the exchange yourself or send a representative? He may want to know who's going to be there for your side."

"I will send a representative."

"Got a name?"

"Our financial manager. Robert Ryder."

McCall was stunned. Paralee's instincts had been right all along. Angela was worked over in Bolivia--Tovolaro's territory--because she knew about an arms deal for the Contras. Javier said Ryder was putting together an arms deal. So *Las Águilas* was backing his play to acquire Banco Dorado. If Tovolaro was still using Ryder . . . would he honor the deal he'd made with McCall on *Isla de la Luna* to steer clear of Banco Dorado? Asking for all this information about the bonds made McCall nervous, like maybe Tovolaro--and Ryder--were going to try to run the bonds without him.

"Ryder? After what he did in Panamá, he's still on your payroll?"

Tovolaro shrugged, his eyes hooded. "His father was our financial adviser for many years, Señor McCall. And we only have the girl's word for what Roberto did. He says she enticed him."

"What about Banco Dorado? You promised me you'd stop trying to acquire it. And *for* that, I only have *your* word." "Yes," Tovolaro said. "We discussed Comercio de Colón and I gave instructions not to pursue Banco Dorado."

McCall fixed Tovolaro with a hard stare, trying not to let his face show the several facets of anger and mistrust suddenly boiling inside him. Angela. The double-cross his bones told him Tovolaro was pulling. He still had one ace in the hole, but if he had any qualms about getting Yanov to forge a travel document, they evaporated.

"How does your man want the money?" Tovolaro asked.

"A small package. Hundreds, in a brief case. That's how they do it in the movies. Where can I reach you?" McCall asked.

Tovolaro tore a page from the notebook he'd been writing in, scribbled a number and handed it to McCall.

McCall read it. "New York?" he asked, noting the 212 area code. Tovolaro nodded. "I'll be in touch," McCall said, pushing back his chair.

****

"Can you talk?" McCall asked when he reached Javier at the bank.

"Mack! I'm glad you called. Wait. Let me close my door."

Javier came back on the line a moment later. "They're buying stock from minority shareholders."

"Shit. How do you know?"

"Carlotta had lunch with the wives of two of them and they told her they had just sold their shares to Morales' lawyer."

"Is Morales buying up shares?"

"I don't think he has the money. The family is hurting." Javier was silent for a long moment. Then he asked, "Didn't you say that *Las Águilas* had agreed not to come after us?"

"That's what Tovolaro told me on *Isla de la Luna* and he confirmed it just today when I met with him. He said he'd given instructions to leave Banco Dorado alone and go after Comercio de Colón. I don't necessarily believe him, though. In fact, I think they might be trying to cut me out of my share of the syndicate. Which probably also means they're reneging on their agreement to stay away from Banco Dorado."

"Could Ryder be doing it on his own?" Javier asked.

"I don't know, but Ryder and Tovolaro are still buddy-buddy, even after what I told Tovolaro about Ryder and Carlotta. There are lots of different ways to tell a lie. I'd like to find a way to cover our asses."

"I think I have a way," Javier said. "But I don't want to talk in the clear on the phone. ¿Entiendes? We need to get together. Right away. Could you fly to Miami? I've been trying to call you for two weeks. We have much to discuss."

"How about tonight? You could fly back in the morning."

"I can take the three-o'clock flight and be there by six. We can have dinner and I can be back here by noon tomorrow."

"Perfect. See you in the Admiral's Club. We can take it from there."

McCall put down the phone and turned to Paralee. "I think you were right," he said. "Not about the drugs. But about torture and killing. Now you can throw in an arms deal for good measure. Our being followed . . . It's all the same people. But we're going to fight back. Want to help?"

She rushed into his arms, almost knocking the breath out of him. There were tears in her eyes. "Do I ever!"

"Then get dressed. We're going to Miami. You'll get to meet an old friend of mine."

Miami

Paralee dressed for comfort in a khaki skirt and brown leather penny loafers with a short-sleeved sweater under a leather jacket. Her makeup was minimal. There hadn't been time or purpose in dressing up and Mack had rushed her every step of the way. Miami International was a melting pot of fashion and, coming off the plane and walking down the concourse, she felt adequately stylish. Then they met Javier in the Admiral's Club and she saw Carlotta.

Carlotta was wearing high heel shoes, a silk blouse, tailored business suit and enough makeup for the cover of two issues of *Vogue*. With her dark hair and almond-shaped, ebony eyes, she was stunning. Paralee knew the type--she'd seen many like her in Paris, dressed off the most expensive and tasteful racks. She appeared to be no more than twenty-five, but she seized control of the meeting as soon as the introductions were made.

"Javier assured me that you had agreed with these people not to continue trying to buy our bank, but apparently you were mistaken. They are still attacking us, Señor McCall," she said, her teeth flashing in bright contrast with the burnished copper of her skin.

What the hell, McCall thought, *'No 'nice to meet you,' just wham-bam, right in the chops.'*

"As Javier may have told you," Carlotta went on. "I am determined to prevent this man from gaining control of Banco Dorado. Since your plans have failed, I have found a way to use the Russian bonds to fight him off."

Paralee sat straight up. *'Who is this girl?'* she wondered. She saw an angry glance pass from Mack to Javier.

"Señorita Benedetti," McCall said, getting up, his face flushed. "Could I get you something to drink? What about you, Paralee?" He didn't wait for either of them to reply. "I'll bring some Cokes." He jerked his head at Javier, a signal to follow him. "Come on, Javier. You can help me."

Once they were out of sight of the women, McCall grabbed Javier's arm and dragged him to a pair of empty lounge chairs. "What the hell's going on here, Javier?" he asked, his anger barely contained. "She knows about the bonds?"

"Mack," Javier said, leaning forward on the edge of his seat. "This is what I needed to talk to you about."

"You told her about the bonds?"

"I had no choice. When they began buying the shares of the minority stockholders, we knew your agreement with *Las Águilas* had been broken.

But listen. She has a good idea," Javier said. "Do you know about options, Mack?"

"Of course I know about options. What the hell do options have to do with anything?"

"We bought call options on the Russian bonds," Javier announced with bright eyes and a gleaming smile. "We were able to buy twenty million dollars worth of Russian bonds for only ninety thousand. Charles Foster did it for us. We have huge position in the market."

McCall took a moment to run the numbers in his head. "You paid four and half percent of current market price for the options? What's your strike price?" he asked, still seething.

"It ranges from twelve to fifteen. They're not all the same because we had to deal with so many people and there is no organized market. Charles' brother is a big collector and knows all the dealers. We'd never have been able to do it with anyone else. It was a great stroke of luck to have gone to Charles in the beginning."

"And you did this without talking to me?" McCall's fury frayed what little patience he had left.

"Mack," Javier protested. "I tried to call you many times before we bought the options. I left a message. When I heard back from you, it was to tell me not to call. Charles said he couldn't hold the deals so we had to go ahead. What should I have done?"

"Damn well sit on it! That's what you should have done," McCall said, the anger spilling over. "Sit on it until we had a chance to talk."

"But we have the chance now, Mack," Javier pleaded, spreading his hands wide. "I couldn't have kept the information from her. I'm sorry about that. I didn't think you would be so angry, Mack. We reserved half the options for you. Give us forty-five thousand--or whatever you want--and we'll transfer them to you. We never intended to cut you out, Mack. You know I wouldn't do that."

McCall sighed, the anger draining away. All he had to do was look at Javier's pained expression to know he'd meant no harm and thought he'd been very, very clever.

"OK," McCall said. "Maybe it can work this way. As I told you on the phone, *Las Águilas* practically want me to guarantee the deal, so I've swotted up a document that should satisfy them. It's bogus, but so what? They're just squeezing me for all the information I'll give them before they screw me. Guess who they're sending to pick up the document?"

"Who?"

"Ryder. The managing director for *Las Águilas* is a Bolivian, General Tovolaro. He's the one I made contact with down there. I put it to him about Ryder raping Carlotta and he promised me he'd take care of it. Obviously, he was just bull-shitting me about laying off Banco Dorado and about getting rid of Ryder."

"Ay, *Dios Mio*," Javier said.

"That's not all," McCall continued. "In La Paz, I ran into a lady I know, a writer. She was investigating a conduit for Contra arms. It has to be Ryder's. Anyway, I brought back some documents for her and delivered them to the Congressional Select Committee on Intelligence. But the Bolivian secret police snatched her and tortured her. She told them everything she knew, including the fact that she'd given me the documents. She got away, but it was a lucky thing. These are bad people. I want to put one in Ryder's ear for this and I want to cut off *Las Águilas'* balls at the same time. I was going to try to get you to talk to all the minority shareholders and put together a syndicate to invest in the bonds with them. I already have the prospectus, the one I put together for *Las Águilas*. Maybe it would keep them from selling if that were part of the deal. But maybe the options will work even better. It's a longer shot, but it's all we've got."

"What are you thinking, Mack?"

"In a minute. Let's get some things straight about these options. Your young lady may have done well in the classroom, but that's not the same thing as doing a deal. You know that. The way it stands, you have every reason to write off that ninety thousand you paid for those options. But if we're lucky--if what I have in mind for Ryder and *Las Águilas* works-- maybe you won't lose it all."

"What do you mean?" Javier asked. "We won't lose the ninety thousand. When they announce the settlement, we exercise our options and submit them to the British. We will make a huge profit and we can buy out the minority shareholders."

McCall shook his head all the time Javier was talking. "It won't work that way, Javier."

"But Mack, I trust your information. There will be a settlement. It's not a speculation. We know the prices will rise."

"You don't know any such thing," McCall told him, a forefinger pressed into Javier's lapel. "This is a settlement between governments, not markets. In fact, the market price is likely to *fall* after the settlement is announced because the only people who'll get anything out of the deal are the ones with eligible claims. You'll have to be a holder of record on the day *before* the announcement--maybe even many days before--not the day after. Do you understand? If you can't afford to exercise those options *before* the settlement is announced, you'd be a damned fool to exercise them afterward because the door to the settlement room will be closed and locked."

Sweat beaded on Javier's forehead. "Dios mío, Mack. What have we done?"

"Look, if I've read Ryder and *Las Águilas* right, if they're going to try to do this deal on their own, maybe we can get them to buy the Russian bonds now. If Ryder goes into the market, you can clear your options selling bonds to him and we can stick him and *Las Águilas* with a bundle of bonds they can't cash when the settlement is announced. Charles Foster will have to help us pull it off. Before we get there, though, I think it might help to give your sassy *señorita* a little scare."

****

Carlotta was disconcerted when McCall and Javier returned and escorted the women back to a bare-bones conference room Mack booked with the reception desk. The room had an oblong table with six chairs. A carafe of water sat on a credenza with two stacks of plastic cups wrapped in cellophane. McCall began speaking right away.

"Señorita Benedetti, I have some bad news for you," McCall began. Then, patiently, he laid out the problem for Carlotta as he had for Javier, watching her flush with anger, then turn pale as the nature and the extent of the bank's exposure became clear.

"What are we to do?" Carlotta asked in a trembling voice when McCall finished.

"I've got an idea how to make them work for us, but you need to understand that if these were ordinary options bought in an organized market, you'd be stuck with them. The price you pay for an option is not, repeat not, refundable. And in this case, you stand to lose the whole ninety thousand. What you need to do is camp out in Charles Foster's trading room and be ready to pounce if you get the chance. Incidentally," McCall added, turning to Javier. "Didn't Charles caution you about this? I'm surprised he didn't warn you off."

Javier shook his head sadly. "He did, but I didn't tell him I knew the price of the bonds would rise. For me at that time, it wasn't a speculation."

"It is my fault," Carlotta said, chagrined at last. "I wanted to stop that man. He's the reason my papá had a heart attack. He's the one who wants to steal our bank. I was too eager . . ." She put her hand on Javier's forearm and looked at him with large, soulful eyes.

Paralee saw Carlotta's look and felt some pity for Javier, but she was more taken with McCall's self-assured, totally-in-control performance. He'd surgically dissected a crisis and put Carlotta in her place, all the while remaining patient but uncompromising. He'd humbled Carlotta, but to

Paralee's surprise, he'd managed to leave her honor intact and given her room to recover.

Javier patted Carlotta's hand and got out of his chair. "I'll be back," he said. "I'm going to book a flight for London."

When he returned, he announced, "We can leave in twenty minutes. We have to hurry, Carlotta. Mack," he added. "If you need to reach me, call Charles Foster's office. I'll leave word there where we are staying."

"*Buena suerte, compadre*," McCall said, rising to walk with them. "We're going to be in Paris in two days. I'll be in touch."

****

The following morning, McCall dialed Tovolaro's New York number from their Miami airport hotel room. "General?" he said when Tovolaro picked up the phone. "The document will be delivered to the Hotel Élysée Ponthieu, 24 rue de Ponthieu, between ten o'clock and twelve o'clock day after tomorrow--that's Thursday. We assume you're still sending Ryder."

"Yes."

"He's to tell the clerk his name is Maurice. The clerk will give him a room key. He's to go to that room and wait for the courier. The courier will ask for Maurice and be told to reply 'Crimson' when your man asks who it is. The courier will give him the document and Ryder will give the courier the money. Are you getting this?"

"I'm writing it down," Tovolaro snapped. "How can we be sure the document is genuine before he gives the courier the money?"

"General, I just don't know what to tell you," McCall said, losing patience. "Tell him to bring his favorite Russian along to read it if he wants to. He can bring Gorbachev himself for all I care, but if he turns it down, our deal is dead. I'll have BITCO release your five million and we'll forget the whole fucking thing." McCall paused, playing the hand to the hilt. Then he added, "Now hear this, General. We're taking risks with people's lives to satisfy you on this, so that ten thousand pounds is due and payable whether Ryder likes the looks of the document or not. You hear me? If he thinks he can take the information and waltz out of there without paying, you tell him people will be watching. He won't make it across the street if he doesn't pay. Am I making myself clear?"

"Yes, Señor. Perfectly clear."

****

"What was all that about somebody watching and him not making it

271

across the street?" Paralee asked when McCall hung up.

"Sudden inspiration. We swotted up a mysterious Russian, might as well give him some sinister credibility. Don't you think Tovolaro would expect something like that?"

"OK. But Russian shooters, Mack," she said, closing the few paces between them and putting her arms around his neck "Isn't that over the top? What if this guy turns it down and doesn't get blown away?"

"It won't matter. They'll have called our bluff and we'll lose the hand. There's no safe way to play it."

New York

Rob Ryder slouched in the overstuffed black leather chair in his World Trade Center office listening to Raul Tovolaro relate the details of his meeting in Washington. The degree of his attention fell short of rapt until Tovolaro mentioned McCall's name.

"McCall?" Ryder said, almost coming out of the chair. "McCall's the guy who brought you the Russian bond deal?"

"Do you know him?" Tovolaro asked.

Chanille entered the office bringing a tray with a coffee service--too late to hear of McCall's connection to the Russian bonds, but just in time to hear Ryder mention his name.

"McCall?" she asked as she arranged the coffee cups and carafe on a sideboard and prepared to serve. "We still don't know what he did with those documents. But nothing's surfaced, so we ought to be hearing from Sandy any day now."

When Chanille turned around, a cup and saucer in each hand, wisps of steam drifting up from the cups, she found both Ryder and Tovolaro staring at her.

"What?"

"McCall. That's what," Ryder said, agitation and astonishment flushing his pale cheeks. "He was in La Paz and now the General says he's the guy putting this Russian bond deal together."

It was Tovolaro's turn to be astonished. "The woman reporter? . . . McCall was the *gringo* in La Paz?"

"I thought you knew," Chanille said.

"No," Tovolaro replied, his brows furrowed. "I met with him the day before she was detained. On *Isla de la Luna*. He would have been in La Paz the next night. But it's not possible the two things are connected. Not possible." He shook his head.

Ryder fell back in the chair. Chanille was still standing at the sideboard, holding the two cups of coffee, mouth slightly agape, as stunned as the other two.

Ryder collected himself first. "I agree. The thing in La Paz was an accident. He was passing through, somebody introduced them or she just grabbed the first American she laid eyes on. He might have helped her just because she was an American and a woman in distress."

"But if he did pick up her documents, they're not at his place. Sandy's people tossed it and came up empty," Chanille said. "They think he FedExed them to a bank in the Bahamas."

"The Bahamas?" Tovolaro asked.

"We had surveillance on him when he got back from Bolivia. He put a package in FedEx right before he hopped another plane. This was just before Thanksgiving."

Tovolaro shook his head. "No, no. That was the prospectus. He sent it to BITCO in Nassau. That was our arrangement. BITCO sent the prospectus to Villaneuva in Miami when we put our money in escrow."

"Then he still has the documents. Of course, he might have passed the stuff before Sandy's surveillance kicked in, but if he did, why haven't we seen a story in the *Washington Post*?" Chanille said.

"Maybe he's waiting for her to pick them up," Ryder said.

"Then where are they?" Chanille asked.

"Stop this!" Tovolaro said. "We will deal with the Russian bonds first."

Ryder walked to the window and stared out at the Hudson River and the broad reaches leading to the Atlantic. When he turned around, he said, "OK. Forget La Paz and the documents. We shouldn't get hung up on that. Maybe he never had the documents or there's no connection between him and the woman in La Paz. There's no question that the bonds are his deal. Think about it. His bank is busted and he's been black-listed with the banking regulators. By now, he's probably on a list with the SEC, too. So he's marginalized in the business. He has to operate off-shore if he's going to operate at all."

Ryder paced back and forth across the panel of windows, waving his arms, oblivious to Tovolaro and Chanille who watched him like spectators at a tennis match. "The inside information is the key to this deal. Without the inside information, there's no play on the bonds." He turned to Tovolaro. "So what's he got that's worth going to Paris for?"

"He claims to have a document that will prove the negotiations are ongoing," Tovolaro replied slowly, his eyes fixed on Ryder. "It is in Russian and it will cost us ten thousand pounds. This is what you are to do." Tovolaro handed Ryder the notes he'd taken while talking to McCall on the telephone that morning.

Ryder scanned them quickly and passed them to Chanille. "Russian, huh? Remember the thing in Vienna?" he said to Chanille. "Magyar Enterprises? Maybe your buddies didn't see him meeting with anybody or maybe that little *fraulein* he took to bed wasn't a graduate student after all. Maybe she was passing information to him." Ryder stopped and looked from Tovolaro to Chanille for a reaction to his reasoning. They each gave him a blank look so he went on.

"Look what we've got here. The bond deal depends on the inside information and we don't know where it came from. We pushed him for proof and now he's showing us a document in Russian. What if the Russians paid McCall to lay this on? Classic disinformation. They dummy up a cross-claims settlement and point McCall toward *Las Águilas . . .*"

"Robbie!" Chanille interrupted. "For God's sake, the man's an American war hero. He's not a Russian agent. You're being totally paranoid. And you're not making sense. You're just looking for reasons not to do this deal."

Ryder turned on her with fury in his eyes, his face suddenly flushed. He took several deep breaths, as if he were going to say something, then changed his mind. Slowly, his color returned and he relaxed. "You're wrong about that, Chanille." Tovolaro fidgeted, impatient with Ryder's speculations about McCall. "Are you going to Paris or not?" he asked Ryder. "The arrangements have been made and time is running out." Ryder looked at Tovolaro and knew there was more at stake than McCall's flaky Russian bond deal. If he didn't go, Tovolaro would think him a coward. It could be the beginning of the end of a profitable relationship. He wasn't ready for that.

"I'll go," Ryder said.

"One last thing, Roberto," Tovolaro said. "You must pay the ten thousand whether you believe the document is genuine or not."

"Oh? Why is that?"

"You will be watched. The Russians will kill you if you double cross them."

"Oh, now I've heard it all," Ryder said, laughing in spite of his resolve to humor Tovolaro. "McCall is really blowing smoke up your ass. If he's got a document, it's phony. The ten thousand pounds is just to make you think it's real. Now it's Russians waiting in the weeds with sniper rifles! That's too much."

"What if you're wrong, Robbie?" Chanille asked. "What if you're wrong about all of it and McCall's on the level? And what if he still has the documents stashed somewhere? You know what that could mean for you."

Tovolaro glared at Ryder. "I agree. You're acting like a child, Roberto. You are the one who demanded proof. He has produced it. He has a right to be annoyed and he has a right to demand some price for the nuisance you have caused."

Ryder fell silent, drawing back into himself. "I don't know. Maybe. Suppose I change my mind after I see his document. What then?"

"The choice is yours, Roberto. You can call me and say you think the proposition is legitimate or not. In either case, you will have done us a service. If you decide the proposition is as McCall has said it is, you have my authority to invest up to ten million in the gold bonds for the account of *Las Águilas* on the terms we mentioned previously--five percent of the net profit. And as I offered before, you may join us with your own investment. As much as a million if you like. The choice is yours."

Tovolaro took Ryder's silence for assent and rose from the chair. "Call me when you have seen the document."

When Tovolaro was gone, Ryder turned to Chanille. "Get me ten thousand pounds in hundreds," he told her when she was halfway across the room. "Charge it to *Las Águilas*. Then get hold of Tommy and tell him to file a flight plan for Paris for tomorrow. Charge the flight to Las Águilas. Two passengers. You and me. Don't pack everything you own, but bring your little Beretta. You think Russians are hiding in the bushes, so you can ride shotgun. Use our Walker identities for the hotel, but we'll be Ryder and d'Orsay for the flight manifest."

"How will I get the Beretta past Customs?" Chanille asked. "They're getting tougher, you know."

"Ask Tommy. I don't think they're so tight at Le Bourget, where the business jets land."

"What'll we do about verifying this document?" she said, turning to leave. Ryder sighed. "I thought you spoke Russian."

"Yeah, but I don't want the responsibility for this one." Ryder gave her a look of disgust. "We'll pick up somebody in Paris, then."

Panamá City

Carlos Sosa's direct line rang at the headquarters of the PDF and he answered gruffly. "Sosa."

"It's Julian. Your bird is flying tomorrow--to Paris. Best guess on his ETA is early morning of the next day. He'll be using Le Bourget. If you get there before him, you can pick him up when he lands. The rest is up to you.'

"*Muchas gracias*, Julian," Sosa said and hung up the phone.

"Consuelo!" he yelled, vaulting out of his chair. He was pulling on his coat when she appeared an instant later. "Call Tocumen. Tell them to hold the Paris flight. I'm leaving now. Call the Foreign Ministry and tell them I'm taking charge of the diplomatic pouches and I want someone from the embassy to meet me in Paris. I don't want any trouble with French Customs." He turned into the hall and headed for the front door. Consuelo trotted after him, writing furiously in her steno pad. "If General Noriega asks for me, tell him I had urgent personal business and that I'll return in three days. Sergeant Rodriguez is standing by?"

"Yes, sir. As you ordered."

Consuelo followed him to the front door of the headquarters and watched him get into the waiting staff car. Then she hurried back upstairs to make the phone calls.

****

"My valise is in the trunk, Rodriguez? And my overcoat?"

"Yes, Comandante," Rodriguez replied, at sharp attention as he opened the door of the sedan, his gold tooth smiling a greeting. "I checked this morning." Rodriguez was almost as old as the major and they'd served together for years, as far back as the days when Sosa was Comandante of the Fifth Zone. Rodriguez and Sosa were comrades-in-arms and brothers in blood, their relationship defined more by their common membership in *Fuerza Ocho* than by their respective ranks.

Rodriguez closed the door for Major Sosa and got behind the wheel. He looked in the mirror, awaiting Sosa's command.

"Tocumen," Sosa barked. "The military terminal. They're holding the plane. Use the siren." Rodriguez grinned, put the car in gear and roared away from PDF headquarters, siren wailing.

Sosa reached under the front seat and withdrew the attaché case he kept there. He opened it, removed his diplomatic passport and tucked it into the inside coat pocket of his uniform. He'd change into civilian clothes on the plane, but it was reassuring to feel the passport against his chest now. Diplomatic immunity was his ticket out of trouble if anything went wrong. Checking the Glock 9mm automatic was his next order of business. He pulled back the slide to see that a round wasn't chambered, removed the clip, made sure it carried a full load, checked the spare clip, then eased the weapon back into its shoulder holster, where the silencer rested in a piggy-back sleeve. It would travel in one of the diplomatic pouches where it would be protected from customs inspection. He was ready.

"May I know your mission, Comandante?" Rodriguez asked, checking the mirror as he sped through the morning traffic.

"A matter of family honor, Emilio. A *gringo* named Roberto Ryder raped the virgin daughter of my *padrino*."

"May I come with you, Comandante?"

"Not this time, old friend," Sosa replied. "Not this time."

Paris

The morning was cold and gray when McCall and Paralee landed at Charles de Gaulle International. Gritty from lack of sleep because of the time difference, they claimed their baggage, loaded it on a cart and trudged through the 'Nothing to Declare' exit. Outside, they found a Peugot taxi and fell into the big back seat.

"I've never been here at Christmas," McCall said, gazing out the window as the cab worked its way toward the city through the morning traffic and the cold, gray dawn.

"It's a little different from the States," she said as they passed huge blocks of apartment buildings. "Parisians don't go crazy with decorations the way we do, but look, there are some strings of lights on the balconies over there."

They arrived at the Hotel Vernet at mid-morning, checked in and fell into bed. They rose to shower and dress around noon.

"We need to get over to the Élysée Ponthieu and book a room," McCall said as he shaved. Paralee stood at his shoulder, watching with fascination.

"You're making me nervous. I'm going to cut myself."

"I like to watch this. You make such funny faces," she said, mimicking him stretching his upper lip and moving his mouth to one side and the other to shave his cheeks.

"Out," he said. "Make yourself useful. See if you can find a courier service that will do this the way we want."

"I'll call Jean-Claude. When I worked for the travel agency, I used him all the time to deliver tickets. He's a small shop, so he'll be eager for the business. He won't mind all the hocus-pocus."

"Big or little doesn't matter as long as he's reliable."

"Not a problem. He'll be fine."

McCall finished shaving and dressed. He could hear Paralee on the phone but couldn't distinguish anything she was saying. She had just hung up when he came out of the bathroom.

"We're set with Jean-Claude," she told him.

"Great. The Élysée Ponthieu's not far. We can walk if you don't mind the weather," he said, looking out the window at a gray sky he knew would be damp and cold.

As they prepared to leave the room, Paralee took him by the shoulders and looked him up and down. "You're cool," she said, admiring the battered felt hat he'd set on his head at a rakish angle, hiding his hair and much of his face. "The white scarf's a nice touch. With that flight jacket, you look like you're headed for the dawn patrol. Where'd you get the hat?"

"I carry it with me. In case it rains. Come on, let's get going," he said, pushing her through the door and down the hall toward the elevators.

"Why'd you pick the Élysée Ponthieu?" she asked when they were outside, striding toward the Champs Élysée.

"It's central and cheap--for Paris, that is. And I've stayed there before. That's all."

"He's only going to be using it for an hour or so, right?"

"That's the plan."

The Élysée Ponthieu was located a block off the Champs Élysées and McCall booked a room for the following day for 'Maurice.' It took less than five minutes. Walking away from the hotel, he said, "Why don't we go on down to the Tuileries?"

Mist hung in the air as they turned onto the Champs Élysées and headed toward the Place de la Concorde. They passed sidewalk cafés, glassed in for winter and just beginning to pick up an early afternoon crowd of Christmas shoppers. The show windows along the way were more gaily decorated for the holidays than the streets and the leafless trees made the vast openness of the Place de la Concorde seem even larger.

Pedestrians hurried along the broad sidewalks beneath black umbrellas. Among them, a woman in a glossy yellow raincoat stood out. Bike rider weaved their way through the Renaults and Citroens, tires sizzling on the wet pavement.

They hurried across the first half of the oval into the grand plaza and stopped in the middle to admire La Madeleine, looking more like a copy of the Parthenon than a church. Another sprint across the traffic speeding along the Place took them onto the wide expanse before the Tuileries.

There were no children romping in the gardens or old men playing checkers, but a few dedicated lovers were there, snuggled into coats, tucked under umbrellas, finding all the warmth they needed in each other's eyes, dreamily ignoring the weather. Paralee took one of McCall's arms in both hands and pressed her body to his as they walked.

He inhaled the damp fragrance of her hair as they circled the rain-spattered pond and returned toward the Place de la Concorde, the gravel of the wide path crunching beneath their feet.

"Go up there," Paralee told him, dragging him along the ramp to the top of the old wall at the edge of the gardens. They stopped near the classic, winged equestrian statue guarding the entrance and looked up the Champs Élysées toward the Arc de Triomphe. It was hidden in the fog, but to their left, the top of the Eiffel Tower rose through the mist.

"Hmmmm. Let's see. Paris, right?"

"Uh huh," Paralee mumbled from behind the high collar of her pea coat.

"How's it feel? Coming back," he asked.

She drew her body to his and McCall felt the warm swelling of her breasts through the tough fabric of the pea coat.

"Familiar," she said, looking up at him. "The good memories are still here, you know, but they don't beckon. Are you cold?" she asked. "I know a little bistro a couple of blocks from here. With any luck, they might have a bottle of cognac."

"Lead on, *ma petite*."

Paralee took him down the Rue de Rivoli to a narrow side street. A block from its mouth, she pointed to a door set in the corner of a low building. Welcoming light radiated from the windows.

"Come on," she said as they passed through the door into the soft coppery glow of the room's polished wood panels. The quiet conversations of a dozen early patrons mingled with a light haze of tobacco smoke that by evening would be a choking fog as thick as the one now on the Champs Élysées. The booths were occupied, so they sat on high stools at one of the round tables in the center of the room. They ordered double cognacs from a bored waiter with a brushy mustache and when he'd gone, Paralee reached across the table and took Mack's hand. It was cold and she rubbed it with both of hers to warm it.

"You're tense," she said. "Is tomorrow really so important?"

He looked at her with sad eyes. "A lot's in the balance. The farm. Banco Dorado. If Ryder believes Yanov's document and they buy the bonds on their own, we might trap them. Javier's got a pot load of options and I think they'll have to go through him to buy Russian bonds. That makes money for Javier, maybe enough to save Banco Dorado."

McCall breathed in the fumes of the cognac and took a small sip. "But suppose Ryder *doesn't* believe Yanov's forgery and they don't buy Russian bonds. That's the worst case scenario. Banco Dorado drops the ninety thousand bucks they paid for the options, I don't make any money out of syndicating the inside information, Ryder and his buddies acquire Banco Dorado, and all I have is the eight hundred thousand in Russian bonds that I own--and on which I owe a hundred thousand to Banco Dorado. If my bonds bring twenty-five percent of face value, I'll only net a hundred thousand. Not enough to do much of anything with. Of course, we'll get the ten thousand pounds for the document, which will cover our travel expenses. There are big downsides all over the place. Even in the best case, if everything works financially, we won't bring anybody back from the dead. It won't stop the killing. Or the torture. I'd like to stop the slaughter and punish the sonsabitches who are responsible for it, but I'm just one ordinary guy and I don't have a cape or a pair of tights."

"I'm sorry I asked. I was having fun showing you a little bit of my Paris."

"Well, don't give up yet."

"I won't, and right now, I'm not going to worry about it. There's an old French saying: *Tout le temps passé en inquiéter, est du temps perdu pour la jouissance.*"

"What's it mean?"

"That all the time you spend worrying is time you lose for being happy."

McCall smiled in spite of himself. "Audrey had a saying something like that. *La mejor venganza estar feliz.* It means 'The best revenge is to be happy.' It's a sweet thought. She made it work. I'm not sure I ever can."

McCall held up his glass to her. "To the moment of truth--or not, if you think about the *bona fides* of Yanov's document."

"Truth," Paralee said. "And happiness. And love."

"All that in one drink?" McCall asked, trying to dispel his somber mood. "I'll give you a better one. Humphrey Bogart said it to Ingrid Bergman in *Casablanca.* 'Here's looking at you, kid.'"

"And she said, 'We'll always have Paris.'"

They let the cognac warm their chilled hands and feet in silence, each thinking their own thoughts. At last, McCall asked, "Do you want lunch or a couple of candy bars, a nap and a good dinner later?"

"There's a drug store at Rond Point. We could get some snacks on the way back to the Vernet and tonight I'll let you take me to dinner at a wonderful little place in my old neighborhood. They have a good wine cellar, too," Paralee said, finishing her cognac and slipping off the stool.

"Do I need to rob a bank before we go?"

"Of course not. Good wine doesn't have to be expensive."

"You haven't proved that to me yet."

****

Chez Nicole was nestled among apartment buildings between Avenue Victor Hugo and Avenue Kleber. Nicole herself greeted her guests as if they were coming to her home for dinner. She made it clear that Paralee was an old favorite.

"*Ma chère,*" she said when Paralee came in. "I knew you could not stay away. You are back for good?"

"*Bon soir,* Nicole. Only a visit, I'm afraid. Nicole, this is my friend, Jack McCall."

"Welcome to *Chez Nicole,*" she said in charmingly accented English, looking him up and down. She turned to Paralee, speaking softly in French. "*Chèrie*, he looks like a real man. Does he satisfy you?"

"*Il est très magnifique, Nicole. Je suis amoureuse et c'est merveileux, incroyable.*"

Nicole smiled with warm brown eyes and turned to McCall.

"This young lady is dear to my heart, Monsieur. Be kind to her or my old friends from the *Maquis* will call on you." She drew a finger across her throat and grinned wickedly. "Come. I will give you my special table." She seated them against the wall, near the piano.

Paralee waited until she had left them and then said, "Nicole was in the Resistance in World War II--you wouldn't think she was old enough would you? She was just sixteen and a *chanteuse*--a singer--in a nightclub the Germans liked. She'd flirt with them, find out where they were stationed and memorize their insignia. Then she'd tell the *Maquis*--the underground--what German units were where. Someone would radio it to London and the Allies. Now she has this little place and after dinner, she sings the old songs."

Nicole wouldn't let them order. She told them they'd have lamb casserole in a flaky crust and brought a red wine, a towel wrapped carefully around the bottle to conceal the label. She uncorked it herself and poured a little into a glass. She ignored Mack and offered it to Paralee.

"If you can name it, *Chèri*, you need not pay," Nicole said and waited while Paralee went through the motions of appraising the wine, holding it to the light, inhaling it, laying it against the back of her throat, swishing it around in her mouth.

Finally, Paralee swallowed, used the tips of her forefinger and thumb to wipe her lips and said, "It's Saint-Émilion. The vintage is '75 or '76. But I'm not sure about the chateau. Samion?"

"*C'est extraordinare!* Such a palate. Enjoy," Nicole said, filling their glasses. "I will return," she added before turning away to attend to her other guests.

"That's impressive. Really impressive. Did you get it right?" McCall said.

"If I missed anything it was the chateau. There are so many in that region. Hard to tell them apart. We'll know if she lets us see the bottle. You can't complain about the price this time, though."

Paris

Dressed in a jogging outfit, Chanille joined Ryder in the salon of the suite they shared in the Hotel San Regis. Ryder was taking breakfast.

"I checked it out," she said. "Windows and roof tops. They all look down on the hotel entrance. It's a narrow street, too. I wish I had some back-up."

"Don't fret about it. This guy's just blowing smoke. Now go get dressed. I need to see the translator and we need to go. It's already nine-thirty and the package is supposed to be delivered between ten and twelve."

Downstairs, the *concierge* met Ryder, whom he knew from his false passport as Walker, and escorted him across the lobby to a sturdy, middle-aged woman in a dark green cloth coat sitting stiffly on the edge of a sofa. The *concierge* introduced her as Irina Suvarova. Ryder passed him a hundred-franc note and turned his attention to Mme. Suvarova, a sturdy, middle-aged woman who, even in Paris, couldn't escape her peasant origins.

"Thank you for coming, Mme. Suvarova," he said to her in awkward French. "Let me explain the assignment to you. I expect to receive some kind of official Soviet document and I want it translated. I expect it to be no more than a page or two, possibly three. Will you be able to do that?" "*Oui*," she answered in a deep voice.

"All right. I also need your opinion of its . . . how do you say? . . . its authenticity. Can you do that?"

Irina Suvarova shrugged. "In Soviet Union, I work for Ministry of Industry. I understand official language."

"Would you be able to tell if it's a forgery?"

Mme. Suvarova shrugged. "Yes, perhaps. If not done well." Ryder thought for a moment, looked at his watch, then said, "That'll have to do. I have another way to see if it's genuine. Shall we go? It's misting. We'll take a taxi." He escorted Mme. Suvarova to the front door. Chanille waited to follow them in another cab.

Sitting behind the wheel of a rented black Peugeot sedan, the engine idling to keep the car warm, Carlos Sosa saw Ryder come out of the hotel with a large woman in a green coat. He slipped the car into gear and pulled into the street, a safe distance behind Ryder's taxi.

****

McCall's eyes popped open. His heart was pounding and he was gasping for breath. Where was he? He looked around the room and slowly understood. Daylight streamed through the window. He looked at his watch and saw with a sickening, empty feeling that it was already a quarter to ten. "Damned jet lag," he muttered.

"Paralee," he called, throwing back the covers and setting his feet on the floor. He rapped on the closed bathroom door. "Paralee. Come on. We've got to get moving." No answer. He opened the door. Empty. Where the hell was she? His nerves ragged, he took a deep breath and tried to calm himself. She must have gone to take the document to the courier, leaving him to sleep. He checked the alarm beside his bed. It had been turned off. He popped the latches on his briefcase. The document was gone. He breathed a sigh of relief. OK. Obviously, she'd taken it to the courier's.

In the bathroom again, he smiled as soon as he saw her message scrawled in soap across the mirror. "Love U!" It was signed with an elaborate "P". He left it there and shaved in the spaces between the letters.

He showered and dressed, expecting her to come through the door at any moment. They'd have breakfast, go back to the courier's office--wherever it was--and wait for the money. *'Would she stay there until the courier returned? Surely not without calling me.'* He settled into a chair by the window and opened yesterday's *Herald-Tribune*.

At ten-thirty, Paralee still hadn't returned. At eleven, with an insistent, eerie feeling jangling his nerves, McCall jammed his hat on his head, wrapped the white silk scarf around his throat and struggled into his leather flight jacket. He left one note on the carpet in front of the door and another at the desk downstairs. Pulse racing, he hurried into the drizzling rain, walked a few steps, sprinted, walked again.

****

A cigarette smoldering between his fingers, the desk clerk of the Hotel Élysée Ponthieu looked at Ryder and Irina without expression. Who was he to understand an American's taste in women? He said nothing to welcome them, but interrogated them by raising his thick, brooding eyebrows.

"Maurice," Ryder announced and was rewarded with a nod. The clerk took a key from a board beside his station and handed it to him. The faded numbers 4-0-3 were etched on the wooden fob. Ryder took out his wallet, but the clerk held up his hand.

"*Ce n'est pas necessaire, Monsieur. La chambre est payée.*"

"*Merci*," Ryder said, putting the wallet back in his coat. He turned away from the clerk and steered Irina into a small, two person elevator. The doors closed and the machinery began to whir, laboriously lifting the cage. The doors opened on a dark corridor. Irina stepped out and found the switch for the hall lights. Room 4-0-3 was two doors away. Ryder crossed its threshold and in two paces stood before one of two tall windows. A sliver of the rue de Ponthieu appeared through wavy imperfections in the 19th century glass. Now and again he caught a flicker of color in the movement of cars and foot traffic on the rain-slick street.

He thought of Chanille below, guarding his flank, checking the roofs and the windows on the other side of the rue de Ponthieu, wondering if she'd seen anyone in position. It seemed so unlikely that he turned away from the window. *'Hell, they could be in the room next door.'* "We might as well be comfortable," he said to Irina. "We may have a while to wait." He checked his watch. Irina unbuttoned her coat and sat on the bed.

****

Chanille, wearing a mannish slouch hat, a short raincoat that hung loose and straight over a skirt slit up the front, scanned every window and every roof top for signs of anyone staking out the Hotel Élysée Ponthieu. She saw no one except two men leaving the hotel and an occasional pedestrian hurrying along the narrow cobblestone street. The driver of a taxi parked down the block, two wheels on the sidewalk, sat motionless behind a newspaper. Probably the one that brought Ryder and the Russian woman, she thought. Ryder must have told him to wait. Funny that the cab didn't have a light on its roof. One of the hotel's cars? She hadn't noticed when they left the hotel. She watched him carefully for some time--a large man with a black mustache. He showed no interest in anything beyond his newspaper.

She checked her watch--eleven-fifteen. The courier could come in the next moment or at five minutes to twelve. She pretended to inspect the menu posted on the glass beside the door of a restaurant that would not open for business until seven that evening. She felt exposed and vulnerable. Some passing *flic* might mistake her for a street walker. She'd have a hell of a time explaining the Beretta Compact nestled in the custom-fitted holster strapped between her thighs.

Movement at a window across from the hotel caught her eye and she was suddenly alert, adrenalin sizzling under her skin. The light was wrong. It was reflecting off the window, turning it into a mirror. Concealed by the reflection, it was a perfect firing position. *'Damn!'*

Pulse suddenly racing, she tensed, slipped her right hand beneath the raincoat into the slit of her skirt. She gripped the Beretta and slowly eased it from its well-oiled holster. She kept it concealed under the folds of her raincoat. From that position, she could fire in the time it took to raise her arm, aim and squeeze off the round.

Then she saw the bicycle, coasting down the street, the rider bent over the handlebars. The brakes squealed and the bicycle came to a stop at the entrance to the hotel. The rider, dressed in a dark, short coat, sunglasses and a helmet, dismounted. *'The courier,'* Chanille said to herself.

The courier pushed the bicycle onto the sidewalk, locked the front wheel, propped it against the wall and disappeared into the hotel. Chanille went on full alert. Perspiration trickled down her sides. The moment of maximum danger would come as soon as the courier returned. *'Would the courier give a signal? Watch what? The courier or the window in the building across the street?'*

****

Ryder and Irina had nothing to talk about and in the silence, Ryder's thoughts drifted. There was a little French restaurant in Vientiane where Lek loved to go. She said it made her feel a proper lady. He saw her across the table from him, ebony eyes dancing in the candlelight, the knowing little smile . . .

The tap on the door startled him.

"Oui?" he called out, sharper than he intended.

"Qui c'est?" asked a contralto voice from beyond the door.

"Maurice," he answered, crossing the room in two quick steps. *"Et vous?"*

"Crimson," was her muffled reply.

He opened the door and saw a petite woman wearing a cyclist's helmet, amber sunglasses and a Navy pea coat, her face illuminated by the light from the windows.

Paralee saw a pale, trim man, wearing an expensive suit under a camel hair coat. For an instant, his eyes had a soft, faraway look, but then they grew cold and hard. She actually thought they changed color--from pale blue to gray. She'd trembled coming up in the elevator. Now so close to him, she was chilled.

"Ah, bien," she said, easing past him, hiding her nervousness and nodding to the large woman sitting on the narrow single bed. She removed the helmet with a spray of fresh rain and turned down the collar of the pea coat. "I have a delivery for you, Monsieur," she said, continuing in French. She withdrew the envelope that had been held in place against her body by the pea-coat, offered it to him and stood back against the door.

Ryder appraised her, thought her saucy, then took the envelope, ripped it open, scanned its incomprehensible Cyrillic characters and handed it to Irina. "What is it?"

Irina read the single page and turned the document over to check the back. It was blank. She looked up at Ryder and said, "It is travel order. Official of Ministry of Finance of Soviet Union travels to London to meet with British Foreign Ministry to finalize terms of a settlement of claims. That is all it says."

"Is it genuine? Authentic?" he asked Irina, studying Paralee.

"If not, is good forgery," Irina replied. "Paper is better than I remember, but is from Finance Ministry." She shrugged.

Ryder took the document and handed it back to Paralee. "There's been a mistake," he told her. "I won't accept this." Paralee looked at him without comprehending. He repeated, "I said I won't accept this."

Paralee composed herself, swallowed hard and found her voice. "But Monsieur," she said, cocking her head to one side. "I am to receive a package from you. Those are my instructions."

"Sorry. I'm not accepting delivery. Take it back. I have nothing for you," Ryder said, coming a step closer and shoving the document at her.

"Monsieur . . ." Paralee protested, suddenly very afraid. The room was too small. He was too close, crowding her, so close she smelled his breath, sour and stale. It was all going wrong. She took the document, laid it against her side and quickly buttoned her coat over it. She fumbled behind her for the door handle, keeping her eyes on Ryder.

"*Au revoir*, Mademoiselle," Ryder smiled, wiggling his fingers at her in a child's imitation of goodbye. Paralee opened the door and backed into the hall, bumping into the opposite wall of the narrow corridor. Only a few steps away the elevator waited, but she didn't want to be caged. Near panic, she swung into the stair well, took them two at a time, adrenalin pumping.

****

Ryder opened his attaché case and slipped a bill from a banded bundle of crisp hundred pound notes. He held it out to Irina. She stared at it for a moment, then at Ryder.

"*Merci, Monsieur. Merci bien,*" she said and smiled. Ryder snapped the attaché case closed, ushered her through the door and into the elevator.

Paralee reached the lobby only seconds before she heard the elevator doors open. She dashed toward the hotel entrance, imagining she could still smell Ryder's breath.

Chanille saw the courier--a girl--emerge from the entrance of the hotel, fumble with the lock on the front wheel, finally take the bicycle by its handlebars and maneuver it toward the street. She mounted the bicycle, began to pedal but almost immediately fell over against a parked car, her pants leg fouled in the sprocket. Dismounting awkwardly, she ripped the material free and pushed the bicycle into the street. The rider would pass by her in a few moments. Then the Russian woman came out, walking away. Chanille checked the window across the street. *'There! A man.'* The sun had moved just enough for her to see him. Her hand tightened on the butt of the Beretta. *'Where's Robbie? Don't come out, Robbie!'*

Chanille saw him come through the hotel doorway and begin to walk toward her. She tried to keep him in the corner of her eye while she watched the window. Then there was movement at ground level. The taxi door swung open. The driver stood up, arms outstretched--a double-handed grip, braced against the roof of the taxi. *'Oh, shit!'* She saw the weapon, extended by a long silencer, heard the hiss as it fired, saw the shot pluck Ryder's coat and chip stone from a wall. Ryder crouched and ran between parked cars into the street. As her own weapon came up, she saw the taxi driver swivel and take new aim. His second shot came an instant later, as Ryder dove for the opposite curb. The courier, pedaling hard, caught the shot meant for Ryder and went down in a clatter, helmet and glasses tumbling into the street.

Then Chanille's Beretta cracked, sending a soft, hollow-point bullet into Major Carlos Sosa's head above the right eyebrow. A bright pink cloud, sprinkled with bits of white, blossomed upward for a moment, then floated to earth as Sosa crumpled. Chanille snapped another shot toward the window. The glass shattered, one large jagged piece falling to the sidewalk like the blade of a guillotine.

****

McCall saw it all from a block away, at the opposite end of the rue de Ponthieu. A man with a briefcase fell and skittered across the pavement, stumbled to his feet and ran. The bicycle rider with the amber glasses went down. He knew immediately that it was Paralee. In almost the same instant--only a few feet away--a man's head exploded, a blossom of blood and bits of brain spewing into the air. Another shot and glass shattered in the street beside him. McCall's legs churned to reach her, a fresh shower of raindrops blurring his vision.

****

Chanille held her position for a few tense moments, the Beretta in both hands, covering the back side in case the man she saw in the window came out of the building. From the corner of her eye, she saw Ryder scramble to his feet and dash for the sidewalk, his camel hair coat soiled with grime from the damp street. In the stillness, the echo of her unsilenced shots reverberated in the narrow street and the sharp, tangy scent of cordite teased her nostrils. Now she saw a man in a leather jacket sprinting hard down the center of the street toward her, his hat flying from his head, a white scarf fluttering over his shoulder, his face grimacing, straining, arms flailing, no weapon that she could see. She crouched, aimed. A simple shot. Not necessary, she decided. She stood up and slipped the Beretta back into its holster, feeling the delicious heat of the gun barrel between her legs, and sprinted after Ryder. She passed within a meter of the courier, sprawled in the street, a rivulet of blood trickling into the seams between the cobblestones. *'Pretty girl. Bad luck to have gotten in the way.'*

****

McCall saw the slender figure in the black raincoat and slouch hat cross the street and run away. Closer and closer, only a few feet more. He threw himself down beside Paralee, ripped open her pea coat and found the exit wound, seeping dark red blood--thank God, a vein, not an artery. The document they'd concocted for Tovolaro was pasted to her sweater. The bullet had passed through it and soaked it in her blood. McCall stuffed it into his pocket, yanked up her turtleneck, folded his silk scarf into a pressure bandage and held it tightly against the wound.

"AMBULANCE!" he yelled at the top of his voice.

Paralee stared at him, eyes wide and bright with fear. "Mack," she moaned. "He wouldn't take it." Rain fell on her face and streaked down her cheeks.

"Hang on, baby. I've got you. You're gonna be OK," McCall told her, the words crisp and clipped. "Get an ambulance, somebody!" he yelled again. Down the street he saw faces peeking out of doorways. One man was waving--at him?

"Hurry!" he called in the man's direction. *"Dépêche! Dépêche!"* He thought that might be French for 'hurry,' but not another appropriate word of the bloody language came into his head. A policeman rounded the corner and came running along the sidewalk from the direction Mack had come, his cape flying, nightstick in hand. The man who'd waved came into the street and shouted, *"Une ambulance est en route!"*

McCall recognized the word 'ambulance' and 'en route' and turned his attention to Paralee. Her blue eyes stared at him, the helmet and her sunglasses six feet away on the cobblestones. He thought he'd stopped the external bleeding from the wound, but he had no idea how much was leaking out inside. She looked scared, breathing in spurts, trying to stem the pain by holding her breath. "I'm cold, Mack," she gasped and he tried to hold her closer to him. Except for a bleeding scrape on her cheek where she'd been thrown into the street, her face was pale with shock and he thought her temperature might be dropping.

Then he heard the on-off wail of a siren and the cold sizzle of tires on the wet street. The rumble of a powerful engine slowed and the hissing tires came to a halt behind him, the siren fading and shutting down, leaving an eerie silence. A moment later he saw the green pants of a paramedic beside him.

"They're here, baby. You're gonna be OK."

McCall allowed the paramedic to pry his hand away from Paralee's belly. His fingers were sticky and cramped, locked around the scarf, now crimson, no longer soft and white. His hands were covered in her blood. And his flight jacket. Like Willie's blood when they went down on the beach, north of Hué. McCall tried to shut out the images of Willie's eyes, scared, pleading with him. Willie's jaw hanging loose in his hands. Willie strangling on his own blood . . . *'No! Not like that. Dear God, please! Not like Willie.'*

He forced himself back to the street, looked up, saw the other body lying in a pool of blood, a second paramedic running toward it. The paramedic stopped and stood looking down, then leaned against the Peugeot and threw up. He turned away, stumbled back toward the ambulance and began pushing a gurney toward Paralee, its wheels clattering on the cobblestones. *"L'homme est mort,"* he said, wiping his mouth. *"Un cas pour la morgue. Et la femme?"*

"C'est grave," the first paramedic said. *"Elle a perdu beaucoup de sang. Allons 'y."* The two paramedics eased McCall to one side, lifted her onto the gurney and pushed it toward the rear of the ambulance.

Paris

McCall sat on his heels in a corner of the ambulance, watching anxiously as one of the paramedics hovered over her, exposing the exit wound and strapping a heavy pressure bandage against it. When the bandage was secure, the paramedic jabbed a small syringe into her arm. Mack assumed it was morphine. The siren started up again with the distinctive eek-onk, eek-onk of European emergency vehicles and the ambulance began to move slowly. The paramedic spread a heavy blanket over her and tucked it in around her legs and torso.

Paralee moaned and opened her eyes. McCall swallowed hard. She looked so pale. The ambulance swayed, rolling her head to one side, and she caught sight of him, her eyes reaching out to him.

"Mack?" she said, her voice weak, almost lost in the siren's wail.

"You're gonna be OK," he said, moving to her side, taking her hand in his, hoping fervently that it was true. "We'll be at the hospital in a minute."

She saw his lips moving, understood nothing and closed her eyes again.

They took her straight into surgery and pushed McCall back into a deserted waiting area.

The policeman from the rue de Ponthieu and a plain clothes detective came in a few minutes later. The detective, speaking passable English, sat down beside McCall and began to draw out his version of what had happened.

"Witnesses say two men were firing. Do you know these men, Monsieur McCall?"

"I saw my friend go down and I ran to her. She was hit by a stray, I guess. I don't know what the shooting was about." McCall knew his answer was partly untrue, but technically correct. A word from him might have put Ryder and whoever had been backing him up in a French court, maybe in a French jail. But Ryder didn't shoot Paralee. Ryder himself was the target and if anyone was to blame for Paralee being in the line of fire, it was him, Jack McCall. *'What can the French police do about that?'*

"I see," the detective said, looking at McCall closely. "It may be necessary for you to speak to the investigating magistrate. You are a visitor here, Monsieur. Is that correct?"

"Yes."

"What is your hotel?"

"The Vernet," McCall said. "Where are we now?"

"The Clinique Victor Hugo, near the Arc de Triomphe. Hotel Vernet is near. Take my card, Monsieur, and call me if you wish to add to your statement." The detective snapped his notebook shut and stood up. "I hope your friend is all right, Monsieur McCall."

The detective left and McCall stared at the clock over the double doors leading to the surgery. Alone, fear and anger went to war within him. His breath came in shallow pants and he could feel his heart thumping against his ribs. He fought it and forced himself to take deep breaths. *'Get a grip, man. Losing it now won't help her.'*

****

Ryder was on the phone to his chief trader, Seth Monroe, when Chanille came into the suite. Flushed and excited, he watched Chanille cross the room, slipping out of her raincoat and throwing it over the back of a chair.

She withdrew the Beretta Compact from the special holster, held it up for Ryder to see. She put it to her nose and inhaled its lethal fragrance with half-closed eyes. Then she laid it on a side table. Velcro ripped as she tore the holster from beneath her skirt and dropped it on the floor. "Robbie, I just killed a man. Did you see it? Awesome. He was just like a target on the range. Better. His head exploded like a ripe melon." The pupils of her eyes were dilated and her breath was coming short and shallow.

He hung up the phone and watched Chanille's languorous walk carry her closer and closer until she stood directly in front of him. He could smell her then--pungent after-action sweat mixed with the powerful aroma of musk.

"Take off your coat," she said. "I want to see where you got hit." Ryder stood up and obeyed, removing his coat and unbuttoning his shirt. Chanille bent down to inspect his blood-stained side, one warm hand on his back holding the shirt away from his body, the other touching the swollen flesh on either side of the wound in his side.

"Mmmmm," she said. "Pretty good crease. Does that hurt?" she asked, squeezing the swelling slightly.

"Owww!" he howled, the stab of pain searing his side. "Yes, damn it."

"It's bloody, but just a scratch really. Get your shirt off. I'll dress it and give you a shot of morphine."

"Never mind about the morphine. Time enough for that when we get on the plane. I can stand it until then. The French cops are going to be asking questions. The desk clerk at the hotel has probably described me by now and they'll be making the rounds of the hotels. If they get me, they've got you. Too bad you had to blow that guy away," Ryder said, scowling. "Call Tommy at Le Bourget or wherever the hell he is and tell him to file a flight

293

plan for immediate departure. You get us packed and checked out of here while I clean up."

****

McCall paced, took deep breaths, yearned for a drink but dared not leave. Other cases came into the hospital and disappeared into the emergency room as Paralee had. He saw them through the haze of his personal horror of having put her in harm's way.

If she died . . .

He had just looked at the clock for the millionth time— two-fifteen— when a blood-spattered, blue-gowned doctor, surgical mask dangling from his neck, pushed through the double doors of the surgery and looked around the waiting room. McCall caught his eyes, held his breath and slowly rose from his seat.

"*Est vous l'homme qui est venue avec la jeune femme qui a eté fusillée?*" he asked McCall.

"*Oui, Doctor, mais je ne parle pas Français bien. Je parle Anglais? Sil vous plais?*"

"*Oui. Bien.* You came with the young lady who was shot?" the doctor asked.

McCall nodded. "How is she?"

"She lost much blood. The bullet touched the renal artery and caused serious internal bleeding and a vein was cut, but no harm to the vital organs. I have repaired the blood vessels and put in the stitches. Now we wait. The bleeding was the great danger." The doctor looked down at McCall's bloody clothes and hands. "You put pressure on the wound?" McCall nodded. The young doctor patted him on the shoulder and added. "You did well, Monsieur."

McCall sagged with relief and, his legs suddenly trembling, sat down quickly.

"Are you all right?" the doctor asked.

McCall nodded numbly.

"We will keep her in this unit to observe her. If the bleeding does not begin again, she will go to another room later today. You must talk to the administrator to admit her. I will send the papers."

"When can I see her?"

"Someone will let you know. Perhaps an hour."

****

The nurse led him into a small ward— the Intensive Care Unit, he assumed. Paralee had just been wheeled in and transferred to a bed. An array of wires leading to monitors were attached to her. She had an IV in one arm and whole blood flowing into the other. She looked small and vulnerable, the skin of her face taut and waxen. The nurse gave him a quick smile and left, drawing a curtain around the bed.

He pulled the straight chair to her bedside, laid his hand next to hers on the crisp, cool sheet and whispered, "I'm here. I'm right here." Then he began to pray, haltingly at first, because he hadn't spoken with God in a very long time.

****

Paralee awoke and found his head on the sheet beside her hand. She tested her fingers to see if they would move and slowly lifted her hand to touch his hair. She couldn't see his eyes open, but she felt him lift his head carefully.

"Hi," she murmured, managing a wan, crooked smile. "Where'd you come from?" He didn't know how to answer her. "How do you feel?"

"Numb. . . . Sleepy. . . . Kinda cold."

"I'll be right back," he said and went into the corridor. He returned with a nurse and a blanket fresh from the warmer.

The nurse spread the blanket over Paralee and tucked it around her with sharp jabs of the flat of her hand. Then she asked a number of questions in French to which Paralee gave groggy, single-syllable responses. The nurse adjusted the IV and left.

"That better?" McCall asked.

"Ummm," she answered. "Warmer . . . Some pain. The nurse said she'd give me something."

He took her hand, being careful of the tubes, and kissed its palm. "Mmmm," she said, staring at the ceiling. "Where am I?"

"The Clinique Victor Hugo," he told her. "Since this morning around eleven. It's almost four now. And you're going to be OK."

"What happened?"

"Somebody tried to take out Ryder and you caught a stray. A bullet made a tunnel from your back to your front. Nicked an artery and a vein, but missed the important stuff. Ryder must have had back-up because the shooter got blown away--literally."

She smiled weakly and answered him in a groggy voice. "How long have you been here?"

"I came in the ambulance. I was with you on the rue de Ponthieu."

"You were there? In the street?" she asked, her voice thin and weak, her lips barely moving.

"Yeah. I was there. Too late."

"I thought you were a dream," she said, closing her eyes. She opened them again and said, "He wouldn't take the document. Do you think he knew?"

"I don't know, baby. I don't know why you went there, either."

"Jean-Claude's rider didn't show. I was afraid everything would get screwed up. So I took Jean-Claude's bike," she mumbled, then grinned crookedly. "Mother said I should find a man I'd walk through fire for. Didn't know she meant gunfire. Have to talk to her about that."

The nurse returned, inserted a hypodermic into a fitting that branched off the IV, injected a clear fluid, withdrew the syringe and left.

Paralee smiled at him stupidly. "Wooooo. I can feel that already. Think I'll take a little nap now. Don't go 'way," she said, her eyelids closing.

Paris

McCall slept in a chair beside her bed through the night. When she awoke alert and hungry in the morning, he chatted with her awhile and then returned to the hotel to clean up, change clothes and make phone calls.

"Good morning, my friend," he said when Chilty answered at his flat in Belgravia. "I'm in Paris. . . . No. I'm not calling about the bonds. Screw the bonds. I almost got somebody killed over those damned things. . . . The girl who's with me. I was trying to put a syndicate together. The deal went to shit city and she got shot . . . No, no. She's going to be OK. It was close, though. . . . Look, it's too complicated. I'll tell you later. Your sterling reputation is not in danger and my Grand Design is dead. I've still got a hundred thousand in the deal, so maybe it will pay off eventually. In time to save the farm, I hope. Anyway, as soon as she can travel, I'm taking her back to the States and I'm going down to the farm. Call me there. . . . Thanks, Chilty. I'll let you know. *Ciao, 'mano.*"

McCall hung up and stared into space. *'What the hell happened here? Ryder looked at the document and then welshed on paying for it. He can't be smart enough to figure out Yanov's forgery but for whatever reason, he didn't go for it. Why was a shooter waiting for Ryder? It couldn't have had anything to do with our deal. Somebody else tried to take him out and it almost got Paralee killed.'*

He could still see her lying in the street, her life ebbing away onto the rain-slick cobblestones. He--John Cooper McCall--had put her there. He felt no redemption in the fact that the doc said he'd saved her.

It wouldn't be pleasant, but he had to let Javier know what happened in Paris.

****

Charles Foster wasn't available, but the receptionist told him that Mr. Banderas and Miss Benedetti were staying at the Dorchester and could be reached there.

Javier's voice was still fogged with sleep and McCall could visualize him rumpled and still in bed.

"It's Mack. How are you?"

"Mack? Ay, *hijo*. Where are you?" Javier asked, suddenly alive.

"Paris. Ryder didn't buy the deal. He even welshed on paying for the document I swotted up. I guess you've been sitting on your butt for two days. Sorry, *compadre.*"

"No, no, no. You can't believe what happened. Early yesterday afternoon, orders for Russian bonds started flooding the market. It was unbelievable. Charles Foster called and we went to his office. Carlotta and I exercised the options and sold as fast as we could, pushing the price every time. It went on all afternoon. All of us, even Charles, worked the phones. Mack--by the end of the day, we made three-point-four million."

McCall sat down heavily, pulling the phone off the table with a crash. It took a few moments for him to find his voice. "I'll be damned. Three-point-four million? . . . Dollars? *American* dollars?"

"Not just dollars, *amigo mío*, but three-point-four net. Did you hear me? I said net. What do you want me to do with your share?"

"No, no. Wait. This doesn't make any sense," McCall said. "Listen, Ryder didn't go for the deal. He wouldn't accept the document I offered him to prove the deal was real. And then there was a war in the street. Some guy was shooting at Ryder and Paralee caught a stray . . . " "

¡ *Dios mío*! She was shot? Is she OK?"

"She lost a lot of blood, but I got her to the hospital and they patched her up. She's there now and she's going to be fine, they say. But who was buying the bonds? It couldn't have been Ryder."

"Ah, but it was," Javier said. "Almost everything we sold went to Ryder and Company. And he paid more than your estimate of what the bonds are going to bring when they make the settlement. It's so good, Mack. He's going to take a loss."

McCall was silent, trying to understand it. *'My fictitious Russians. He thought they were the ones shooting at him because he didn't pay. Unbelievable. But now what?'*

Finally he said, "I don't think this is going to stop him coming after Banco Dorado. Anyway, we don't know when the settlement will be, so he won't know he's taking a loss for . . . well, however long it is before the announcement."

"Yes, but we have his cash," Javier said. "We have a--¿ *Como se dice?*--a war chest--¿ *No?*--to go after the minority shareholders. We will fight him with his own money!"

"Incredible," McCall said. "I don't understand it at all."

"Your share, Mack. What do you want me to do with it?"

"What share, Javier? You bought the options. I didn't."

"No, no, Mack. We reserved half for you. Never mind how the books will balance. Half of the net profit is yours."

"Then let it ride. Keep it in the war chest until Banco Dorado is safe. You might need to give me an advance of a couple hundred thousand, though.

My grandfather's farm--it's got that mortgage I need to pay."

"*No te preocupe, 'mano.* We have more than enough for that and to buy the ten or fifteen percent from the minority shareholders to keep Ryder from getting control. You'll own a bigger piece of Banco Dorado. Are you sure you don't mind?"

"We'll sort all that out later. I've got to get over to the hospital and tell my lady." McCall paused, then said, "This is crazy, you know it? We don't deserve any of this. We've been screwing up right and left and we're still coming up roses."

"Mack, just say *Gracias á Dios y no hace ni una pregunta.* Thank God for watching over us. Don't ask why."

****

There was one more call to make before he went back to the hospital.

"Colonel Campbell? This is Jack McCall. Sorry to wake you . . . Yes, sir. That's correct. Paralee and I are in Paris, Colonel, and she's had an accident. . . . Yes, sir. Somewhat serious. She's in the hospital, but she's awake and alert and she's going to be fine. I just wanted to call and let you know. . . . Actually, sir, she got in the middle of a gunfight and caught a stray. I know that sounds more like Beirut than Paris, but that's what happened. . . . No, sir. No permanent damage. Not even much of a scar, they say. . . . No, sir. I'm not at the hospital right now. I'm at the hotel. . . . She's at the Clinique Victor Hugo. I promise to have her call you, sir. . . . I think they want to keep her a few more days before they let her travel. I'd guess we'll be home in a week at the outside. . . . She's been doing research for me--I think you knew that--and our reason for being in Paris had to do with the project. Look, Colonel, I feel responsible. I couldn't feel any worse. . . . Yes, sir. I understand. . . . No, sir. I'd feel the same way in your place. . . . Yes, sir. . . . No, sir. . . . Yes, sir. I will, sir. . . . No, sir. Not at all, sir. I felt it was my duty to call you. . . . Yes, sir. I'll tell her. . . . Goodbye, Colonel."

McCall couldn't remember anything he'd dreaded so much as making that phone call. It was over now and he hoped he'd made it easier for Paralee to talk to her parents. He stripped off his shirt and went for a shower. He could see her in half an hour.

****

"Your father's a tough old bastard, isn't he?" McCall said as he came through the door, grinning. He carried a bouquet of long-stemmed red roses and a paper bag.

299

Paralee's face lit up at the sight of the roses. "Where did you find them?"

"You can find anything in Paris. Except Krispy Kreme doughnuts. I tried, but the closest I could come was glazed *croissants*. The *concierge* steered me to a little *boulangerie* ¾ is that how you say it? Not far from the hotel. Anyway, I thought they might do in a pinch. He held up the paper bag.

Her eyes widened to match her smile. "You're unbelievable. The roses must have been outrageously expensive."

"Worth every franc."

"They're gorgeous," she said, holding up her arms to him, still dangling an IV tube. "Come kiss me." He tucked the roses out of the way behind his back and gently pressed his lips to hers. She surprised him when the tip of her tongue reached out to him.

"Well," he said, straightening up and smiling broadly. "You're feeling pretty frisky for somebody who was two quarts low yesterday."

"Wait'll I get out of here. I'll show you frisky."

"Don't get ahead of yourself, kid. You've got a ways to go."

"Hey, what was that you said about my dad?" she asked.

"I said he's a tough old bastard."

"How would you know?"

"I just got off the phone with him."

"You called him?" Paralee asked, bolting upright in the bed. "Owww! Damn!" she howled as the stitches and tender muscles around the wound reminded her why she was in a hospital bed. "What did you *say* to him?"

"I told him Paris was a tough town."

"Stop kidding around, Mack. You didn't tell him I got shot, did you?"

"Take it easy," McCall said, grinning. "I told him the truth, including the prognosis that you're going to be fine."

The phone rang beside Paralee's bed and she answered it.

"*Oui?* . . . Oh, Mom. . . . Yes, I'm fine. Don't worry. . . . I would've called you later . . . . Yes, he said he talked to Dad. He's with me right now. Just brought a dozen long-stemmed red ones. They're luscious. Must have cost a French fortune. . . . Well, I told you I was fine. . . . OK, let me talk to him. . . . Hi, Dad. Mack says you're a tough old bastard." She cut her eyes at McCall, who glared back. "Yeah. I guess he might be. . . . Thanks, Dad. . . . You bet. I'll be home for Christmas and not just in my dreams. . . . I'll try to bring him if you promise to be nice. . . . OK. 'Bye, Dad. Give Mom a hug. I'll call tomorrow."

She put the phone on its cradle and smiled at him. "My dad looked up your Air Force record. He's impressed."

"How did your father get into my records?" McCall shot back, frowning.

"He was in Personnel at the Pentagon for awhile. He knows which buttons to push. If *you* were my father, wouldn't you want to know something about the man your daughter was madly, irretrievably, desperately in love with?"

"Madly, irretrievably, desperately? Is that what you said? When did that start?"

"Maybe just madly," she teased, an immense pride welling up in her. Her dad was impressed with her guy. She never thought *that* could happen with any man she brought home. And Mack had called him, man to man.

The West Country

Once clear of London, the Jaguar XJ6 sped swiftly along the M4, Tchaikovsky's 6th, the "Pathetique," reverberating through the leather lined cabin. The rain was little more than heavy mist and the ground fog came in grey wisps that threw a shroud of mystery over the landscape.

After yesterday, Charles Foster had cut his ties to the firm and the City. The fresh breeze of freedom was beneath his wings, lifting him to giddy heights. He knew the smile on his face was a stupid grin, but there was no one to see it and he wouldn't have cared if there had been.

He couldn't have asked for a better day to conclude his long career trading bonds and he ran the visions of that frantic, exhilarating day through his mind. There was Roddy, standing cool and firm in the trading room, like the captain of a fighting ship in the heat of battle, his uniform shirt sleeves and garish suspenders. The ones he wore yesterday were plum colored with gold flowers, certainly one-up on his Wall Street colleagues who settled for bright red.

Banderas and his chairman's daughter, Carlotta, adapted quickly to the headsets of veteran traders and lent eager assistance, both bright-eyed with the pace of the trading.

And when the market closed and they adjourned to his paneled office . . . Roddy, flushed with his victorious campaign. Banderas, coatless, tie askew, slouched in one of Charles' spindly chairs, exhausted. Even Carlotta's sophisticated mask had slipped. She sat primly, legs crossed at the ankles, angled and tucked under her chair, back straight, the way she'd been taught, but the surge of adrenalin that had carried her through the afternoon had ebbed and her eyes were glazed with fatigue.

Charles himself was sure he showed no such signs of wear and tear. If anything, he was more alive than when he awoke that morning, troubled by his client's predicament. He remembered opening the small bar hidden in the paneling, withdrawing two chilled bottles of Bollinger's. He threw grace to the winds and popped the corks, one by one. If he'd had fireworks at hand, he would have set them off, too. Everyone took a celebratory glass of champagne and turned to him, beaming.

"Dad," Roddy said, lifting his glass. "To you--the Leopard of Lombard Street."

Javier had straightened up to add, "More than a leopard. Master of the Universe."

Carlotta brightened and smiled her agreement.

He took it as a warm and satisfying salute, but he shook his head and refused to take credit for their extraordinary stroke of luck. "Thank you, one and all. But surely you know it was great good fortune, not my genius, that carried the day. And perhaps Mister McCall had something to do with it. I don't know how it happened, but without that intense demand, we'd never have been able to unwind your positions. And I must say, you all performed quite brilliantly."

"Come on, Dad. Didn't you have a hunch this was going to turn out as it did?" Roddy asked, beaming an admiring smile toward his father.

"They say I have a 'nose' for such things," he'd replied, wiggling his eyebrows and touching his long, slender nose. "But one shouldn't make too much of that. Actually, one never *knows*. The options, of course, made it far more exciting." He nodded toward Javier and Carlotta. "You two and McCall . . . I certainly didn't have had the stomach for that play."

While Roddy poured another glass, Charles brought out the humidor from beneath the bar and offered Cohiba cigars all around, even to Carlotta, who smiled and shook her head.

"You didn't take the options, Dad, but you took a heavy position in the bonds. You've never been a plunger, so what was your fallback?" Roddy asked.

"You know we're establishing the museum your uncle has always wanted. If the collector's market wouldn't take them back, I would have donated the lot to William's museum and let the Inland Revenue argue with me over their value. Speaking of value, have you put up the day's numbers?"

"They're still working on them," Roddy said. "Banco Dorado's profits will cover its outlay for the remaining options and leave quite a handsome balance. No doubt of that. As for you, Dad, your personal net gain should be about half a million pounds, give or take. An honest day's wage, wouldn't you say?"

"You cleared my position today?"

"Of course," Roddy said, drawing on the Cohiba and releasing a blue-gray stream of fragrant smoke into the room.

Javier was slow to react, but finally understood what Roddy Foster had said.

"You bought our Russian bonds for your own account?" he asked.

He'd smiled and waved his cigar like a conductor's baton. "Why of course, dear boy. You don't imagine bond traders live on commissions alone, do you?"

Javier turned to Roddy and asked, "And all our sales were to Ryder and Company? No one else?"

Roddy shook his head. "There were some fast followers who came in on the rise. But far and away, the biggest buyer was Seth Monroe, chief trader at Ryder's. He was the mover and shaker. All his purchases will be registered to Ryder and Company. I imagine the funds are clearing through Barclay's as we speak."

Charles hadn't fully understood why this was important, but Banderas had fallen back in his chair, allowing a splatter of champagne to escape from the glass and stain his tie. Banderas had muttered something about McCall's being cut out of some commission, but he hadn't really paid much attention to that. He was savoring the sight of his only son, strong and mature in his profession, the product of his long training. He couldn't help but feel pride and a certain sadness, thinking this would be the last time they would work together. He knew then that he would be away in the morning and here he was, the dream becoming a reality.

He was on his way to Bristol to see the yacht dealer who had the forty-four foot Cheoy Lee. It was a handsome sloop, with teak decks, commissioned five years ago, lavishly equipped and rigged for single-handed sailing at sea. The first sight of it had brought her vividly to his mind, that wild, gangly girl with the falsetto voice. She had loved to sail, but he'd lost her suddenly--overnight--with so much left to be said and barely a letter of goodbye. For all these years, she lived in his memory of golden days on Bideford Bay where they'd braved the wind and the water and dreamed of sailing over the western horizon together.

His eyes were focused on the road, but his mind held a vision of her running along the beach where she always waited for him, her shoes in one hand, her skirts in the other, splashing through the water as she ran to the little sloop, laughing as he pulled her over the gunwale into the cockpit. So free and vibrant, so full of life.

He'd have the artist paint her name on the transom of the Cheoy Lee just as she had signed that long-ago letter to him, with the neat slanting lines and swirls of her name--*Audrey.*

New York

The fading winter light caught the stubble of Ryder's blond beard and deepened the shadows beneath his eyes as he rose from the desk where he'd spent most of a long day. Chanille was sprawled on one of the couches in Ryder's office. They were both exhausted.

They'd come directly from the airport to the office in the World Trade Center, weary and reeking of the scent of high altitude sex. Ryder had barely settled into the chair behind the desk when his private line rang. It was Sandy Hammond. He'd been livid.

"Where the hell have you been? I've been trying to reach you for two days." Hammond hadn't waited for a reply. "Get on to that captain of yours down in Montevideo and tell him to weigh anchor. By the time your boat gets to Cape Town, I'll have a cargo waiting on the docks ¾ mortars, RPGs, AK47s and enough ammo to keep the Contras fighting for six months.

Ryder's adrenalin had surged and the fatigue that had weighed him down lifted quickly. "That's great," Ryder said. "We'll get right on it. I don't even want to know what changed your mind."

"Nothing's come out in the papers from that fiasco in La Paz and Secord's all tangled up again. He can't move the stuff the Israelis have stashed in Portugal on schedule, so the powers that be decided to let us go ahead. Now move your ass!"

Ryder heard the click and set the phone on its cradle. "Chanille," he called into the outer office. "Bring coffee. Sandy just called. We've got a green light."

There had been no time to discuss the Russian bond deal with Seth Monroe, but Ryder knew they'd picked up seven million at an average price of thirty-three. The details could wait until his ship cleared Montevideo harbor and was on the way to Cape Town.

A doc who didn't ask questions came to the office with a needle and thread and a bottle of pain pills that let Ryder continue to function and he and Chanille put the wheels in motion to get the *Sturmpetrel* to sea. For openers, they'd had to find the captain. Once the captain was sober, there had been problems with the harbor master which had only been resolved after three long telephone conversations in Spanish and a transfer of cash to the harbor master's account. Finally, the crew had been located and the ship got under way, steaming down the Rio de la Plata toward the Atlantic. With the project launched, Ryder went to the bar beside his executive wash room, dropped ice cubes in a tumbler and poured it half full of Scotch. He called across the room to Chanille. "Do you want a drink?"

"Yes," she mumbled. "And a large glass of ice water. Did the doctor say you could mix alcohol with those pills?"

"I couldn't care less," he said. He took the drinks across to the couch and handed her the water and the Scotch. "I just got word that the SS *Sturmpetrel* has left the estuary of the Rio de la Plata and has entered the South Atlantic bound for Cape Town," Ryder said. "She'll load ten million worth of small arms and ammo in a few days, which means two-point-five million for us on delivery. Not bad. Not bad."

"It's great," she said, clicking her glass against his in a weary salute. "Captain What's-his-name can handle it for a few days now, can't he? I want a long hot soak, clean sheets and twelve hours sleep. Oh. I forgot. I called a friend in Paris this morning. You'll be interested to know it wasn't a Russian who shot you in Paris."

He frowned, pressing the chilled glass to his forehead. "Sure it was. One of McCall's Russians. He said there'd be Russian shooters if we didn't pay for the document. That's how I decided the bond deal was for real."

"I know that's what you thought," Chanille persisted, reviving a little. "There was nothing in the newspapers about it and the reason was that the French Foreign Ministry put a lid on it. The shooter had diplomatic immunity." Chanille paused to let that soak in. "His name was Carlos Sosa. He was a Major in the Panamanian Defense Force. More than that. He was a Comandante in the *Fuerza Ocho*--Noriega's special death squad. Noriega put out a contract on you."

"No way," Ryder replied, shaking his head, angry with Chanille for raising the issue. "McCall set things up in Paris. Noriega wouldn't have known about that. Besides, there was no reason for Noriega . . ."

"You're not thinking this through, Robbie. They didn't get you, so the contract's still out there. Maybe it has to do with the arms deal. Would Noriega think you were cutting him out of anything?"

"No. The CIA's taking care of Noriega. We're working for the same people. That's just not it."

"This affects us both, you know. I'm the one who took out one of Noriega's top lieutenants. They may not know that now, but they will sooner or later."

Ryder didn't hear her. He was gazing out the window, thinking hard. "The bank? Would the old man know Noriega?"

"It's a small country. Everybody knows everybody and you know what they say about Noriega--you can't buy him, you can't sell him, but you can rent him. Maybe Benedetti just signed a short-term lease. There's another thing," Chanille said. "McCall must have figured out by now that you and *Las Águilas* are screwing him. What if he still has the documents? There won't be anything to stop him using them now. In fact, he has a lot of incentive to do just that."

"Damn it, Chanille! One thing at a time. We don't know that McCall has the damned documents. And the *Sturmpetrel* is already at sea. Nobody's going to stop it now."

"Not necessarily. If there's a big stink in the papers, the powers that be might wash their hands of your conduit. You might be on the hook for a boat load of small arms and ammo."

Washington

Dixie was in the kitchen of the townhouse she shared with Kurt Sorensen, an apron tied around the wool skirt she'd worn to the Hill that day. A streak of flour ran like a gash of war paint across one cheek. She was pounding a glob of bread dough as if it were a living thing about to attack her. Kneading bread dough was Dixie Davenport's way of venting her anger. She'd spent the day in closed session listening to one senior official after another disclaim knowledge of arms shipments to the Contras. Dixie knew--but couldn't prove--that they were lying. She had Angela's notes from her "Deep Throat" that named names and gave shipment dates. And the information that Angela got in South America showed the whole sorry network down there. She was tempted to go for half a loaf, but she dared not use the information on the White House linkage because she didn't know who Angela's "Deep Throat" was and didn't want to lead the hounds to him. Angela might come up with something more in South Africa. She was a resourceful gal.

Kurt had the misfortune of arriving before Dixie was through with her homemade therapy. "Hello, hello," he called as he came through the door, his cheery mood squelched as soon as he smelled the yeast and heard the heavy thud of a wad of bread dough being slammed against the cutting board. He set his briefcase on the floor and hung his overcoat in the closet while he mustered the courage to deal with Dixie in one of her bread-making moods. He wanted a drink badly, but he wouldn't get it without facing her--the booze was in the kitchen.

She gave him an angry glance as he made his way to the pantry. Kurt found the vodka and held up the bottle to her, asking if she would join him. She didn't respond. He filled a tumbler with ice cubes and poured a triple for himself, letting it chill for the absolute minimum amount of time before taking a large swallow. He winced at the fiery liquid's passage down his gullet. There might not be courage in a bottle, he thought to himself, but it was a damned good substitute.

"Hard day at the office?" he asked.

"They haven't learned a damned thing from the last time, that adventure of Nixon's and Kissinger's in Chile, trying to keep Allende out of office. Now they're running another rogue operation out of the National Security Council, enthusiastically abetted by Bill Casey and the CIA. What in the *hell* is the President thinking of? Doesn't he realize we're sponsoring bloody repression? His precious Contras are nothing more than the dregs of Somoza's death squads. Goons and thugs. Can you believe they're calling this policy disaster 'Operation Democracy'? I know he's supposed to sleep fifteen hours a day, but Kurt, really! Doesn't he know what's going on?"

"Contra hearings again," Kurt surmised. "You know I've discussed it with the Secretary. He took it up with the President and got his head handed to him. Incidentally, he's persuaded the President's in the dark on the details."

Dixie gave the dough ball a rest and heaved a sigh. "Maybe he doesn't know. I'm not the one to judge that. But if he *doesn't* know, he *ought* to."

Sorensen rushed through the opening with the best news he could muster. "We have the conference coming up in Venezuela next month--another go at making some progress on the Contadora peace process. They're going to call for an end to external support for paramilitary forces in the region. That means the Contras."

"Oh, bullshit, Kurt. Maybe you can engineer some sweet-smelling resolution out of that bunch, but you don't really think you can sell it at the White House, do you? The Contadoras are going to ask Reagan to behave and you think he's going to go along?" Dixie shook her head. "The Contadora process isn't going anywhere. We have to stop it *here*." She brought her arm up over her head and pounded her index finger into the dough.

"I don't know what else to do, Dixie. We've got a lot of other fish to fry. Maybe last month's Geneva Summit looked like a love fest, but we still have major problems with the Soviets over the ABM treaty and Star Wars. The President likes Gorbachev. Mrs. Thatcher likes Gorbachev. Hell, even I like Gorbachev. We have a chance to make something good happen with this guy if we focus on it. I hate to put it like this, but it really does seem more important to avoid killing millions of people in this country and the Soviet Union with nuclear weapons than to save a few hundred in Central America."

"Damn it all to hell, Kurt," Dixie shouted, banging a fist into the bread dough, her eyes blazing. "It's not just about the bloody body-count and the kill-ratio. The President of the United States has been breaking his oath of office from the day he moved in. Somewhere in that oath it says he swears by God Almighty that he will preserve and protect the Constitution and faithfully execute the laws of the land. The Congress has duly enacted laws against what his administration is doing in Central America--he even signed the damned things. His people are flaunting those laws, violating them every damned day. If we don't call the President to task on this, how is it any different from giving Soviet missiles a free shot at our major cities? Either one will destroy us. One's just quicker than the other."

Dixie was walking him backward, a flour-coated forefinger punching his chest. He managed to finish his vodka on the rocks in one swallow just before he hit the wall.

"You say the President doesn't know the true extent of this debacle in the making. But every time we try to shine a light on this mess from Capitol Hill, people in his administration who are supposed to tell us the truth tell us lies. They're being *told* to lie. You don't come before the Senate of the United States and just automatically lie. Maybe they're lying to the President, too. I don't know. But let me tell you something, Mr. Stripedy Pants, secrecy and duplicity allow stupidity to go unchallenged. What's going on here is stupid and it's very dangerous to our democracy." Dixie stood glaring at him, breathing hard.

Kurt saw the anger draining from her then and he reached out to her, pulling her to him. Her head fell against his chest and she cried.

"I'm just so frustrated," she said, looking up at him.

"Go wash your face. I'm going to take you to The Palm, pour a couple of very dry Martinis down you and buy you the best steak in town. Then we're going to settle in at Charlie Byrd's and listen to some good music. After that, we're coming back here. I'm going to take you to bed and we're going to forget about all this stuff until after the holidays. Come on. Let's have some fun."

She smiled uncertainly at him, then she laughed. "Should I change clothes?"

"No," he said. "But you might want to take that apron off."

The Shenandoah Valley

McCall stared out of the frosted windows of the library at the great white blanket being drawn over the Valley. The snow had begun sometime during the night and was still falling heavily. The cornfield was already covered and there was a good chance he'd be snowed in by morning. He'd had a difficult time for a few days after their return from Paris. The memory of Paralee bleeding through his scarf had brought back the nightmares of Willie dying in his arms on the beach. He ordered a case of Cardhu from the Virginia ABC store and crawled inside several bottles trying to drown the memories. Eventually, he realized the Scotch was doing more harm than good. He'd have to find redemption somewhere else.

He picked up the phone and dialed Paralee's number in Winchester.

"How do you feel?" he asked.

"I'm going crazy. Mother and I will be pulling hair in another couple of days if I don't get out of here. Dad's retreated to his bunker in the basement and won't come out. My brothers went to visit friends and won't be back until Christmas. They say I'm not good company. What are *you* doing?"

"Sitting by the fire in the library. Looks like the skiers are going to get some deep powder. Is it snowing at your place?"

"Of course it's snowing! I'm only fifty miles away," she snapped, then fell silent for a moment. In a sweeter voice, she said, "Mack, can I come to the farm before we all get snowed in? I miss the hell out of you."

"I don't know. You sound toxic to me."

"I won't be toxic with you," she pleaded. "I promise."

"OK. I'll bring the pickup. The Mercedes won't make it through this snow and they won't plow until it stops. Be a little while. Think you can wait?"

"I'll be on the doorstep," she said and hung up without waiting for him to reply.

As he prepared to head out into the storm, McCall filled a thermos with hot beef bouillon and pulled two thick alpaca blankets from the closet in the master bedroom. He still thought of it as Josh's, but it had been the first room in the house he'd tackled. Josh's things had now been replaced by his own and he'd been sleeping there since they returned from Paris.

He put on light-weight snow boots, took his heavy coat from the peg in the kitchen and pulled on a Chicago Bears stocking cap. He went through the dog trot into the garage and pushed open the doors. Four inches of snow were already on the ground. At the rate it was coming down, there'd be a foot by the time they got back. He threw a snow shovel into the truck bed just in case. He thought about putting on chains, but decided against taking the time to do it. Chains were a pain in the ass.

****

Their return to the farm grew increasingly hazardous as the flakes continued to fall, but they arrived at last, slithering up the hill into the open garage.

"Go on ahead," McCall told Paralee. "I'll bring your stuff."

Paralee threw a blanket over her head and shoulders and hurried through the dog trot into the kitchen. From the door, she turned back to watch him pulling her bags from behind the seat and struggling into the house.

"Whew!" he said. "I'm glad that's over. Get on in. I've got to stoke up the fire."

He shut the door, dropped her bags and stripped off his cap. She came into his arms then and kissed him hard. "I missed you, Jack Mack McCall," she whispered, leaning back in his arms and fixing her dark blue eyes on him.

"Does that mean I can put your stuff in the master bedroom?"

"Josh's room?"

"Yeah. I put Josh's things away. It's a nice bed. You should try it."

"All right," she said, smiling. "I'll take a chance. Put my stuff in there-- right after you throw some logs on the fire. I'll call Mom and tell her we made it."

"Want to make something hot to drink?" he asked, helping her out of her coat and hanging it on one of the pegs by the door. "Or would you rather have a Scotch?"

"You've got Cardhu?"

"In the kitchen."

"I'll pour us both a double. Deal with the fire, my man."

He brought the wood into the library where Paralee was stirring the coals. "What did your mom say?" he asked.

"Couldn't get through. I guess the lines are down. We had some icing before the snow started. We really are snowed in."

Mack had rearranged the library to create a sitting area in front of the fireplace and Paralee curled up against him on the old, cracked leather couch, a thick, Peruvian alpaca blanket tucked around her feet. The firelight and a vague reflection from the snow outside softly lit their faces.

He looked down at her, touched his glass to hers and said, "Here's looking at you, kid."

She smiled, took a small sip and snuggled against him. "And we'll always have Paris," she said and they sat in silence for a long time, watching the orange and red and blue of the dancing flames, content simply to be together. Finally, Paralee changed positions, resting her head in his lap and looking up at him. He smoothed the blanket over her and left his hand on her stomach.

"I need you to tell me slowly what happened," she said. "I did a lot of research on those blasted bonds and I've got a quart of French blood in my veins to go with the sweat and toil and tears. What finally happened with Ryder and Tovolaro?"

"I guess they were going to screw me from the get-go. Right after we got back, I faxed Tovolaro twice that I wanted a decision. I gave him my fax number and called him every day for a week. He was never available. Which is fine because they're stuck with a bunch of bonds they can't cash when and if the settlement's announced. Wellington, Winchester still has about eight hundred thousand dollars worth of bonds and if there's a settlement, I'll cash them. But who knows when that'll be. Until then, I'm asset rich and cash poor in a very significant way."

"And Javier? What about the bank?"

"He's going great guns, buying up minority shares. He and I now have twenty percent of the bank--that's double what we started with--and when we add in Don Francisco's thirty five percent, we're in control. Ryder's cut off at the pass. What I don't know is how pissed Ryder and Tovolaro are going to be when they find out how screwed they are. I don't know how they can blame me--they sowed the wind and reaped the whirlwind--but you never know. I'm still going to keep looking over my shoulder for awhile."

New York

"Are you sure about this?" Ryder howled at Chanille, waving the fax at her.

"It's straight from London Station. Looks like an exact copy to me," she said, taking detached pleasure in Ryder's dilemma. "You got shagged, didn't you? You bought too late and you're not British. Want me to call a decorator and start papering the walls with Russian bonds?"

Ryder read the document again.

Russian Compensation

The Foreign Compensation
(Union of Soviet Socialist Republics)
(Registration and Determination of Claims)
Order 1985

Her Majesty's Government announces that this Order is due to come into effect on 1 January 1986. Copies are available from HMSO.

A fund of about £ 46 million will become available for distribution to those who can satisfy the terms of the Order. Claims may be made by:

Original British or Commonwealth claimants or their successors in respect of financial and property claims arising before 1939 which were registered with the Foreign Office Claims Department or the Russian Claims Department of the Board of Trade between 1918 and 1951. British or Commonwealth holders on 15 December 1985 of bonds issued or guaranteed by Russian authorities prior to 7 November 1917.

It is not possible to forecast what percentage of the assessed value of successful claims will be made. Claims registered between 1918 and 1951 were valued by the claimants at approximately £ 400 million. This did not include all the bonds for which claims can legitimately be made. It follows that the payout as a percentage of the amount claimed is likely to be small.

Application forms and explanatory leaflets may be obtained by sending the coupon below to the Foreign Compensation Commission, c/ o Price Waterhouse, 134 Buckingham Palace Road, London SW1 9SA (telephone 01-823 4181)

Please note that completed application forms in respect of bonds must be received by 31 March 1986. Those in respect of property, debts and other claims must be received by 30 June 1986.

"If you mean I'm screwed because we weren't holders of record on December 15, yes, damn it! But McCall's syndicate is screwed, too, assuming he ever got it off the ground."

"Yeah, but now Tovolaro and *Las Águilas* are going to want your *cojones*, not McCall's. You're the one who finally approved the deal and you're the one who dragged his feet so long you didn't make the deadline. You think Tovolaro's going to forget about that? And that's not your only problem. That other shoe hasn't fallen yet."

Two heavy lines developed between Ryder's eyebrows as he looked at her, perplexed and growing angry. "What do you mean?"

"The documents. The ones that woman gave McCall in Bolivia. They haven't surfaced, so as nearly as we can tell, he's still got them. This would be a good time for him to blow your conduit. The *Sturmpetrel* hasn't even made port in Cape Town."

"Haven't you got a line on him yet?"

"We're working on it," she said. "I thought he'd run to Panamá and hide out with his buddies at Banco Dorado, but we checked everywhere in Panamá, starting with that guest house you're so fond of, and we came up dry. As far as that's concerned, he didn't fly anywhere commercially. He might have taken a charter flight, but he's not on any commercial manifests. Not Panamá, not Perú, not Texas. Of course, he could be driving. That would make him all but invisible."

Chanille rested her buns against the back of one of the armchairs, slouching her pelvis forward in the habitual posture that so distracted Ryder. "We found a farm that belonged to his grandfather down by Mt. Jackson, in the Shenandoah Valley. I was going to put somebody on that today, but there was a big snow storm out there and I haven't been able to get it done."

Ryder looked at Chanille intently for several moments. "Do you ski?" he asked.

"Of course," she answered.

"Then go home and get a ski suit. A white one if you've got it. If not, go buy one. I'll rent a four-wheel drive Jeep and pick you up early tomorrow morning."

"We're going skiing?"

"Aren't you listening? We're going after those documents. Didn't you say he's out in the Virginia boondocks? The weather report this morning said the whole East Coast is clearing. They'll have the roads plowed by tomorrow."

"I didn't say he was there," Chanille protested. "He could be anywhere. He could be in Montana."

Ryder shook his head. "No, I don't think so. He's parked the documents with Grandpa. Maybe he's there, too. If he is, we can take care of him right there. They won't find the bodies until spring comes. We'll get Banderas and the old man in Panamá later. First, I want those documents."

The Shenandoah Valley

In the billowing folds of the goose-down comforter, she looked like a golden currant in a puff pastry. He touched her cheek carefully, wanting to wake her, but not startle her. He smiled when her eyes opened.

"Good morning," he said.

"This is the most marvelous bed," she replied. "If I weren't starving, I'd stay here all day."

"You'd better hope there's enough to eat around here, because we're not going past the woodpile today. It's snowing again. Look," he said, pointing to the skylights over their heads where the wind had blown away the overnight accumulation. The flakes were still falling. "There's got to be more than a foot out there already."

"Mmmmm," she said, snuggling closer to him.

He kissed her. Then the phone rang.

"Let it ring," he muttered.

"No," she said, rolling out of bed and grabbing her robe. "It's probably Mom. The phone lines must be back up. She'll go ballistic if I don't answer it."

McCall heaved a sigh and fell back into the feather bed.

"Mack," she called, her voice excited. "It's London. Ross Chesley. Hurry."

****

"No, that's OK. We're snowed in and the phones have been down for a couple of days . . . You're kidding . . . So it's on? Congratulations, 'mano! You pulled it off. Is the PM pleased? . . . That's great. I can't wait to see it. I've got Audrey's bonds and the eight hundred thousand I bought on the open market and I managed to make a killing at someone else's expense after all. I'll tell you about it later. . . . Yeah, that was her. She's pretty well healed. She was recuperating up at her folks' house, but they were about to put her in a tow sack with a big rock and drop her in the river. Actually, she's just randy. We're taking care of that."

"Maa-ack!" Paralee howled and punched his arm--hard.

McCall grinned and went back to his conversation with Chilty. "Yeah. I'll let you know. . . . I haven't got a fax machine down here. Can you read it to me?"

McCall put his hand over the mouthpiece and grinned at Paralee.

"So?" she asked, bouncing up and down beside him.

"It's on," McCall told her. "Chilty's going to read the announcement to me."

McCall held the phone away from his ear so that Paralee could hear Chilty's recitation.

When Chilty finished, McCall shook his head. "Holders as of December 15. Even if Tovolaro had come on board, it would have been too late. And no gold, huh?"

"It's just as I told you, Mack, no gold," Chilty replied, paused and went on, sly laughter in his voice. "But suppose the gold were there . . . Do you think we'd tell the Russians?" Chilty waited a moment to let that settle in, then added, "You haven't asked about the settlement price. Aren't you interested in that?"

"Hell, yes, I'm interested. It's just a lot to absorb all at once. What is it?"

"It's not finally set, but it looks like it will be in the neighborhood of fifty on the bonds."

"I can't believe it," McCall said. "If it's fifty, I'll make four hundred thousand. Do you know how soon?"

"I wouldn't start spending it just yet," Chilty said. "There'll be some sort of advance payment on the bonds soon. The rest to come later, when all the dust clears."

Chilty had to go and when McCall hung up the phone, he grinned at Paralee. "No gold, but we're still golden," he said. "We can even afford a few bottles of that Montrachet you like so much."

"I didn't understand what he said about the gold."

McCall shook his head. "He didn't say it actually, but I think it's still there. It's just that the Brits aren't going to tell the Russians."

"Can they do that?"

"Are you kidding?" McCall laughed. "Read some British history. But what's best is that all those bonds Ryder bought are going to be worthless in the settlement. He's screwed two ways."

"How?"

"First, the settlement will be for holders of record on the 15th of December. He didn't buy until the 18th. That's the real killer. But my ace in the hole was that the Brits are only going to accept bonds submitted by British holders." McCall grinned, waiting for Paralee to make the connection.

"But you're not British. How will you cash the bonds you bought before the 15th?" "Wellington, Winchester is a British Commonwealth company. I don't own the bonds. Wellington, Winchester does." "But you own Wellington, Winchester."

McCall wiggled his eyebrows. "Indeed I do, but that's a state secret of the Bahamanian government and irrelevant for this deal. Now come here, there's something I want to show you."

McCall put his arm around Paralee's shoulder and drew her gently toward the library table beside the windows. "Look," he said, holding up two simple frames. "I had these done last week."

Paralee's hand went to her mouth. "Audrey's bonds," she said. "The prettiest ones. You're going to keep them?"

"I think she'd like that, don't you?"

As Paralee took each framed bond in her hands to examine it, something caught McCall's eye in the cornfield below. He left her at the table and went to the window. Two hunters were slogging through the snow, a man and what looked like a boy, tall and slender.

The boy held a rifle with a scope, obviously a hunting rifle, but the man was carrying something shorter and smaller than a rifle. The snow was up to their knees and they were making a deep track from the road through the cornfield. *'They must be stuck in a drift,'* McCall thought, watching them approach. When they were fifty yards from the house, McCall went to the door to greet them.

"What is it, Mack?" Paralee asked, putting down the bonds and going to the window.

"A couple of guys coming up to the house. Hell of a day to go hunting. Car must be stuck in the snow. You better go make another pot of coffee."

When McCall opened the door and stepped onto the front porch, the pair stopped and the man moved around in front of the boy, who had bent down. McCall strained to see what the matter was. Suddenly, he saw the barrel of the rifle come up, screened by the man. Reflexively, McCall stepped back in the doorway just as the rifle fired. In the next instant, the bullet hissed beside his ear and he felt its sting. He dove back through the opening as another shot screamed after him. His ear was on fire and a warm, sticky ooze of blood ran down his jaw. *'Sonafabitch. That was a head shot. They're trying to kill me!'*

Paralee came out of the kitchen. "Mack, what the . . .?"

"Get down!" he yelled at her from the shelter of the wall beside the door, adrenalin surging through his veins. With one hand he slammed the door closed just as a hail of assault weapon fire shattered the leaded glass and splintered the wood.

'You bastards! That's my door!'

Josh's 30-30 rested in the corner. Behind the disintegrating front door, McCall fell to the floor, snatched the rifle with his left hand and kept rolling into the library. Sitting with his back to the wall beside the big window, he levered the breech half open, praying Josh kept the gun loaded. He peered inside the chamber. The shiny brass of a shell casing winked back at him.

'Thanks, Pa.'

With the rifle at his shoulder, he rose quickly, broke a window pane and sighted down the barrel at the snow-covered front yard. The two men were trying to rush the house, but the snow was too deep and they were foundering, making little progress. The man stopped and unleashed another burst at the front of the house to cover the boy as he waded forward through the snow.

McCall heard the shots strike the stone, the door and the living room windows, but he held steady. As the sights lined up against the boy, McCall thought his vision had never been sharper, more acute. He squeezed the trigger slowly, the barrel steady and the sights locked onto the target. He scarcely heard the explosion of the round or felt the recoil. The bullet struck the young hunter, throwing him back. He sat down awkwardly in the snow, the rifle falling from his hands. As McCall levered another round into the chamber and shifted his aim to the man, he saw the boy's torso fall back and disappear in the snow.

He fired again and saw his shot rip the material of the man's ski suit at the shoulder a moment before the library window exploded, showering the room with a thousand shards of broken glass.

He spun away from the window and took cover behind the wall, his skin stinging from the razor-sharp bits of glass imbedded in his face and hands. The display case with the first Joshua's bayonet and the bullets they'd taken out of Thomas was knocked over, its glass broken. Bits of book bindings and paper floated in the rays of sun streaming through the window casing.

'Ay, ay. Damn it! Damn it! DAMN IT!'

"Maaaaack!" he heard Paralee scream.

"Stay in the kitchen!" he yelled at her, but she was already scurrying into the library on all fours.

McCall worked the lever of Josh's rifle. A spent casing flew across the room, but the breech closed too easily and he knew the magazine was empty. *'Oh, shit. Now what?'* He had no idea where Josh kept his shells.

Mack, your ear . . . your face . . . you're all bloody. What's happening?" Paralee wailed, frantically dabbing at the blood spatters on his cheeks and forehead, smearing it into war paint stripes before she pulled back, realizing she wasn't helping.

"They're not hunters," he said, squatting with his back against the wall. "Get behind the couch. I put one down, but the other one's got an Uzi. I'm going to have to get him into the house."

"What?" she said, her eyes wide with fright.

"I'm out of ammo. I can't kill the sonofabitch out there! I've got to get him inside."

"No, Mack. No," Paralee cried. "Not in here!"

Mack shook his head, jaw clenched, the pause in the action letting fear seep in. "Listen to me. Even if he thinks we're dead, he'll have to come in to make sure. At least look through the windows. It won't take long. It's colder than kraut out there. Now move your ass. Get behind that couch and stay there. Don't make a sound. You hear me?"

McCall laid the empty 30-30 against the wall and stretched into the room. He could just reach the tip of the old bayonet. He dragged it across the floor to him. Gripping it at the socket, he examined the long triangular blade. Almost a short sword. *'This is lethal. I just have to get close enough.'*

Icy wind whistled through the broken window. McCall shivered, straining to hear movement outside the house. For a long time there was nothing but the wind. He prayed his teeth wouldn't chatter or the frost of his breath give him away. As his fingers grew colder, he flexed them again and again against the socket of the bayonet.

Then he heard the crunch of a boot on the snow. Another. The shooter was on the porch. Near the sun room, only a few steps away.

McCall tensed his legs and came out of the squat. He stood against the wall, his knuckles white against the socket of the bayonet. If the gunner were careless enough not to look through the crack where the door was hinged against its frame . . .

There was a flurry of footsteps, followed immediately by an ear-splitting burst from the Uzi. McCall squinted his eyes and gritted his teeth watching splinters and bits of glass fly into the living room. There was a momentary silence before he heard a shout and the gunner came bursting through the door, spraying the room with fire from the Uzi.

McCall sprang off the wall, throwing his whole body against the shooter's back, knocking him sprawling, face down, plunging the bayonet into his back with every ounce of strength he had. It went in deep. The shooter grunted. The Uzi went skittering across the floor and came to rest against the living room hearth. McCall held on and straddled him.

The shooter lay still, stunned, gasping for air. A red mist of anger clouding his eyes, McCall pressed hard against the shooter to hold him down, gripped the socket of the bayonet with both hands to pull it free, feeling it scrape against bone. With both arms above his head, he drove the bayonet into the shooter again. The blade imbedded in the floor, nailing him to the ancient planking.

The man gave another short cry, gasped for air and flailed one arm, trying in vain to reach behind him to get at the bayonet. Then the breath went out of him and he lay still.

Slowly, McCall felt the anger and the fear drain away. He rose and backed away, leaving the bayonet quivering in the man's back.

Warily watching the shooter, McCall retrieved the Uzi from the base of the hearth. He held it loosely in one hand and walked back to the lifeless body on the floor. Reaching down with one hand, he pulled back the hood of the ski jacket. Dead eyes stared back at him.

'Whoever you are, why the hell did you make me do this?'

In the corner of his eye, he saw Paralee in the frame of the library doorway, holding Josh's 30-30 by the barrel, ready to use it as a club.

She came toward him then, a slow step first, then a headlong rush into his arms, Josh's rifle clattering to the floor.

McCall held her close to him, squeezing her tight to stop her shaking, beginning to feel the freezing cold himself. "Come on," he said. "Let's get a coat on you. You're freezing."

****

Sheriff Templeton took less than an hour to make his way up to the farm. The driveway was too deep for his patrol car or Ezra Cunliffe's, the deputy from Woodstock. McCall watched them slogging up the driveway like a two-man skirmish line, guns drawn, but hanging loose in their hands. McCall waved and stepped off the porch, the hood of his parka thrown back, his breath steaming the frosty air.

"Hey, Bobby," he greeted Templeton.

"Damnation, Jack Mack, are you OK?" he asked, taking in the bloody spatters and scabbing streaks on McCall's face.

"Glass splinters," McCall replied. "It looks worse than it is. Two bodies, Bobby. I haven't moved them. One's out there in the cornfield. Maybe you want to look at it first. The other one's inside."

Chanille d'Orsay lay on her back in apparent peaceful repose. A fluff of down protruded from the hole in her ski jacket where Mack's bullet had crashed through the middle of her chest. If there was blood, it was all beneath her.

Templeton bent over to look at the Sig Sauer beside her. "This is a woman, Jack, and that's a sniper's rifle." He patted the pockets of the ski jacket and found an ID case. "Chanille d'Orsay," he mumbled and looked up at McCall. "Know her?"

McCall shook his head. "Never heard of her."

Templeton looked back down the line of deep footprints in the snow that led to the Jeep Cherokee. "Looks like they missed the driveway and couldn't turn around. No matter, they weren't making much of a secret of it, were they? Let's have a look in the house."

The two officers stopped short of the porch and inspected the damage to the library window and what was left of the leaded-glass front door. "What caused all that?" Cunliffe asked.

"The guy inside had an Uzi. Packs a hell of a punch," McCall replied, following them into the living room.

Paralee stood in the library doorway, her coat pulled close around her, shivering, watching McCall and the two deputies. Cunliffe was taking pictures of everything, the strobe flash winking brightly every few seconds. Templeton walked slowly around the lifeless body nailed to the floor by the bayonet, shaking his head. "I'll be damned. I'll be damned," he kept muttering to himself.

Finally, he squatted down beside the dead man and removed a wallet from his hip pocket. He flipped it open and found the New York driver's license.

"Robert McKinsey Ryder, it says here."

"Holy shit!" McCall said. "Ryder?"

"You know him?" Templeton asked.

"Not really. Not personally. But, yeah, I sort of know him."

"Ryder?" Paralee said, moving two tentative steps closer to the body. "The man in Paris?"

McCall looked at her. "Want to see?"

"No. . . Yes. . . I don't know," she said, taking another step closer. Then she stood straight and added. "Why not? He won't be the first dead man I've ever seen."

McCall knelt down and pulled back Ryder's hood.

"That's the man in the hotel, in the Élysée Ponthieu."

McCall dropped the hood back over Ryder's face and stood up. "Did you make some coffee?" he asked Paralee, as much as anything to get her mind off the corpse in the living room and the whole violent morning.

She took the hint, slipped past Ryder's dead body and disappeared into the kitchen. The two policemen stepped gingerly around the wreckage of the library and the living room, Cunliffe taking more pictures. Paralee served them coffee in the sun room and Templeton reminded Paralee that they'd met on her first visit to the farm, when she was looking for Josh. But he didn't let it get social. He took out his notebook and wrote down their account of what had happened.

Finally, Templeton raised his eyebrows to look at Ezra Cunliffe. Then he turned to McCall. "Clear cut case of self-defense, Mack. I don't think it'll have to go much farther than that. We'll have some stuff for you to sign down at the office and the judge may want to do an inquest for the record. You think they've got any friends who might want to come after you now?"

"I don't know, Bobby," McCall said. "I sure as hell hope not. But just in case, I'm going to reload Pa's thirty-thirty if I can find where he keeps his cartridges. If you'll let me keep the Sig Sauer and the Uzi, I'd feel better."

Templeton nodded. "Good idea. I've got some .30-. 30 ammo in my cruiser. I'll go down and get it. I'm going to have to have the weapons for evidence sooner or later, but you keep them for now. The meat wagon's on the way. They'll get these bodies out of here. We've got what evidence we need from the scene and you can start putting things back together as best you can. Damn cold in here. What are you going to do about that window in the library? The front door's sure a mess. I always loved that door. How old you figure it is?"

McCall shrugged. "It goes back to the Civil War."

"That where that ugly bayonet came from?" Templeton asked. "I'm going to have to borrow it for awhile. I'll take real good care of it, though."

"It's from the Revolution. The first Joshua brought it out here to the wilderness with him," McCall said. "Took it away from a dead Redcoat, I think. Hadn't been used in a long time, but it sure came in handy today."

The ambulance arrived in the road below and two attendants, stretchers on their shoulders, tramped up the drive, following Templeton's and Cunliffe's trail.

"We'll hang around until the bodies are out of here," Templeton said. "If I were you, Mack, I'd go get inside a whiskey bottle and try to forget all about this sorry day."

* * * * * * * * * * *

McCall nailed a tarp over the library window and managed to get what was left of the front door back into its frame, a sheet of plywood covering the destroyed leaded glass. He built up one fire in the living room and another in the sun room and sent Paralee there with a bottle of Cardhu. It was one of the few places in the house that was undamaged by that morning's carnage.

With a stiff brush from under the sink and a bucket filled with soapy water he scrubbed the blood from the planks in the living room floor. It was easier than he thought. Ryder's blood hadn't penetrated the varnish except where the bayonet had made a three-cornered hole in the wood. That reminder would be with them for a long, long time unless he replaced the plank.

Paralee was sitting at one end of the stone hearth holding a tumbler of Cardhu in both hands, the blazing logs crackling beside her. She was pale and edgy. McCall knelt beside her.

323

"I'm still scared, Mack," she said, quivering slightly. "Please tell me your life isn't like this."

"It's not," he said, taking the tumbler from her and holding both of her hands in his, his eyes begging her to believe him, hoping it was true.

"Why did they want to kill us?" she said. "Was it that thing about the Russians in Paris? Was it because they thought you tricked them into buying the bonds?"

McCall shook his head. "I don't know. Maybe. We did nick them for more than three million bucks and they probably know that they're looking at a dead loss now. Maybe it was about Banco Dorado. We cut them off at the knees there. We've got the majority of shares and we bought them with their money. It could have been about the documents I brought out of Bolivia It's all sort of wrapped up together. "

"You don't still have them, do you?"

"The documents? No. They've been swallowed up in the maw of our intelligence establishment. Or one of the maws, at least. I took them up to the Hill. After that, I don't know what happened to them."

"I just want to know if this is over," Paralee said.

"To be honest, I don't know. But I haven't heard from Tovolaro--and Ryder . . . well, let's just say he's no longer a factor. Who else is there?" He waited a long moment, then added, "So, I guess it's over."

"Then hold me, Mack. I want to feel safe again."

****

Later, Paralee found Mack standing at the windows of the sun room, a tumbler of Cardhu on the small table beside Josh's chair. She wrapped her arms around his waist and laid her cheek between his shoulder blades.

"What's going to happen now?" she asked.

He turned in her grasp to face her. His arms came to rest on her shoulders. She looked up into his eyes, the light in the room a mixture of icy white moonlight and the flickering orange and yellow of the fireplace.

"That depends on you."

"On me? What do I have to say about it?"

"I've known for awhile what I wanted . . ."

"I know," she said. "To feel that you belonged to this family, that you were worthy of the farm and all your ancestors."

"Be quiet, Paralee. Let me finish. When I was here by myself, before the blizzard hit and you came down here, I took a long step back and looked at my life. I don't have anyone to answer to any more. The farm is mine now, free and clear. It's the way Pa wanted it to work out. I can come back here

324

when and if I want to. Or one of my kids."

"You don't have any kids, do you?"

"Will you be quiet? I'm trying to say something here."

"OK. I'll be quiet."

"When we were in Paris, I started to know what I wanted--what I wanted, not what somebody else wanted for me. I almost lost you there. But I'm hard-headed and it took awhile before I could say to myself that what I really want is a lifetime with you, whether it's here or somewhere else--anywhere else--on the planet."

She closed her eyes and leaned into him, feeling his heart beat, breathing the aroma of his skin.

"Have you ever been to Tuscany?" she murmured. "No. What's in Tuscany?"

"There's a little inn, south of Livorno, on the coast road. It's so old I think the Etruscans built it. Anyway, it has a wonderful stone terrace where you can have a glass of Toscano and watch the sun set on the sea. I was there once--by myself--and I always imagined that would be the most wonderful place to be with the man I loved when he asked me to marry him."

"I see."

"The light's best in early summer. June, say."

"It's a long way for a lover to go if he doesn't know the answer to the question."

"Oh, the answer would be yes. Definitely yes. Unquestionably yes if he comes all the way to Livorno and kneels on the old stones of the terrace of the Villa Antico just at sunset."

"I could do that."

"*Would* you do that?"

"Maybe," he replied, grinning.

THE END

AUTHOR'S NOTE

The United Kingdom and the Soviet Union did, in fact, settle their joint claims and while the author took literary license in moving forward the date of the announcement of the settlement, the particulars of the agreement, signed July 15, 1986, were exactly as described in the book. The Foreign Compensation Order came into effect February 1, 1987. The settlement was concluded in June, 1994, with some £ 62 million ultimately paid against all claims. Registered bond claims of £ 28.5 million returned £ 15.7 million--approximately 55 percent of face value, significantly more than the Commission's initial estimate of 20 percent on which Chilty and McCall based their estimates in the book.

Although the first reference I found to the settlement was in Robert K. Massie, *The Romanovs: The Final Chapter* (New York: Random House, 1995), the most complete discussion of the subject I know is contained in an excellent work by William Clarke, *The Lost Fortune of the Tsars* (New York: St. Martin's Griffin, 1996). In particular, Clarke is the source of the story of the gold shipments and Lili Dehn's affidavit.

Data regarding the value of foreign claims outstanding against Tsar Nicholas II in his final days were drawn from Herbert Feis, *Europe, the World's Banker 1870-1914* (New Haven: Yale University Press for the Council of Foreign Relations, 1930).

Keith Hollander's Scripophily: *The Art of Finance* (New York: Museum of American Financial History, 1994) served as my primary reference on scripophily.

David Arkley of the British Embassy in Washington was extremely helpful in putting me in touch with Her Majesty's Foreign Compensation Commission and A. N. Grant, Secretary to the Commission, most graciously provided the official documents about the terms of the settlement and other details that enriched and validated the story.

Among the numerous sources I consulted on events in Central America, the most important to me were: Lawrence E. Walsh, *Final Report of the Independent Counsel for Iran/ Contra Matters* (Washington, DC, 1993); Peter Kornbluh, *Nicaragua: The Price of Intervention* (Washington, DC: Institute for Policy Studies, 1987); Jonathan Marshall, Peter Dale Scott and Jane Hunter, *The Iran Contra Connection: Secret Teams and Covert Operations in the Reagan Era* (Boston: South End Press, 1987); Frederick Kempe, *Divorcing the Dictator: America's Bungled Affair with Noriega* (New York: G.P. Putnam's Sons, 1990); Bob Woodward, *Veil: The Secret Wars of the CIA, 1981-1987* (New York: Simon & Shuster, 1987); and Bob Woodward, *Shadow: Five Presidents and the Legacy of Watergate* (New York: Simon & Schuster, 1999). Special thanks are due to those stalwart friends who read the manuscript in various stages and offered not only helpful comments, but support and encouragement--

Amy, Howard, Jim, Jeri, Sam, Jim and Michele. Special thanks to Claude for his comments and corrections. Jo read it over and over, helped find the glitches and the typos and, most importantly, was there when the mountains seemed the highest.
Fair Oaks Ranch
August 2013

ABOUT THE AUTHOR

James Christian holds BA, MA and PhD degrees in Economics from the University of Texas at Austin. His travels have taken him to fifty countries in Latin America, the Near East, Europe, Africa, Asia and the former republics of the Soviet Union. He was Chief Economist of the US League of Savings Institutions during the turbulent period of the 1980s when US financial institutions struggled to survive loan defaults occasioned by historically high interest rates, the collapse of oil prices and the deregulation of the financial system. These events, combined with the run-up to the scandal of the Iran-Contra affair, provide the realism of personal experience to create a tapestry for the story of *Audrey's Bonds*.

Dr. Christian has been Professor of Economics at Iowa State University, the University of Texas at Austin and the University of the Incarnate Word. He has also been Professor of Business Administration at Texas A

9 781955 459181